Hatter III
Seeking Wonder

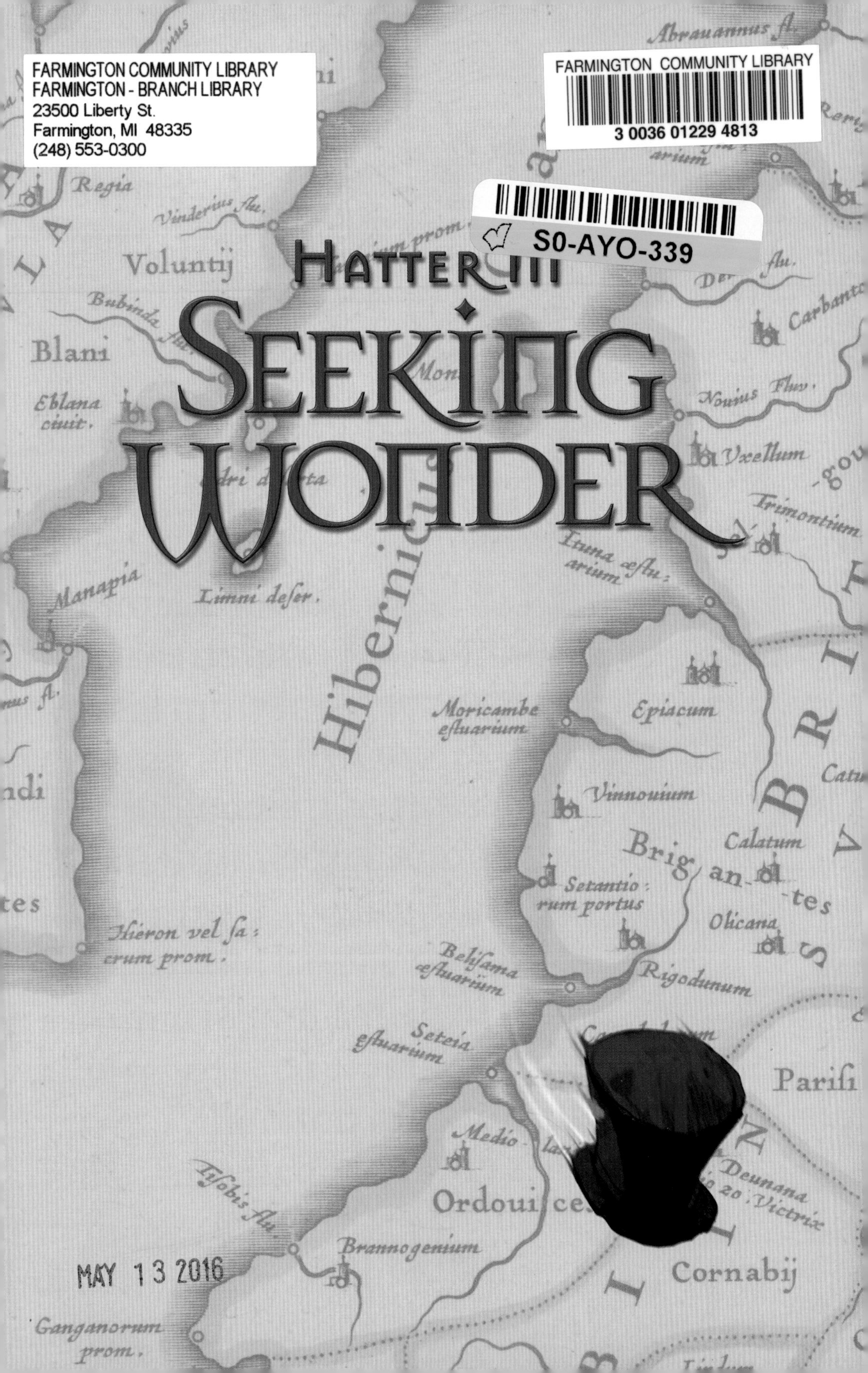
Abrauannus fl.
Regia
Vinderius flu.
Voluntij
Bubinda flu.
Blani
Eblana ciuit.
Manapia
Limni deser.
Hibernicus
Nouius Fluv.
Vxellum
Trimontium
Ituna æstu: arium
Moricambe æstuarium
Epiacum
Vinnouium
Brig an-tes
Calatum
Setantio: rum portus
Olicana
Hieron vel sa: crum prom.
Belisama æstuarium
Rigodunum
Seteia æstuarium
Parisi
Deunana
Ordoui ces
Brannogenium
Tisobis flu.
Cornabij
Ganganorum prom.

Vanduara

Dam—

Clota æstuarium

NICA

Colania

Coria

Curia

Bremenium

Otadeni

Vedra flu.

Itunnus flu.

Bodotria æstuarium

Lindum

ij

Gadini

Caledonia Silua

Cale — donij

Banatia

Alauna

Victoria

...emia

...cemagi

Alata

Orrea

Venni cones

Deuana

Celnius flu.

Tae...

Taua æstuarium

Diua fluuius

Dunum Sinus

O C E...

Gabrantuicorum portuosus sinus

...um leg. ...ictrix

Abus flu.

Petuaria

Ocelum prom.

G E R M...

...euchlani

Saline

Metaris æstuarium

Venta

Garienus flu.

"The World is a book, and those who do not travel read only a page" -Saint Augustine

Hatter M
SEEKING WONDER

Created by
Frank Beddor

AUTOMATIC
PUBLISHING

Hatter M: Seeking Wonder

Creator
Frank Beddor

Artists
Sami Makkonen
Tyson Schroeder

Cover Art
Bill Sienkiewicz

Writers
Shaun Manning
Nate Barlow
Stephen Jarrett
Curtis A. Clark
Jordan M. Doronila
Sis Kipling
Jake Hart

Letterer
Tom B. Long

Mirror Keeper
Lucas San Juan

Code Breaker
Kelly Contessa

Logo Design by
Christina Craemer

Interiors Designed by
Tom B. Long

The Looking Glass Wars ® is a trademark of Automatic Pictures, Inc.
Copyright © 2015 Automatic Pictures, Inc.
All rights reserved.

Printed in Korea.

ISBN: 978-0-9912729-1-4

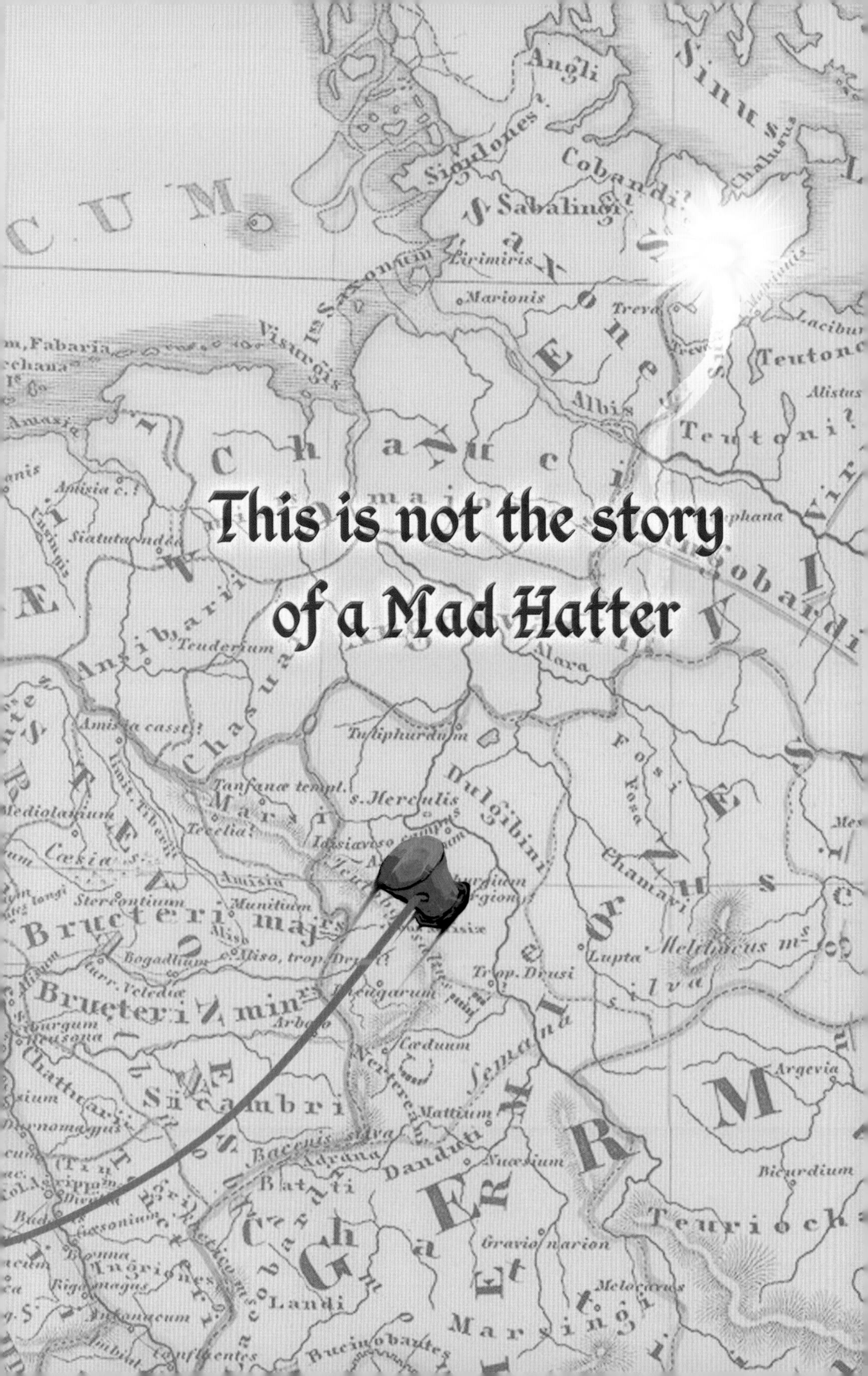
Angli
Sinus
Sigulones
Cobandi?
Chalusus
Sabalingi
Saxones
Pirimiris
Marionis
Treva
Visurgis
Teutoni?
Teutono
Laciburg
Alistus
Albis
Chauci
Amisia c.?
Siatutanda
Teuderium
Ansibarii
Alara
Amisia castl.?
Tuliphurdum
Chasuari
Tanfanæ templ.
s. Herculis
Marsi
Mediolanium
Dulgibini
Fosi
Cæsia s.
Amisia
Stereontium
Munitium
Bructeri majores
Aliso
Bogadium
Aliso, trop. Drusi?
Trop. Drusi
Lupta
Melibocus m.
Chamavi
Bructeri minores
Arbalo
Cæduum
Sicambri
Mattium
Semana
Argevia
Bacenis silva
Adrana
Nuæsium
Batavi
Bicurdium
Teuriochæ
Gravionarion
Bonna
Ingriones
Rigomagus
Landi
Meloravus
Marsingi
Antonacum
Confluentes
Bucinobantes

This is not the story of a Mad Hatter

Thank You

Crystal Gazers, Mirror Skryers,
Looking Glass Diviners and Prismatic Oracles

Contents

The Quest

Who are we?

The Hatter M Institute for Paranormal Travel is a devout assemblage of radical historians, cartographers, code breakers and geo-graphic theorists pledged to uncovering and documenting through the medium of sequential art the full spectrum journey of Royal Bodyguard Hatter Madigan as he traversed our world from 1859 – 1872 searching for Princess Alyss of Wonderland.

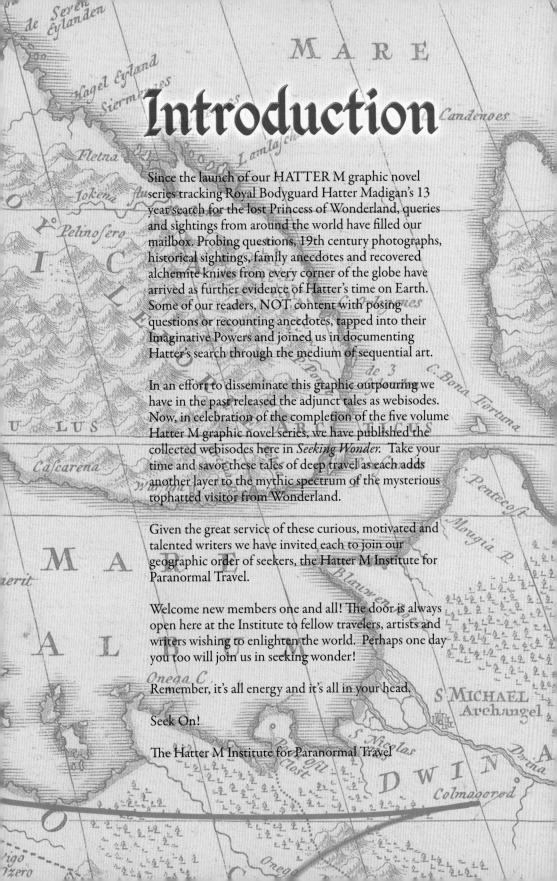

Introduction

Since the launch of our HATTER M graphic novel series tracking Royal Bodyguard Hatter Madigan's 13 year search for the lost Princess of Wonderland, queries and sightings from around the world have filled our mailbox. Probing questions, 19th century photographs, historical sightings, family anecdotes and recovered alchemite knives from every corner of the globe have arrived as further evidence of Hatter's time on Earth. Some of our readers, NOT content with posing questions or recounting anecdotes, tapped into their Imaginative Powers and joined us in documenting Hatter's search through the medium of sequential art.

In an effort to disseminate this graphic outpouring we have in the past released the adjunct tales as webisodes. Now, in celebration of the completion of the five volume Hatter M graphic novel series, we have published the collected webisodes here in *Seeking Wonder*. Take your time and savor these tales of deep travel as each adds another layer to the mythic spectrum of the mysterious tophatted visitor from Wonderland.

Given the great service of these curious, motivated and talented writers we have invited each to join our geographic order of seekers, the Hatter M Institute for Paranormal Travel.

Welcome new members one and all! The door is always open here at the Institute to fellow travelers, artists and writers wishing to enlighten the world. Perhaps one day you too will join us in seeking wonder!

Remember, it's all energy and it's all in your head.

Seek On!

The Hatter M Institute for Paranormal Travel

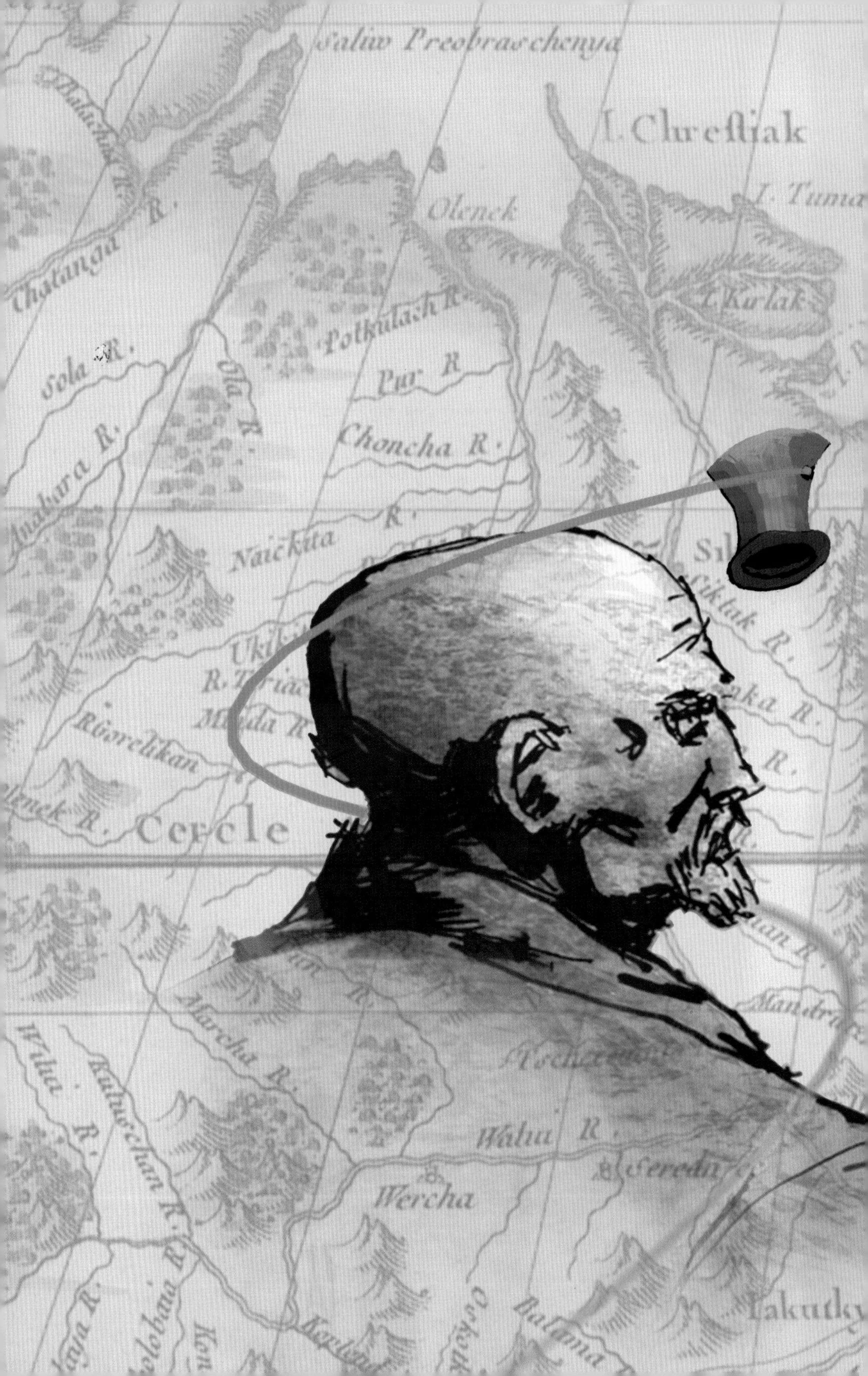
Saliw Preobraschenya
I. Chreſtiak
Olenek
Chatanga
Sola R.
Polkulach R
Pur R
Choncha R.
Anabara R.
Naickita
Cercle
Wercha

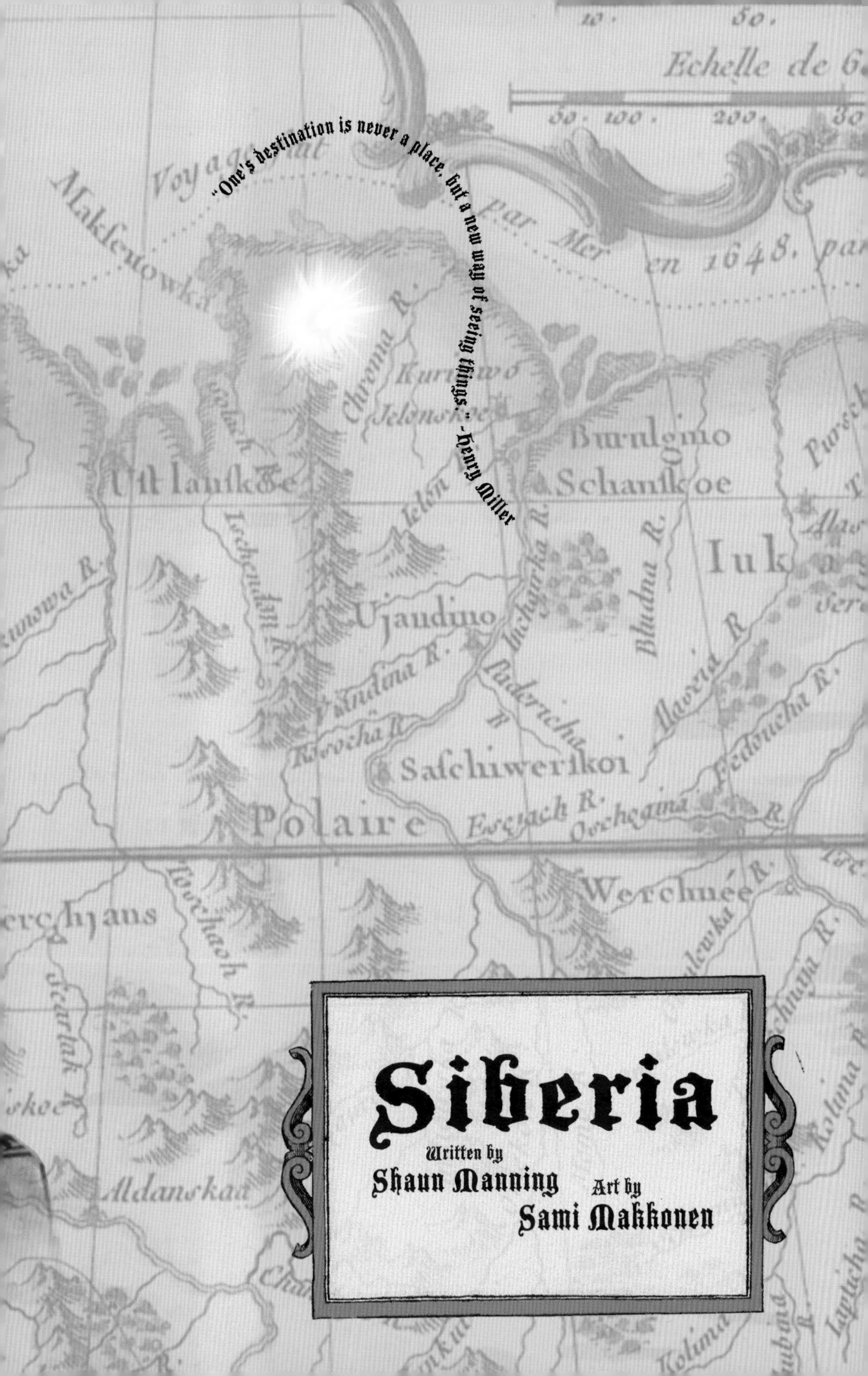
Echelle de
par Mer en 1648, par
Burulgmo
Schankoe
Ujaudino
Saschiwerikoi
Polaire
Aldanskaa

"One's destination is never a place, but a new way of seeing things." - Henry Miller

Siberia

Written by
Shaun Manning

Art by
Sami Makkonen

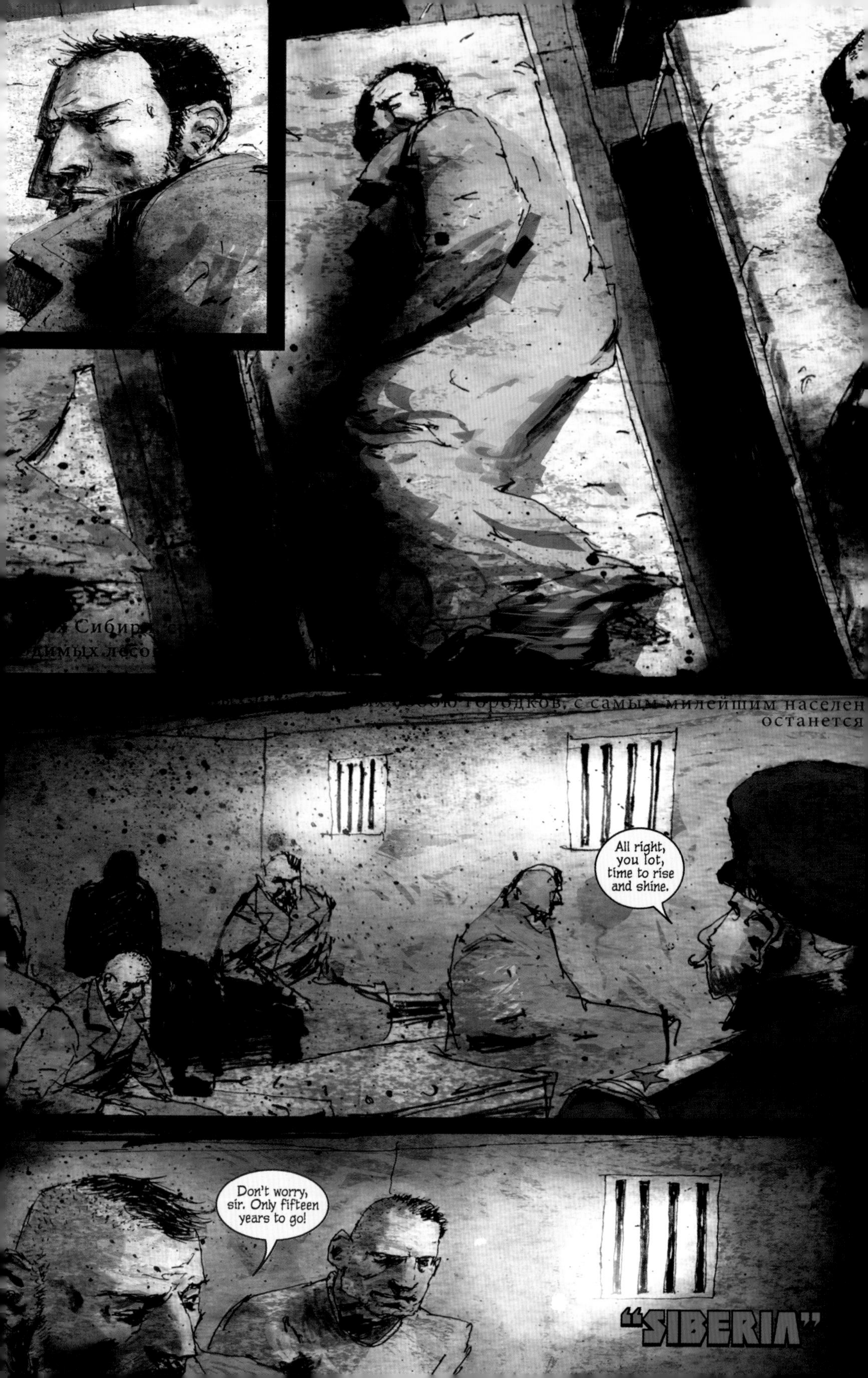
All right, you lot, time to rise and shine.
Don't worry, sir. Only fifteen years to go!
"SIBERIA"

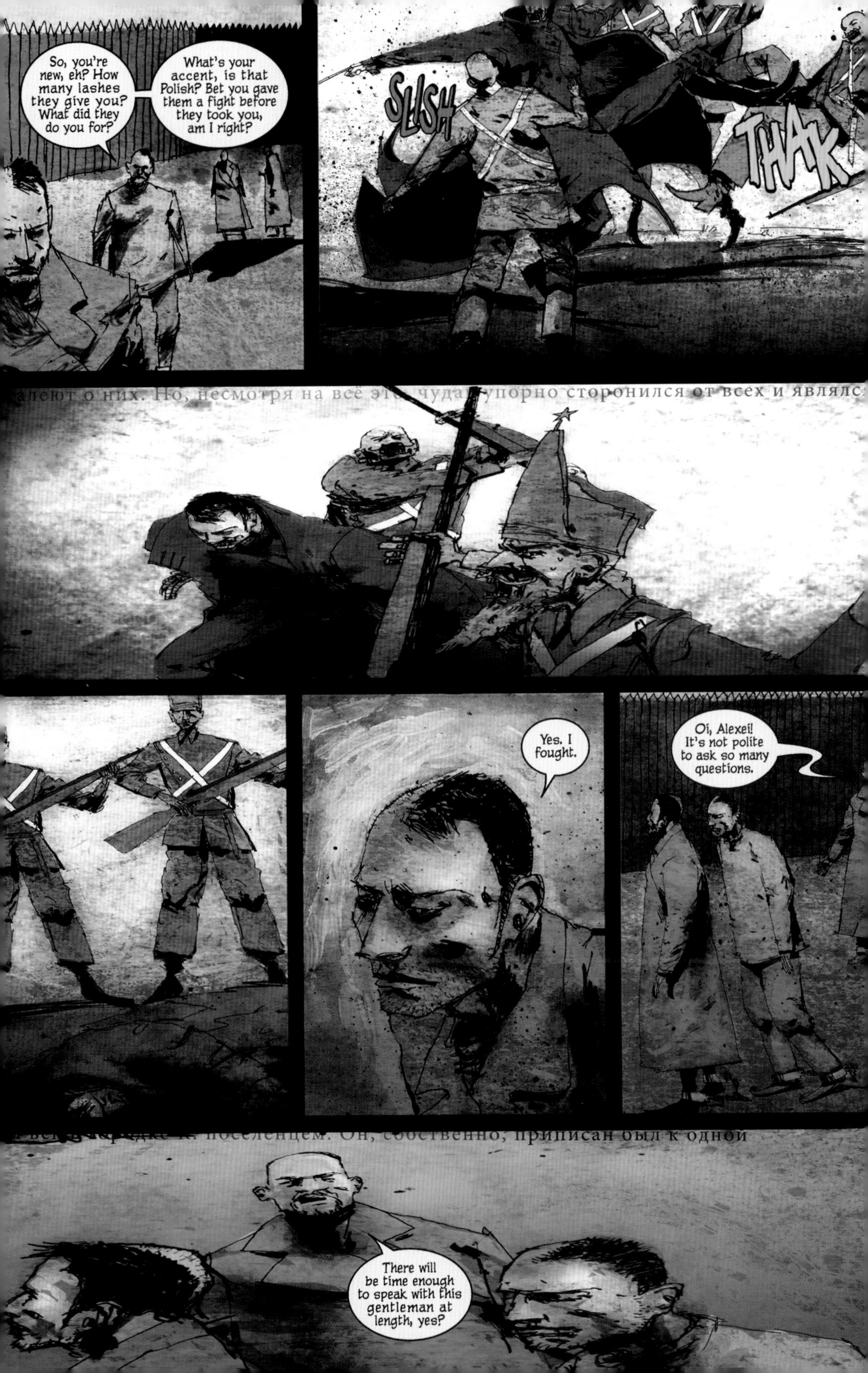
So, you're new, eh? How many lashes they give you? What did they do you for?
What's your accent, is that Polish? Bet you gave them a fight before they took you, am I right?
SLISH
THAK
Yes. I fought.
Oi, Alexei! It's not polite to ask so many questions.
There will be time enough to speak with this gentleman at length, yes?

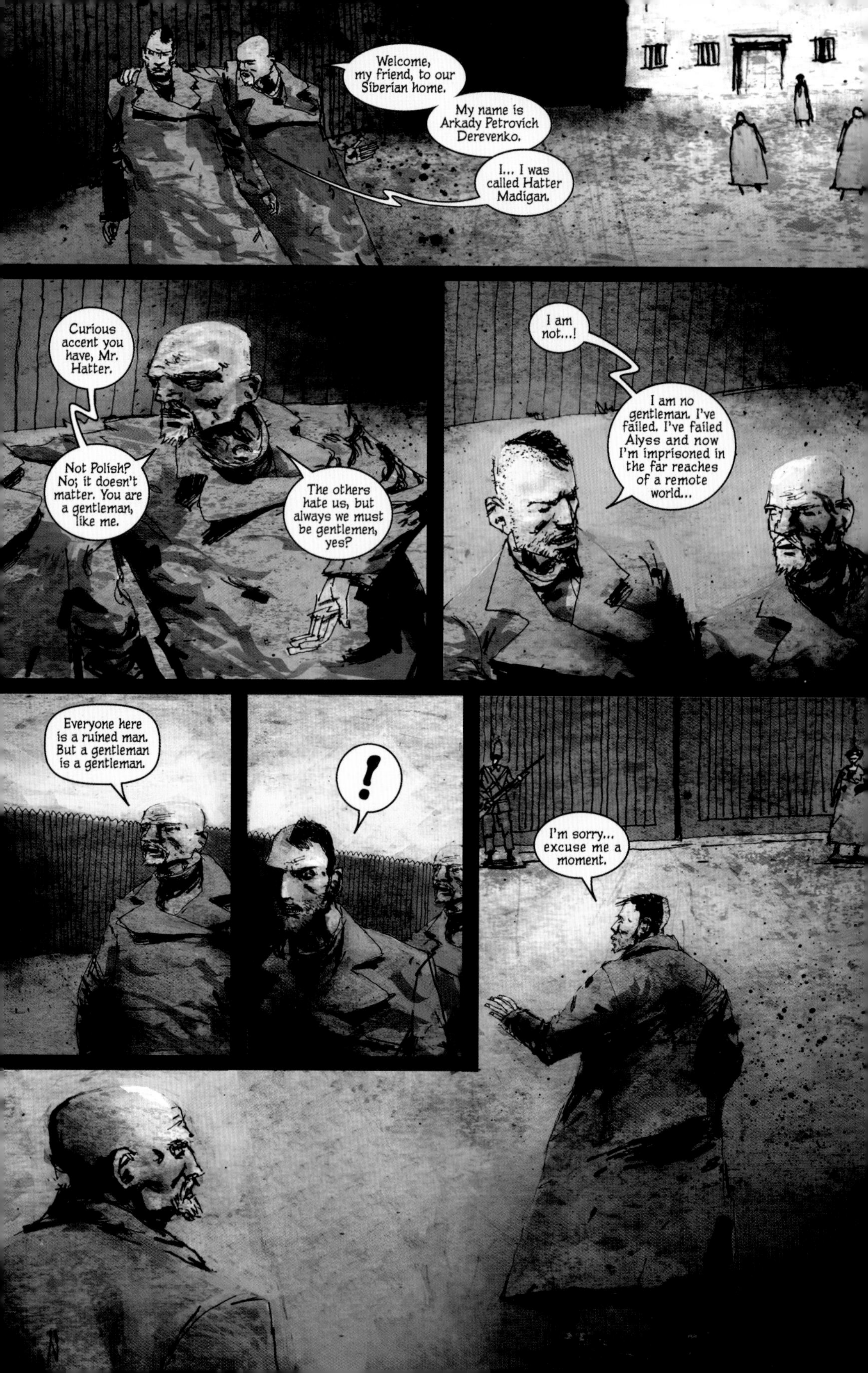
Welcome, my friend, to our Siberian home.
My name is Arkady Petrovich Derevenko.
I... I was called Hatter Madigan.
Curious accent you have, Mr. Hatter.
Not Polish? No; it doesn't matter. You are a gentleman, like me.
The others hate us, but always we must be gentlemen, yes?
I am not...!
I am no gentleman. I've failed. I've failed Alyss and now I'm imprisoned in the far reaches of a remote world...
Everyone here is a ruined man. But a gentleman is a gentleman.
!
I'm sorry... excuse me a moment.

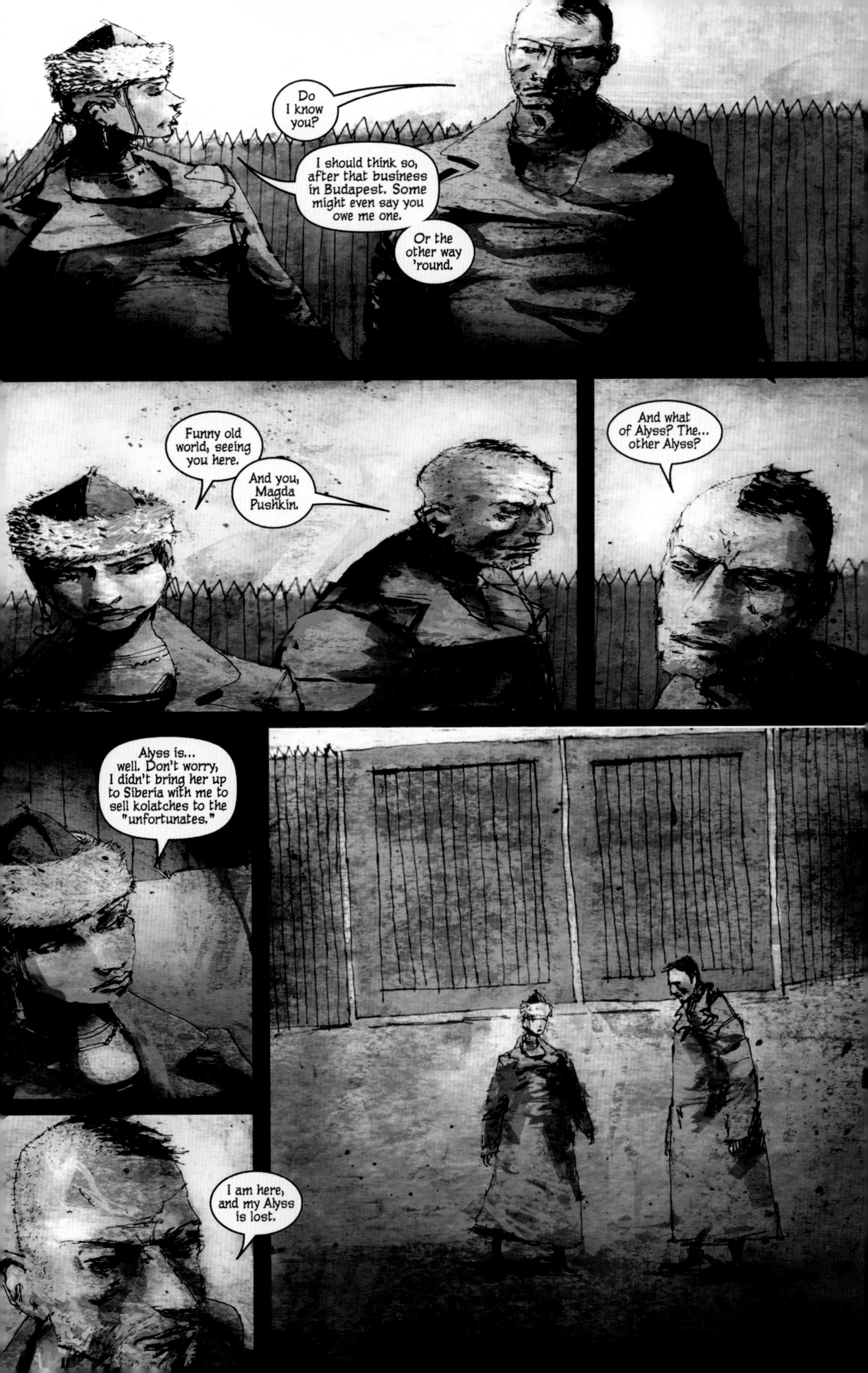
Do I know you?
I should think so, after that business in Budapest. Some might even say you owe me one.
Or the other way 'round.
Funny old world, seeing you here.
And you, Magda Pushkin.
And what of Alyss? The... other Alyss?
Alyss is... well. Don't worry, I didn't bring her up to Siberia with me to sell kolatches to the "unfortunates."
I am here, and my Alyss is lost.

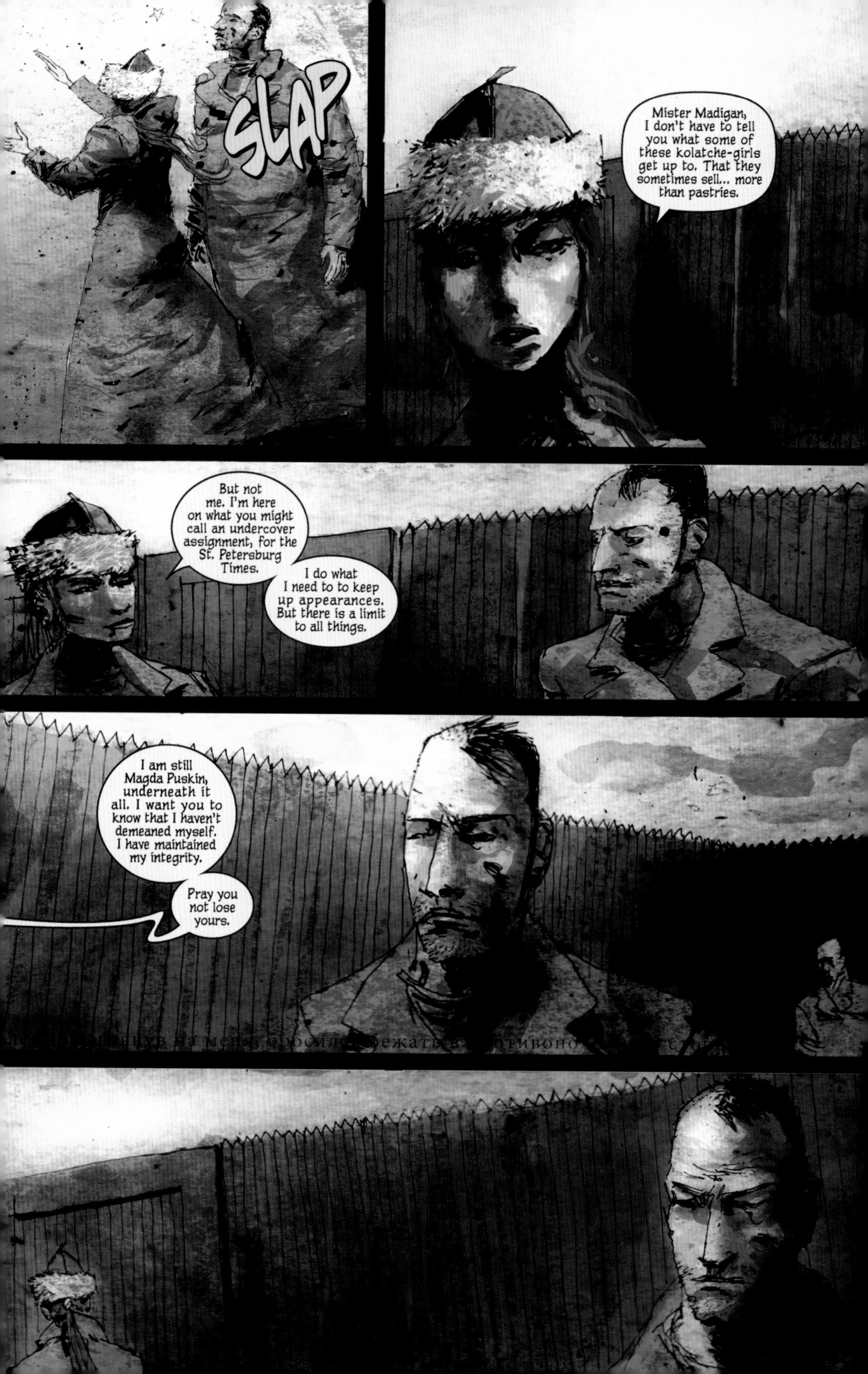
SLAP
Mister Madigan, I don't have to tell you what some of these kolatche-girls get up to. That they sometimes sell... more than pastries.
But not me. I'm here on what you might call an undercover assignment, for the St. Petersburg Times.
I do what I need to to keep up appearances. But there is a limit to all things.
I am still Magda Puskin, underneath it all. I want you to know that I haven't demeaned myself. I have maintained my integrity.
Pray you not lose yours.

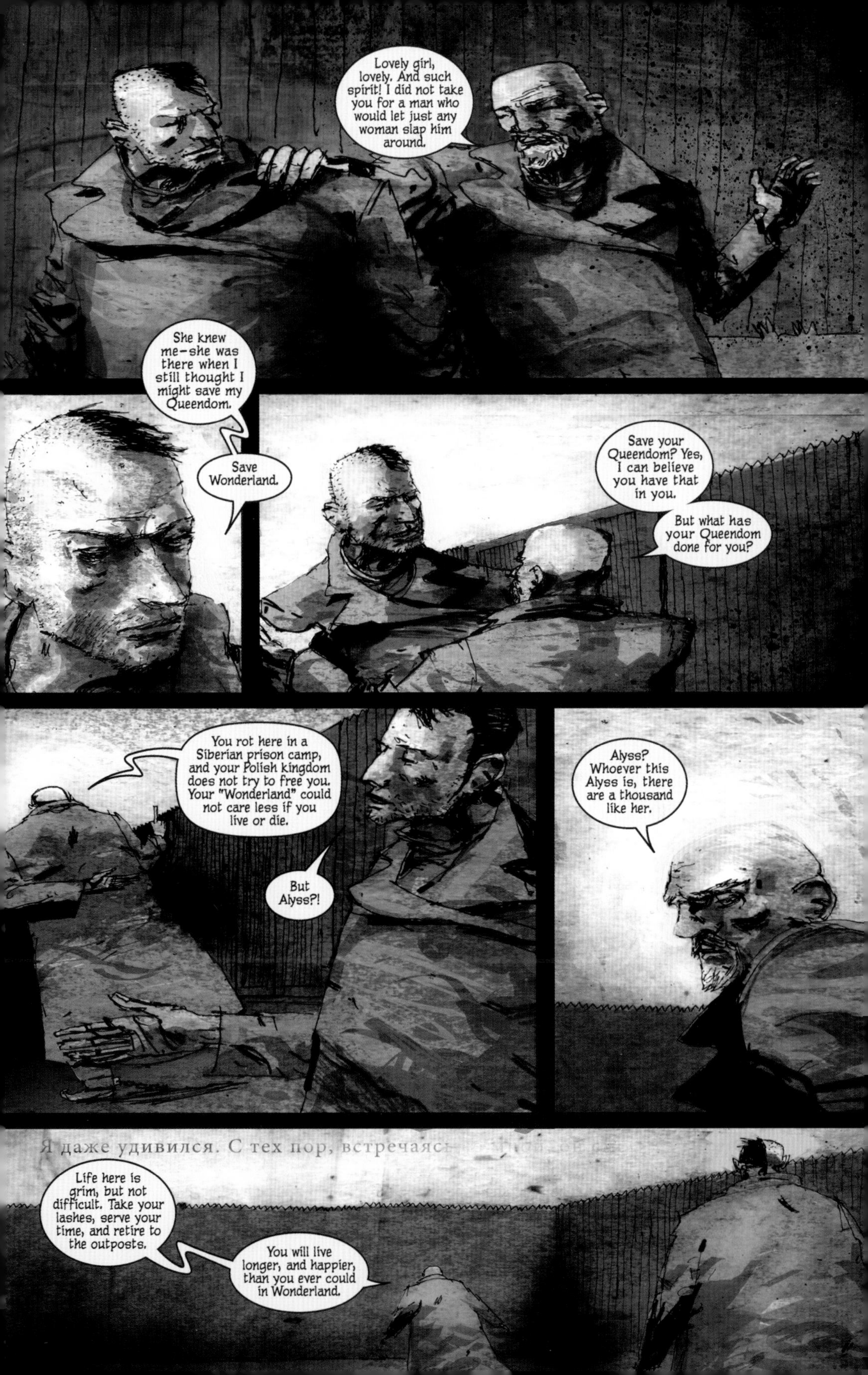
Lovely girl, lovely. And such spirit! I did not take you for a man who would let just any woman slap him around.
She knew me—she was there when I still thought I might save my Queendom.
Save Wonderland.
Save your Queendom? Yes, I can believe you have that in you.
But what has your Queendom done for you?
You rot here in a Siberian prison camp, and your Polish kingdom does not try to free you. Your "Wonderland" could not care less if you live or die.
But Alyss?!
Alyss? Whoever this Alyss is, there are a thousand like her.
Я даже удивился. С тех пор,
Life here is grim, but not difficult. Take your lashes, serve your time, and retire to the outposts.
You will live longer, and happier, than you ever could in Wonderland.

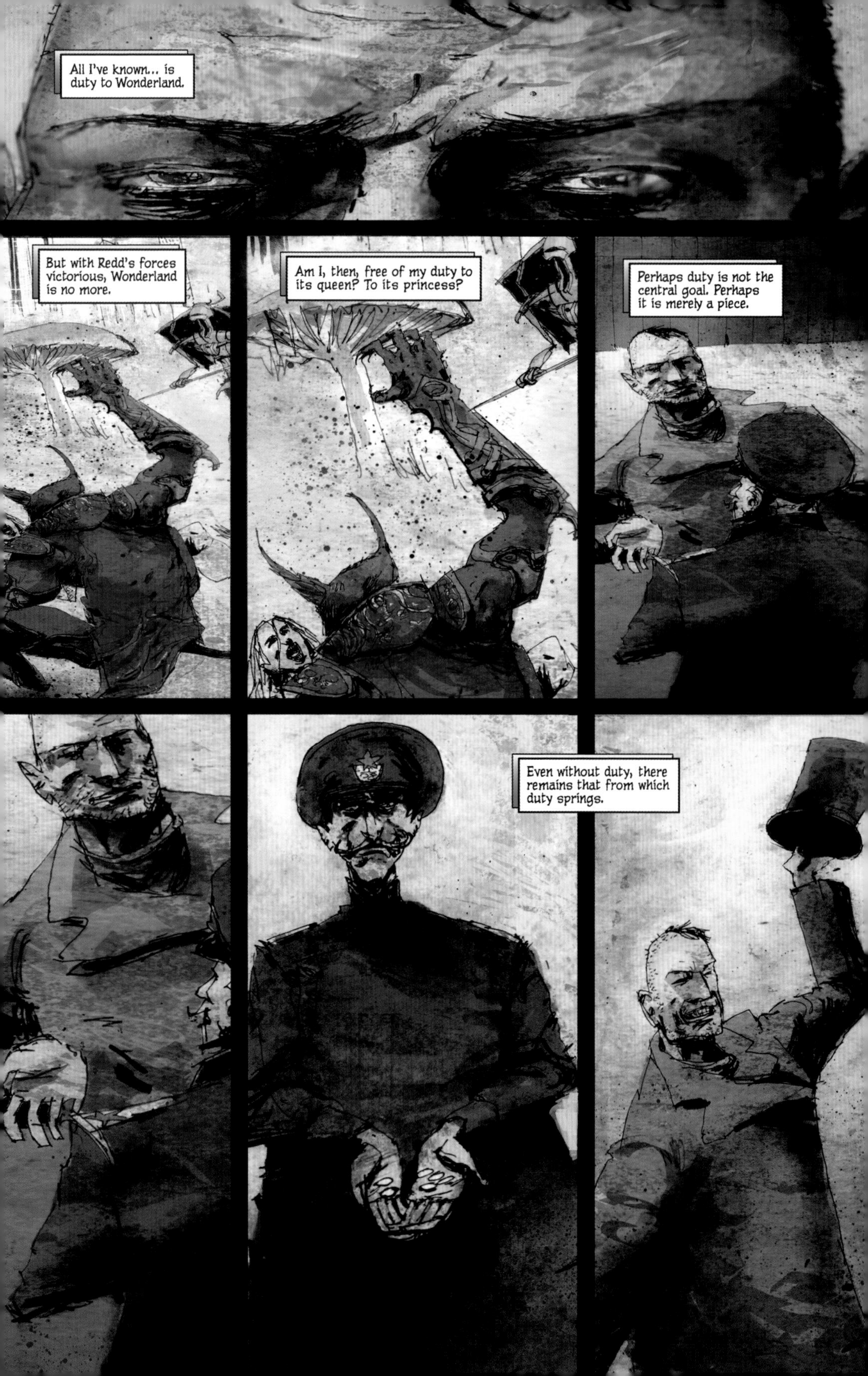
All I've known... is duty to Wonderland.
But with Redd's forces victorious, Wonderland is no more.
Am I, then, free of my duty to its queen? To its princess?
Perhaps duty is not the central goal. Perhaps it is merely a piece.
Even without duty, there remains that from which duty springs.

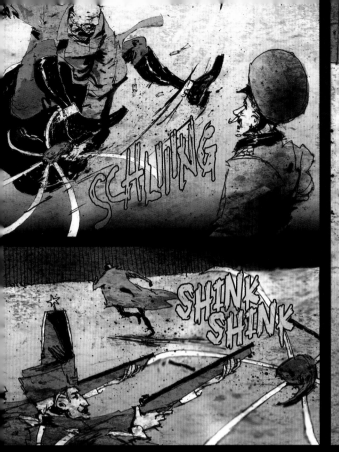

SCHLIING

SHINK
SHINK

I can not separate what I am from who I am. And I would not do so even if I could.

I am Hatter Madigan, bodyguard to the royal family of Wonderland.

"Only he that has traveled the road knows where the holes are deep." ~Chinese proverb

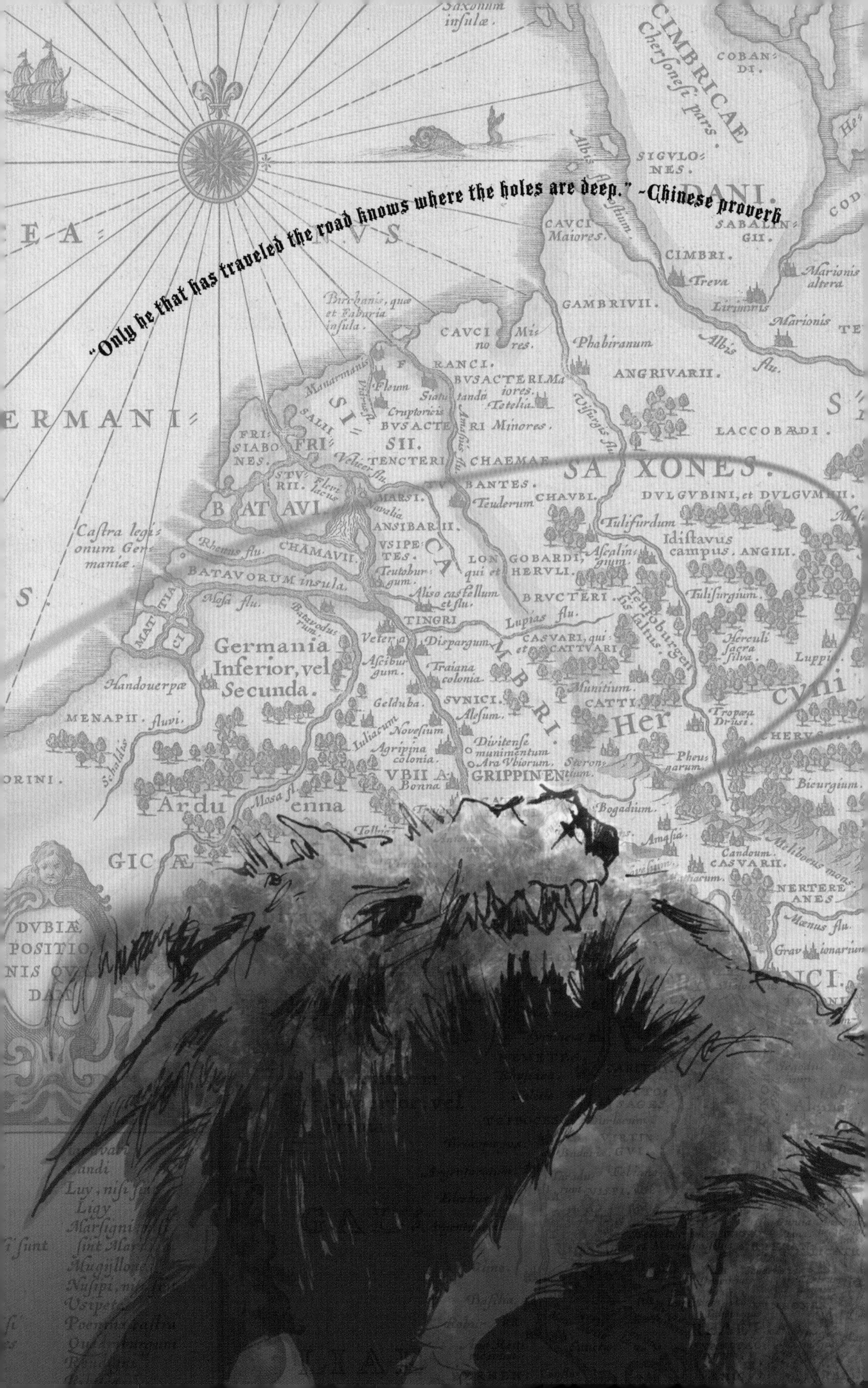

CIMBRICAE
Cherfonefi pars.
DANI.
SAXONES.
ERMANI
BATAVI
Germania
Inferior, vel
Secunda.
Ardu
enna
BATAVORVM insula.
CHAMAVII.
TENCTERI
CHAEMAE
LONGOBARDI,
qui et HERVLI.
BRVCTERI
Idistavus
campus.
ANGILI.
TINGRI
SVNICI.
VBII A
GRIPPINEN
Agrippina
colonia.
Bonna
Teutoburgensis saltus.
Hercinii sacra silva.
MENAPII.
GAMBRIVII.
ANGRIVARII.
LACCOBARDI.
CAVCI Maiores.
CIMBRI.
DVBIAE
POSITIO
NIS QV
DAM

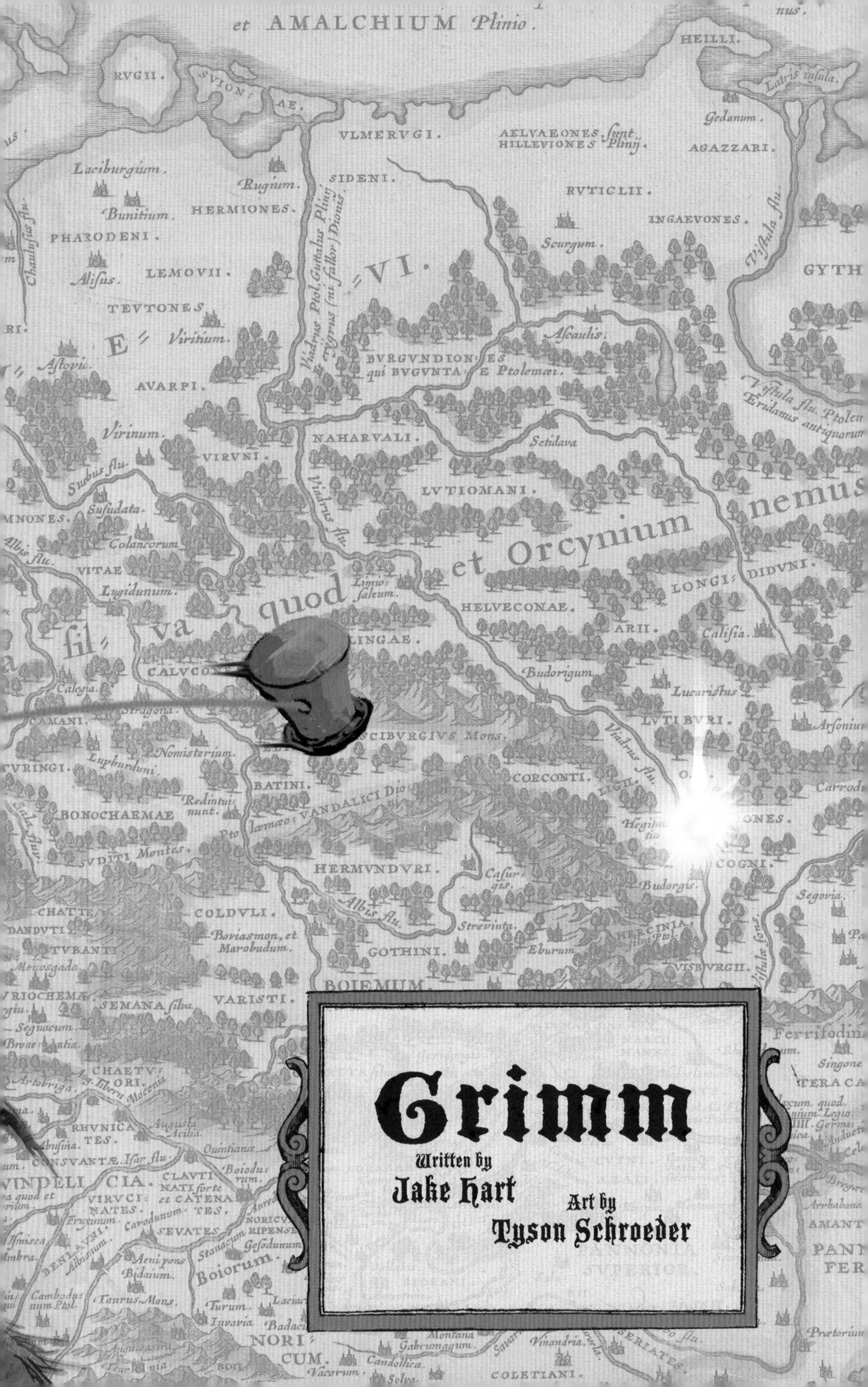
Grimm
Written by
Jake Hart
Art by
Tyson Schroeder
et AMALCHIUM Plinio.
HEILLI.
RVGII.
SVION
AE.
Latris insula.
Gedanum.
VLMERVGI.
AELVAEONES sunt
HILLEVIONES Plinij.
AGAZZARI.
Laciburgium.
Rugium.
SIDENI.
RVTICLII.
Bunitium.
HERMIONES.
INGAEVONES.
PHARODENI.
Scurgum.
Chalusius flu.
Viadrus Ptol. Guttalus Plinij & cygnus (ni fallor) Dionis.
Vistula flu.
Alisus.
LEMOVII.
VI.
GYTH
TEVTONES
E
Viritium.
Ascaulis.
Astovia.
BVRGVNDIONES
qui BVGVNTAE Ptolemaei.
AVARPI.
Vistula flu. Ptolem
Eridanus antiquorum
Virinum.
NAHARVALI.
Setidava
VIRVNI.
Suebus flu.
Viadrus flu.
LVTIOMANI.
Susudata.
Colancorum.
Albis flu.
et Orcynium nemus
VITAE
Limiosaleum.
LONGI
DIDVNI.
Lugidunum.
fil va quod
HELVECONAE.
ARII.
Calisia.
LINGAE.
CALVCO
Budorigum
Calegia.
Lucaristus
CAMANI.
Stragona.
LVTI BVRI.
Arsonium
ASCIBVRGIVS Mons.
Nomisterium.
Luphurdum.
CVRINGI.
BATINI.
CORCONTI.
LIGII.
Carrod
Redintuinum.
BONOCHAEMAE
VANDALICI
ONES.
Ptolemaeo
SVDITI Montes.
COGNI.
HERMVNDVRI.
Casurgis.
Budorgis.
Segovia.
CHATTE
COLDVLI.
Albis flu.
Strevinta.
DANDVTI
Boviasmon, et Marobudum.
HERCINIA silva Ptol.
TVBANTI
GOTHINI.
Eburum
Vistulae fons.
Menosgada
VISBVRGII.
BOIEMUM.
VARISTI.
SEMANA silva.
Seguacum.
Ferrifodin
CHAETVORI.
Singone
Artobriga.
TERACA
RHVNICATES.
Augusta Acilia.
Abusina.
Quintianae
CONSVANTAE. Isar flu.
Boiodurum.
VINDELICIA.
CLAVTINATI forte et CATENATES.
VIRVCINATES.
NORICVM RIPENSE
SEVATES.
Carodunum.
Gesodunum
Boiorum.
Aeni pons
Bidaium.
PANN
FER
Cambodunum Ptol.
Taurus Mons.
Turum.
Iuvavia
Badaci
Montana
Gabrumagum.
Vinandria.
NORICUM.
Candollica.
Praetorium
Vacorum.
Solva.
COLETIANI.

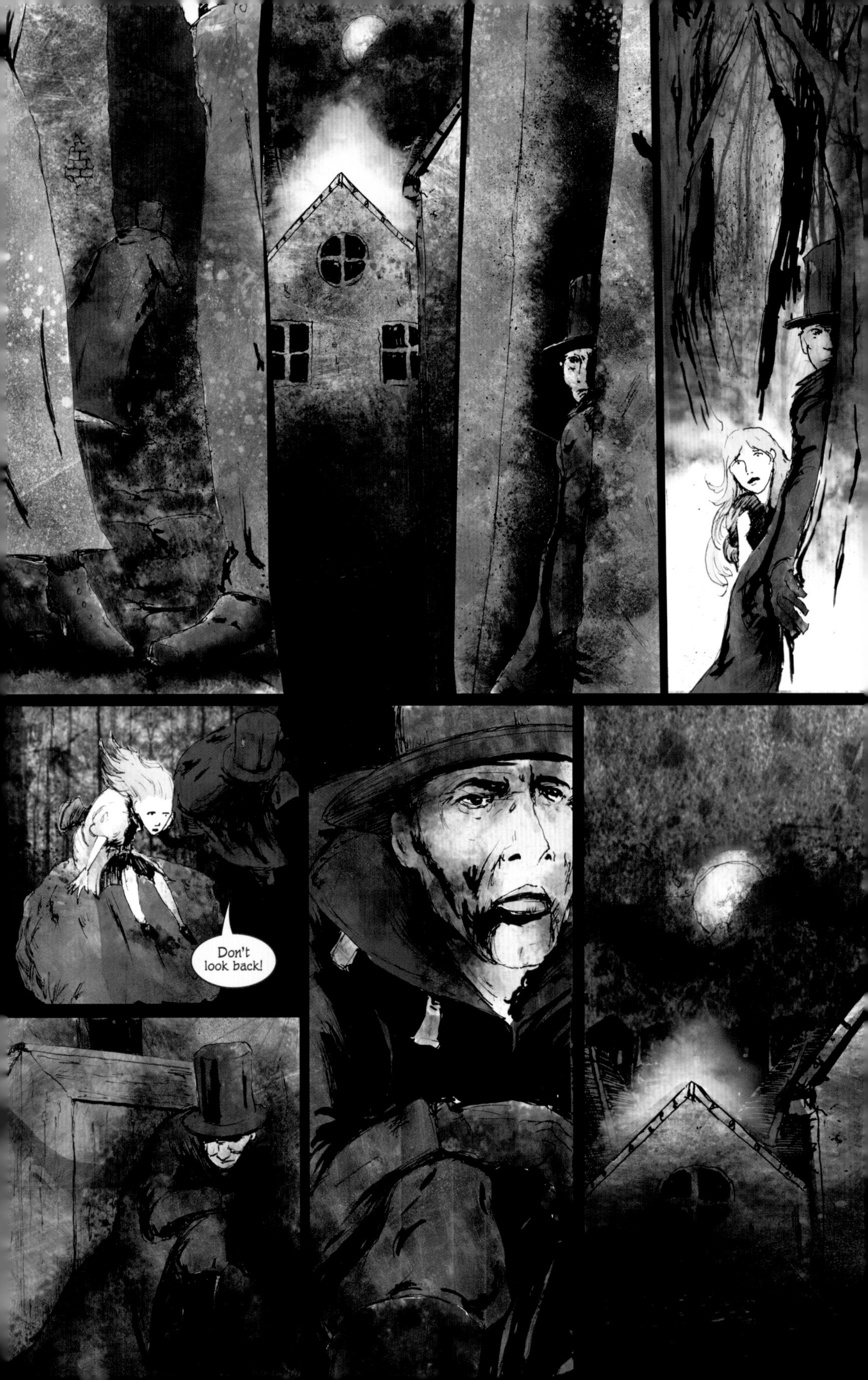
Don't look back!

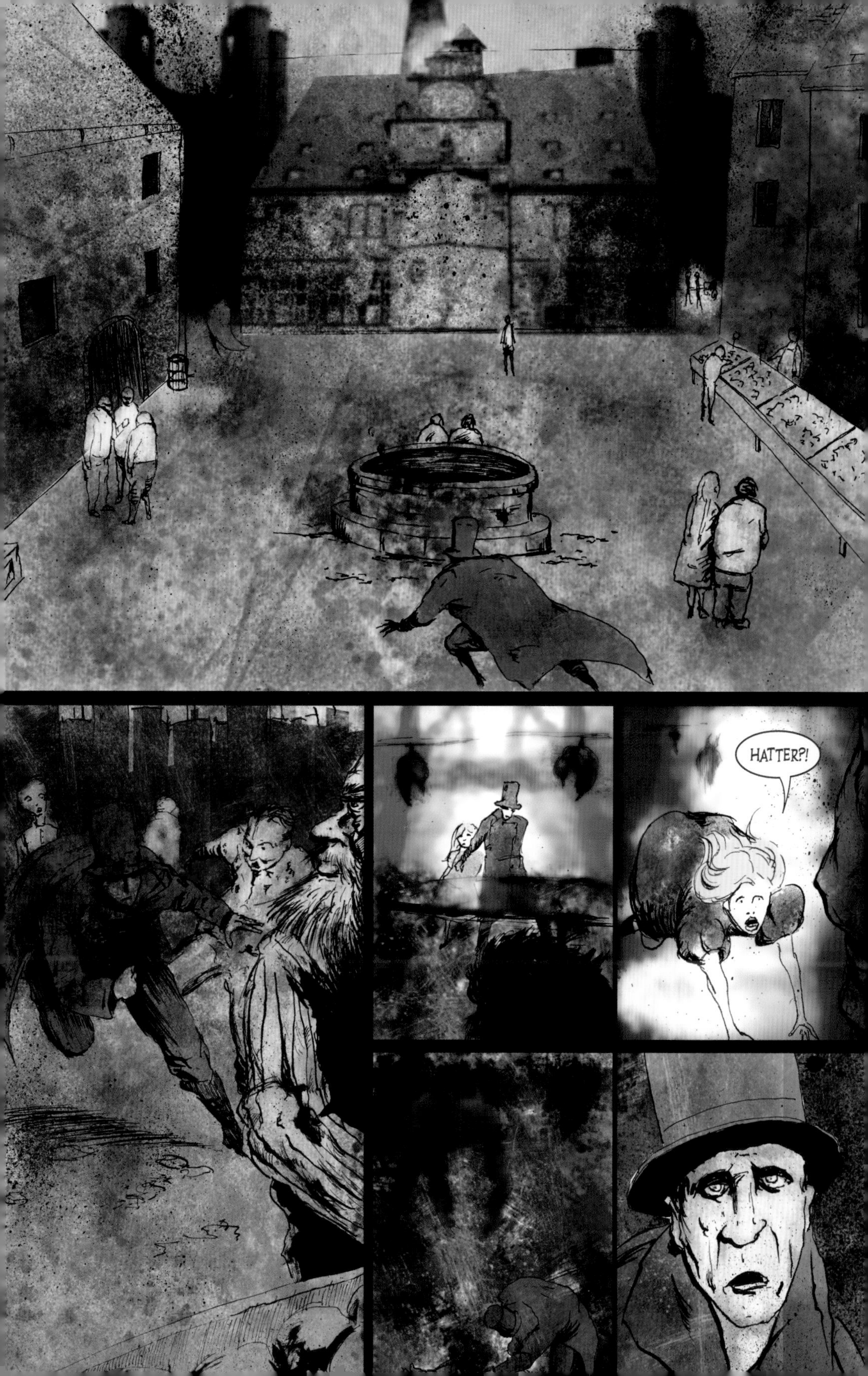
HATTER?!

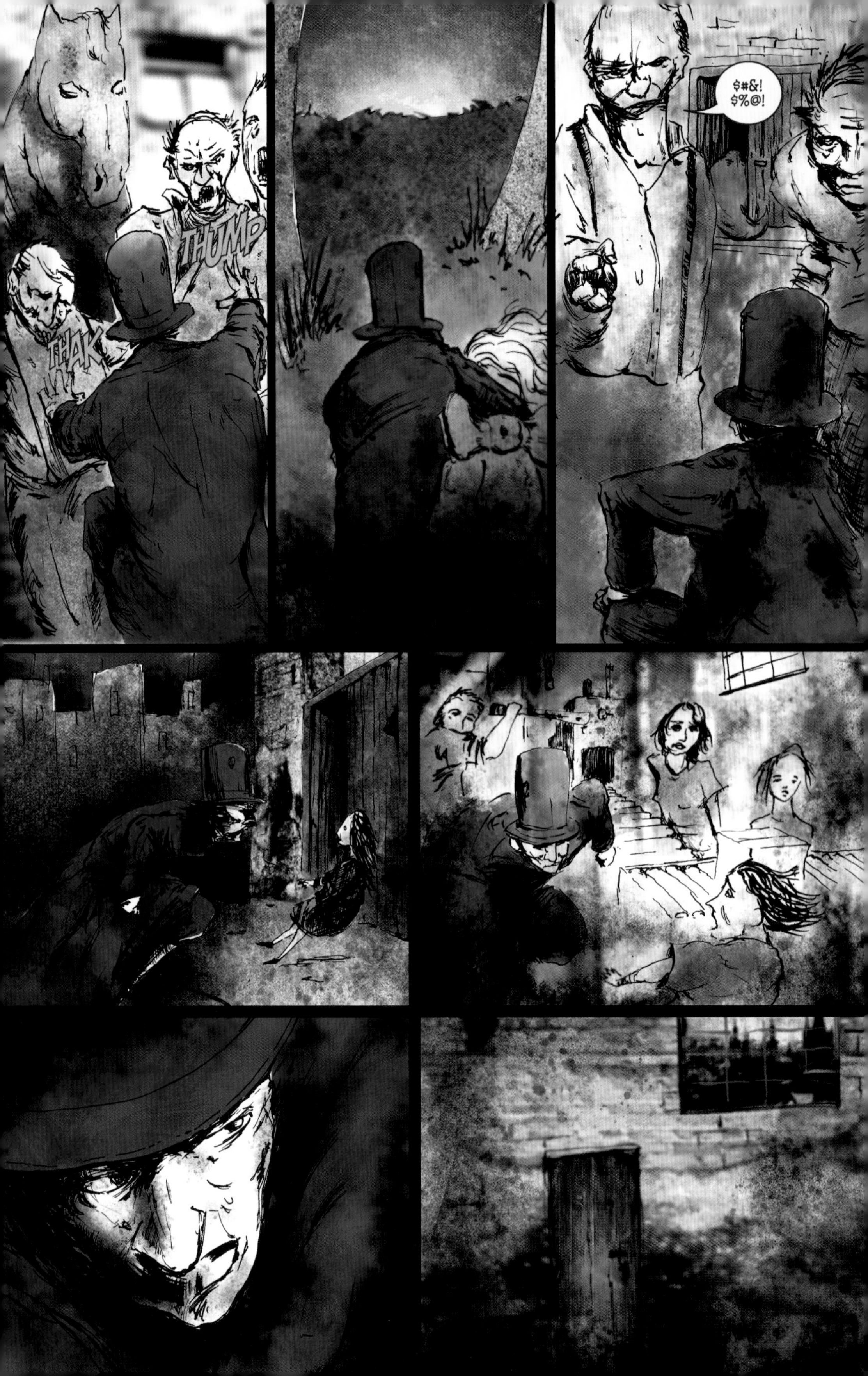
THUMP
THAK
$#&!
$%@!

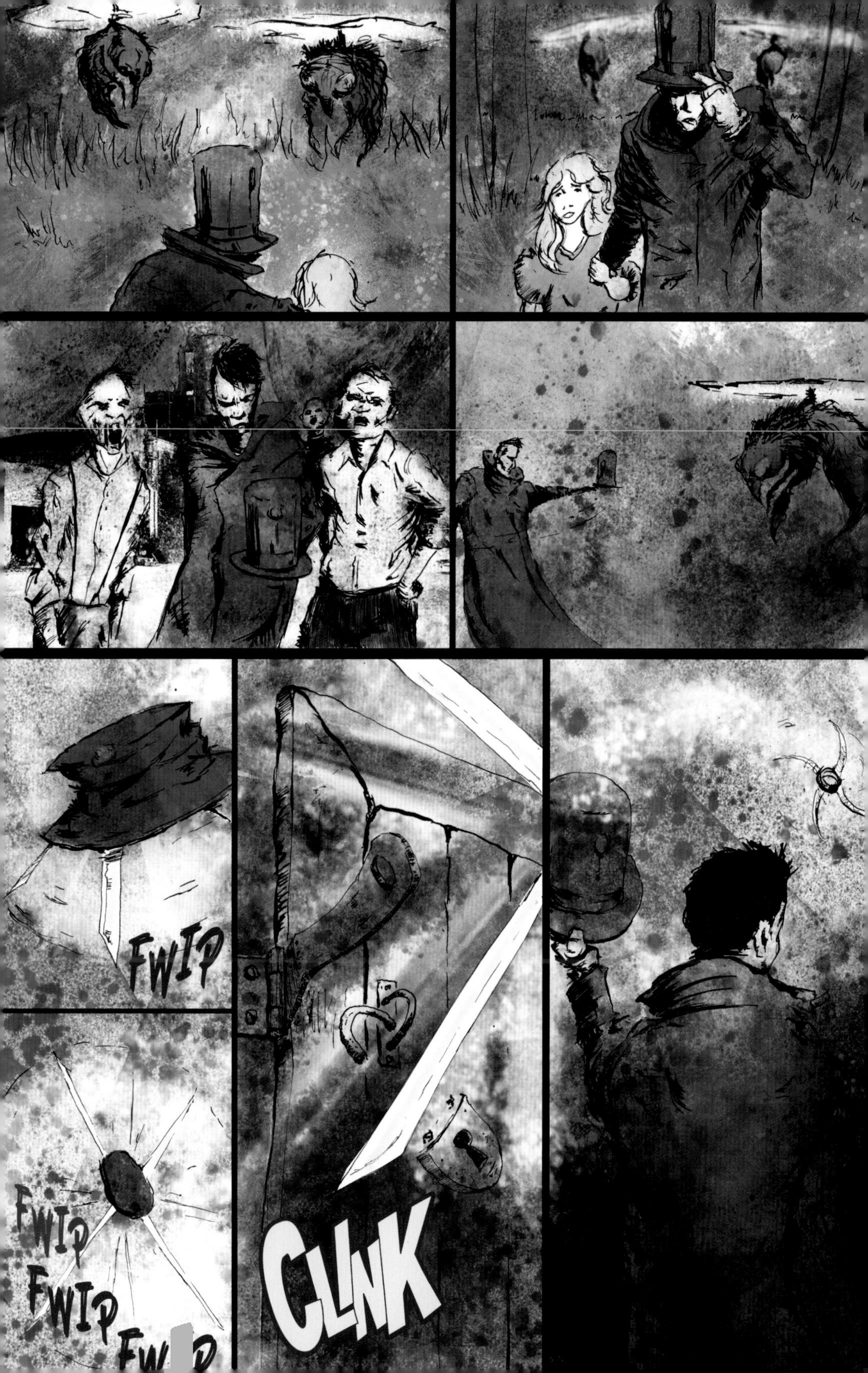
FWIP
FWIP
FWIP
CLINK

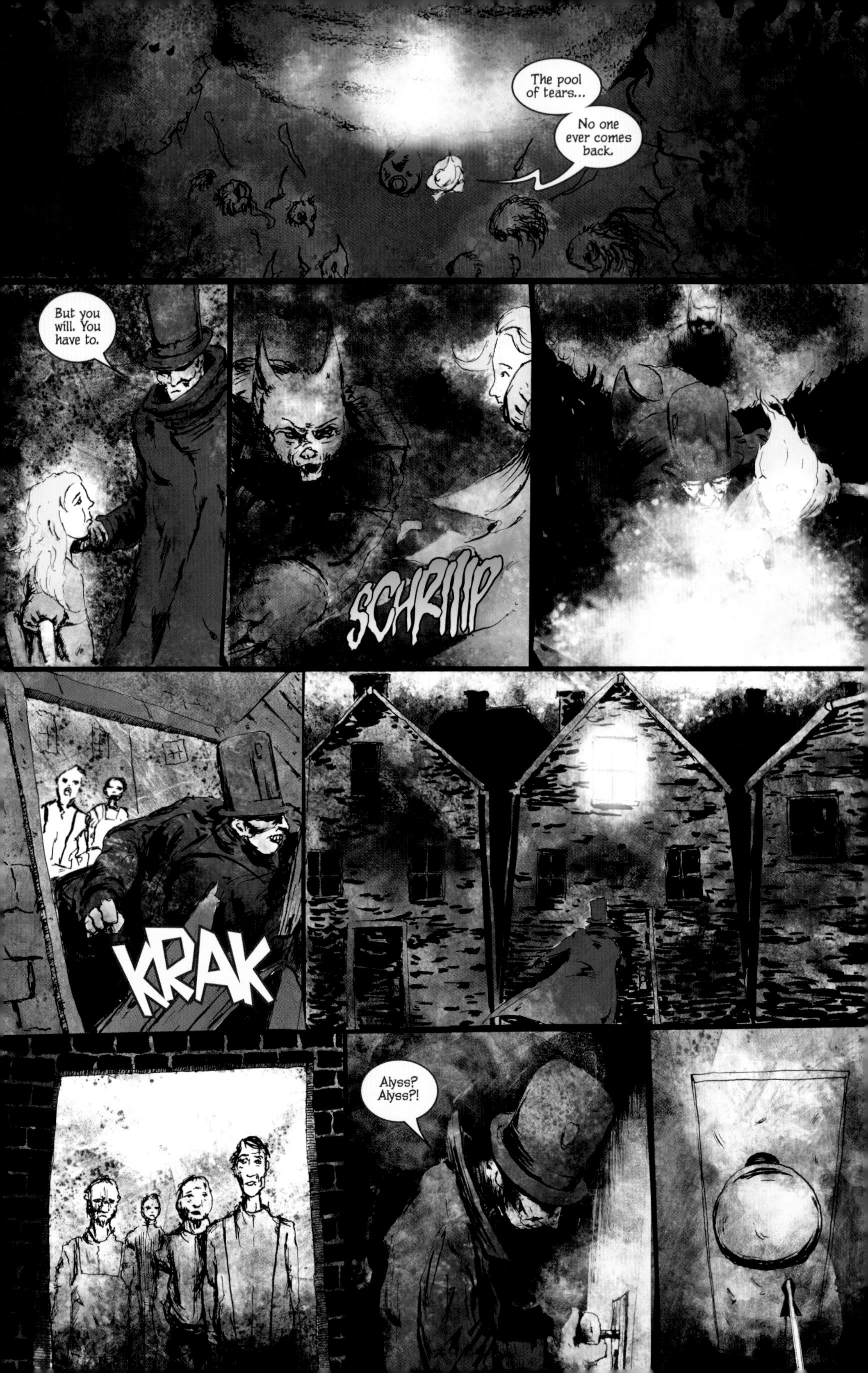
The pool of tears...
No one ever comes back.
But you will. You have to.
SCHRIIIP
KRAK
Alyss? Alyss?!

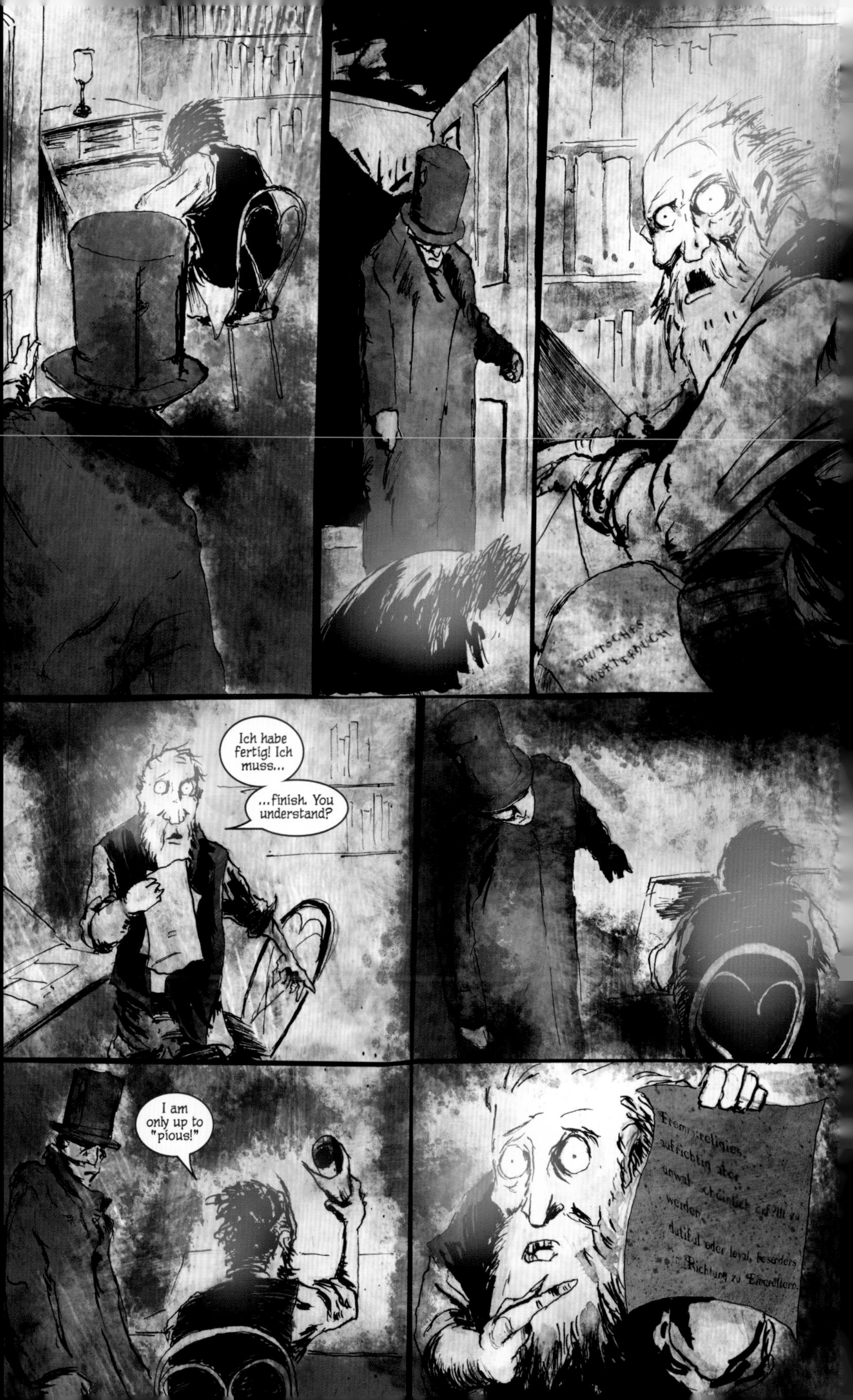
DEUTSCHES
WORTERBUCH
Ich habe fertig! Ich muss...
...finish. You understand?
I am only up to "pious!"
dutiful oder loyal, besonders

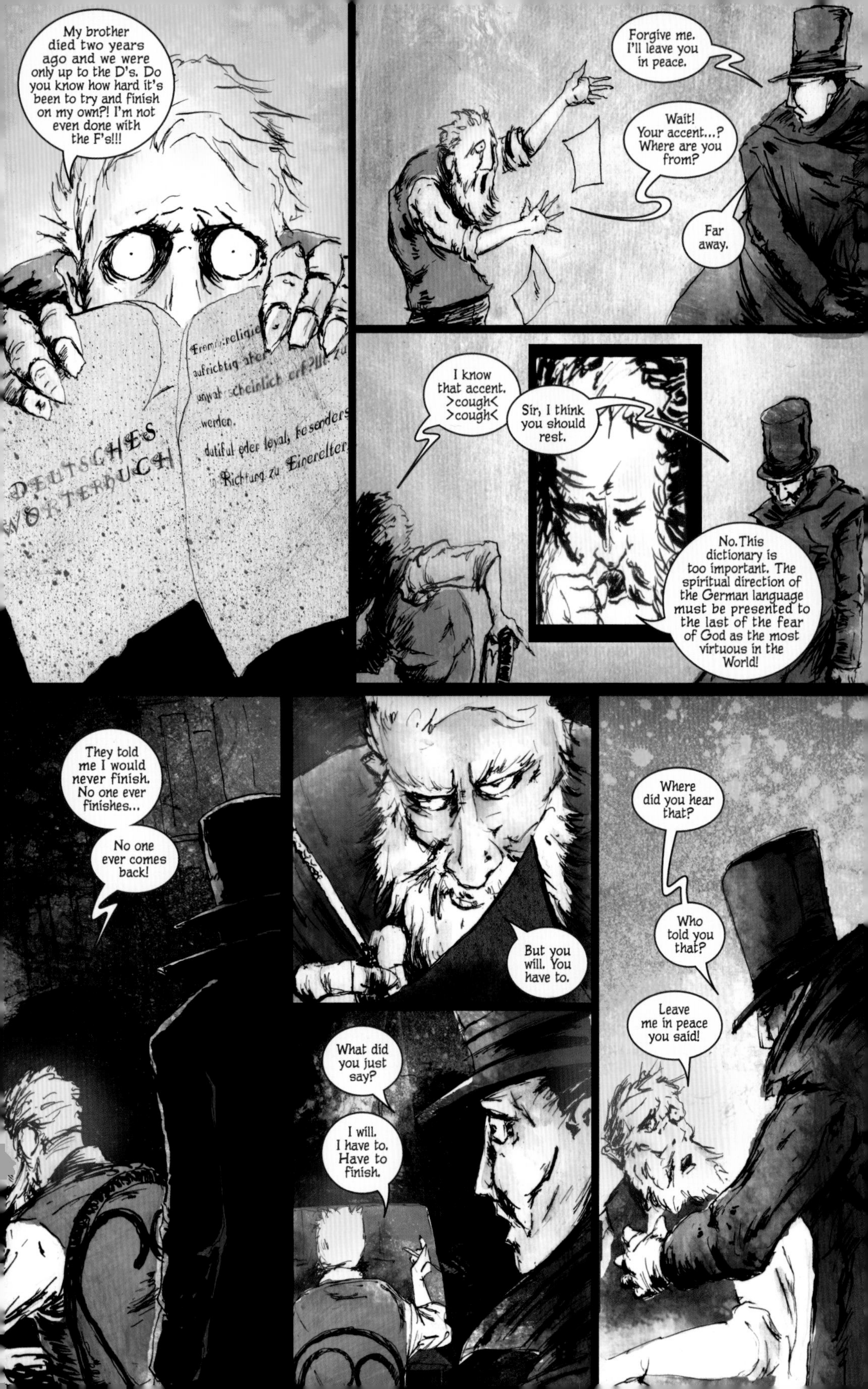
My brother died two years ago and we were only up to the D's. Do you know how hard it's been to try and finish on my own?! I'm not even done with the F's!!!
DEUTSCHES WÖRTERBUCH
Forgive me. I'll leave you in peace.
Wait! Your accent...? Where are you from?
Far away.
I know that accent. >cough< >cough<
Sir, I think you should rest.
No. This dictionary is too important. The spiritual direction of the German language must be presented to the last of the fear of God as the most virtuous in the World!
They told me I would never finish. No one ever finishes...
No one ever comes back!
But you will. You have to.
What did you just say?
I will. I have to. Have to finish.
Where did you hear that?
Who told you that?
Leave me in peace you said!

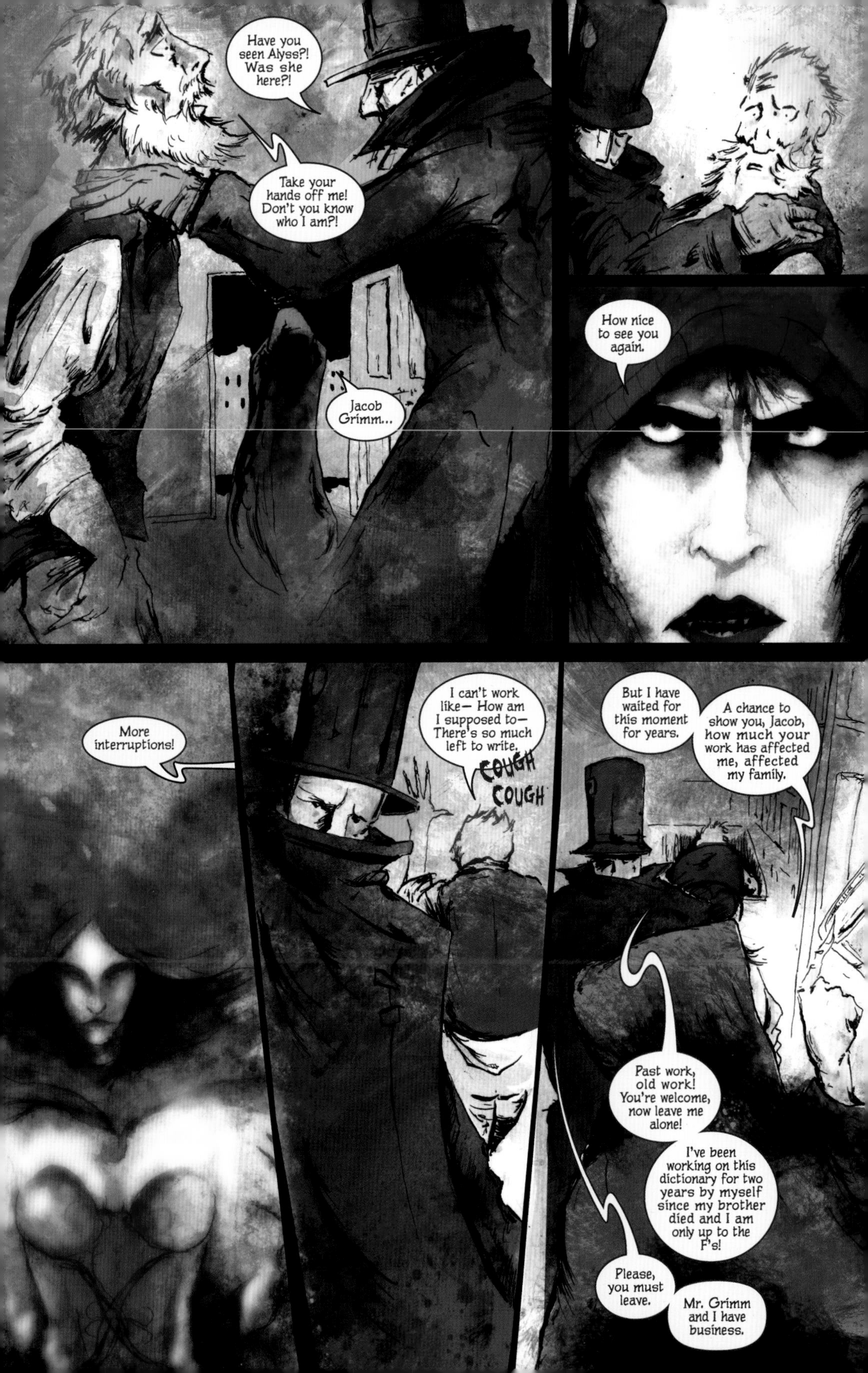
Have you seen Alyss?! Was she here?!
Take your hands off me! Don't you know who I am?!
Jacob Grimm...
How nice to see you again.
More interruptions!
I can't work like— How am I supposed to— There's so much left to write.
COUGH COUGH
But I have waited for this moment for years.
A chance to show you, Jacob, how much your work has affected me, affected my family.
Past work, old work! You're welcome, now leave me alone!
I've been working on this dictionary for two years by myself since my brother died and I am only up to the F's!
Please, you must leave.
Mr. Grimm and I have business.

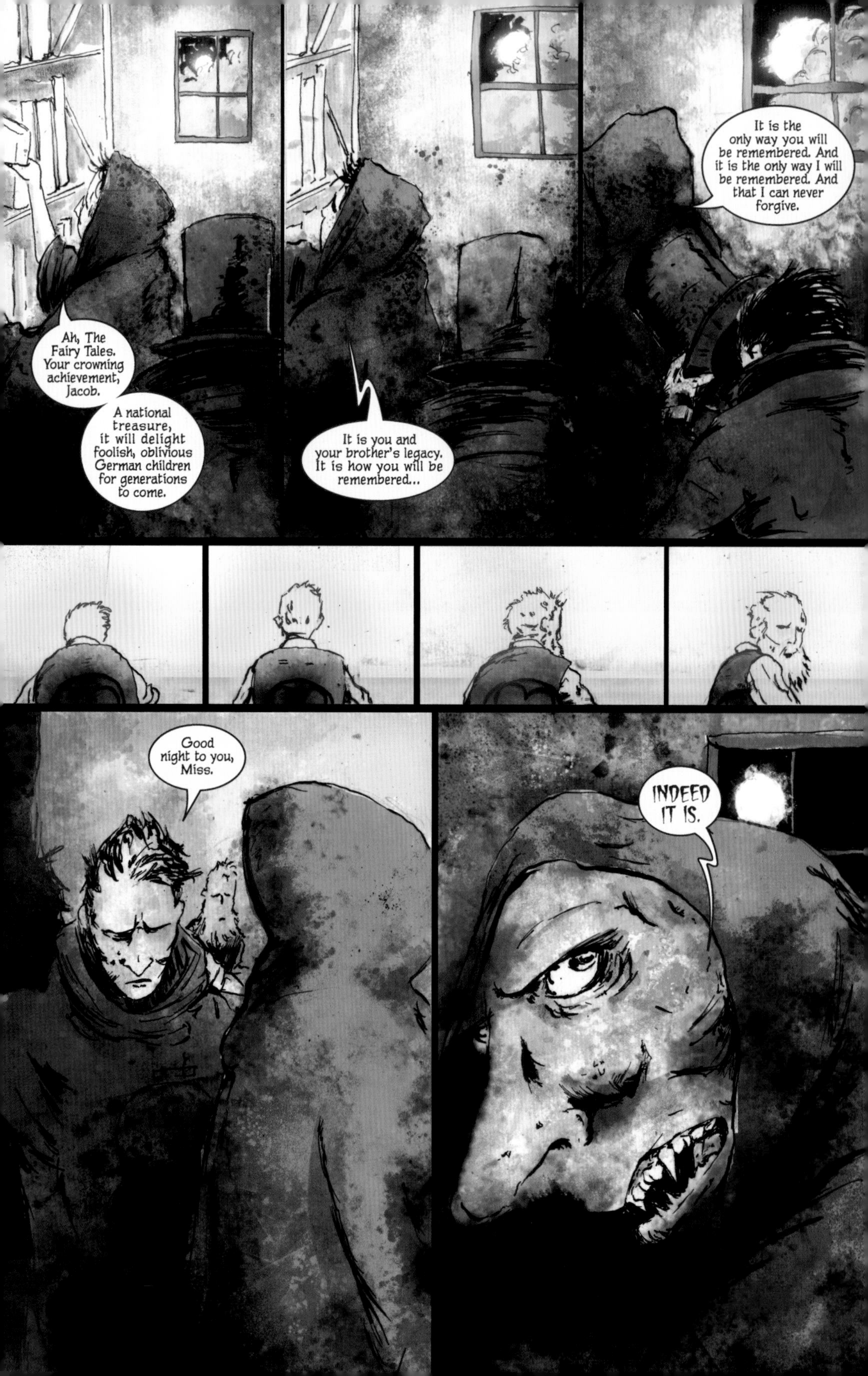
Ah, The Fairy Tales. Your crowning achievement, Jacob.
A national treasure, it will delight foolish, oblivious German children for generations to come.
It is you and your brother's legacy. It is how you will be remembered...
It is the only way you will be remembered. And it is the only way I will be remembered. And that I can never forgive.
Good night to you, Miss.
INDEED IT IS.

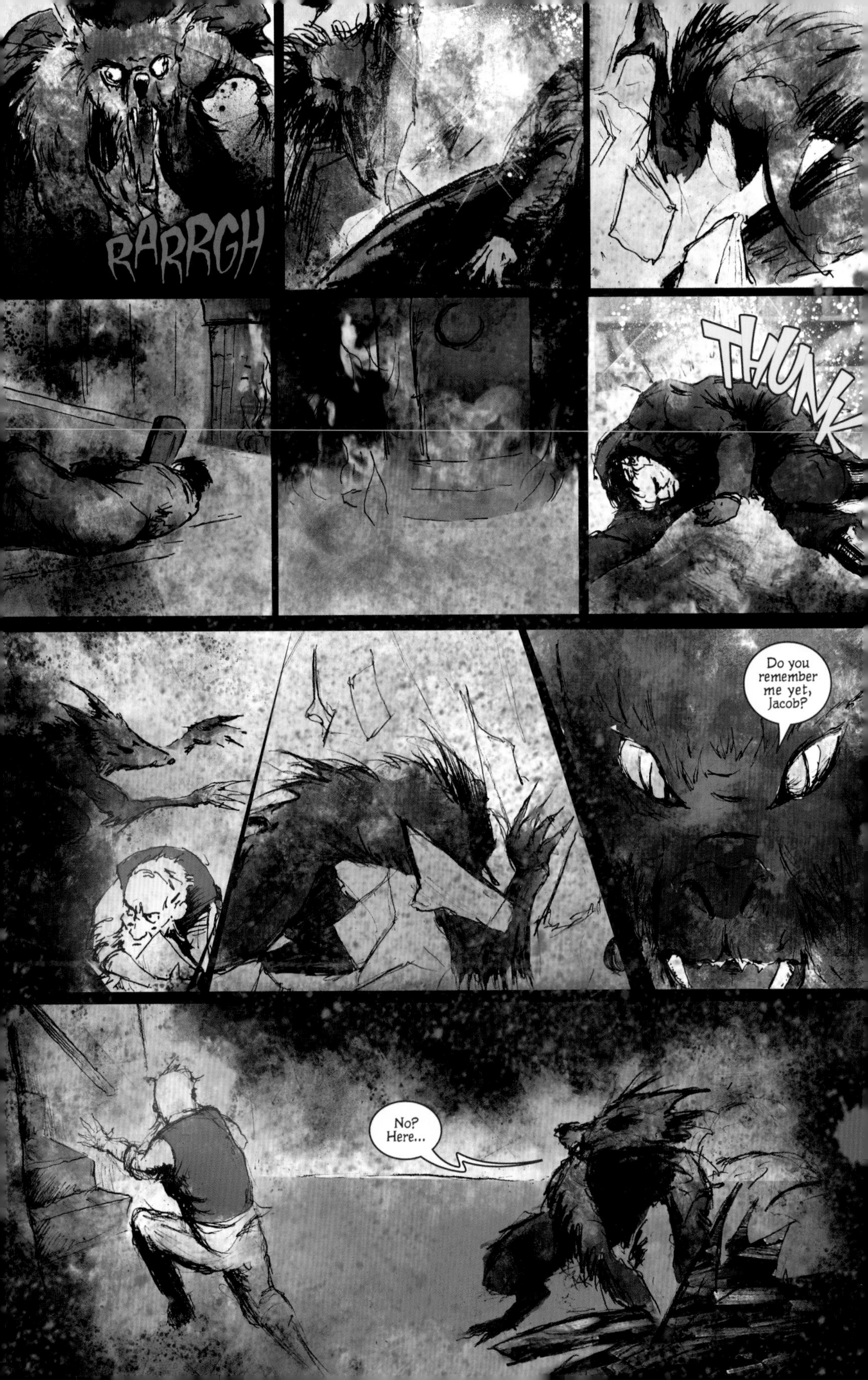
RARRGH
THUNK
Do you remember me yet, Jacob?
No? Here...

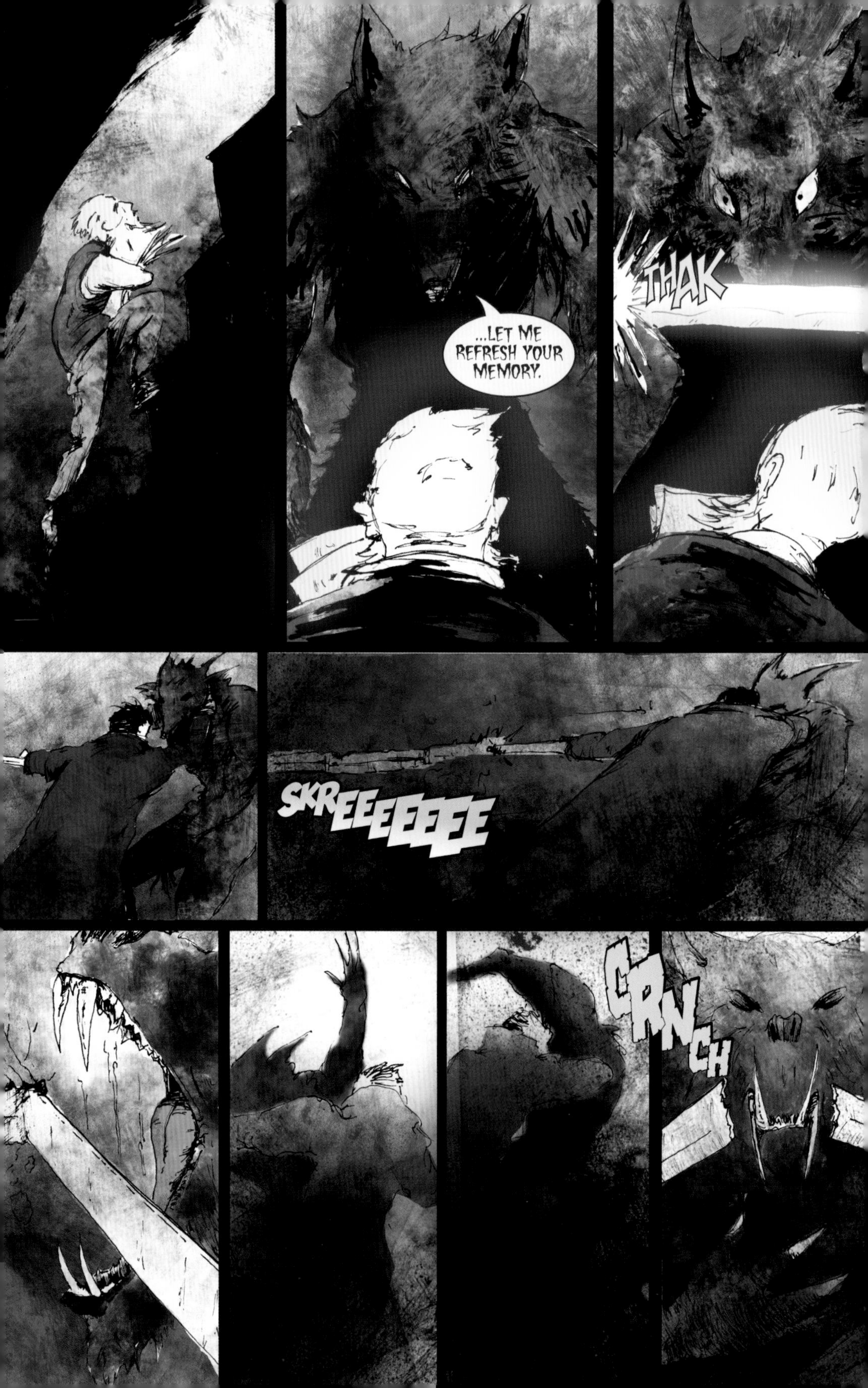
...LET ME REFRESH YOUR MEMORY.
THAK
SKREEEEEEE
CRNCH

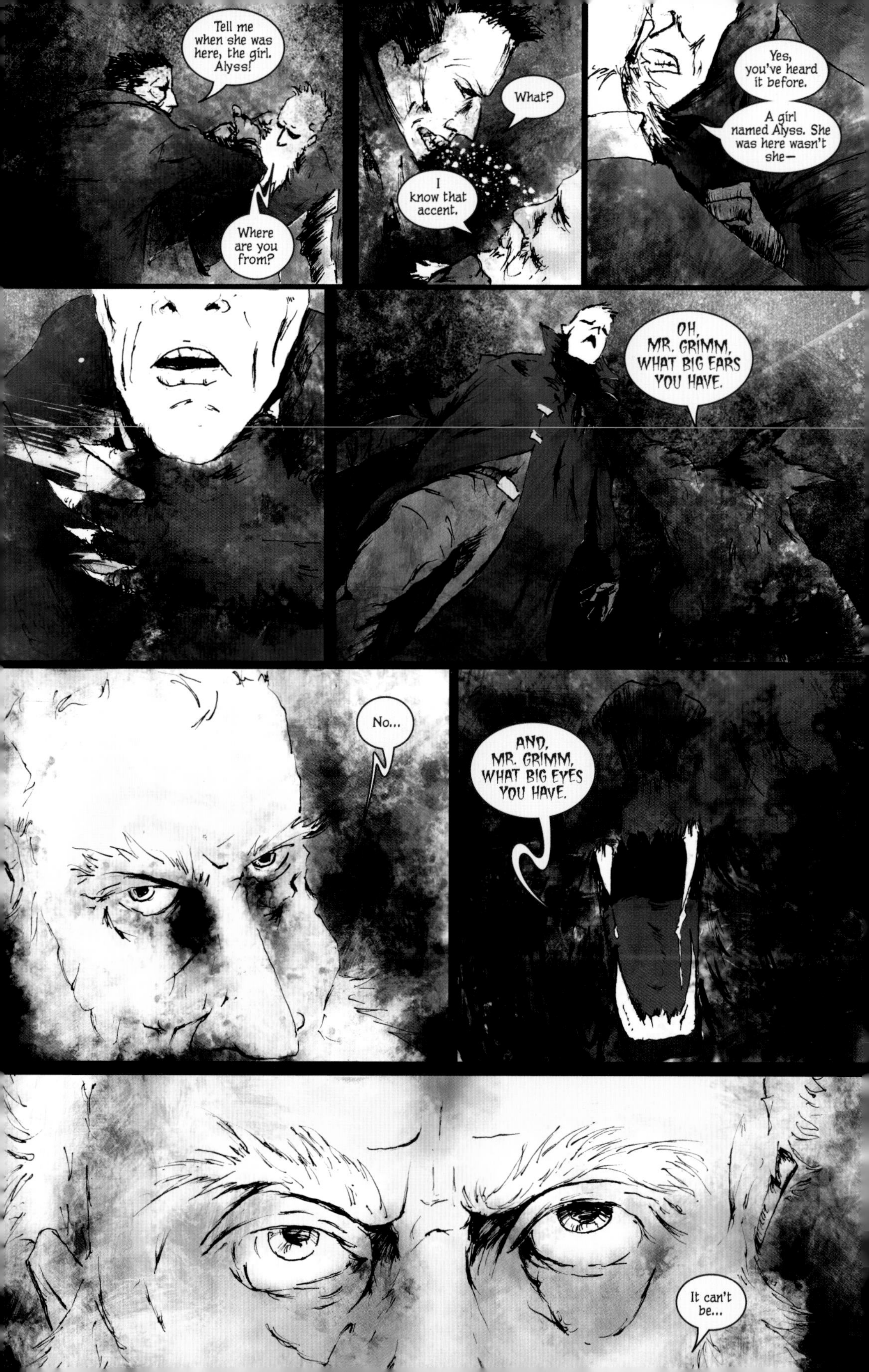
Tell me when she was here, the girl. Alyss!
Where are you from?
What?
I know that accent.
Yes, you've heard it before.
A girl named Alyss. She was here wasn't she—
OH, MR. GRIMM, WHAT BIG EARS YOU HAVE.
No...
AND, MR. GRIMM, WHAT BIG EYES YOU HAVE.
It can't be...

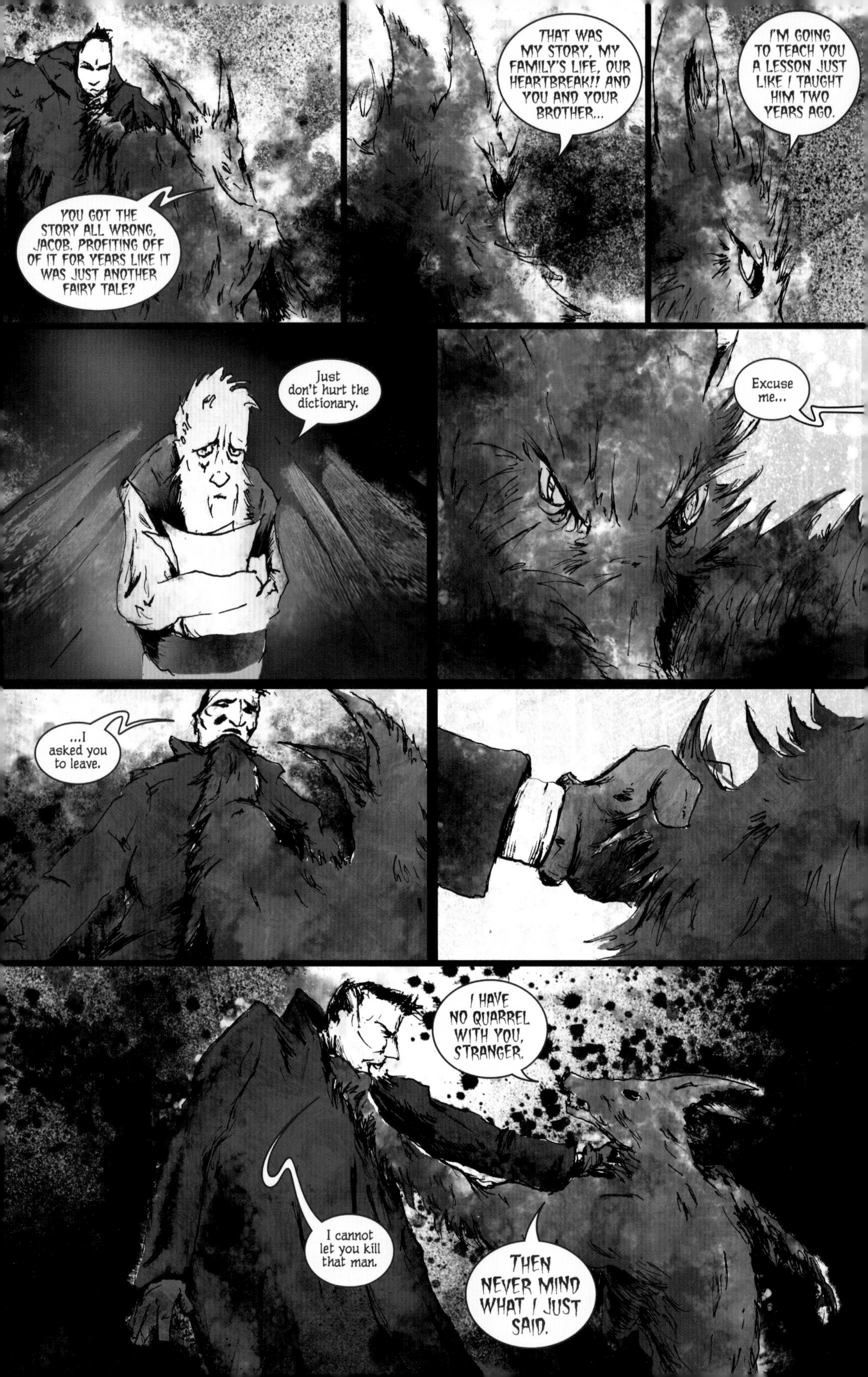
YOU GOT THE STORY ALL WRONG, JACOB. PROFITING OFF OF IT FOR YEARS LIKE IT WAS JUST ANOTHER FAIRY TALE?
THAT WAS MY STORY, MY FAMILY'S LIFE, OUR HEARTBREAK!! AND YOU AND YOUR BROTHER...
I'M GOING TO TEACH YOU A LESSON JUST LIKE I TAUGHT HIM TWO YEARS AGO.
Just don't hurt the dictionary.
Excuse me...
...I asked you to leave.
I HAVE NO QUARREL WITH YOU, STRANGER.
I cannot let you kill that man.
THEN NEVER MIND WHAT I JUST SAID.

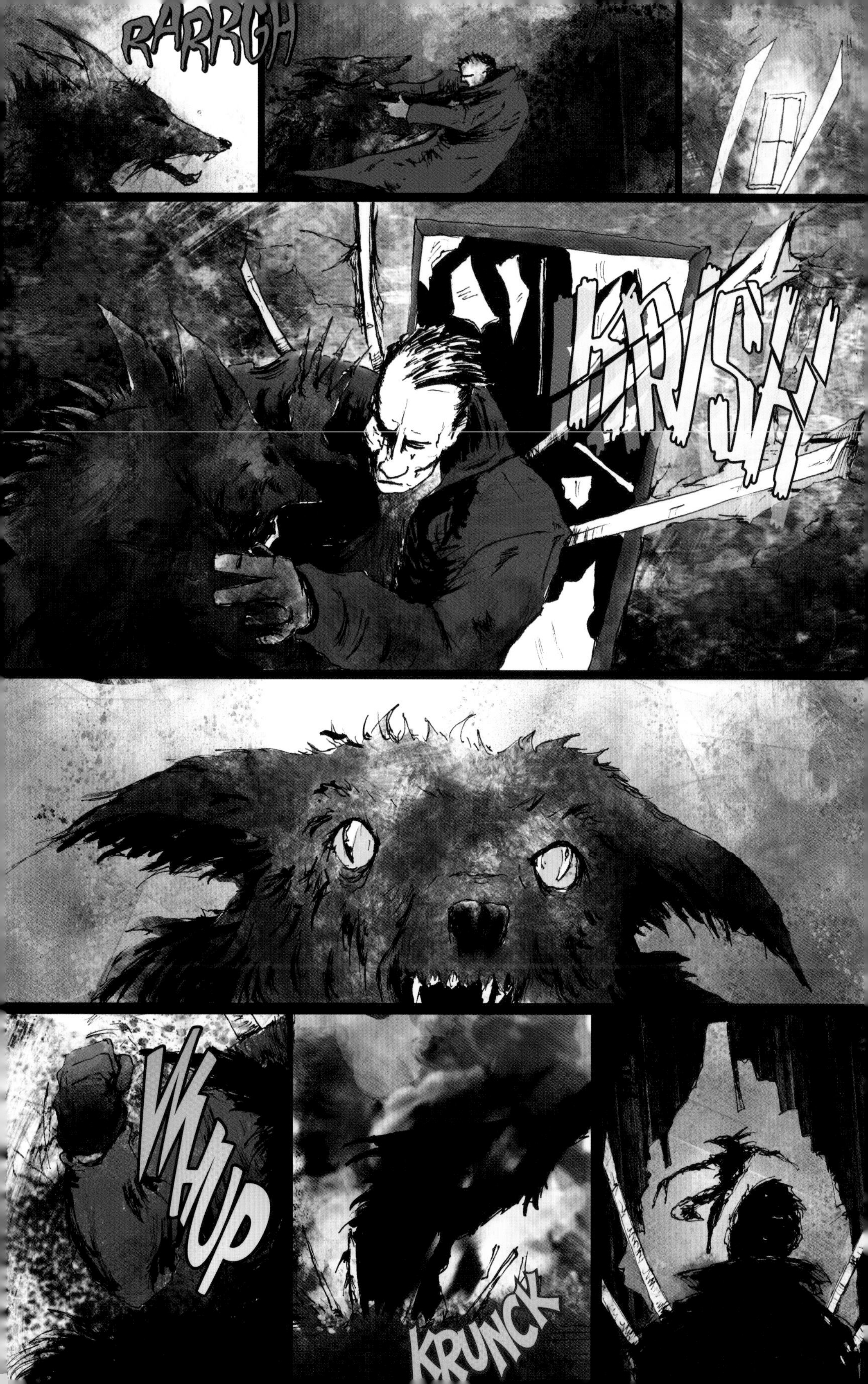
RARRGH
KRISH
WHUP
KRUNCK

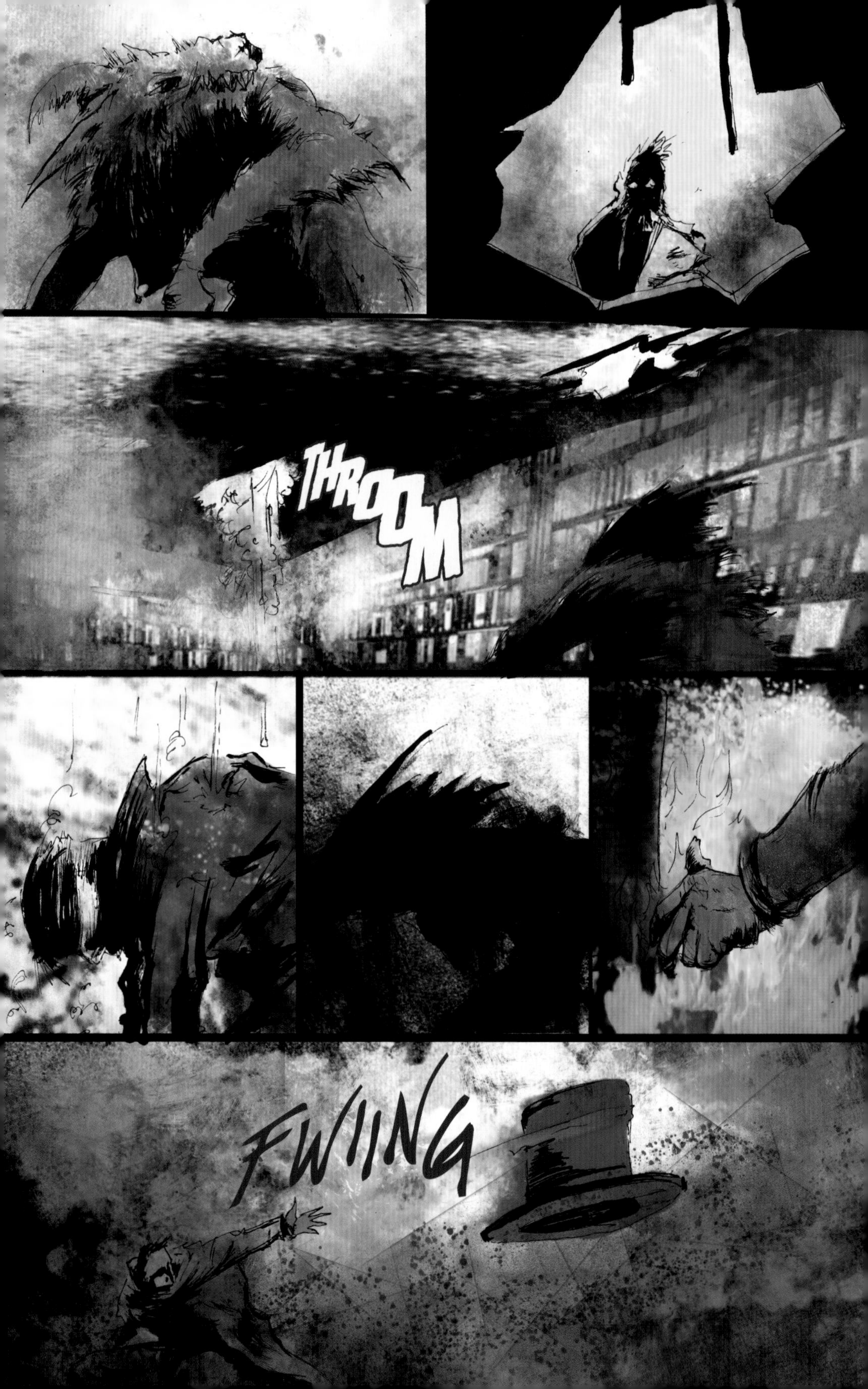
THROOM
FWING

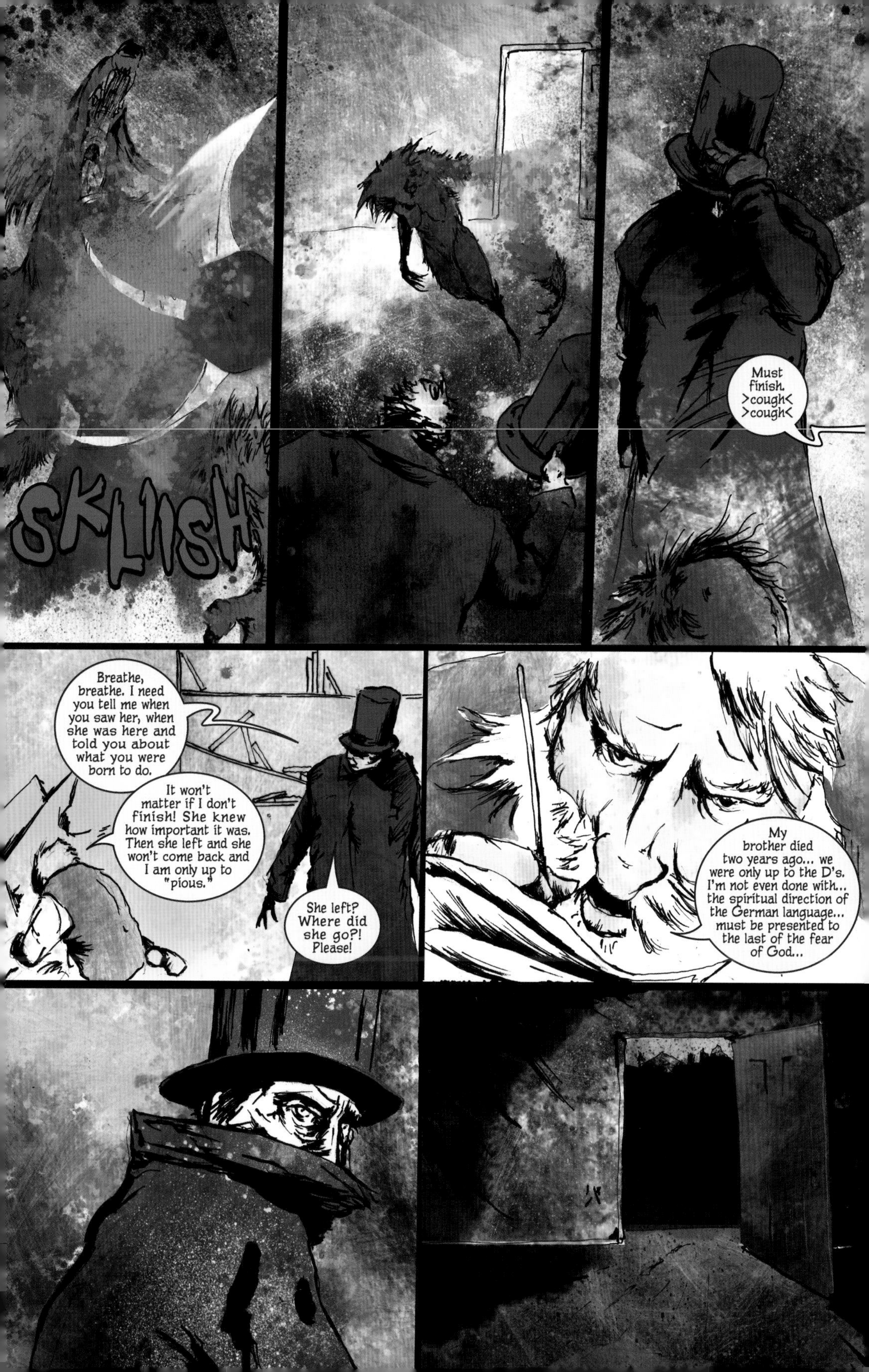
SKLISH
Must finish. >cough< >cough<
Breathe, breathe. I need you tell me when you saw her, when she was here and told you about what you were born to do.
It won't matter if I don't finish! She knew how important it was. Then she left and she won't come back and I am only up to "pious."
She left? Where did she go?! Please!
My brother died two years ago... we were only up to the D's. I'm not even done with... the spiritual direction of the German language... must be presented to the last of the fear of God...

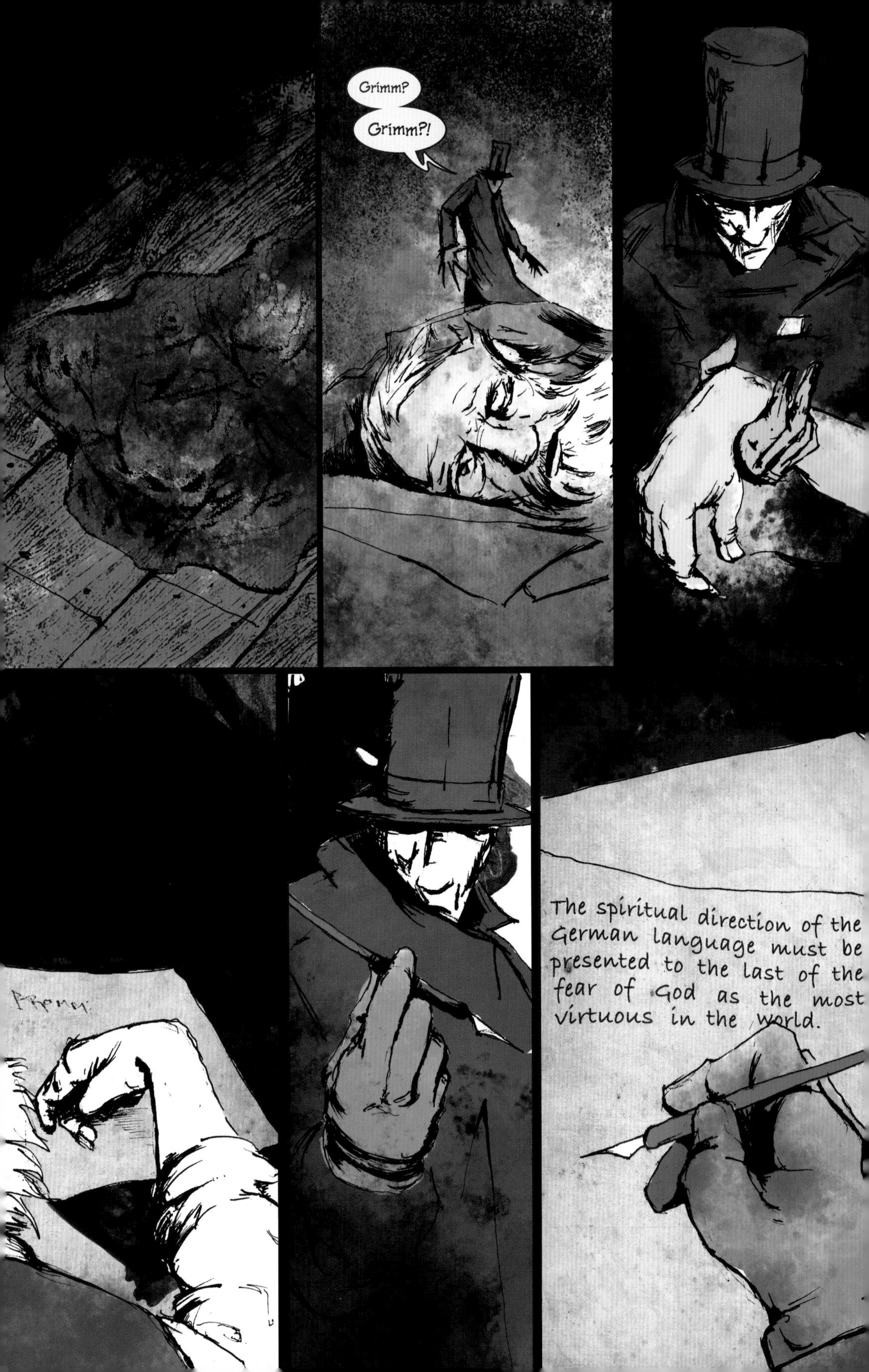
Grimm?
Grimm?!
The spiritual direction of the German language must be presented to the last of the fear of God as the most virtuous in the world.

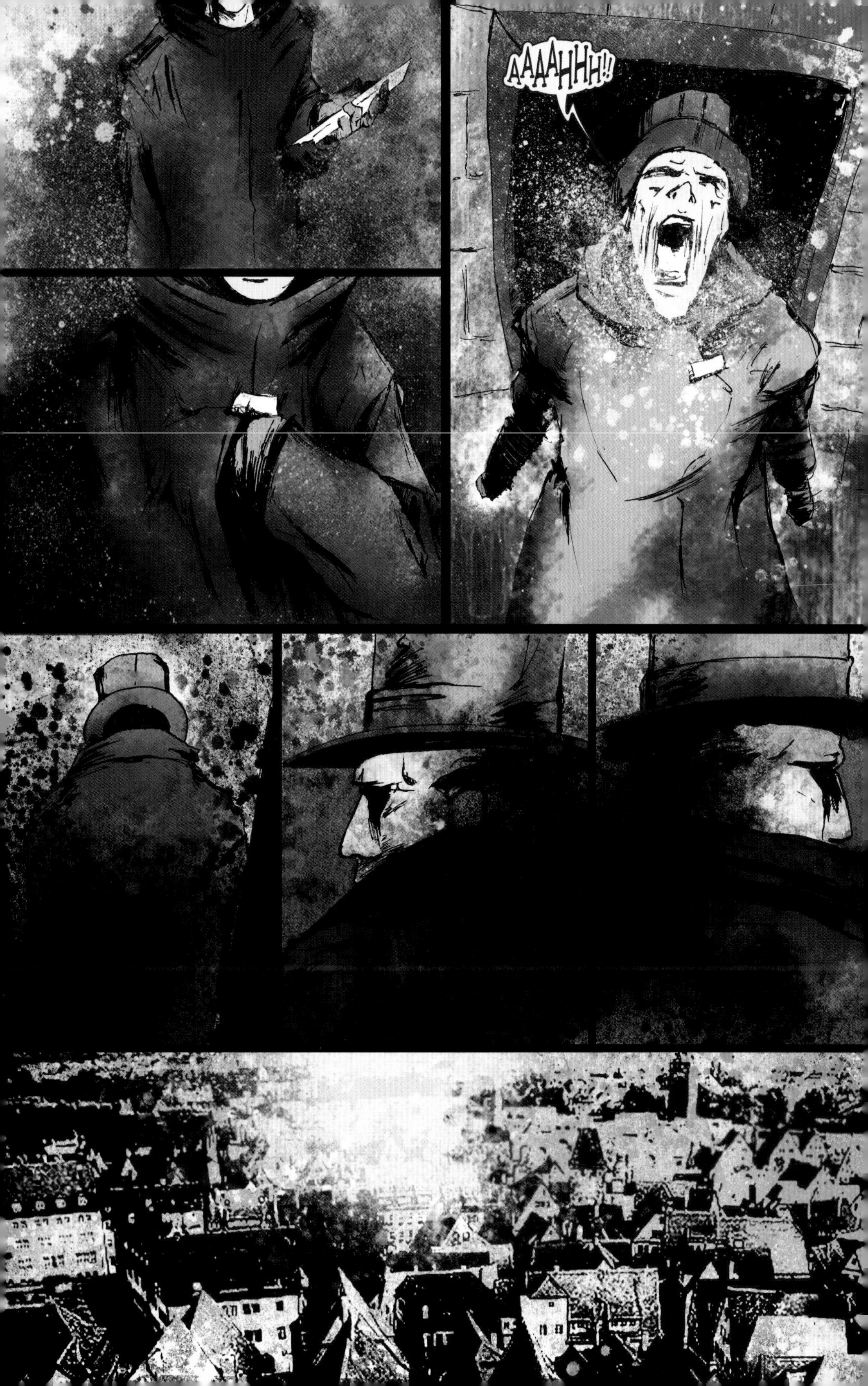
AAAAHHH!!

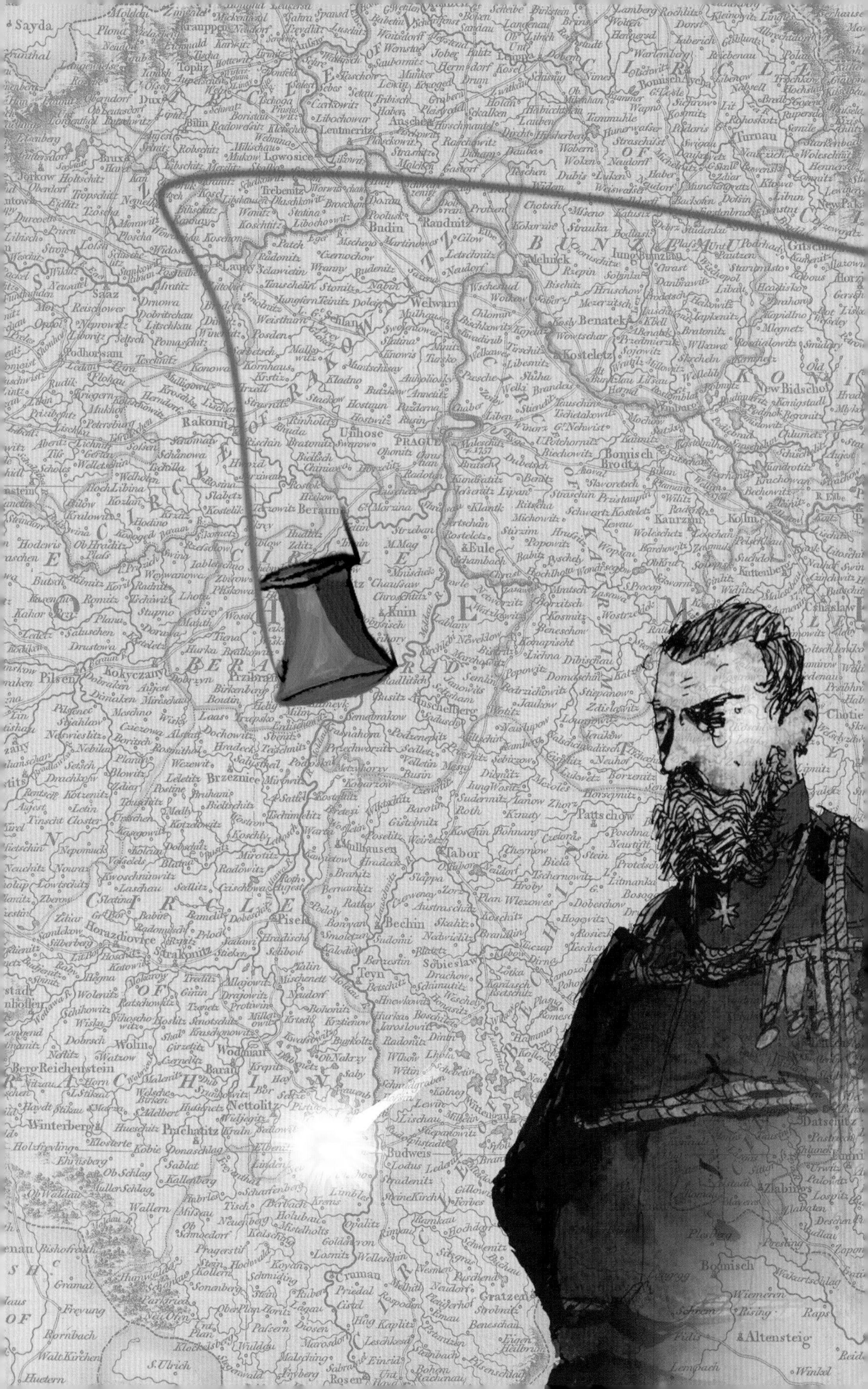
PRAGUE
Rakonitz
Unhose
Budin
Welwarn
Jung Bunzlau
Benatek
Kosteletz
Bomisch Brodt
Kaurzim
Kolin
New Bidschof
Beraun
Pilsen
Kokyczany
Przibram
Brzeznice
Strakonitz
Pisek
Bechin
Tabor
Teyn
Budweis
Winterberg
Prachatitz
Nettolitz
Wodnian
Gratzen
Saaz
Bilin
Leutmeritz
Lowositz
Trebenitz
Raudnitz
Turnau
Czaslaw
Pattschow
Sobieslaw
Altensteig
Horazdiowice
Wolin
Podhorsam
Sayda

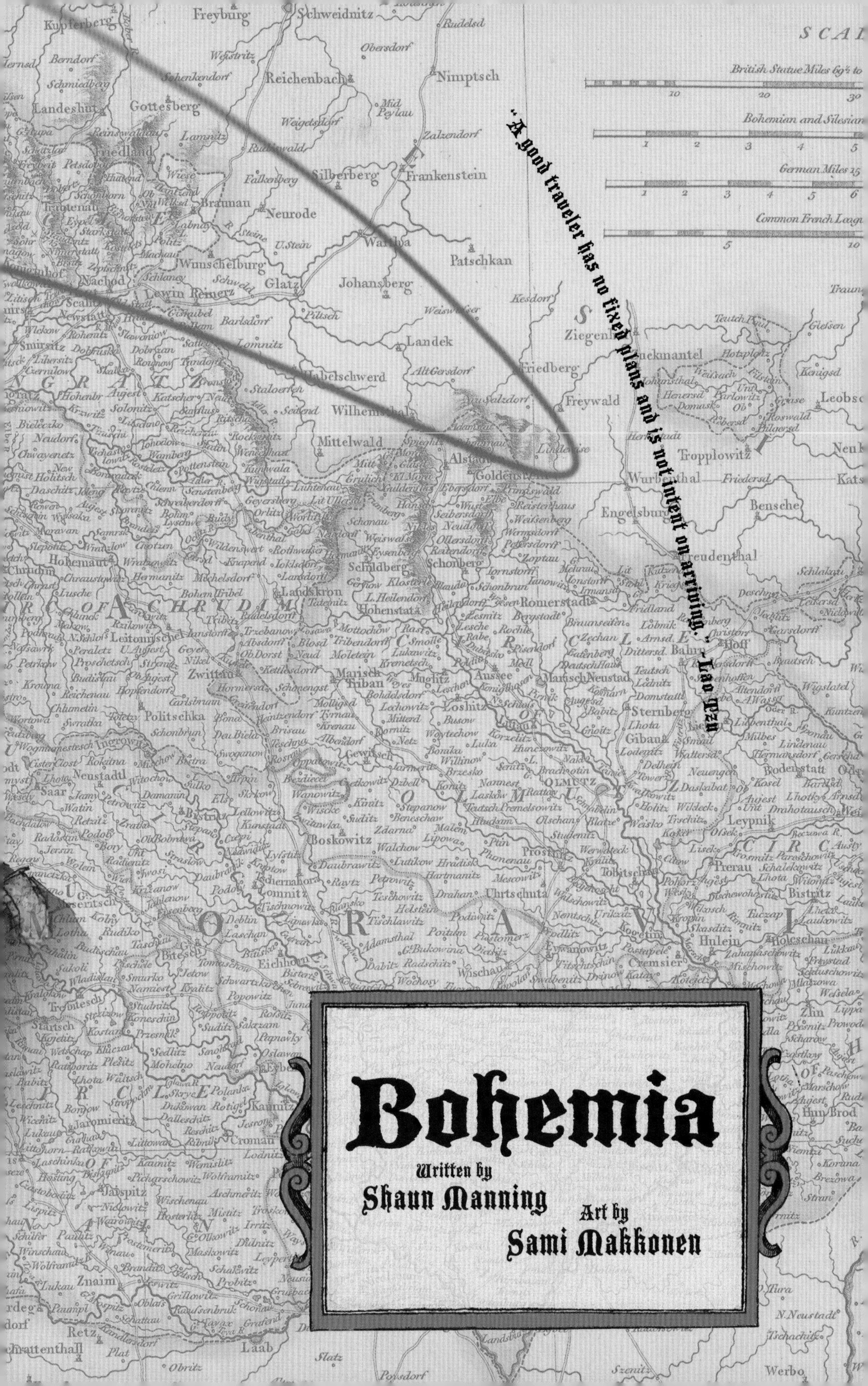
"A good traveler has no fixed plans and is not intent on arriving." -Lao Tzu
Bohemia
Written by
Shaun Manning
Art by
Sami Makkonen

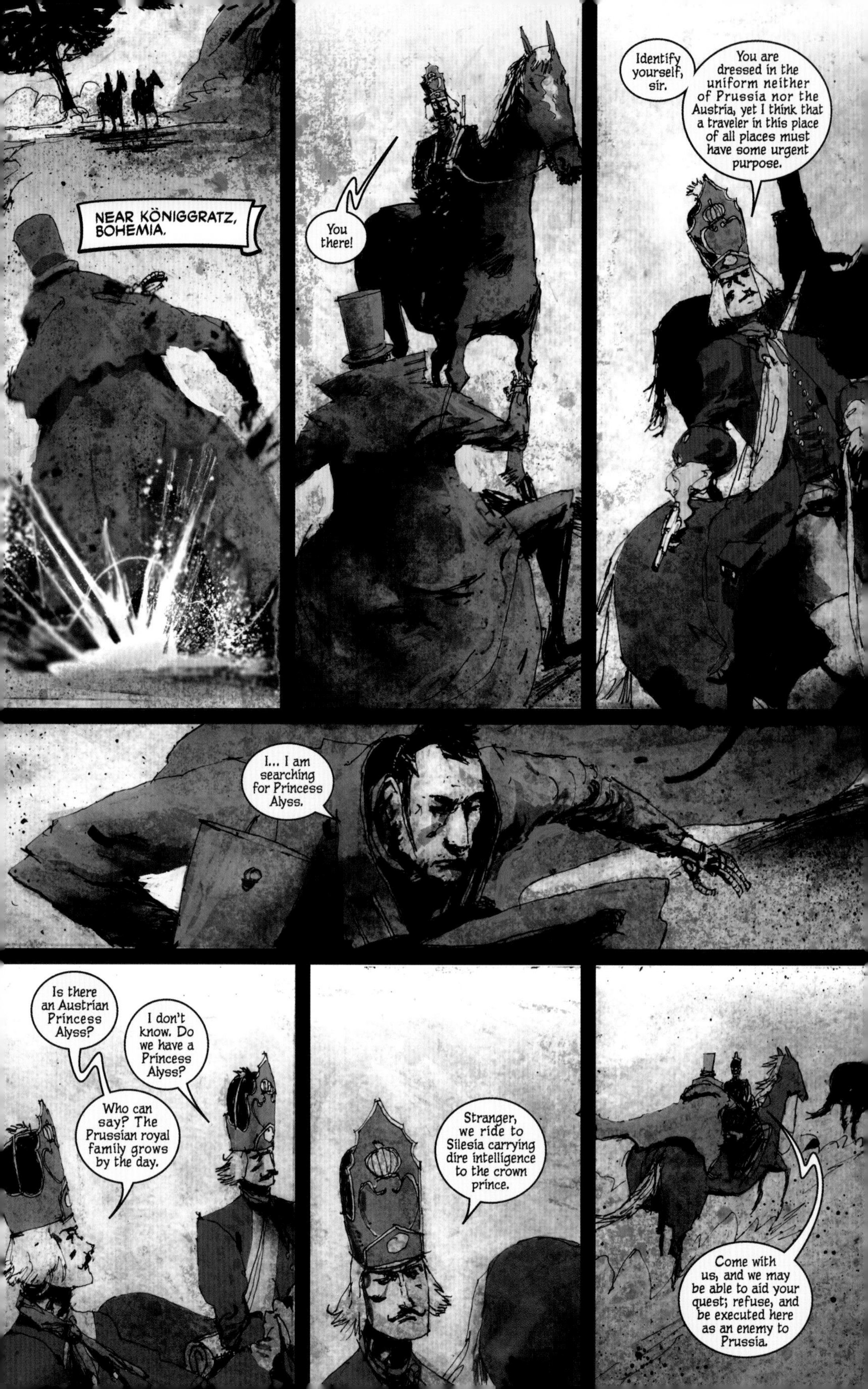
NEAR KÖNIGGRATZ, BOHEMIA.
You there!
Identify yourself, sir.
You are dressed in the uniform neither of Prussia nor the Austria, yet I think that a traveler in this place of all places must have some urgent purpose.
I... I am searching for Princess Alyss.
Is there an Austrian Princess Alyss?
I don't know. Do we have a Princess Alyss?
Who can say? The Prussian royal family grows by the day.
Stranger, we ride to Silesia carrying dire intelligence to the crown prince.
Come with us, and we may be able to aid your quest; refuse, and be executed here as an enemy to Prussia.

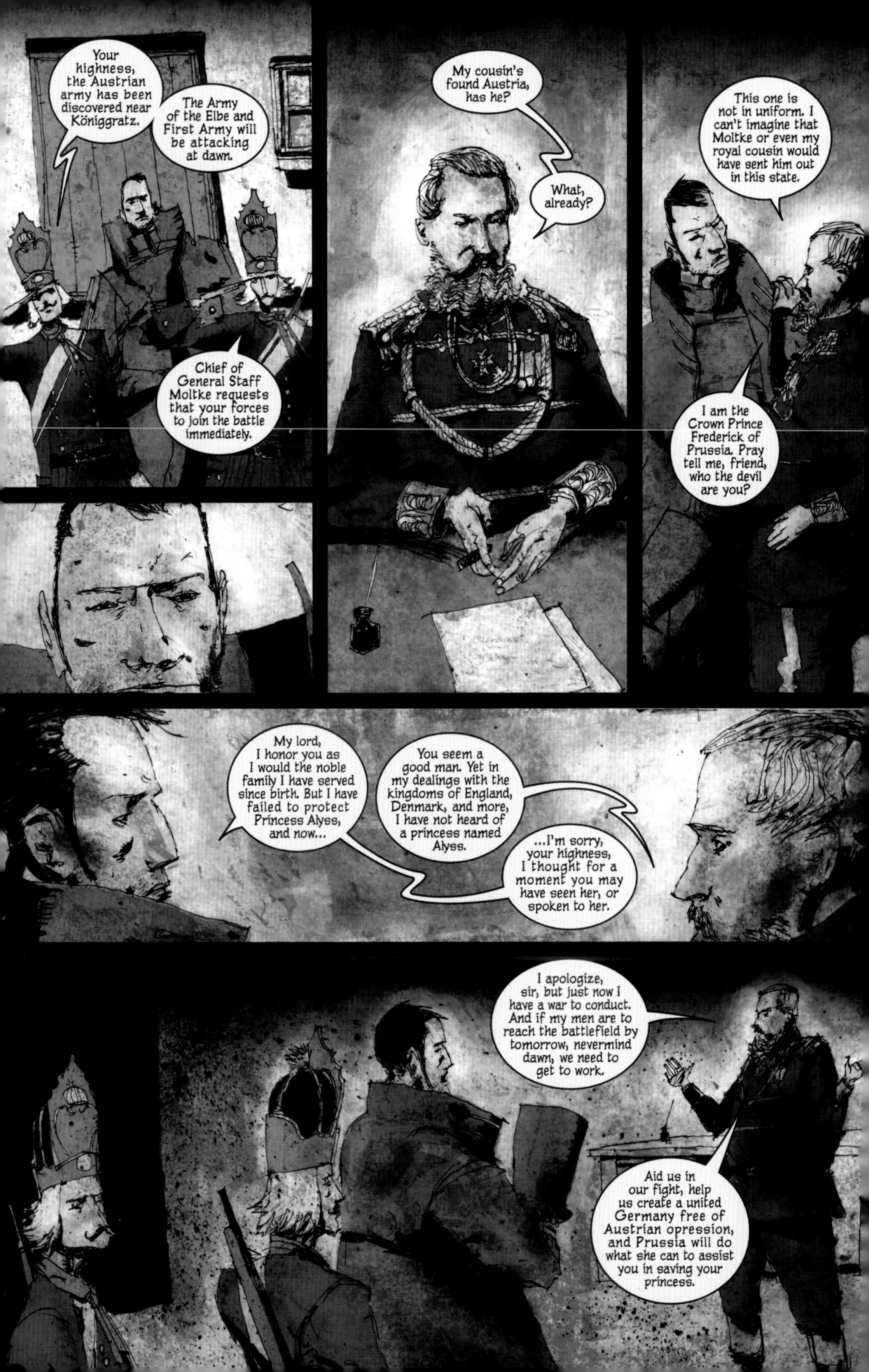
Your highness, the Austrian army has been discovered near Königgratz.
The Army of the Elbe and First Army will be attacking at dawn.
Chief of General Staff Moltke requests that your forces to join the battle immediately.
My cousin's found Austria, has he?
What, already?
This one is not in uniform. I can't imagine that Moltke or even my royal cousin would have sent him out in this state.
I am the Crown Prince Frederick of Prussia. Pray tell me, friend, who the devil are you?
My lord, I honor you as I would the noble family I have served since birth. But I have failed to protect Princess Alyss, and now...
You seem a good man. Yet in my dealings with the kingdoms of England, Denmark, and more, I have not heard of a princess named Alyss.
...I'm sorry, your highness, I thought for a moment you may have seen her, or spoken to her.
I apologize, sir, but just now I have a war to conduct. And if my men are to reach the battlefield by tomorrow, nevermind dawn, we need to get to work.
Aid us in our fight, help us create a united Germany free of Austrian opression, and Prussia will do what she can to assist you in saving your princess.

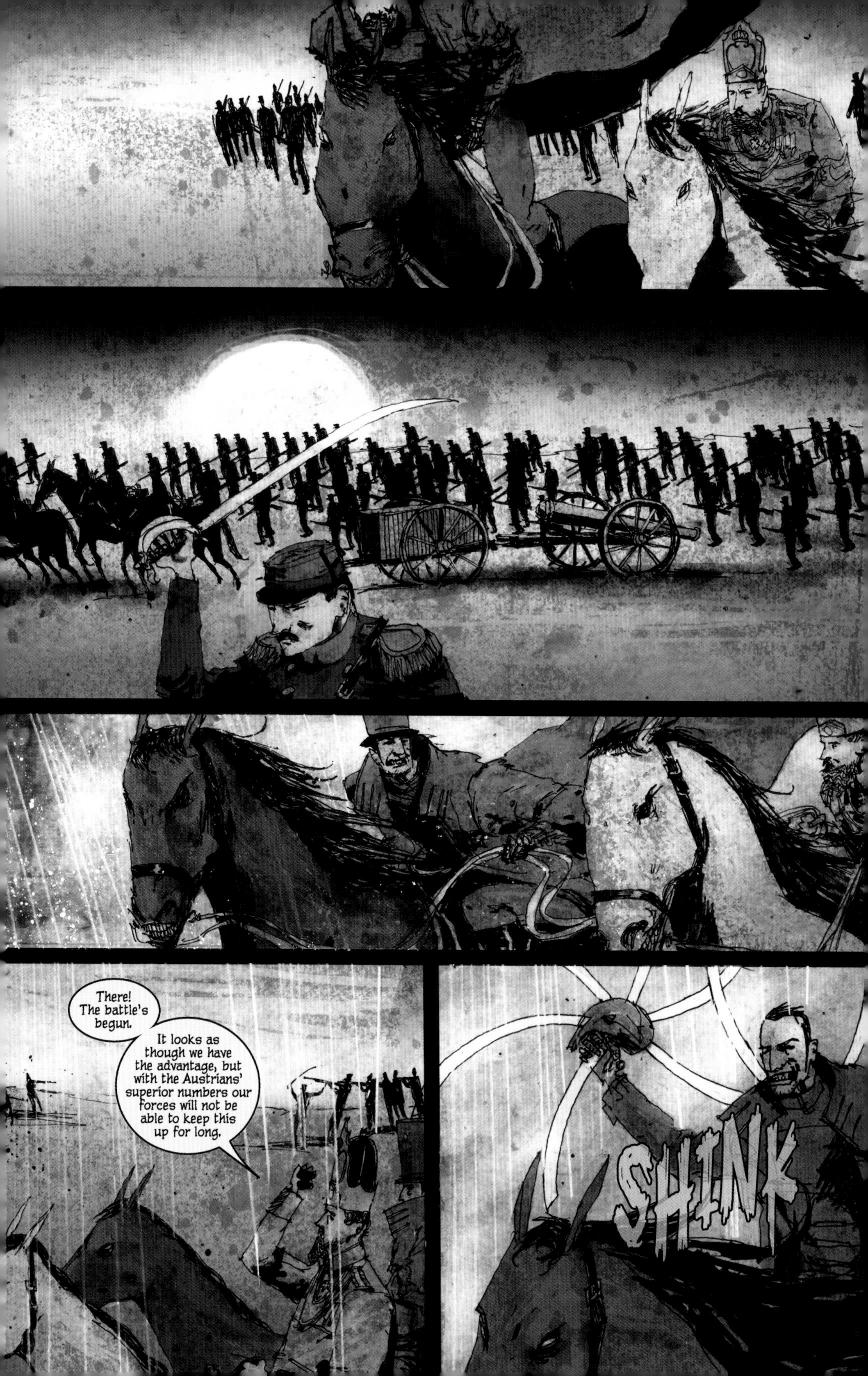
There! The battle's begun.
It looks as though we have the advantage, but with the Austrians' superior numbers our forces will not be able to keep this up for long.
SHINK

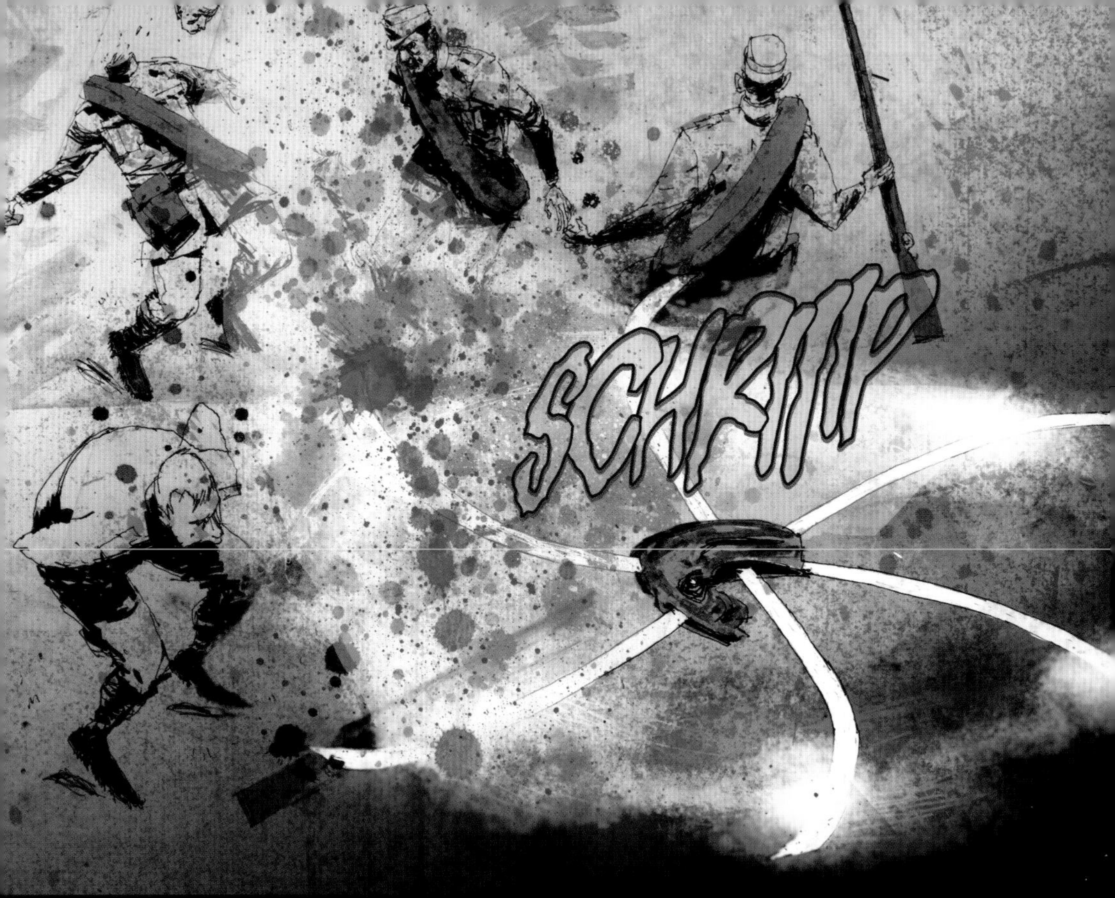
SCHRIIP

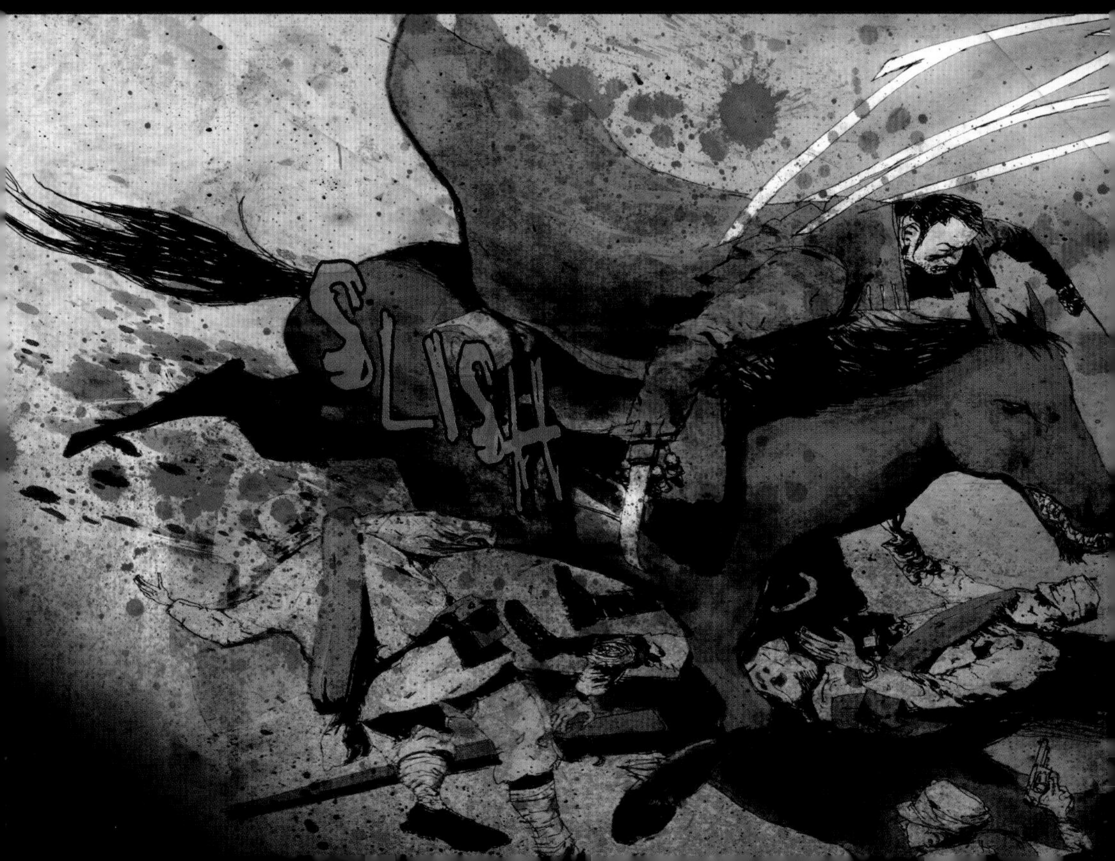
SLISH

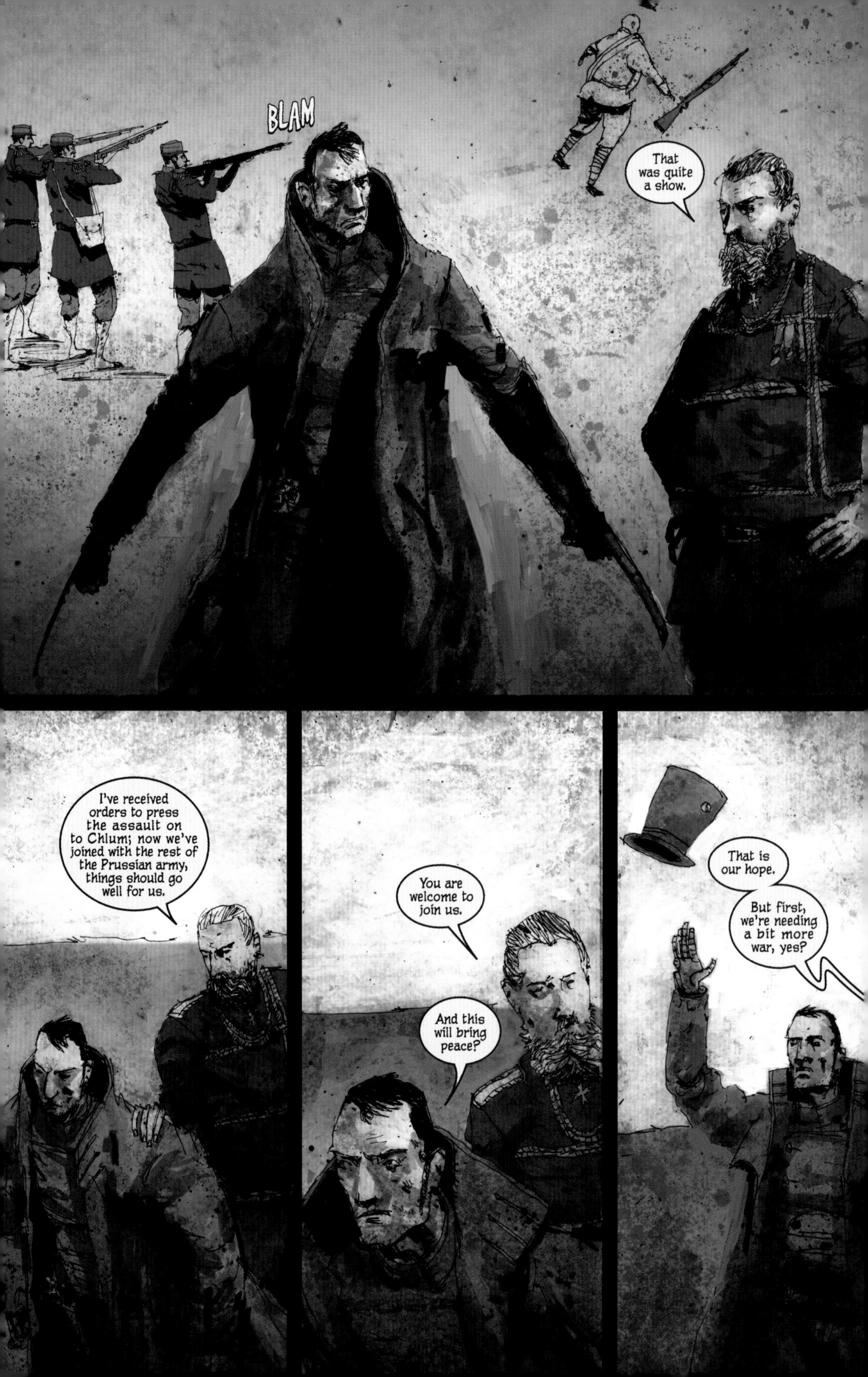
BLAM
That was quite a show.
I've received orders to press the assault on to Chlum; now we've joined with the rest of the Prussian army, things should go well for us.
You are welcome to join us.
And this will bring peace?
That is our hope.
But first, we're needing a bit more war, yes?

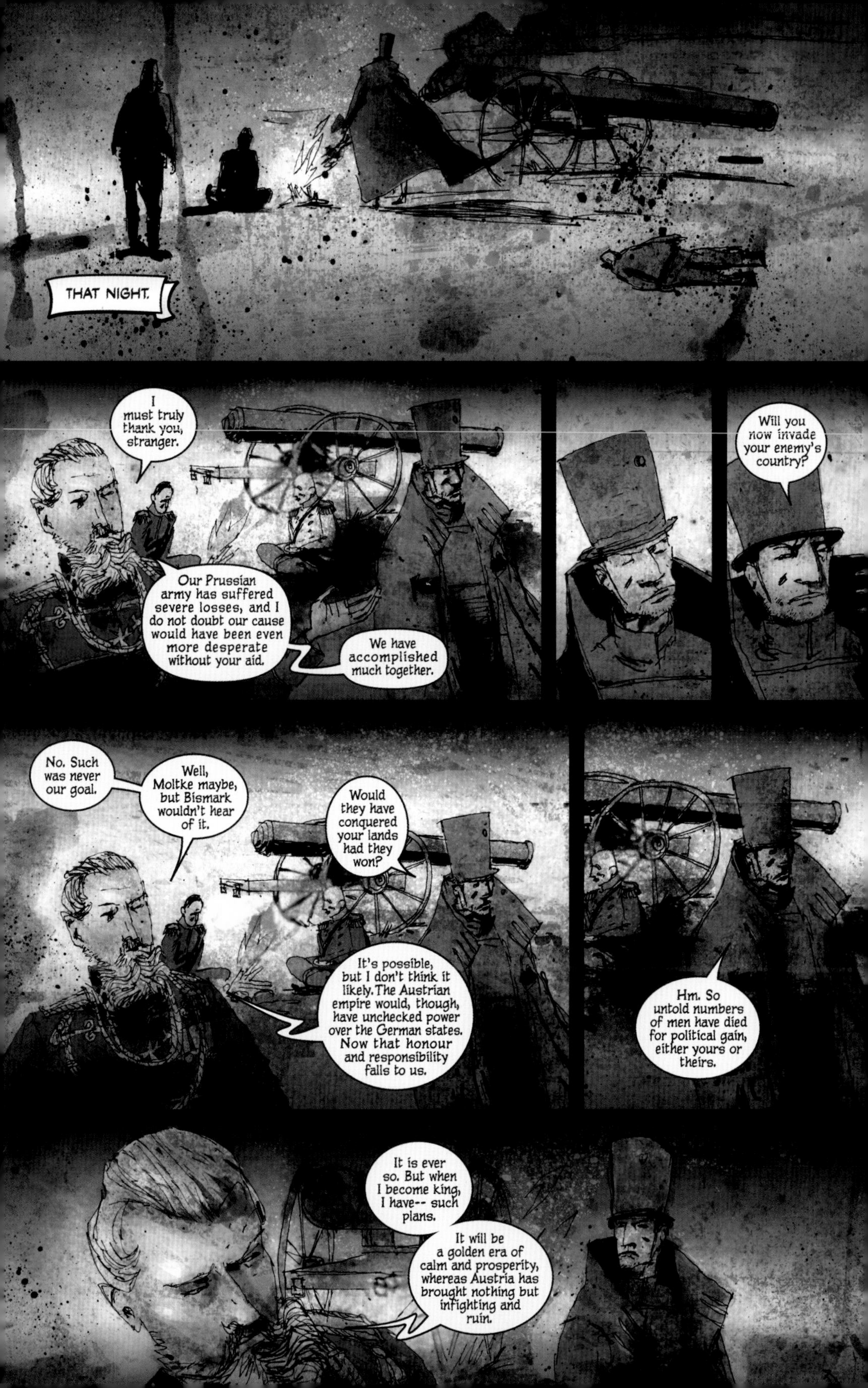
THAT NIGHT.
I must truly thank you, stranger.
Our Prussian army has suffered severe losses, and I do not doubt our cause would have been even more desperate without your aid.
We have accomplished much together.
Will you now invade your enemy's country?
No. Such was never our goal.
Well, Moltke maybe, but Bismark wouldn't hear of it.
Would they have conquered your lands had they won?
It's possible, but I don't think it likely. The Austrian empire would, though, have unchecked power over the German states. Now that honour and responsibility falls to us.
Hm. So untold numbers of men have died for political gain, either yours or theirs.
It is ever so. But when I become king, I have-- such plans.
It will be a golden era of calm and prosperity, whereas Austria has brought nothing but infighting and ruin.

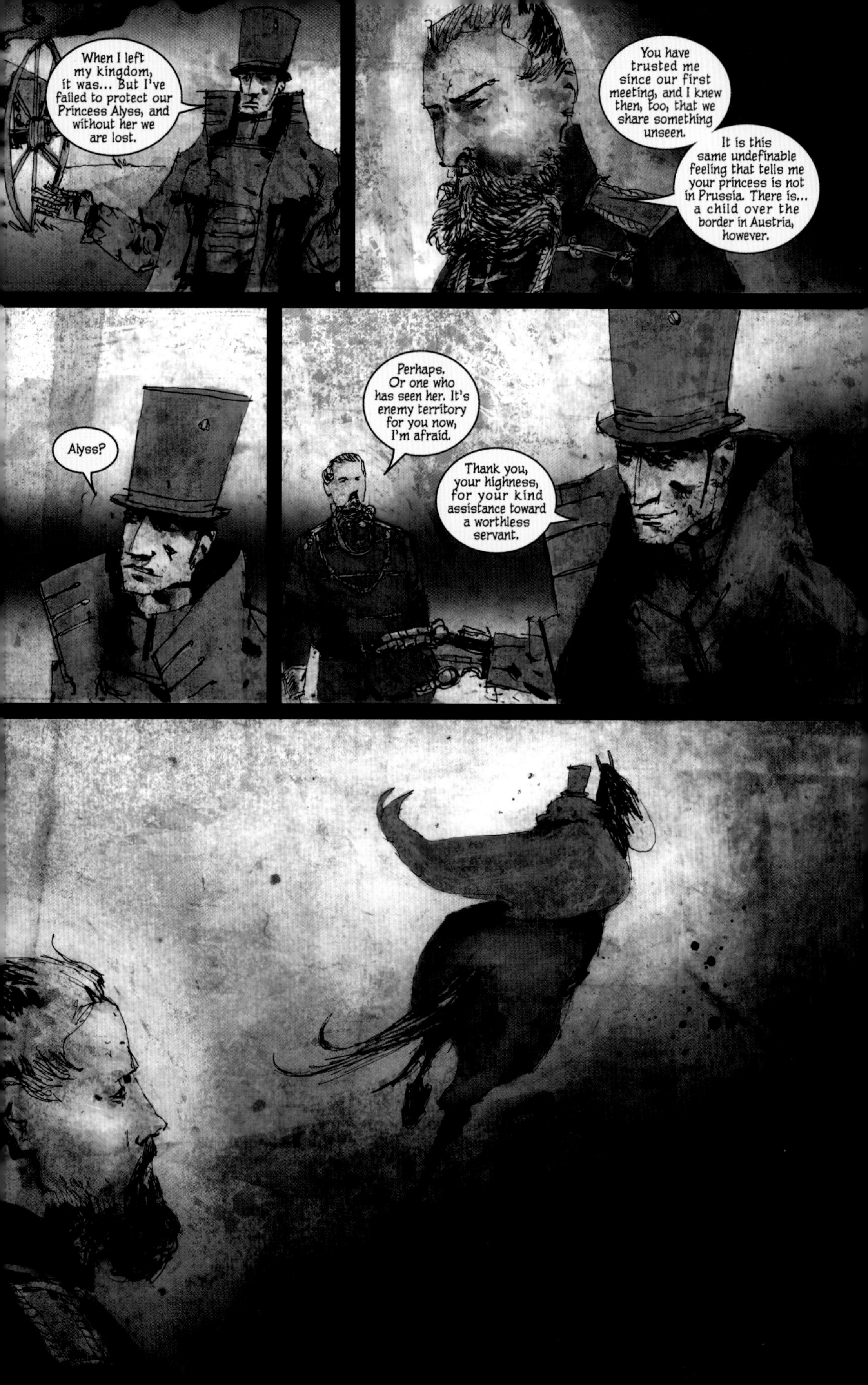
When I left my kingdom, it was... But I've failed to protect our Princess Alyss, and without her we are lost.
You have trusted me since our first meeting, and I knew then, too, that we share something unseen.
It is this same undefinable feeling that tells me your princess is not in Prussia. There is... a child over the border in Austria, however.
Alyss?
Perhaps. Or one who has seen her. It's enemy territory for you now, I'm afraid.
Thank you, your highness, for your kind assistance toward a worthless servant.

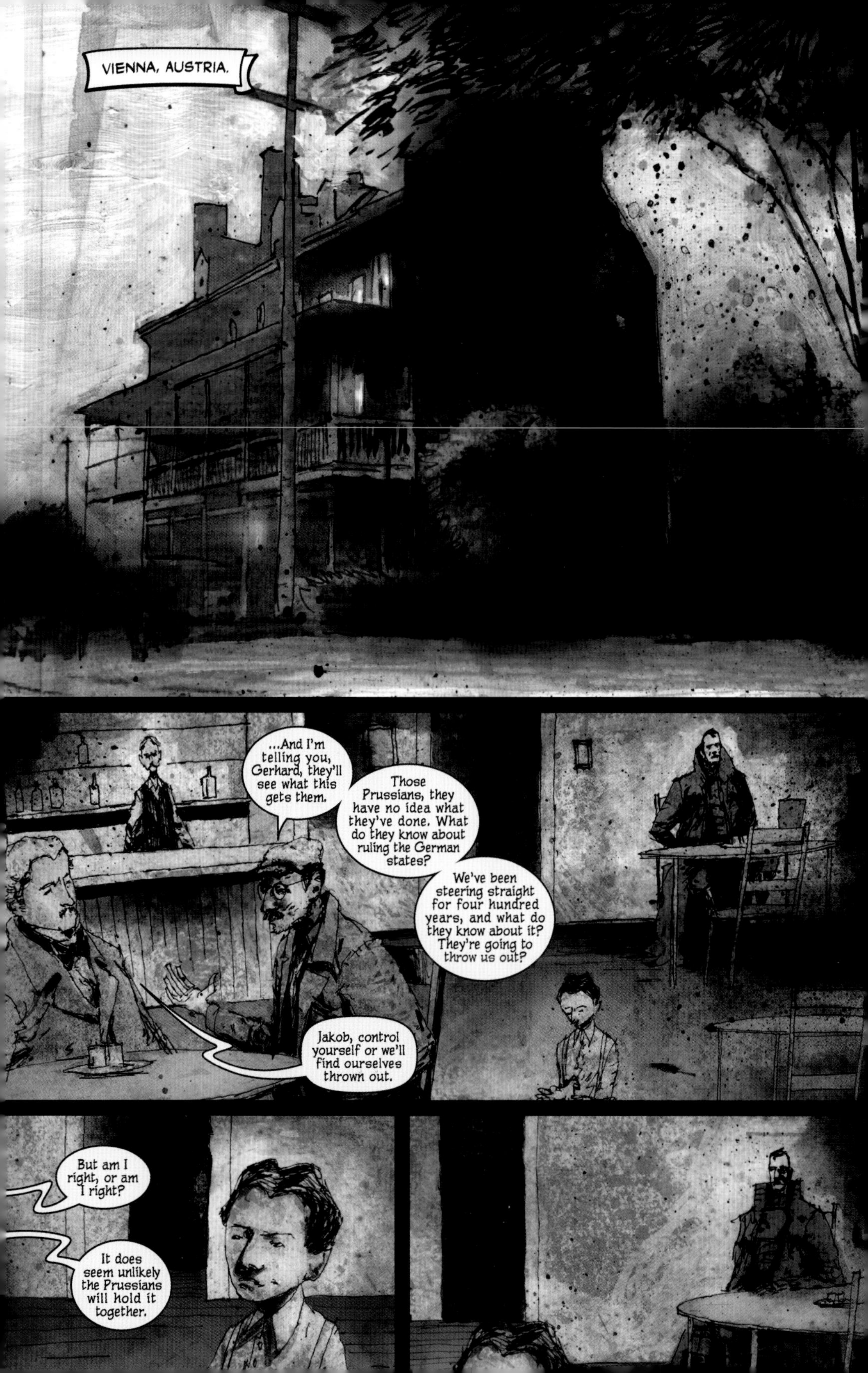
VIENNA, AUSTRIA.
...And I'm telling you, Gerhard, they'll see what this gets them.
Those Prussians, they have no idea what they've done. What do they know about ruling the German states?
We've been steering straight for four hundred years, and what do they know about it? They're going to throw us out?
Jakob, control yourself or we'll find ourselves thrown out.
But am I right, or am I right?
It does seem unlikely the Prussians will hold it together.

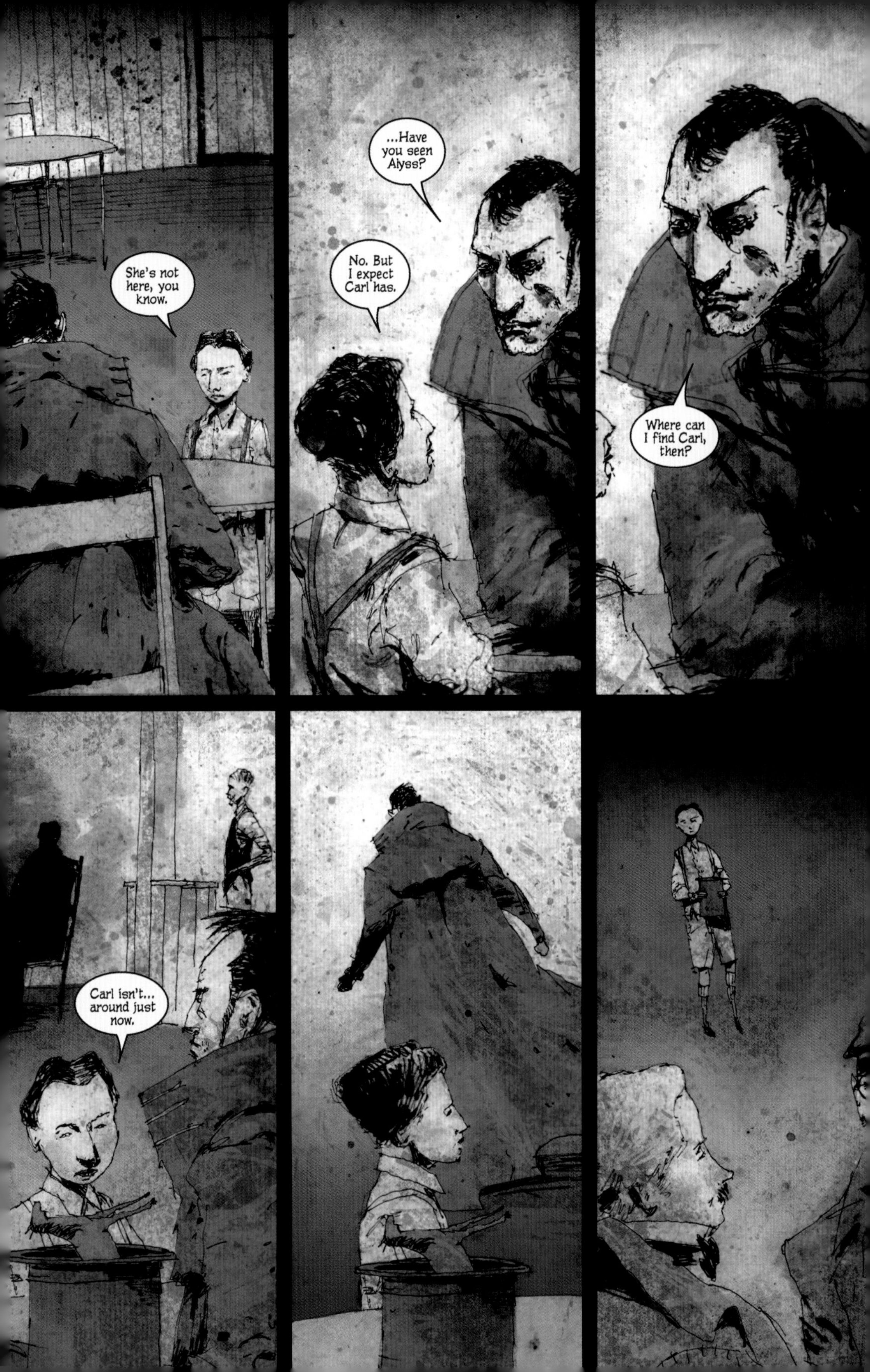
She's not here, you know.
...Have you seen Alyss?
No. But I expect Carl has.
Where can I find Carl, then?
Carl isn't... around just now.

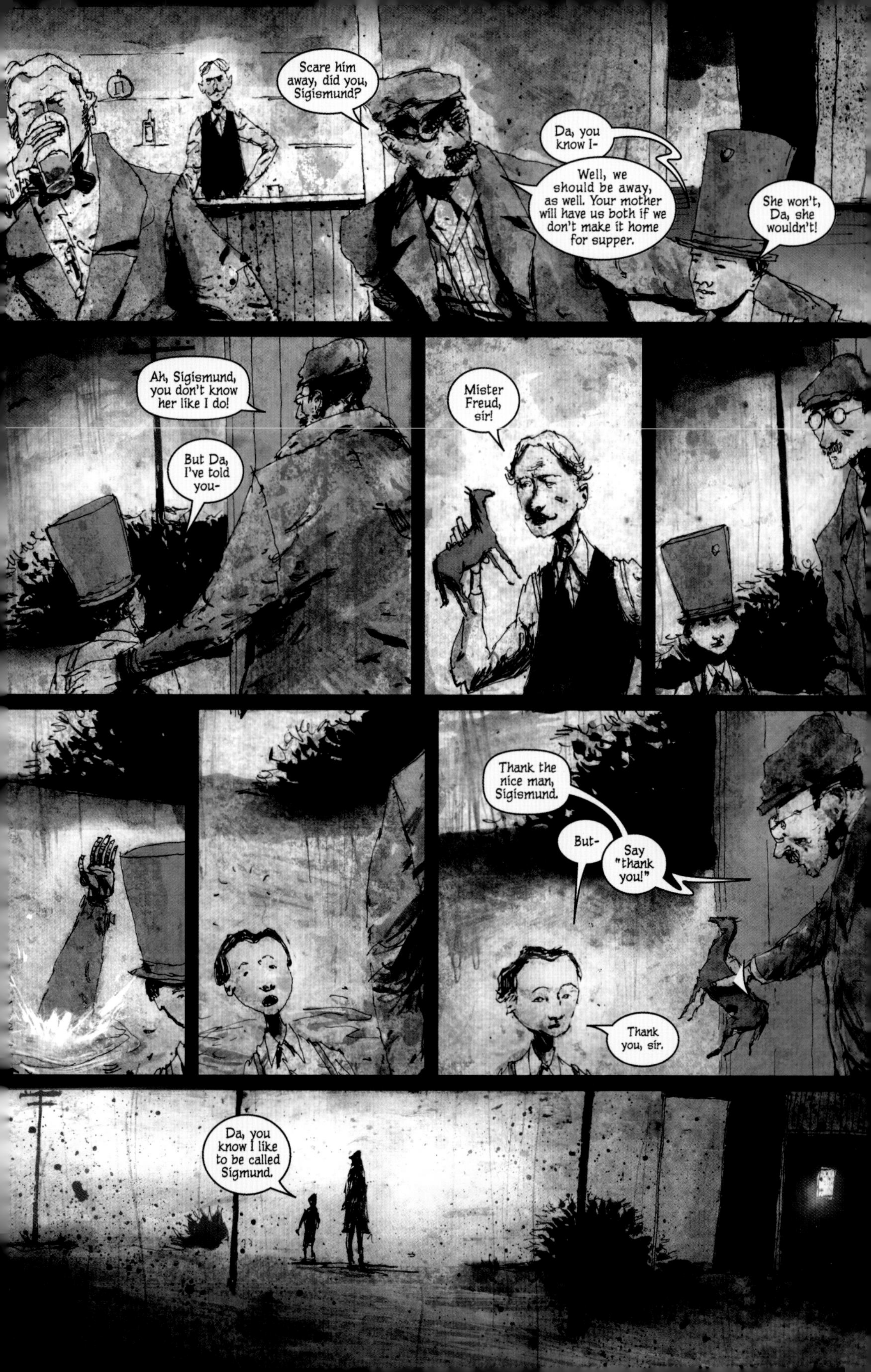
Scare him away, did you, Sigismund?
Da, you know I-
Well, we should be away, as well. Your mother will have us both if we don't make it home for supper.
She won't, Da, she wouldn't!
Ah, Sigismund, you don't know her like I do!
But Da, I've told you-
Mister Freud, sir!
Thank the nice man, Sigismund.
But-
Say "thank you!"
Thank you, sir.
Da, you know I like to be called Sigmund.

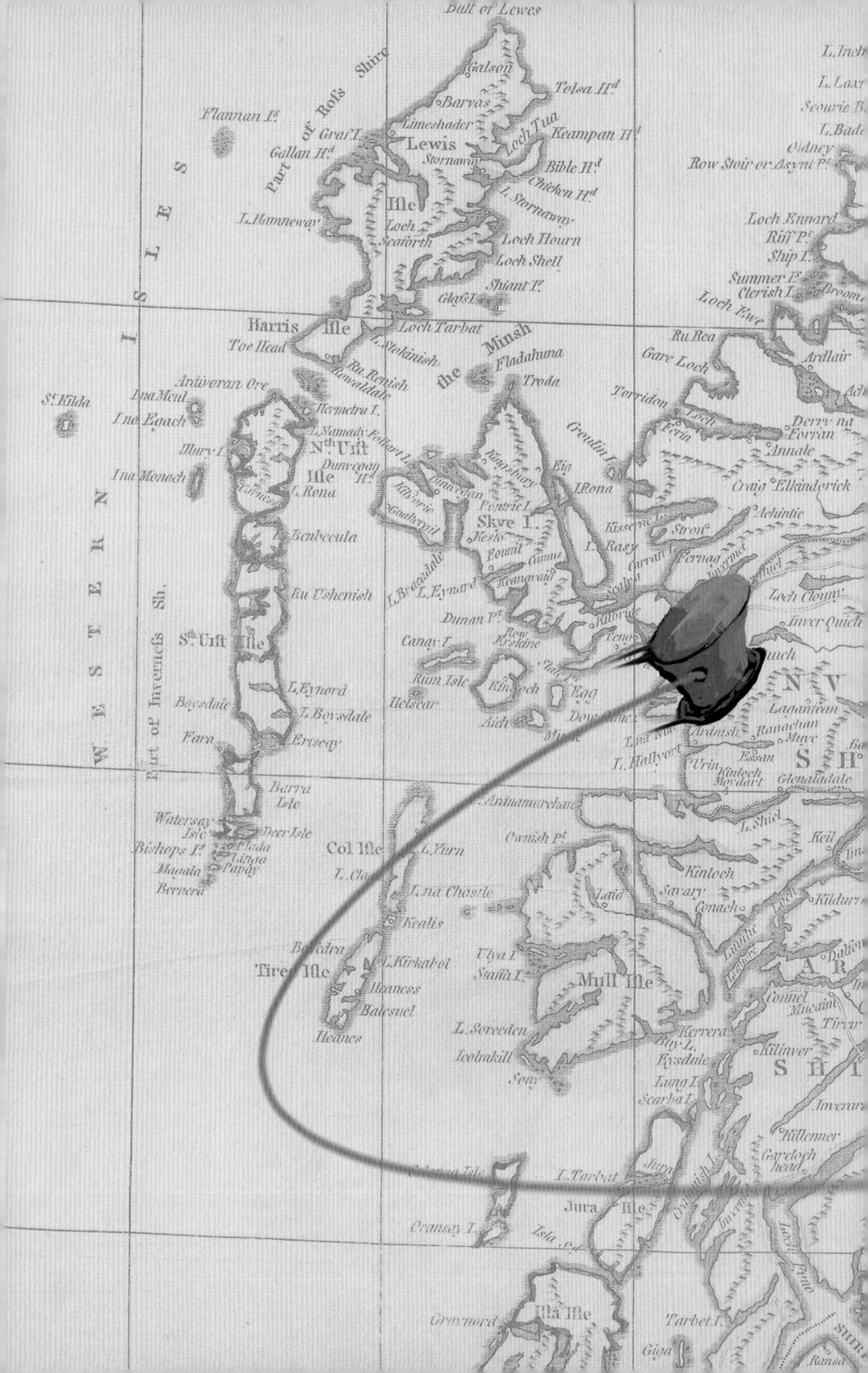

Butt of Lewes
Galson
Barvas
Tolsa Hd.
Flannan Is.
Part of Ross Shire
Graf I.
Limeshader
Lewis
Loch Tua
Keampan Hd.
Gallan Hd.
Stornaway
Bible Hd.
Chicken Hd.
L. Stornaway
Isle
L. Hanneway
Loch Seaforth
Loch Hourn
Loch Shell
Shiant Is.
Harris Isle
Loch Tarbat
Toe Head
L. Stokinish
the Minsh
Fladahuna
Troda
Ru Renish
Rowaldale
St. Kilda
Ardivoran Ore
Hermetra I.
Ina Eaach
Nth. Uist Isle
Dunvegan Hd.
Ina Monach
L. Rona
Benbecula
Ru Ushenish
Sth. Uist Isle
L. Eynord
L. Boysdale
Boysdale
Fara
Eriscay
WESTERN ISLES
Part of Inverness Sh.
Barra Isle
Watersay Isle
Deer Isle
Bishops Is.
Bernera
Skye I.
Dunvegan
Kingsbury
Portrie I.
Eig
I. Rona
L. Rasy
L. Bracadale
L. Eynard
Dunan Pt.
Canay I.
Rum Isle
Helsear
Egg
Muck
Col Isle
L. Yurn
L. na Chostle
Kealis
Tiree Isle
L. Kirkabol
Heaness
Balesuel
Ulva I.
Staffa I.
Mull Isle
L. Screeden
Icolmkill
Kerrera
Fysdale
Lung I.
Scarba I.
L. Tarbat
Jura Isle
Oransay I.
Isla Isle
Tarbet I.
Giga
Ardnamurchan
Cwnish Pt.
Kinloch
Savary
Conach
L. Shiel
Kilinver
Inverary
Killenner
Gareloch head
Loch Ewe
Gare Loch
Ardlair
Terridon
Derry na Forran
Annale
Craig Elkinderick
Achintie
Stron
Loch Clouny
Inver Quich
Laganfean
Ranachan
Glenaladale
Connel
Mucairn
Loch Ennard
Riff Pt.
Ship I.
Summer Is.
Clerish I.
Broom
Ru Rea
Scourie B.
L. Laxt
L. Inch
Oldney
Row Stoir or Asynt Pt.

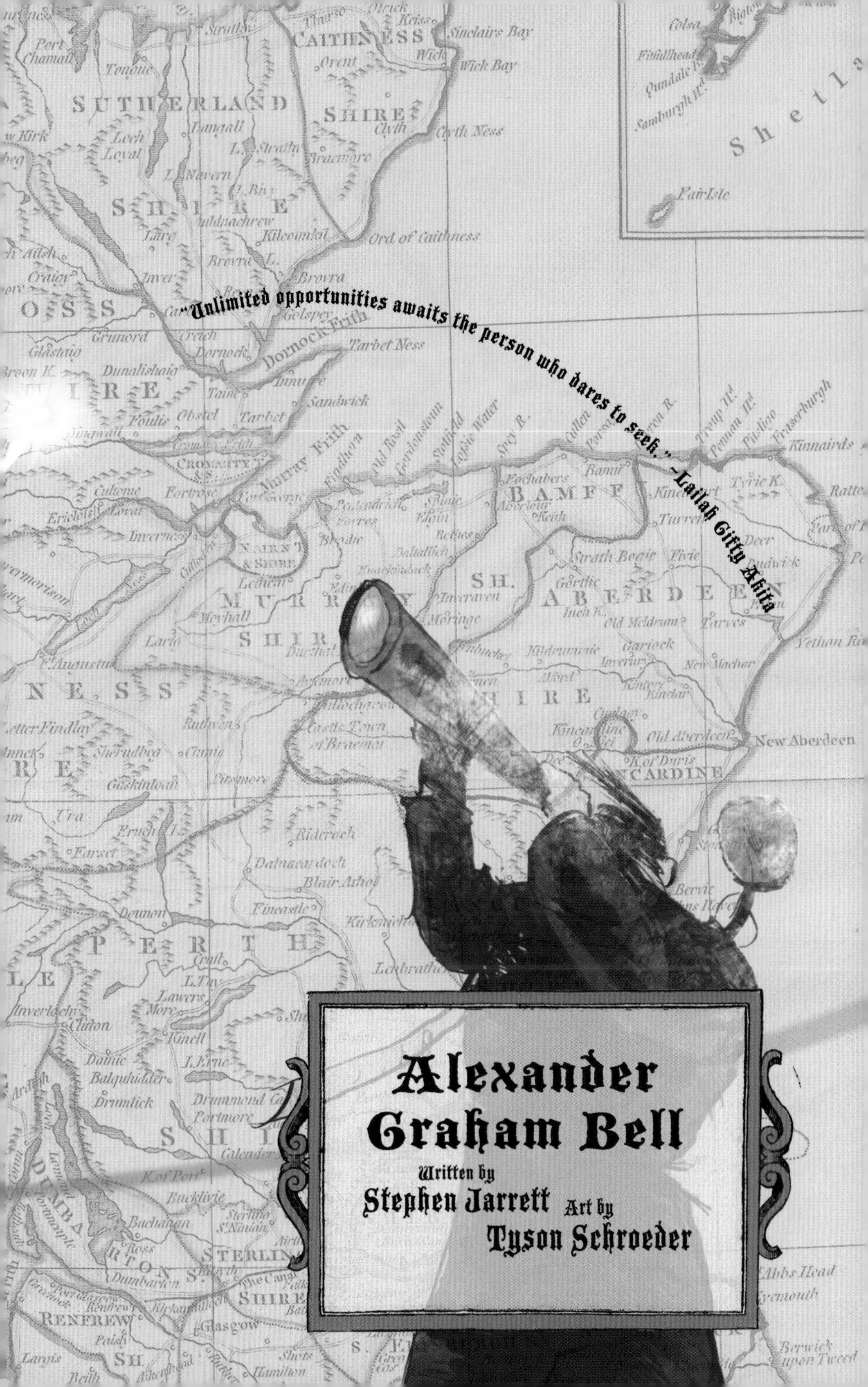
CAITHNESS SHIRE
SUTHERLAND SHIRE
ROSS SHIRE
CROMARTY
NAIRN SHIRE
MURRAY SHIRE
BAMFF SH.
ABERDEEN SHIRE
NESS
PERTH SHIRE
STERLING SHIRE
DUMBARTON SH.
RENFREW SH.
KINCARDINE
Shetla
Fair Isle
Dornock Frith
Murray Frith
Tarbet Ness
Wick Bay
Sinclairs Bay
Ord of Caithness
Inverness
Dingwall
Fort George
Old Aberdeen
New Aberdeen
Old Meldrum
Strath Bogie
Blair Athol
Dalnacardoch
Glasgow
Dumbarton
Paisly
Hamilton
Berwick upon Tweed

"Unlimited opportunities awaits the person who dares to seek." –Lailah Gifty Akita

Alexander Graham Bell

Written by
Stephen Jarrett

Art by
Tyson Schroeder

SCOTTISH HIGHLANDS

AWWROOWOOO

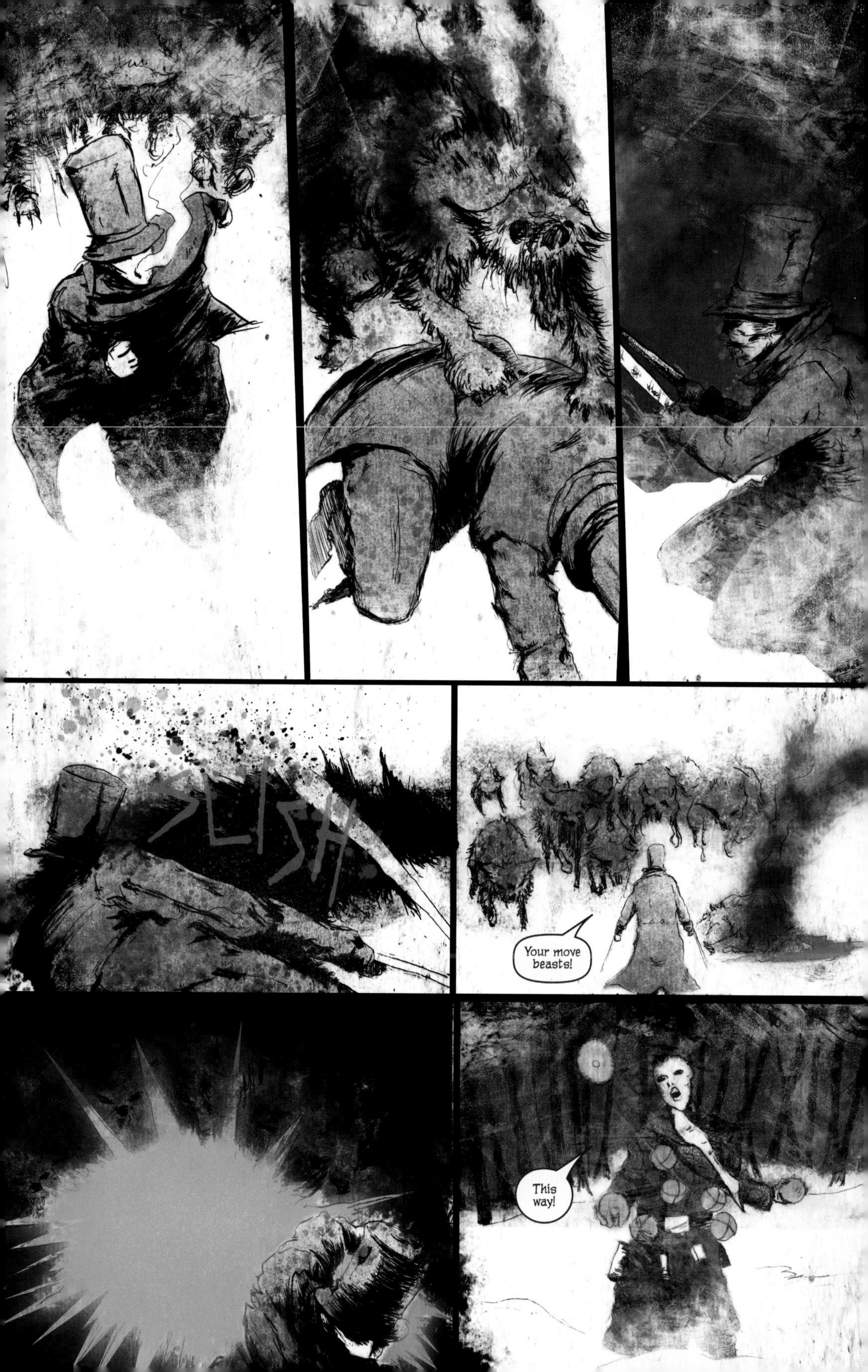
SLISH
Your move beasts!
This way!

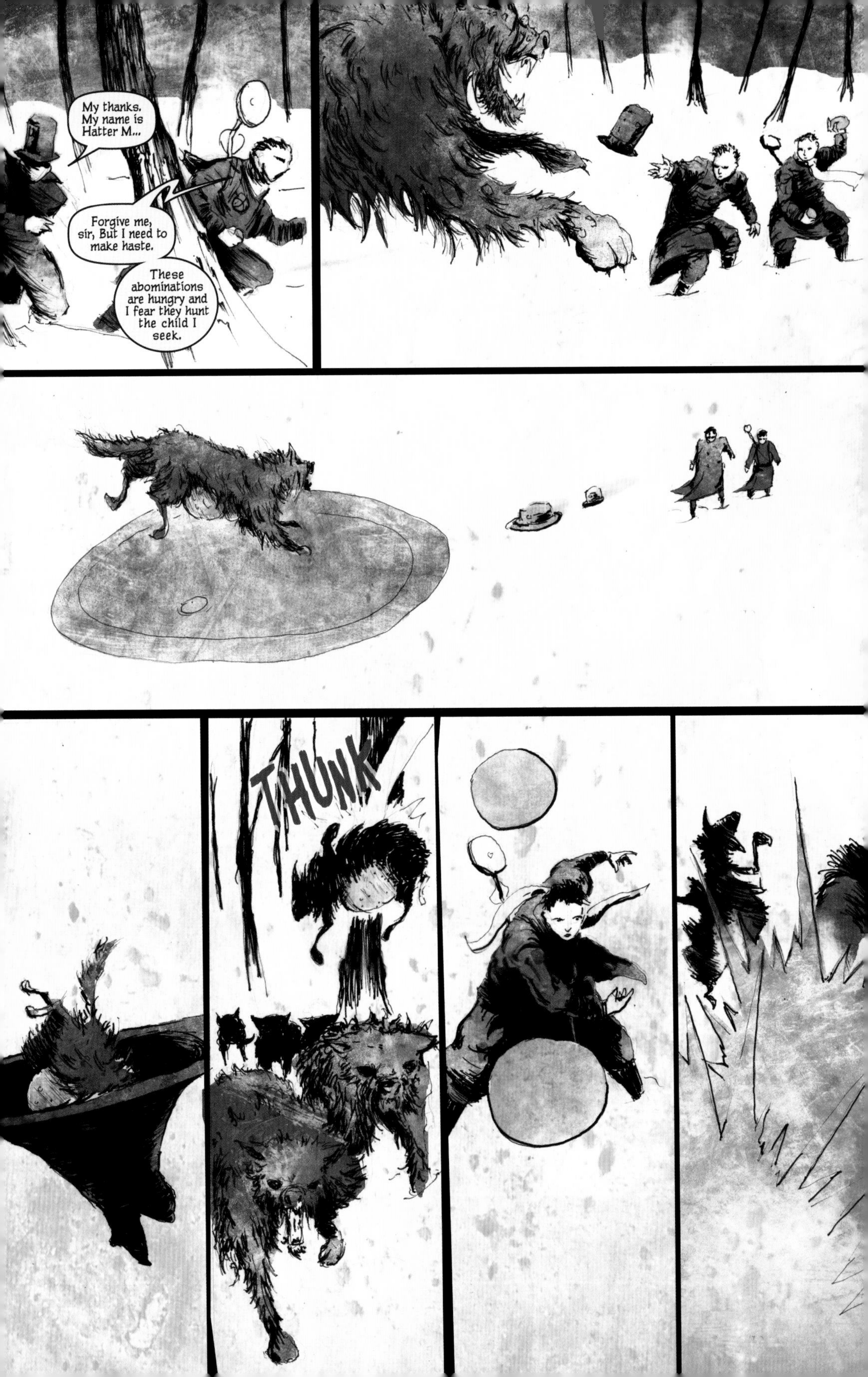
My thanks. My name is Hatter M...
Forgive me, sir, But I need to make haste.
These abominations are hungry and I fear they hunt the child I seek.
THUNK

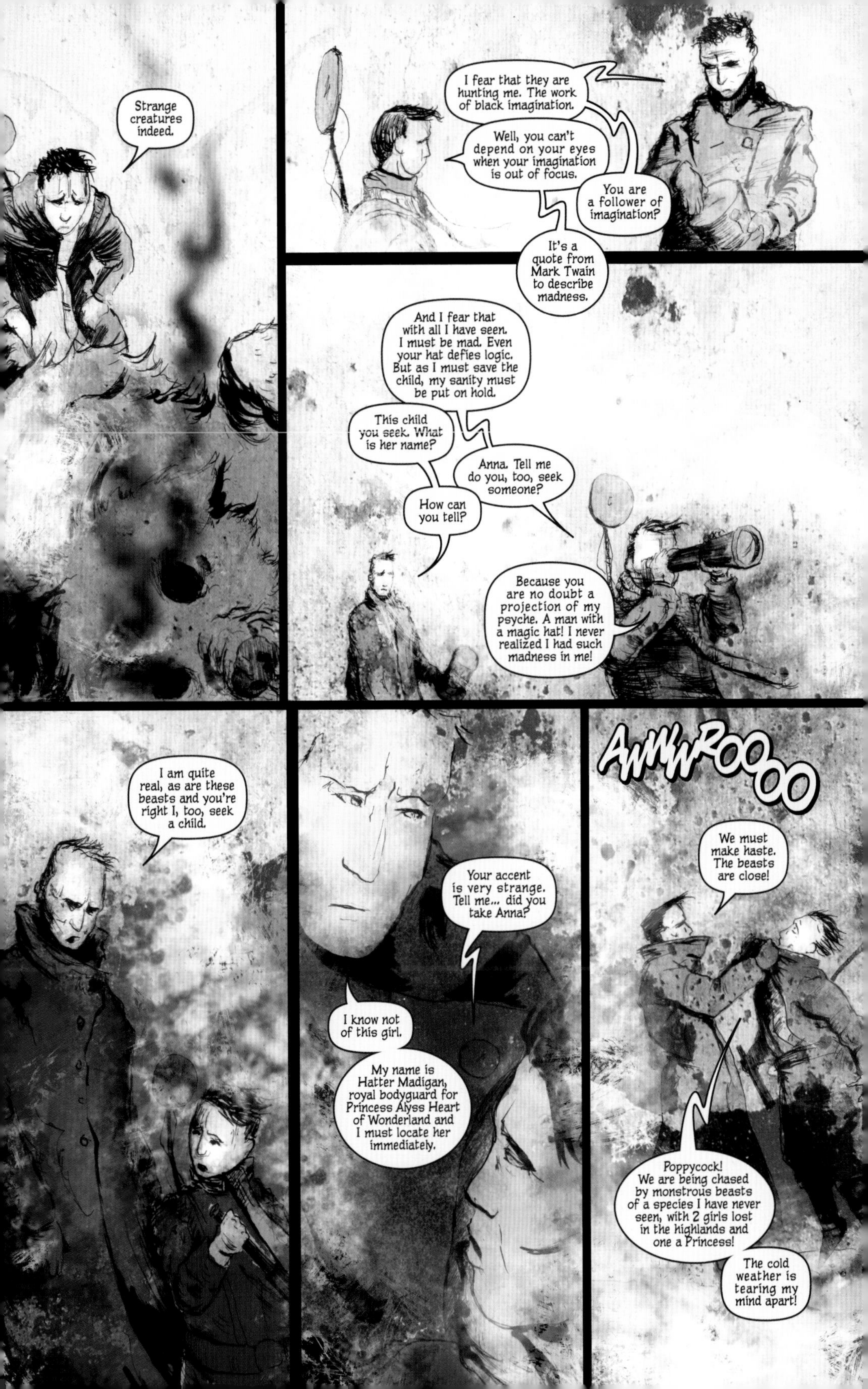
Strange creatures indeed.
I fear that they are hunting me. The work of black imagination.
Well, you can't depend on your eyes when your imagination is out of focus.
You are a follower of imagination?
It's a quote from Mark Twain to describe madness.
And I fear that with all I have seen. I must be mad. Even your hat defies logic. But as I must save the child, my sanity must be put on hold.
This child you seek. What is her name?
Anna. Tell me do you, too, seek someone?
How can you tell?
Because you are no doubt a projection of my psyche. A man with a magic hat! I never realized I had such madness in me!
I am quite real, as are these beasts and you're right I, too, seek a child.
Your accent is very strange. Tell me... did you take Anna?
I know not of this girl.
My name is Hatter Madigan, royal bodyguard for Princess Alyss Heart of Wonderland and I must locate her immediately.
AWWROOOOO
We must make haste. The beasts are close!
Poppycock! We are being chased by monstrous beasts of a species I have never seen, with 2 girls lost in the highlands and one a Princess!
The cold weather is tearing my mind apart!

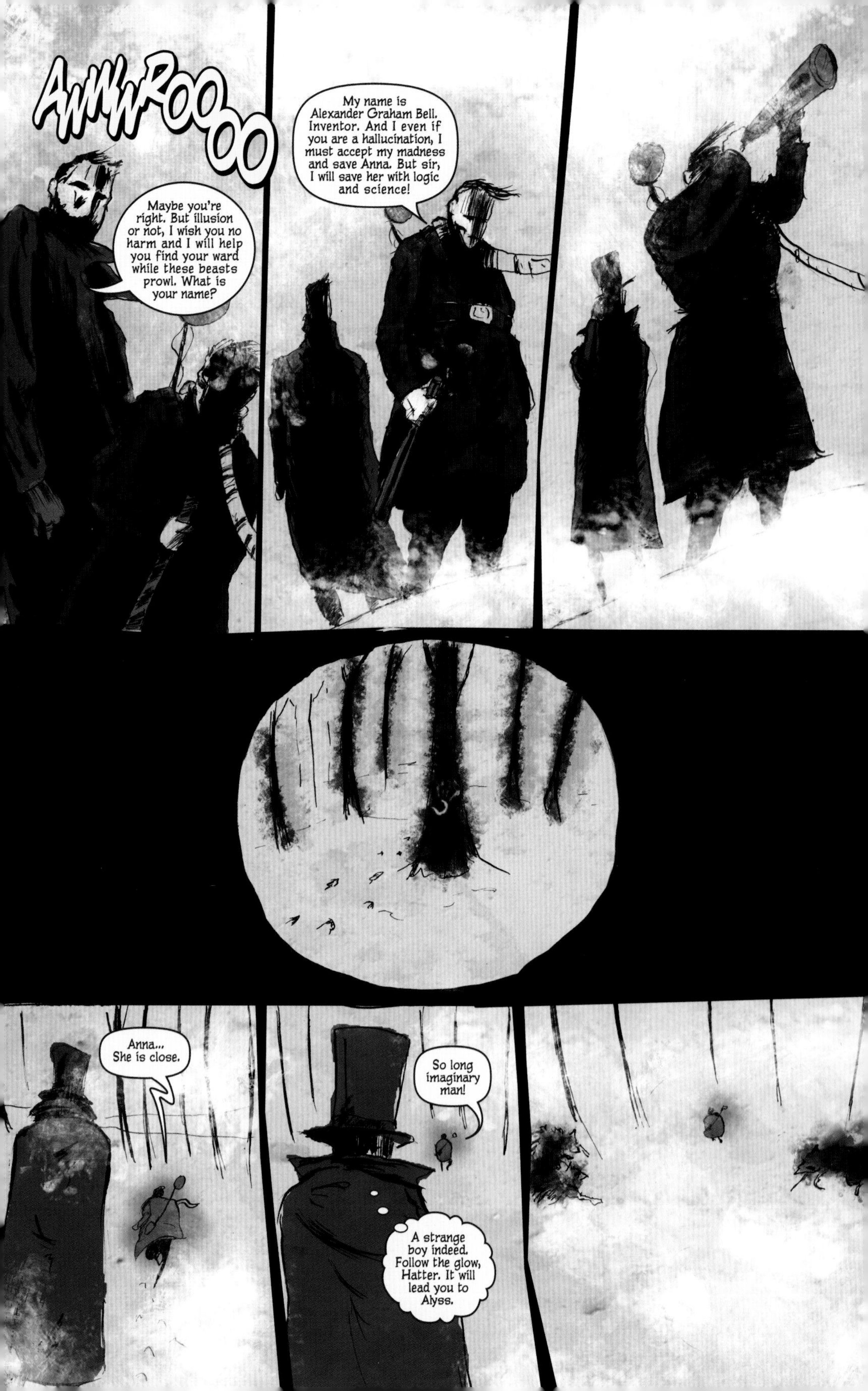
AWWROOOOO
Maybe you're right. But illusion or not, I wish you no harm and I will help you find your ward while these beasts prowl. What is your name?
My name is Alexander Graham Bell. Inventor. And I even if you are a hallucination, I must accept my madness and save Anna. But sir, I will save her with logic and science!
Anna... She is close.
So long imaginary man!
A strange boy indeed. Follow the glow, Hatter. It will lead you to Alyss.

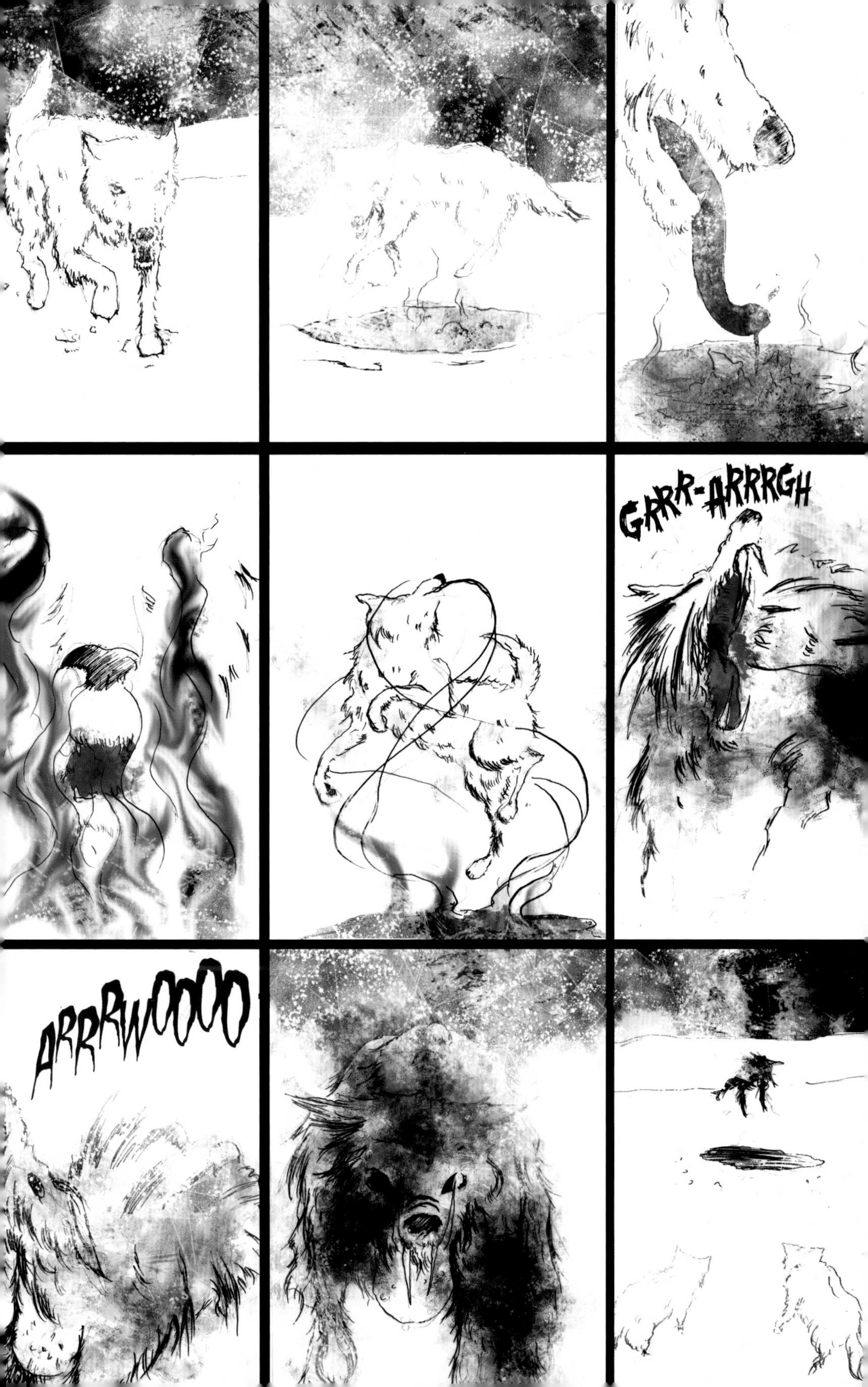
GRRR-ARRRGH
ARRRWOOOO

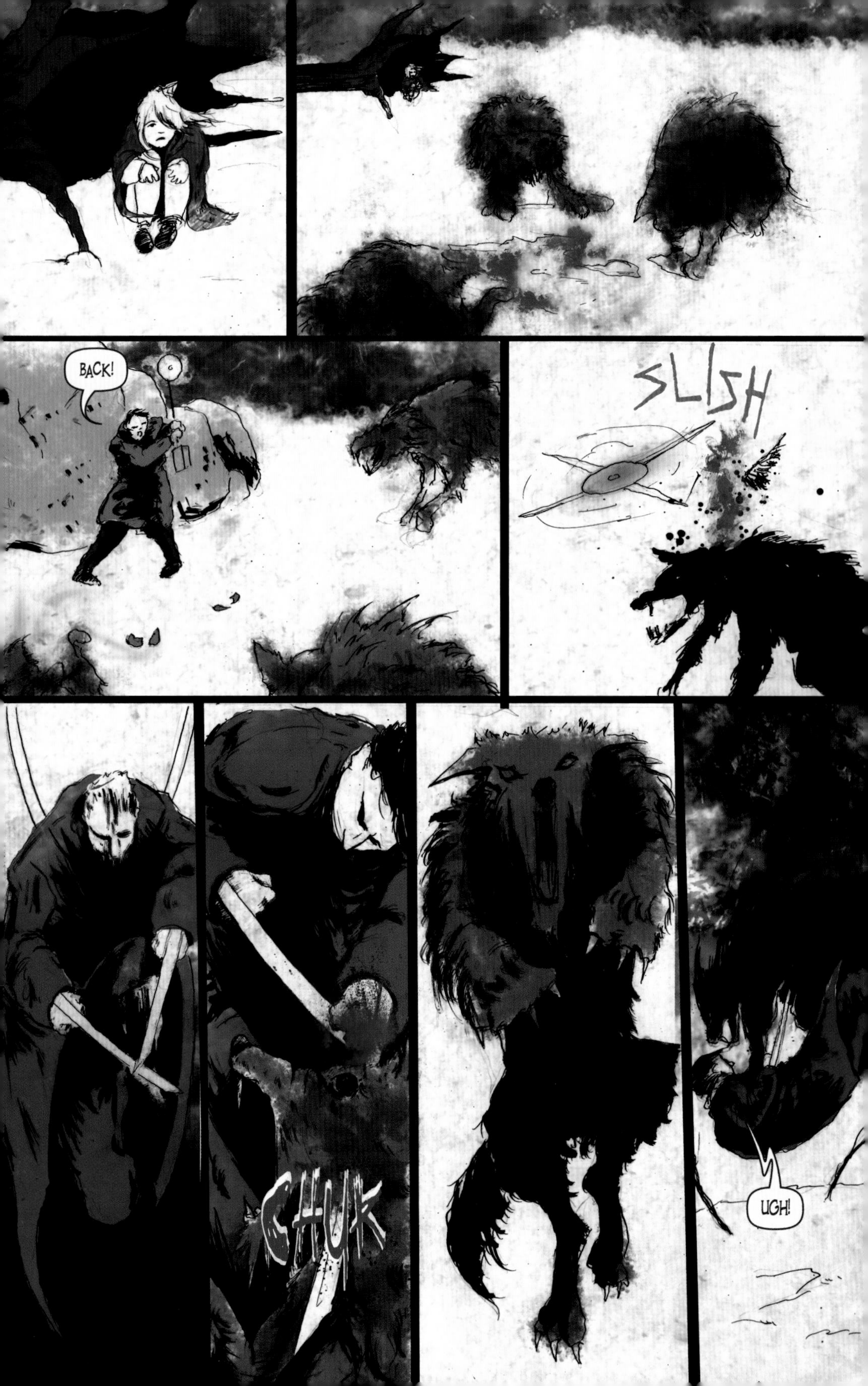
BACK!
SLISH
CHUK
UGH!

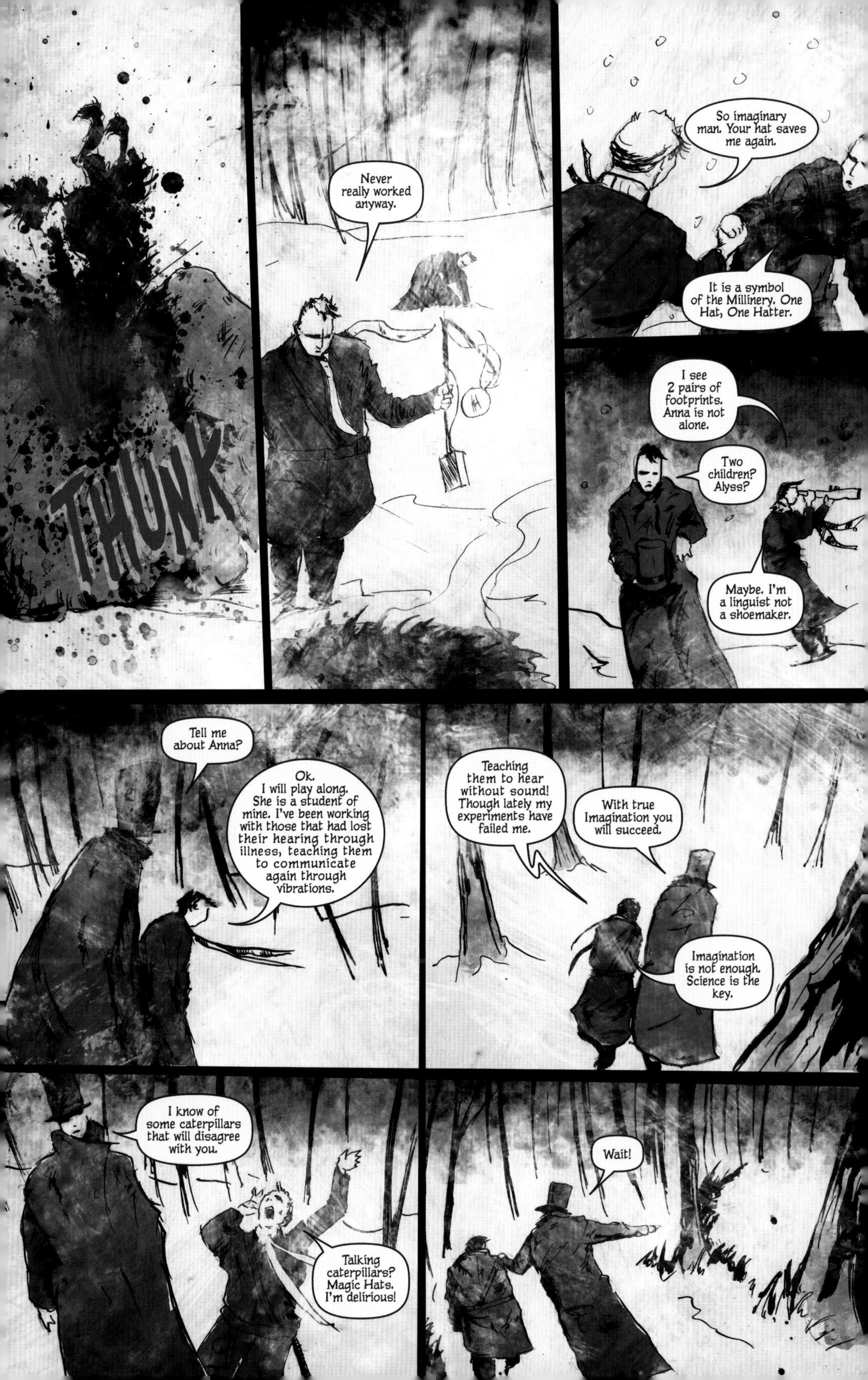
THUNK
Never really worked anyway.
So imaginary man. Your hat saves me again.
It is a symbol of the Millinery. One Hat, One Hatter.
I see 2 pairs of footprints. Anna is not alone.
Two children? Alyss?
Maybe. I'm a linguist not a shoemaker.
Tell me about Anna?
Ok. I will play along. She is a student of mine. I've been working with those that had lost their hearing through illness, teaching them to communicate again through vibrations.
Teaching them to hear without sound! Though lately my experiments have failed me.
With true Imagination you will succeed.
Imagination is not enough. Science is the key.
I know of some caterpillars that will disagree with you.
Talking caterpillars? Magic Hats. I'm delirious!
Wait!

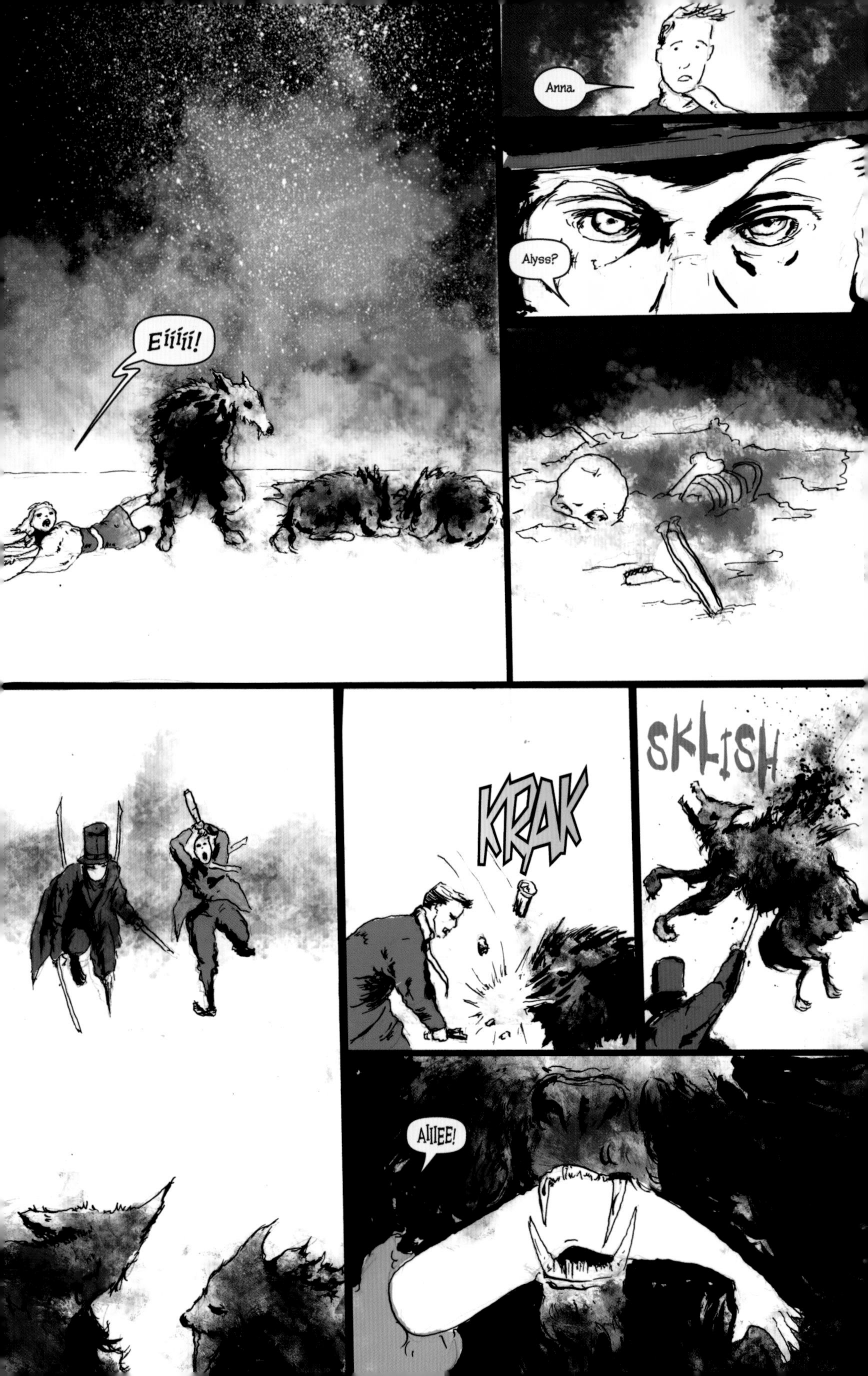
Eiiiii!
Anna.
Alyss?
KRAK
SKLISH
AIIIEE!

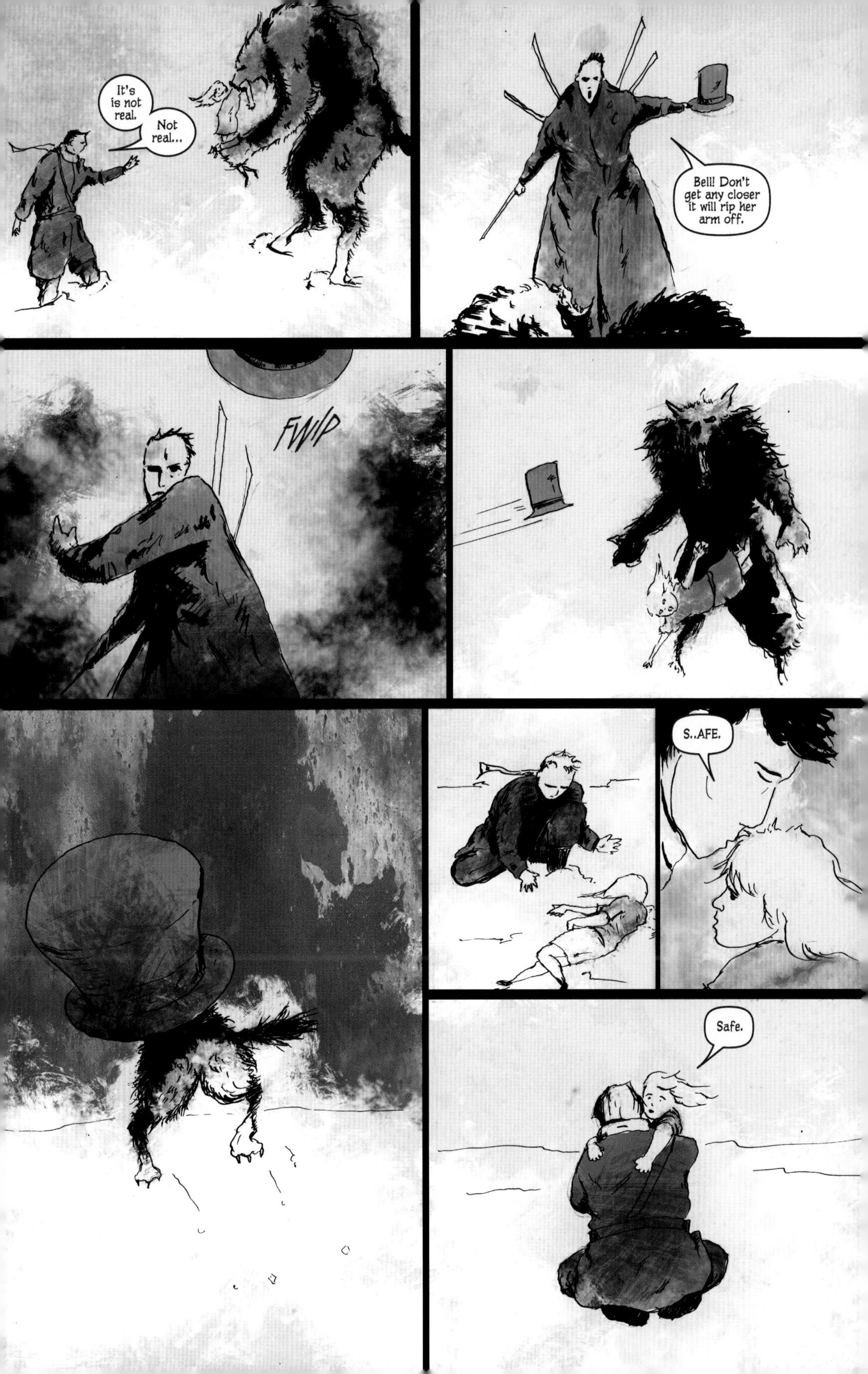
It's is not real.
Not real...
Bell! Don't get any closer it will rip her arm off.
FWIP
S..AFE.
Safe.

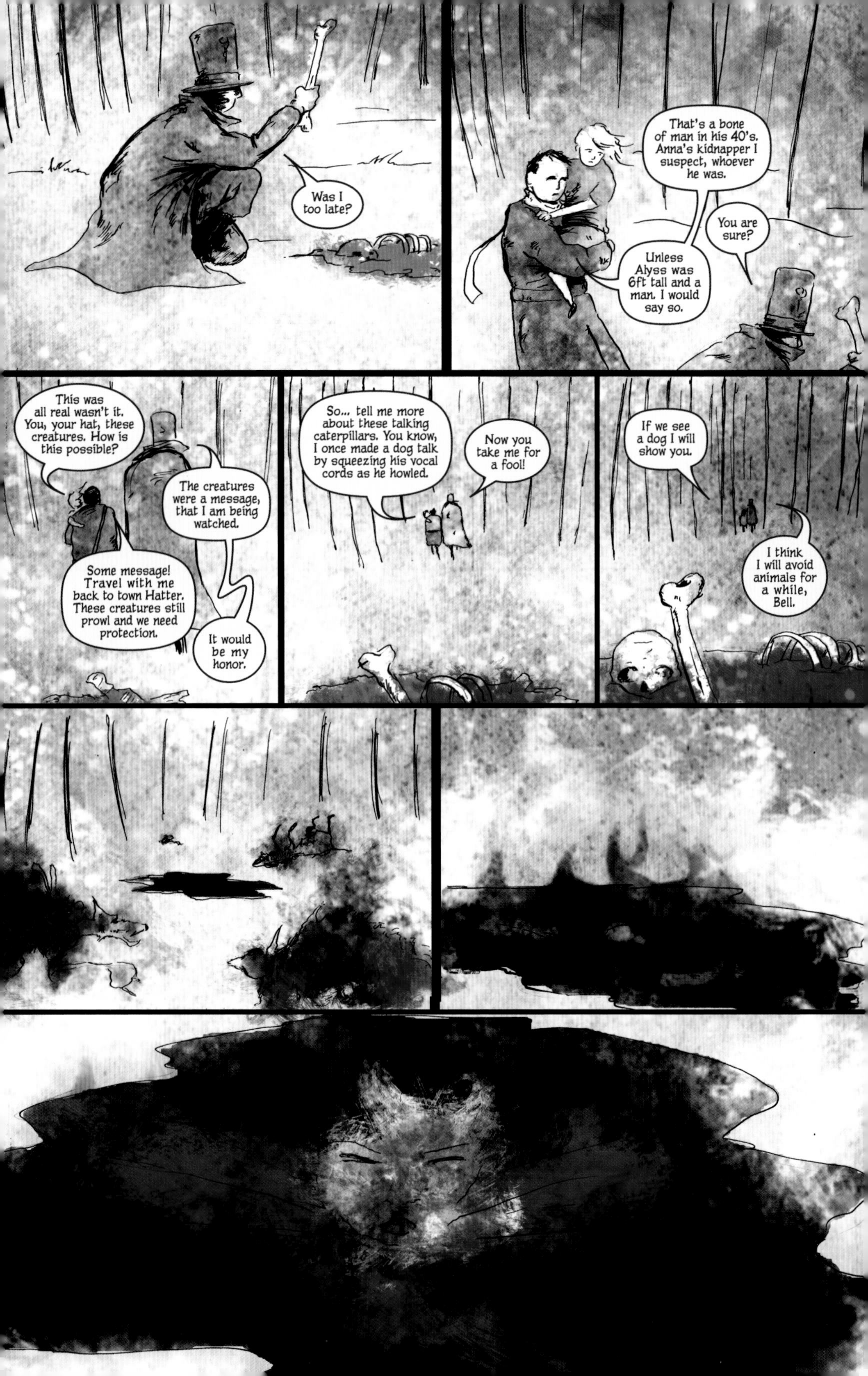
Was I too late?
That's a bone of man in his 40's. Anna's kidnapper I suspect, whoever he was.
You are sure?
Unless Alyss was 6ft tall and a man. I would say so.
This was all real wasn't it. You, your hat, these creatures. How is this possible?
The creatures were a message, that I am being watched.
Some message! Travel with me back to town Hatter. These creatures still prowl and we need protection.
It would be my honor.
So... tell me more about these talking caterpillars. You know, I once made a dog talk by squeezing his vocal cords as he howled.
Now you take me for a fool!
If we see a dog I will show you.
I think I will avoid animals for a while, Bell.

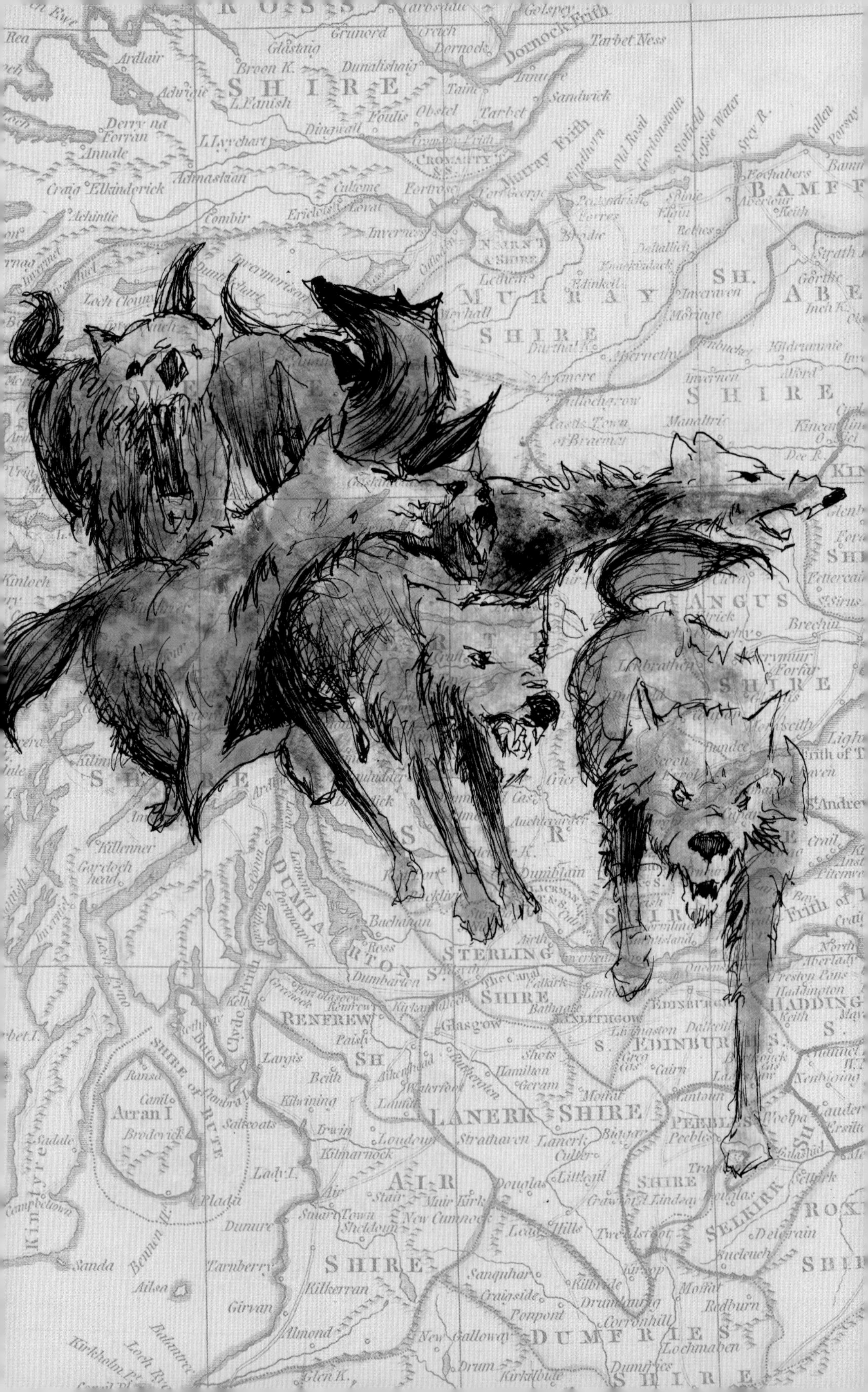

SHIRE
Glastaig
Grunord
Dornock Frith
Tarbet Ness
Ardlair
Broon K.
Dunalishaig
Dornock
Achrigie
L.Fanish
Foulis
Obstel
Tain
Tarbet
Sandwick
Derry na
Forran
L.Lyvchart
Dingwall
Annale
Murray Frith
Achnaskian
Craig Elkinderick
Culeome
Fortrose
Fort George
Fochabers
BAMF
Achintie
Combir
Ericlots
Lovat
Inverness
Forres
Elgin
Keith
Brodie
Rothes
Invermoriston
Loch Cloun
NAIRN & SHIRE
MURRAY
SHIRE
SH.
Inveraven
Moringe
Abernethy
Strath
ABE
Kildrummie
Invernen
Alford
SHIRE
Aviemore
Manaltrie
Castle Town of Braemar
Kincardine
Dee R.
Kinloch
ANGUS
Brechin
Forfar
SHIRE
Dundee
St. Andrews
Crail
Frith of Tay
Killenner
Gareloch head
DUMBARTON
Buchanan
Ross
Dumbarton
Dumblain
Auchterarder
STERLING
SHIRE
The Canal
Falkirk
Linlithgow
Renfrew
RENFREW
SH.
Paisly
Glasgow
Kirkintilloch
Greenock
Port Glasgow
Kelly
Clyde Frith
Largis
Beith
Kilwining
Shots
Hamilton
S. EDINBURGH
Edinburgh
Dalkeith
Livingston
Preston Pans
Haddington
HADDING
North Berwick
Aberlady
Aran I
Canil
Brodevick
Ransa
Saltcoats
Irwin
Kilmarnock
Loudoun
LANERK SHIRE
Strathaven
Lanerk
Biggar
Culter
PEEBLES
Peebles
SHIRE
SELKIRK
Selkirk
Galashiel
Lauder
Kintyre
Saddale
Campbeltown
Lady I.
Plada
AIR
Air
Stair
Muir Kirk
New Cumnock
Douglas
Littlegil
Lindsay
Crawford
Lead Hills
Tweedsoot
Dunure
Sanda
Bennan H.
SHIRE
Tarnberry
Ailsa
Kilkerran
Girvan
Sanquhar
Craigside
Ponpont
Kilbride
Drumlanrig
Moffat
Corronhill
Redburn
Delorain
Bucleuch
ROX
Almond
New Galloway
DUMFRIES
Lochmaben
Dumfries
Drum
Kirkholm
Balantrae
Glen K.
Kirkbride
SHIRE

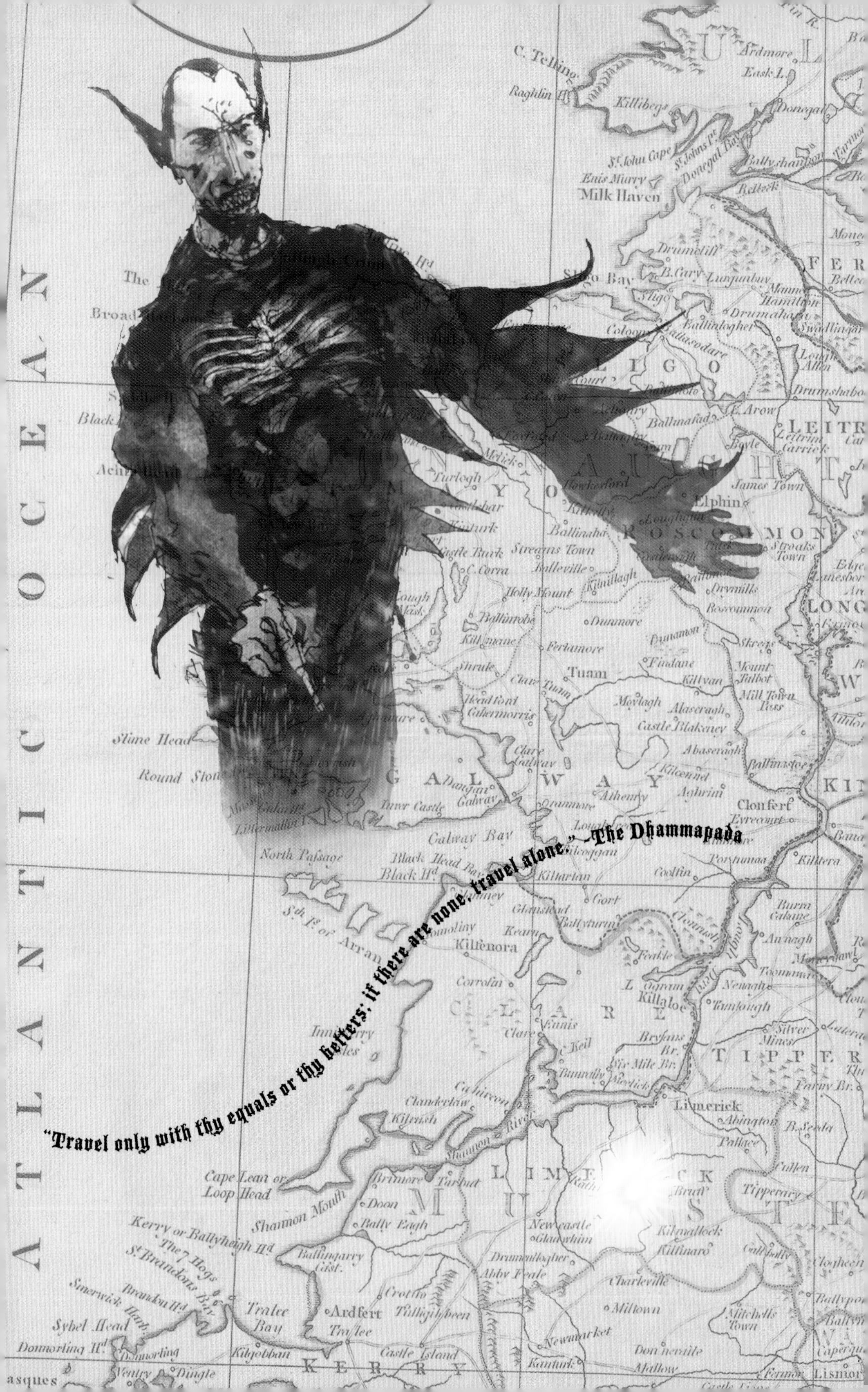
"Travel only with thy equals or thy betters; if there are none, travel alone." -The Dhammapada
ATLANTIC OCEAN
C. Telling
Raghlin Hd.
Killibegs
Ardmore
Donegal
St. John Cape
St. Johns Pt.
Donegal Bay
Bally shannon
Enis Murry
Milk Haven
Drumcliff
Sligo Bay
Sligo
SLIGO
Ballinafad
Boyle
LEITR
Leitrim
Carrick
James Town
Elphin
ROSCOMMON
Strokestown
LONG
MAYO
Turlogh
Hollymount
Ballinrobe
Dunmore
Tuam
Ballinasloe
Slime Head
Round Stone
GALWAY
Galway
Athenry
Aghrim
Clonfert
Eyrecourt
Galway Bay
North Passage
Black Head Bay
Kiltartan
Gort
Portumna
Killaloe
Kilfenora
Corrofin
CLARE
Ennis
Clare
Keil
Six Mile Br.
Limerick
Abington
Tipperary
TIPPER
Clanderlaw
Kilrush
Shannon River
Tarbut
Cape Lean or Loop Head
Shannon Mouth
Kerry or Ballyheigh Hd.
The 7 Hogs
St. Brandons Bay
Brandon Hd.
Smerwick Harb.
Sybel Head
Donnorling Hd.
Tralee Bay
Ardfert
Tralee
Castle Island
Kilgobban
Ventry
Dingle
KERRY
Newcastle
Kilmallock
Charleville
Milltown
Newmarket
Kanturk
Mallow
Doneraile

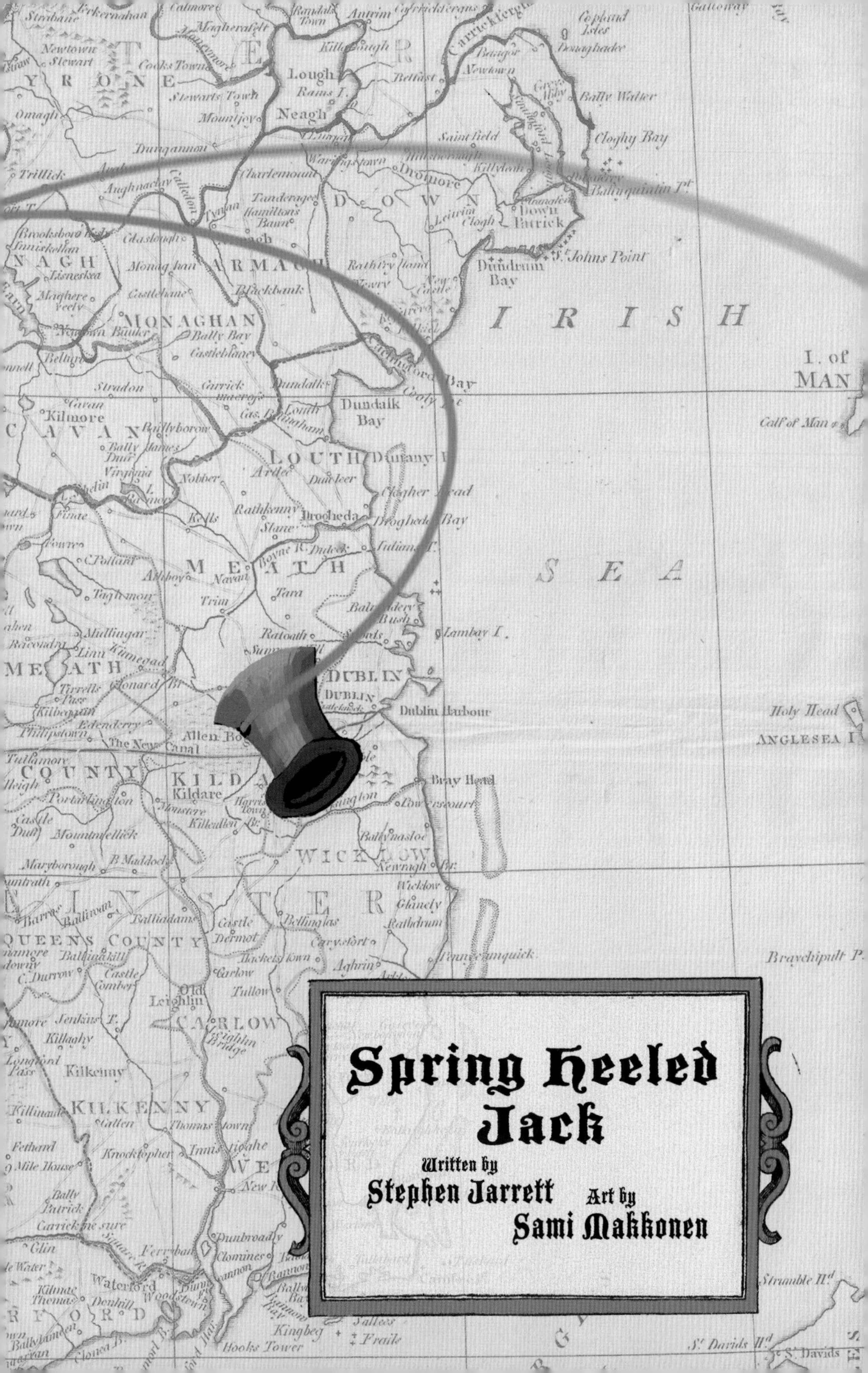

Spring Heeled Jack

Written by
Stephen Jarrett

Art by
Sami Makkonen

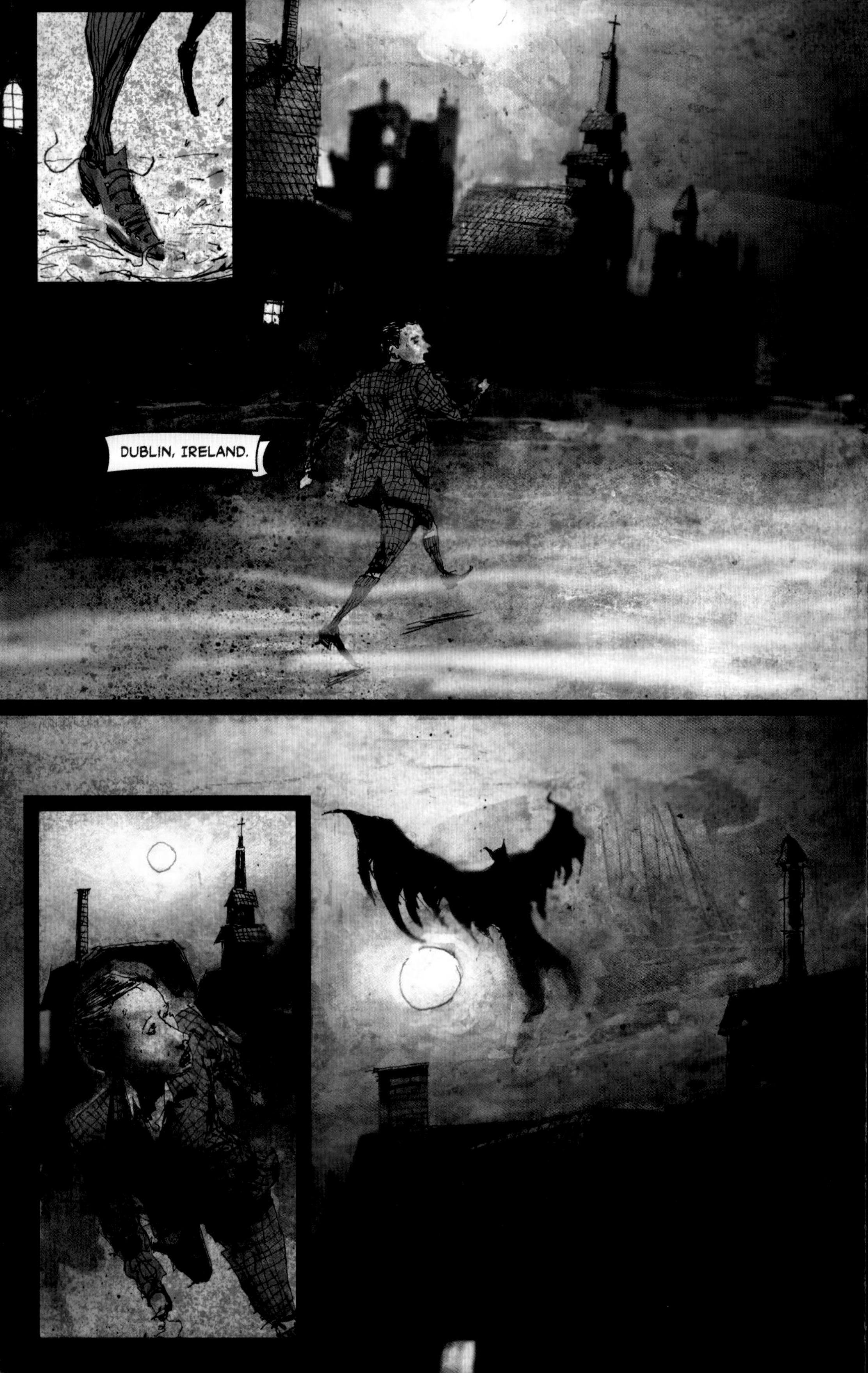
DUBLIN, IRELAND.

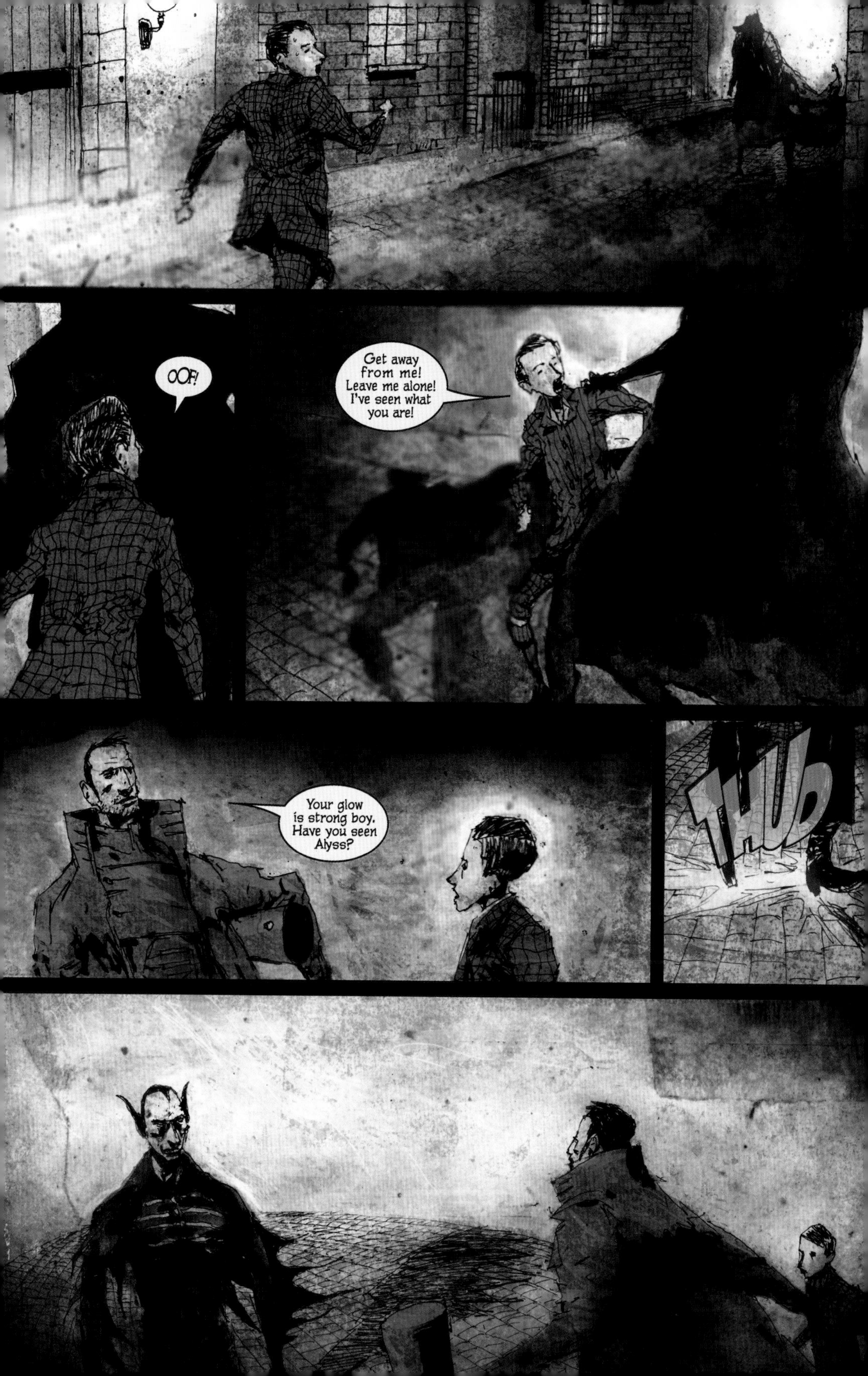
OOF!
Get away from me! Leave me alone! I've seen what you are!
Your glow is strong boy. Have you seen Alyss?
THUD

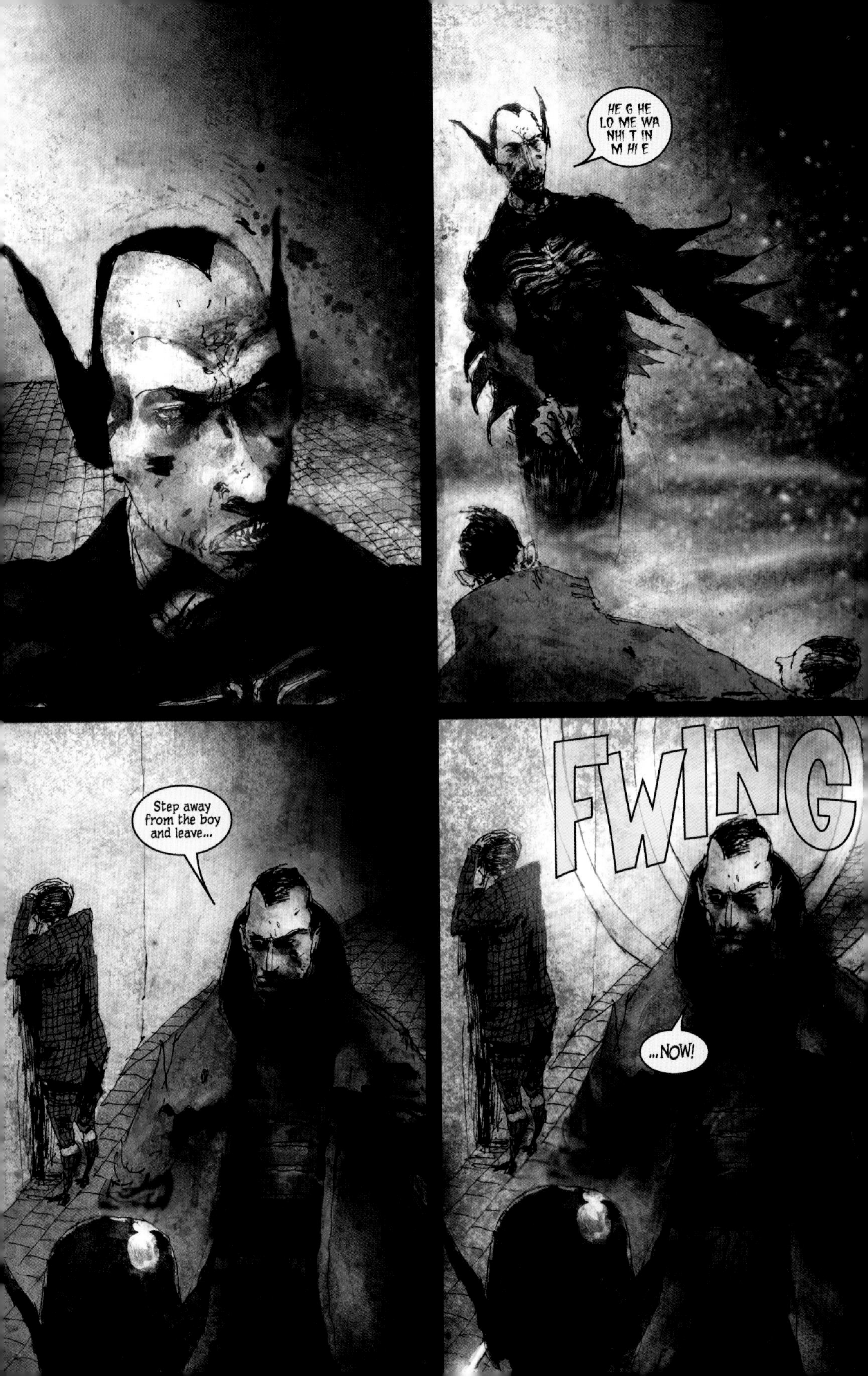
HE G HE LO ME WA NHI T IN M HI E
Step away from the boy and leave...
FWING
...NOW!

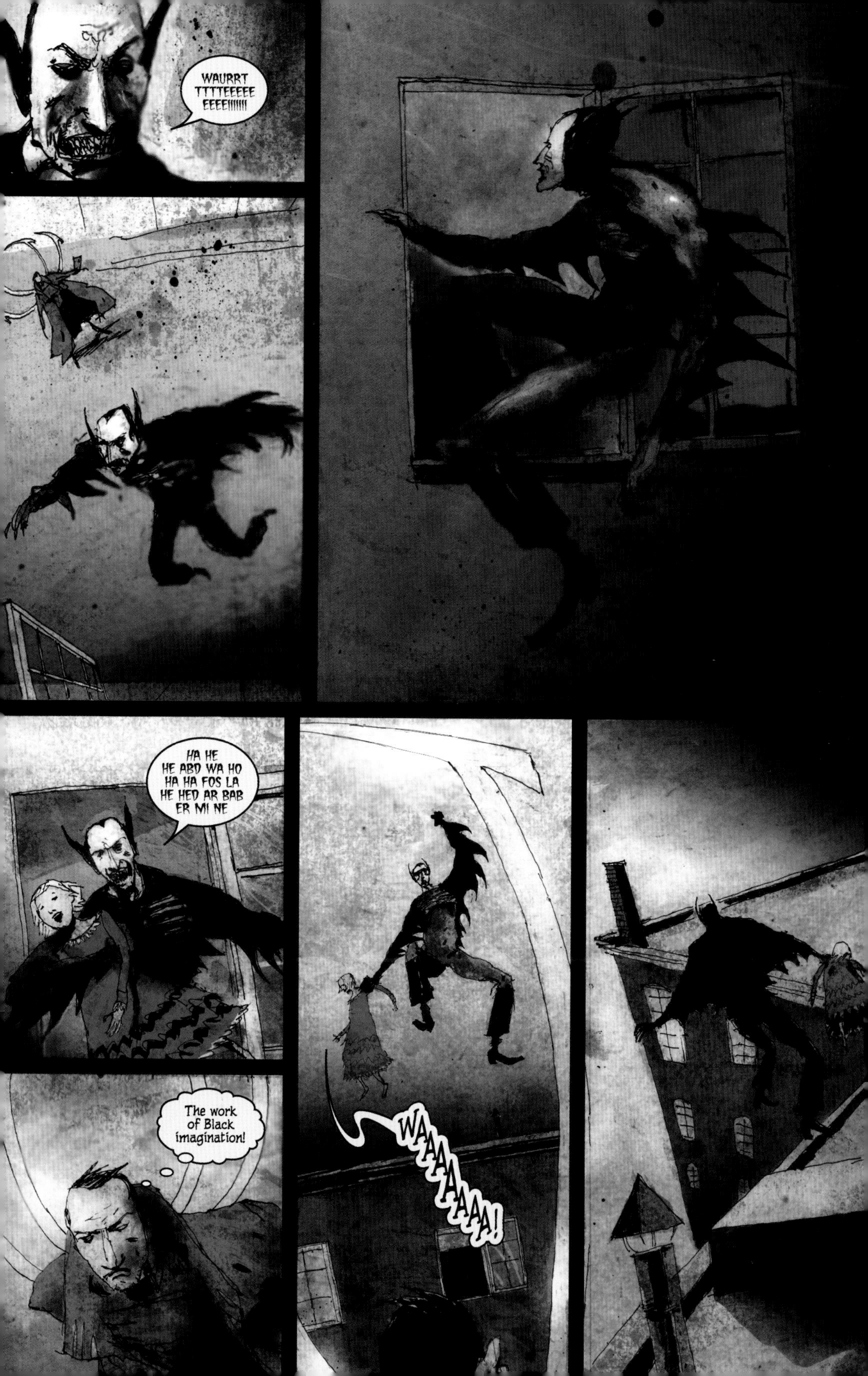
WAURRT TTTTEEEEE EEEE!!!!!!
HA HE HE ABD WA HO HA HA FOS LA HE HED AR BAB ER MI NE
The work of Black imagination!
WAAAAAAAA!

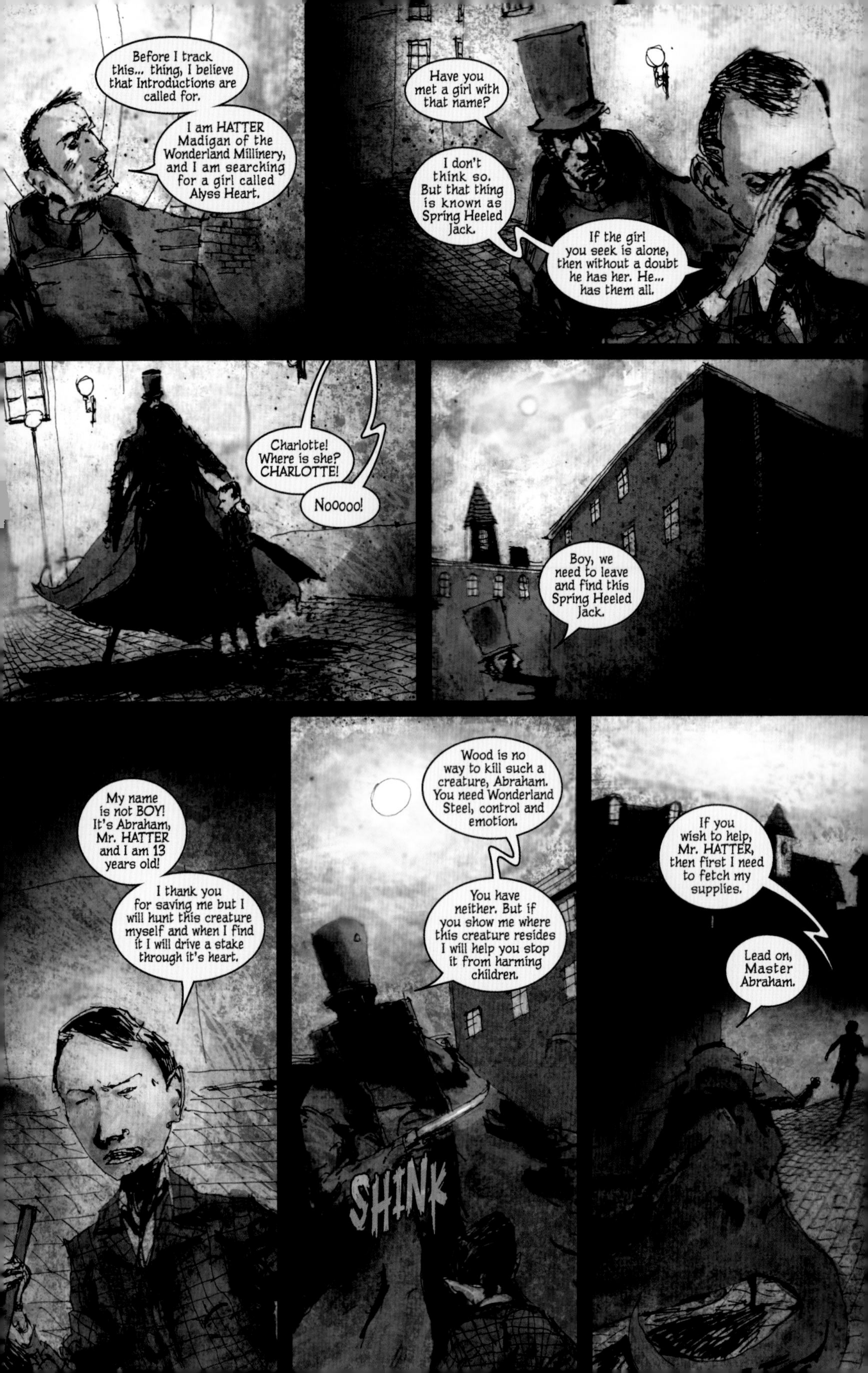

Before I track this... thing, I believe that Introductions are called for.
I am HATTER Madigan of the Wonderland Millinery, and I am searching for a girl called Alyss Heart.
Have you met a girl with that name?
I don't think so. But that thing is known as Spring Heeled Jack.
If the girl you seek is alone, then without a doubt he has her. He... has them all.
Charlotte! Where is she? CHARLOTTE!
Nooooo!
Boy, we need to leave and find this Spring Heeled Jack.
My name is not BOY! It's Abraham, Mr. HATTER and I am 13 years old!
I thank you for saving me but I will hunt this creature myself and when I find it I will drive a stake through it's heart.
Wood is no way to kill such a creature, Abraham. You need Wonderland Steel, control and emotion.
You have neither. But if you show me where this creature resides I will help you stop it from harming children.
SHINK
If you wish to help, Mr. HATTER, then first I need to fetch my supplies.
Lead on, Master Abraham.

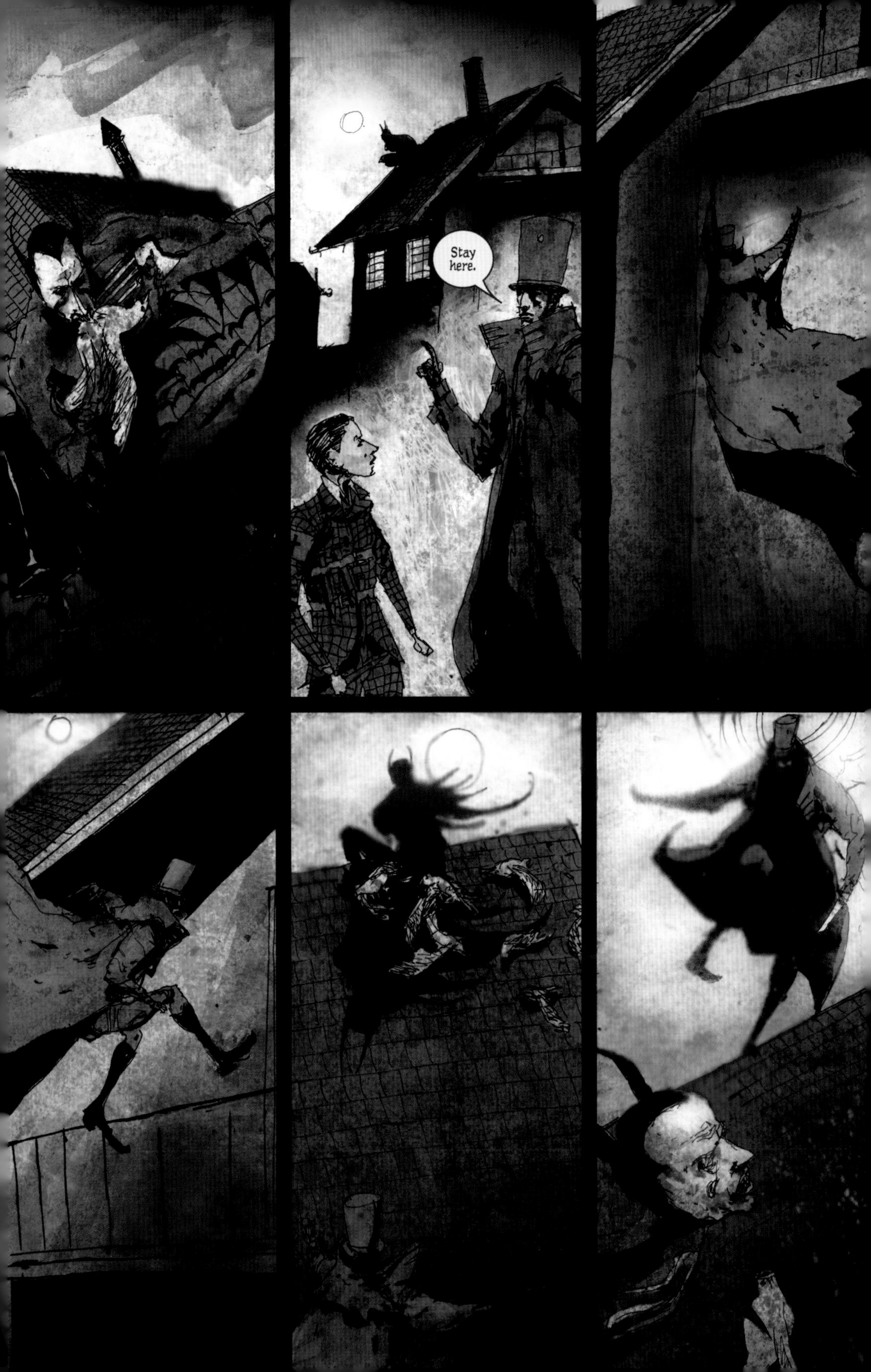
Stay here.

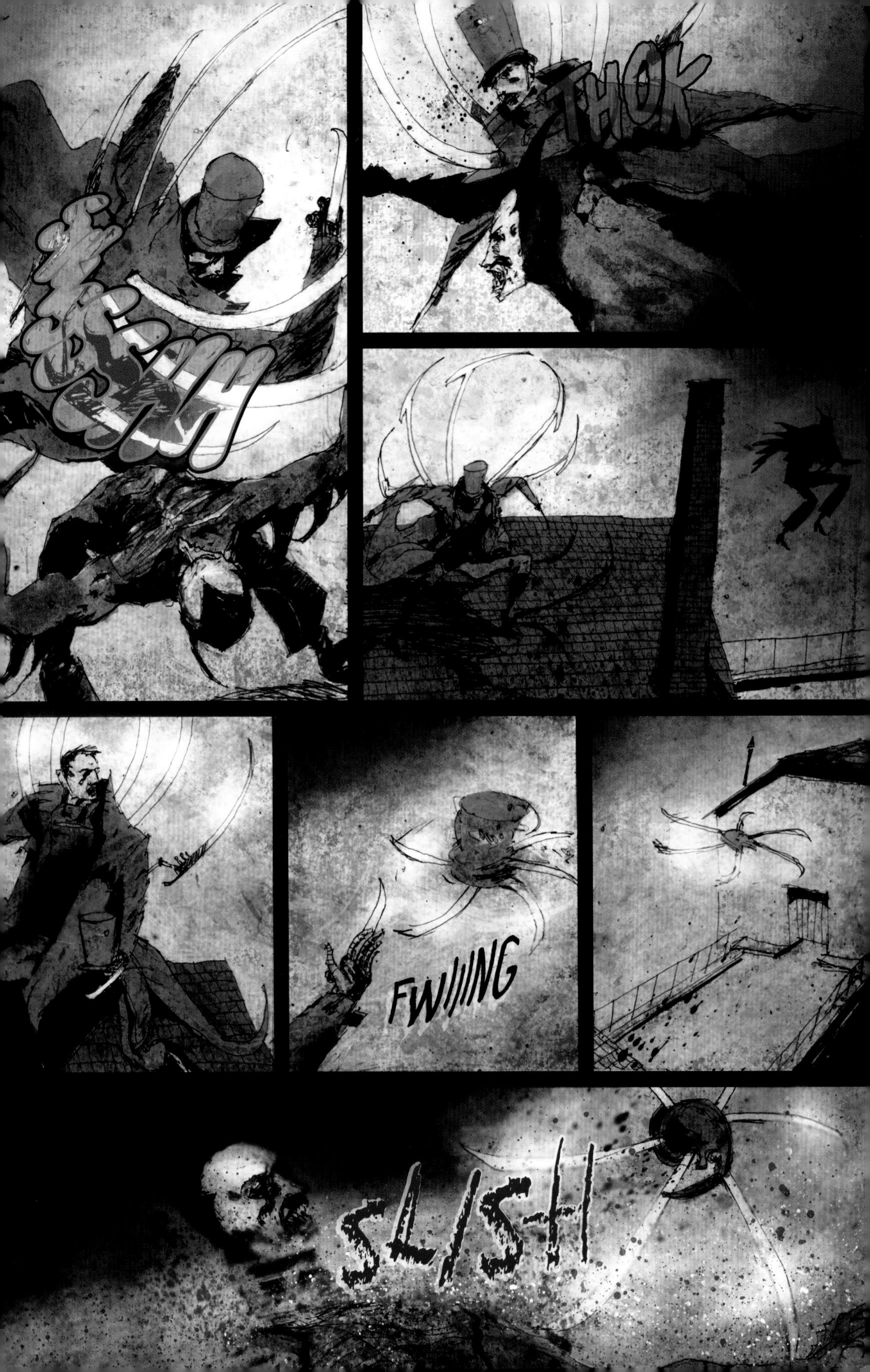
THOK
FWIIIING
SLISH

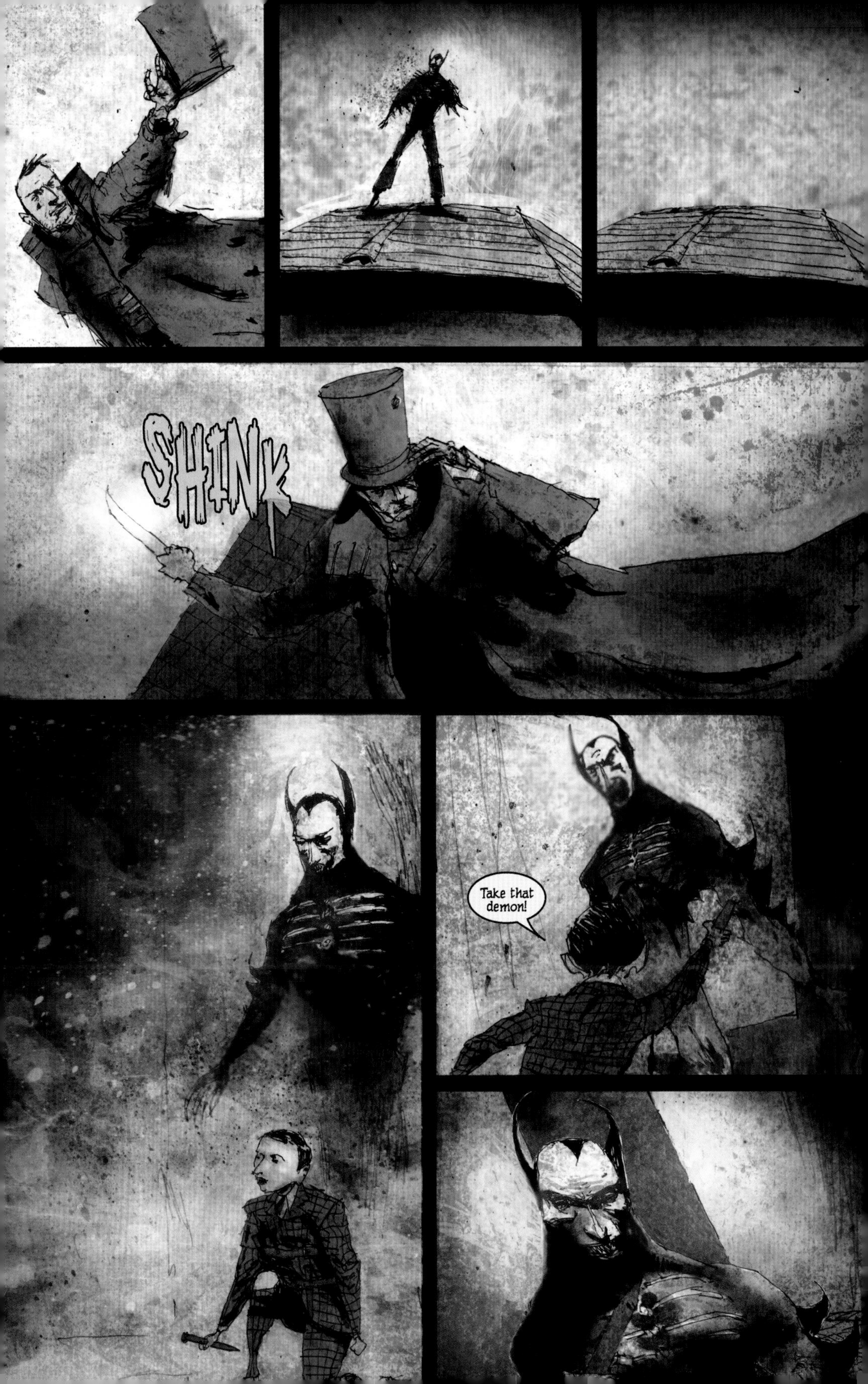
SHINK
Take that demon!

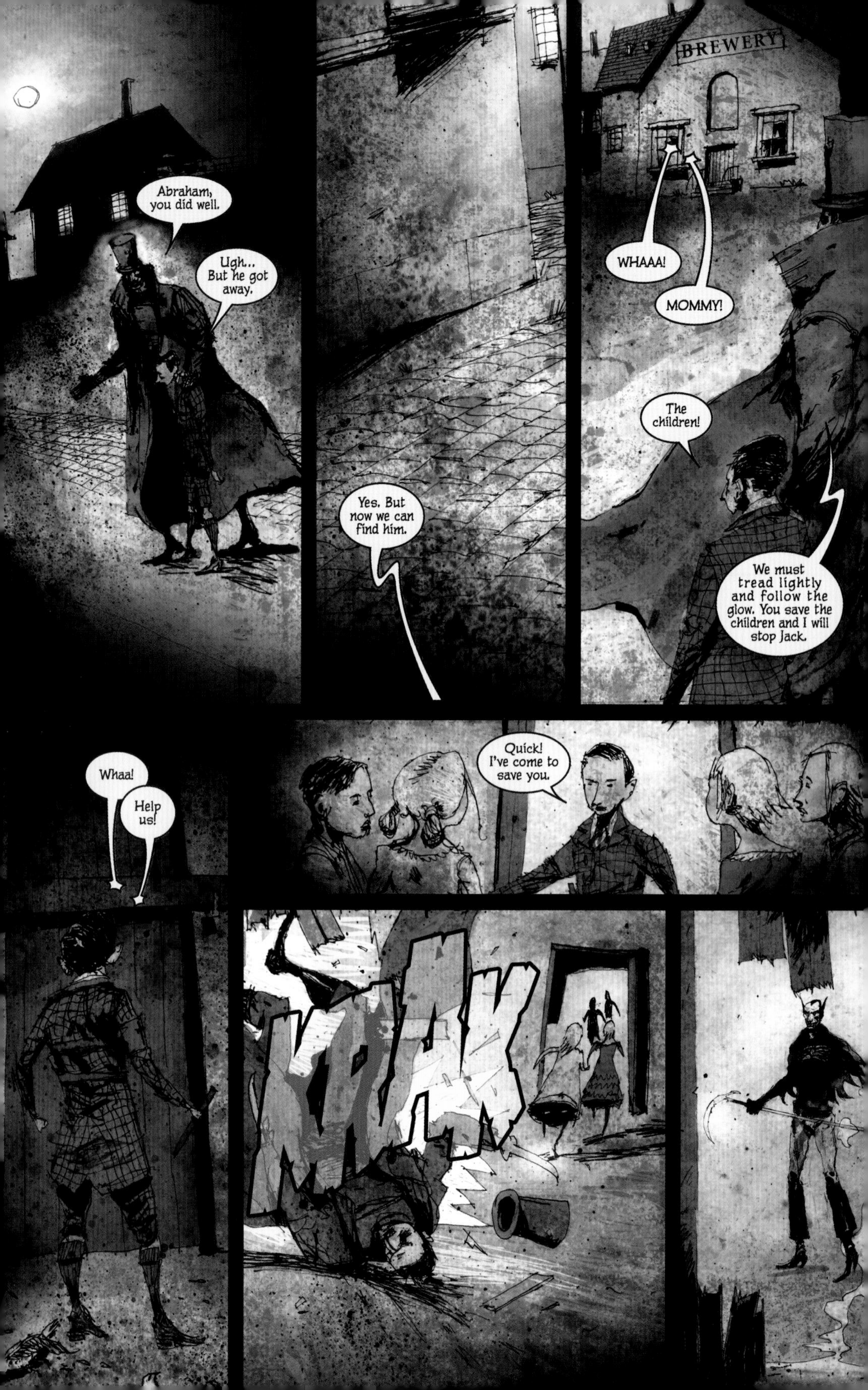
BREWERY
Abraham, you did well.
Ugh... But he got away.
Yes. But now we can find him.
WHAAA!
MOMMY!
The children!
We must tread lightly and follow the glow. You save the children and I will stop Jack.
Whaa!
Help us!
Quick! I've come to save you.
WHAK

AAHAGHEEE!

Now you will answer my questions!

Gone. But what's this?

I'm sorry you didn't find your Alice but you did save these children... and me.

Do you think Jack will return?

If he does then so will I. You fight well, Abraham.

My friends call me Bram. Mr. Madigan. Bram Stoker and you are most definitely a friend.

I am honored, Bram.

Now, let's get you and these children home.

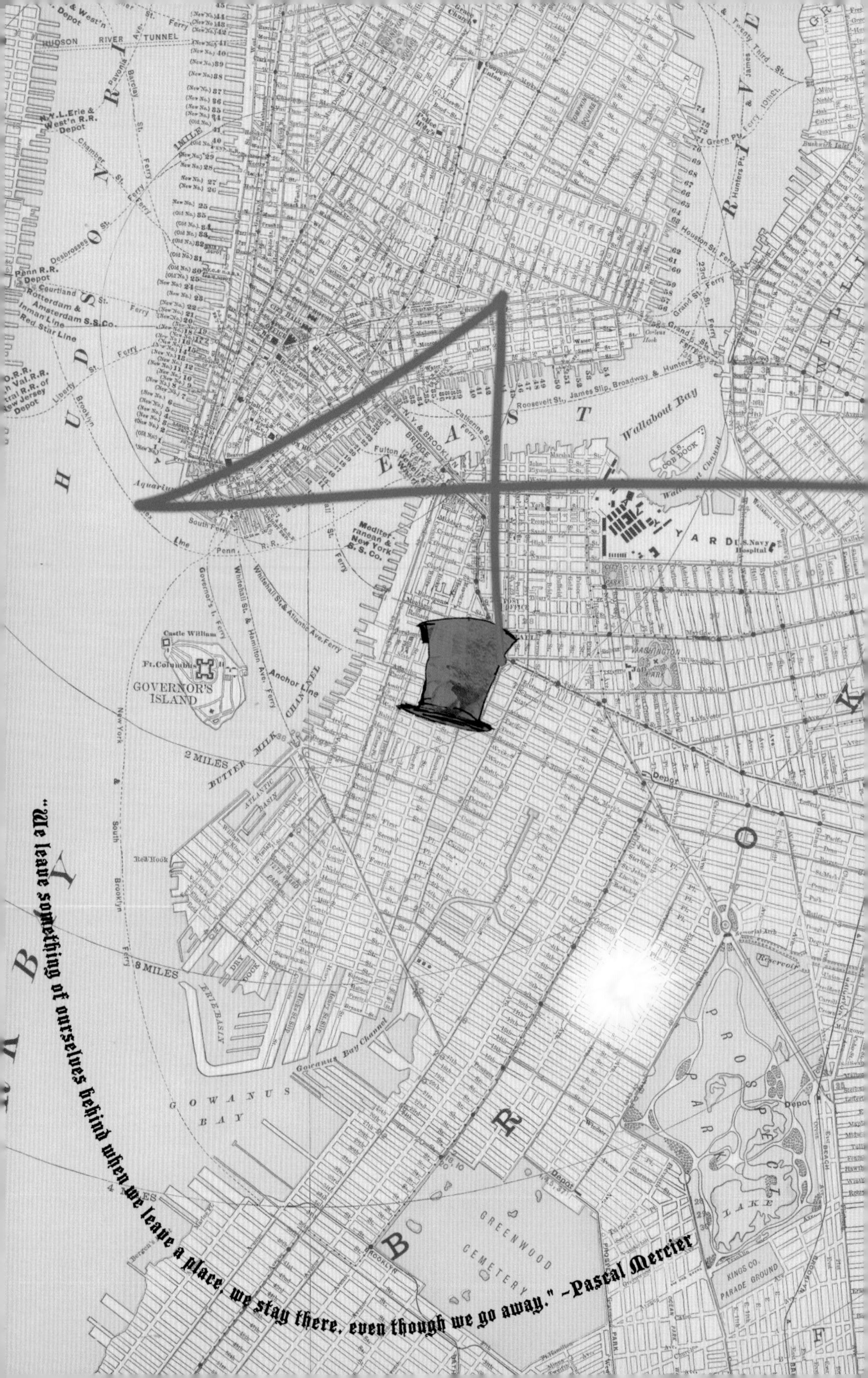

HUDSON RIVER TUNNEL
EAST RIVER
Wallabout Bay
U.S. NAVY YARD
U.S. Navy Hospital
GOVERNOR'S ISLAND
Castle William
Ft. Columbus
BUTTER MILK CHANNEL
ATLANTIC BASIN
ERIE BASIN
Red Hook
GOWANUS BAY
Gowanus Bay Channel
GREENWOOD CEMETERY
PROSPECT PARK
LAKE
KINGS CO. PARADE GROUND
2 MILES
3 MILES
4 MILES
N.Y. & BROOKLYN BRIDGE
WASHINGTON PARK
CITY PARK
Reservoir
Memorial Arch

"We leave something of ourselves behind when we leave a place, we stay there, even though we go away." –Pascal Mercier

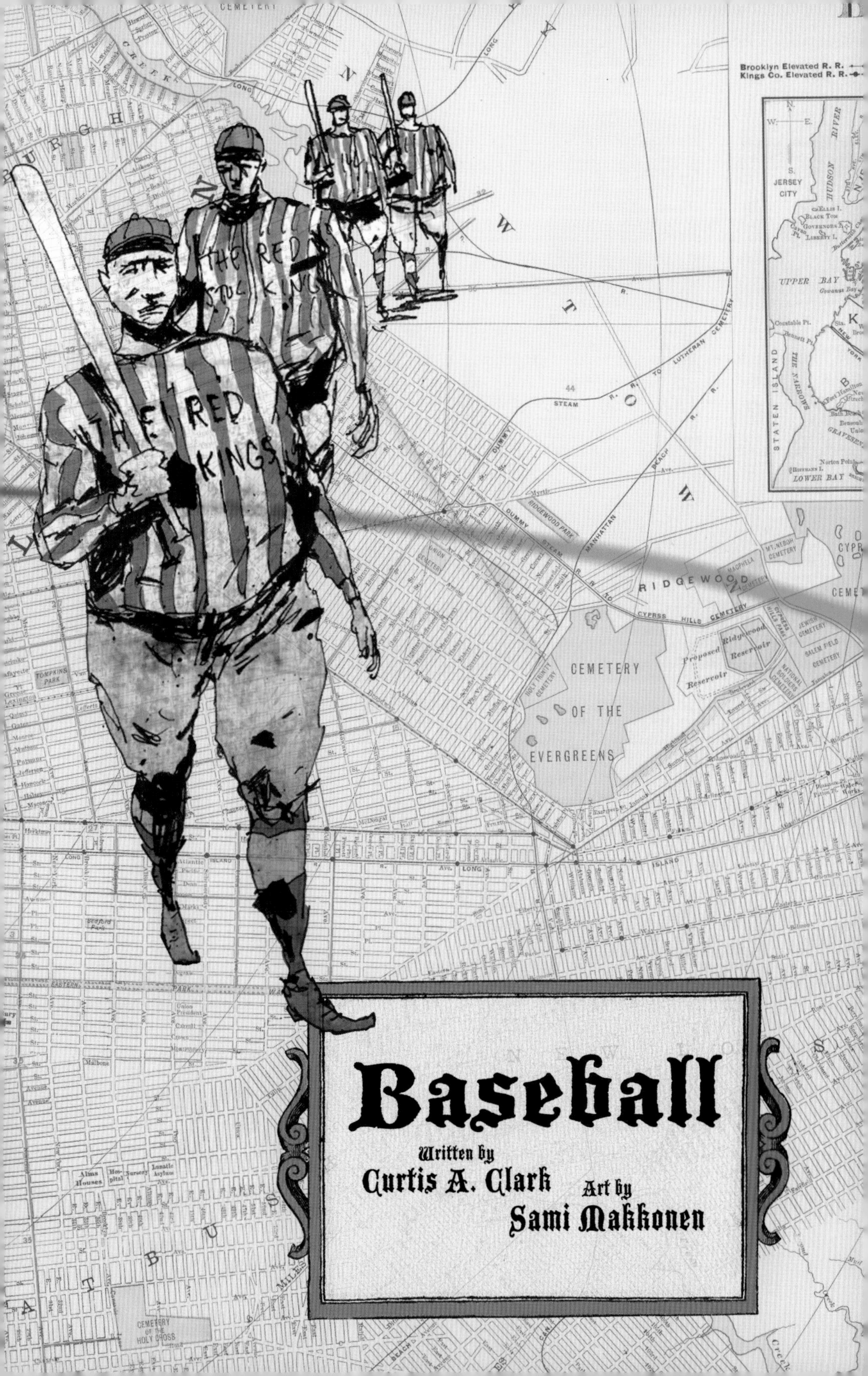
THE RED KINGS
THE RED KINGS
Brooklyn Elevated R. R.
Kings Co. Elevated R. R.
JERSEY CITY
HUDSON RIVER
UPPER BAY
STATEN ISLAND
THE NARROWS
LOWER BAY
RIDGEWOOD
CEMETERY OF THE EVERGREENS
CYPRSS HILLS CEMETERY
Proposed Ridgewood Reservoir
TOMPKINS PARK
CEMETERY OF THE HOLY CROSS
STEAM R. R. TO LUTHERAN CEMETERY

Baseball

Written by
Curtis A. Clark

Art by
Sami Makkonen

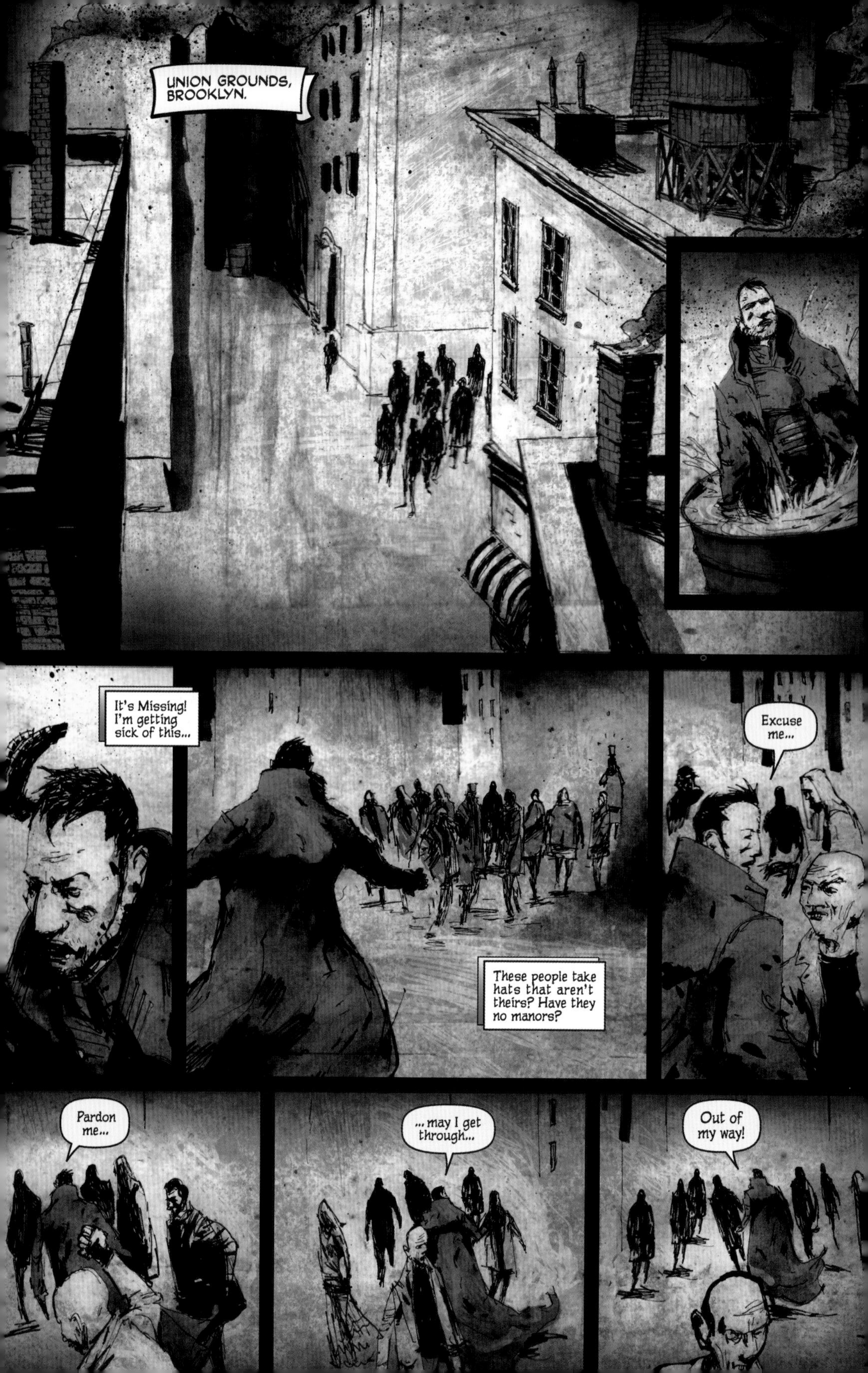
UNION GROUNDS, BROOKLYN.
It's Missing! I'm getting sick of this...
These people take hats that aren't theirs? Have they no manors?
Excuse me...
Pardon me...
...may I get through...
Out of my way!

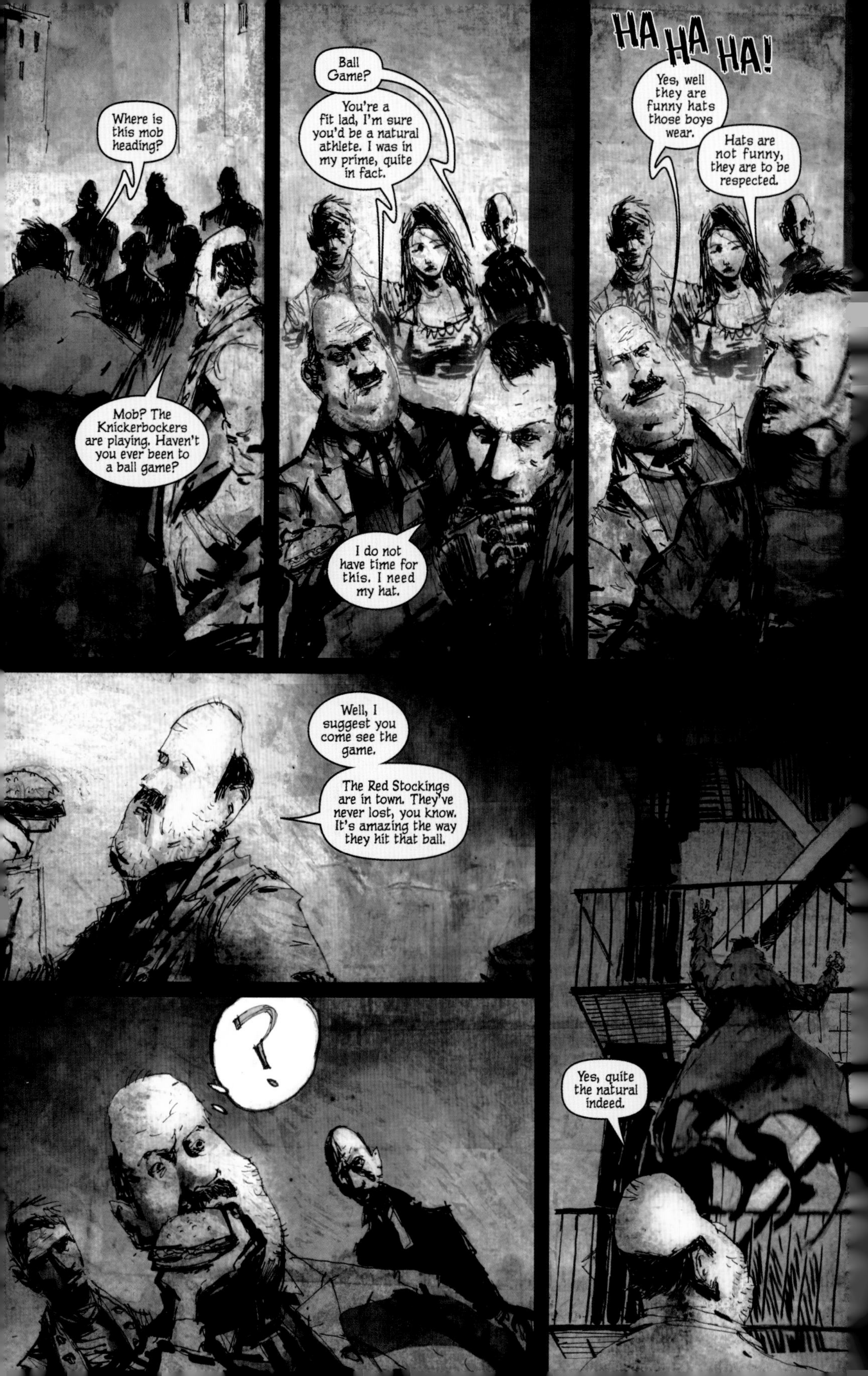
Where is this mob heading?
Mob? The Knickerbockers are playing. Haven't you ever been to a ball game?
Ball Game?
You're a fit lad, I'm sure you'd be a natural athlete. I was in my prime, quite in fact.
I do not have time for this. I need my hat.
HA HA HA!
Yes, well they are funny hats those boys wear.
Hats are not funny, they are to be respected.
Well, I suggest you come see the game.
The Red Stockings are in town. They've never lost, you know. It's amazing the way they hit that ball.
?
Yes, quite the natural indeed.

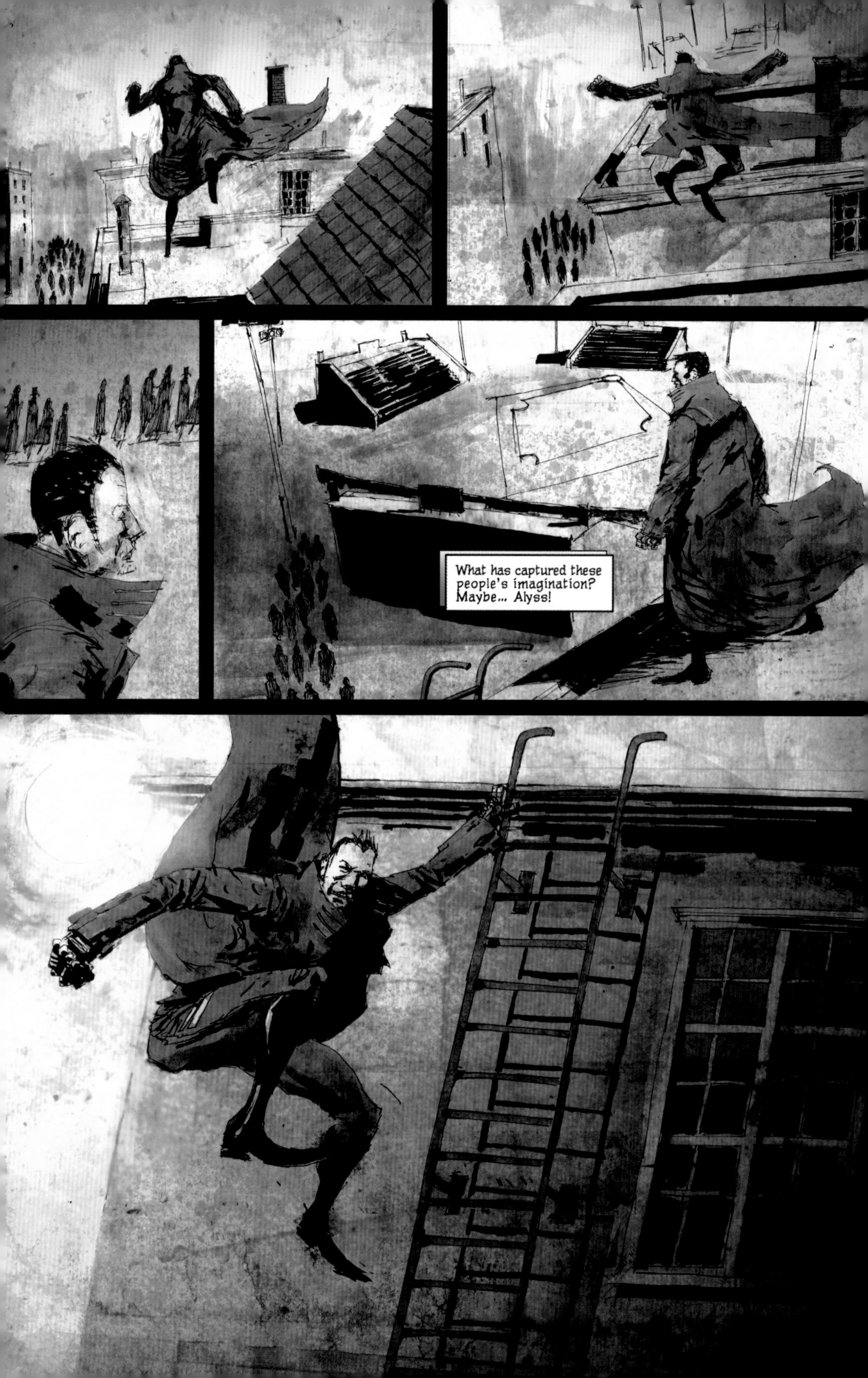
What has captured these people's imagination? Maybe... Alyss!

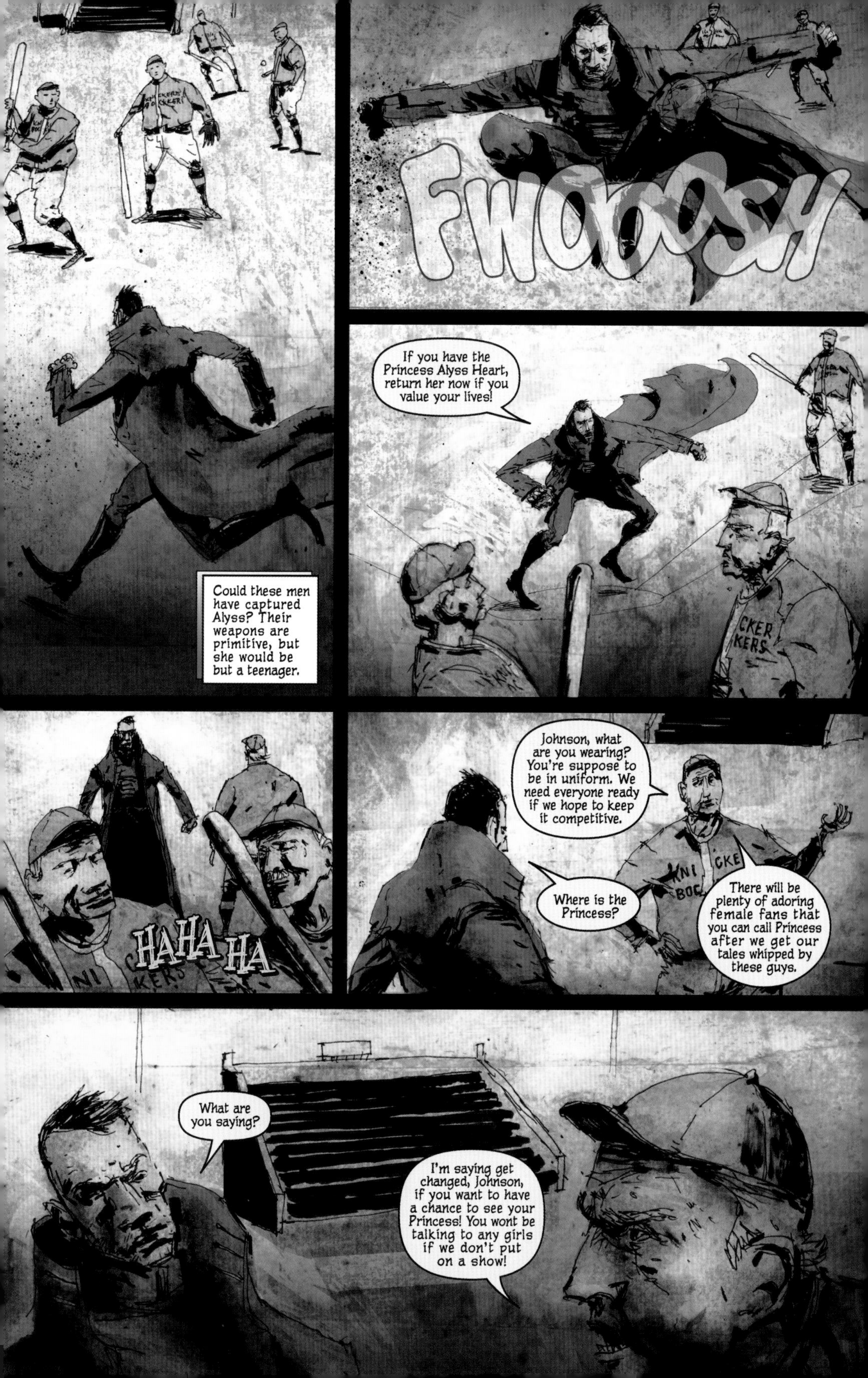
FWOOSH
Could these men have captured Alyss? Their weapons are primitive, but she would be but a teenager.
If you have the Princess Alyss Heart, return her now if you value your lives!
HAHA HA
Johnson, what are you wearing? You're suppose to be in uniform. We need everyone ready if we hope to keep it competitive.
Where is the Princess?
There will be plenty of adoring female fans that you can call Princess after we get our tales whipped by these guys.
What are you saying?
I'm saying get changed, Johnson, if you want to have a chance to see your Princess! You wont be talking to any girls if we don't put on a show!

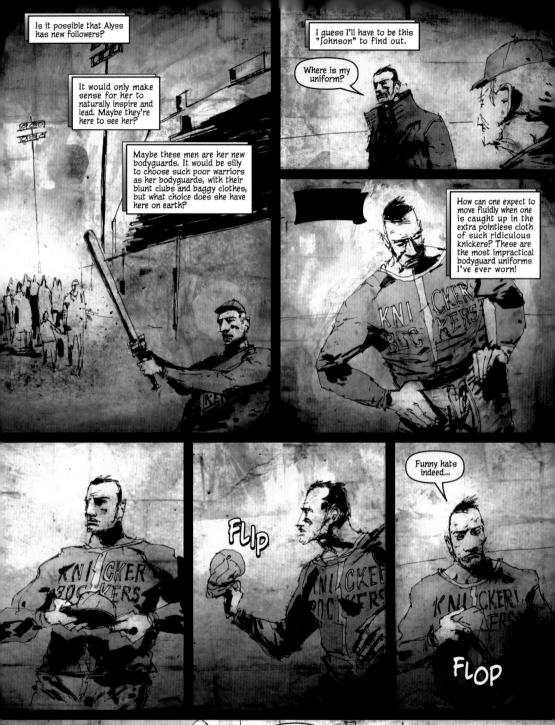

Is it possible that Alyss has new followers?

It would only make sense for her to naturally inspire and lead. Maybe they're here to see her?

Maybe these men are her new bodyguards. It would be silly to choose such poor warriors as her bodyguards, with their blunt clubs and baggy clothes, but what choice does she have here on earth?

I guess I'll have to be this "Johnson" to find out.

Where is my uniform?

How can one expect to move fluidly when one is caught up in the extra pointless cloth of such ridiculous knickers? These are the most impractical bodyguard uniforms I've ever worn!

FLIP

Funny hats indeed...

FLOP

Take a few practice swings, Johnson. I'm putting you in right. Try not to fall asleep out there.

Right? Sleep? What?

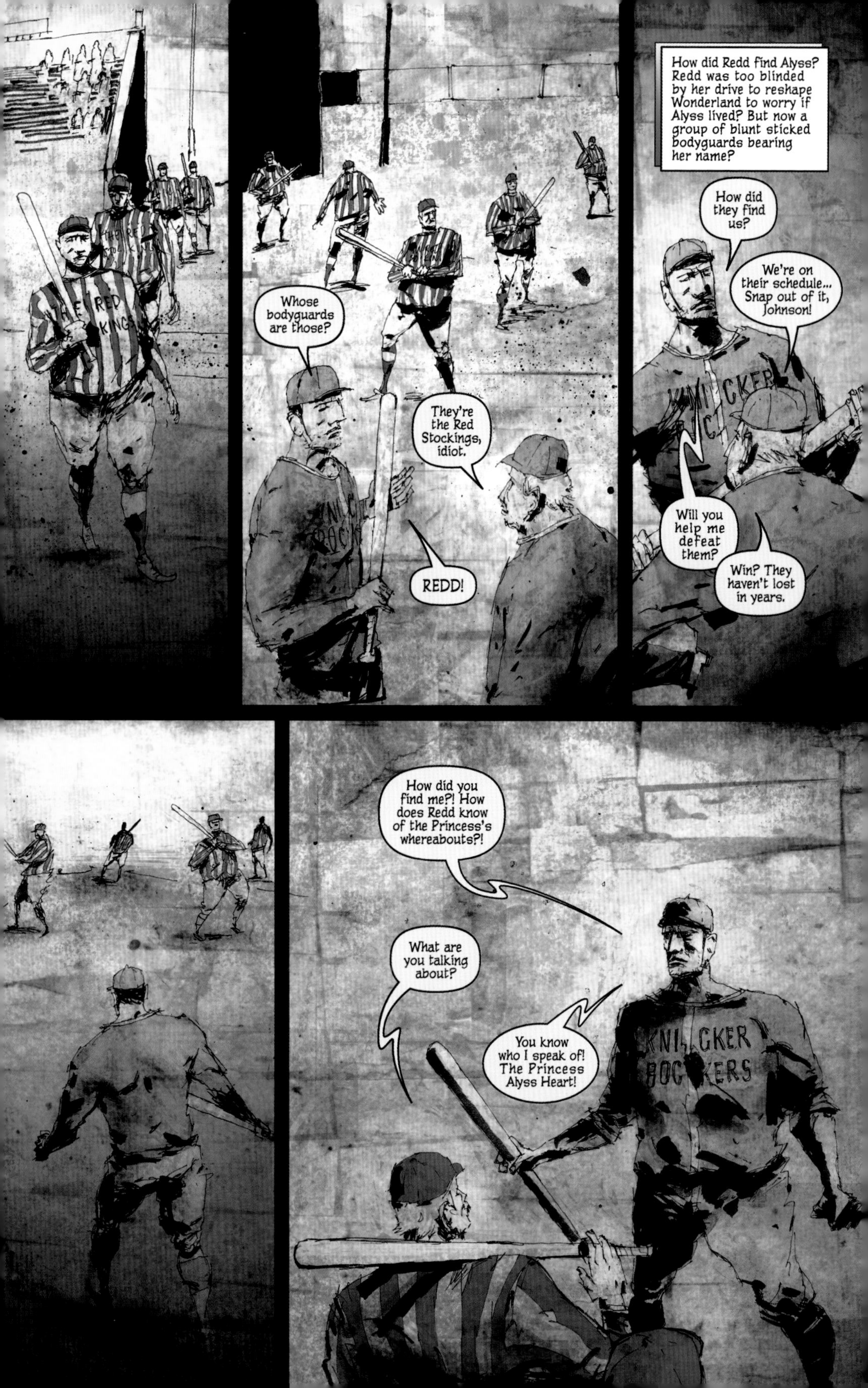
How did Redd find Alyss? Redd was too blinded by her drive to reshape Wonderland to worry if Alyss lived? But now a group of blunt sticked bodyguards bearing her name?
Whose bodyguards are those?
They're the Red Stockings, idiot.
REDD!
How did they find us?
We're on their schedule... Snap out of it, Johnson!
Will you help me defeat them?
Win? They haven't lost in years.
How did you find me?! How does Redd know of the Princess's whereabouts?!
What are you talking about?
You know who I speak of! The Princess Alyss Heart!

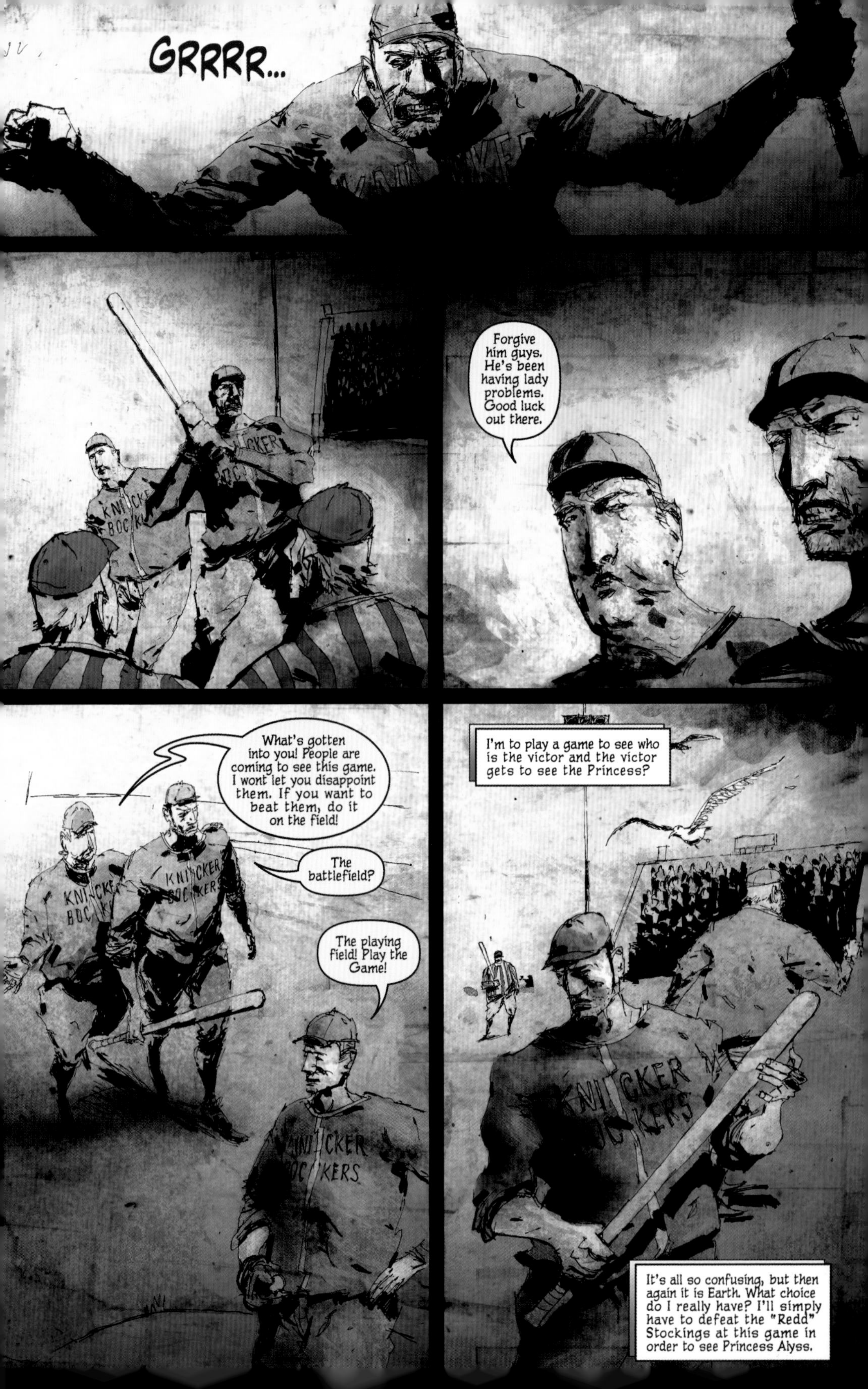
GRRRR...
Forgive him guys. He's been having lady problems. Good luck out there.
What's gotten into you! People are coming to see this game. I wont let you disappoint them. If you want to beat them, do it on the field!
The battlefield?
The playing field! Play the Game!
I'm to play a game to see who is the victor and the victor gets to see the Princess?
It's all so confusing, but then again it is Earth. What choice do I really have? I'll simply have to defeat the "Redd" Stockings at this game in order to see Princess Alyss.

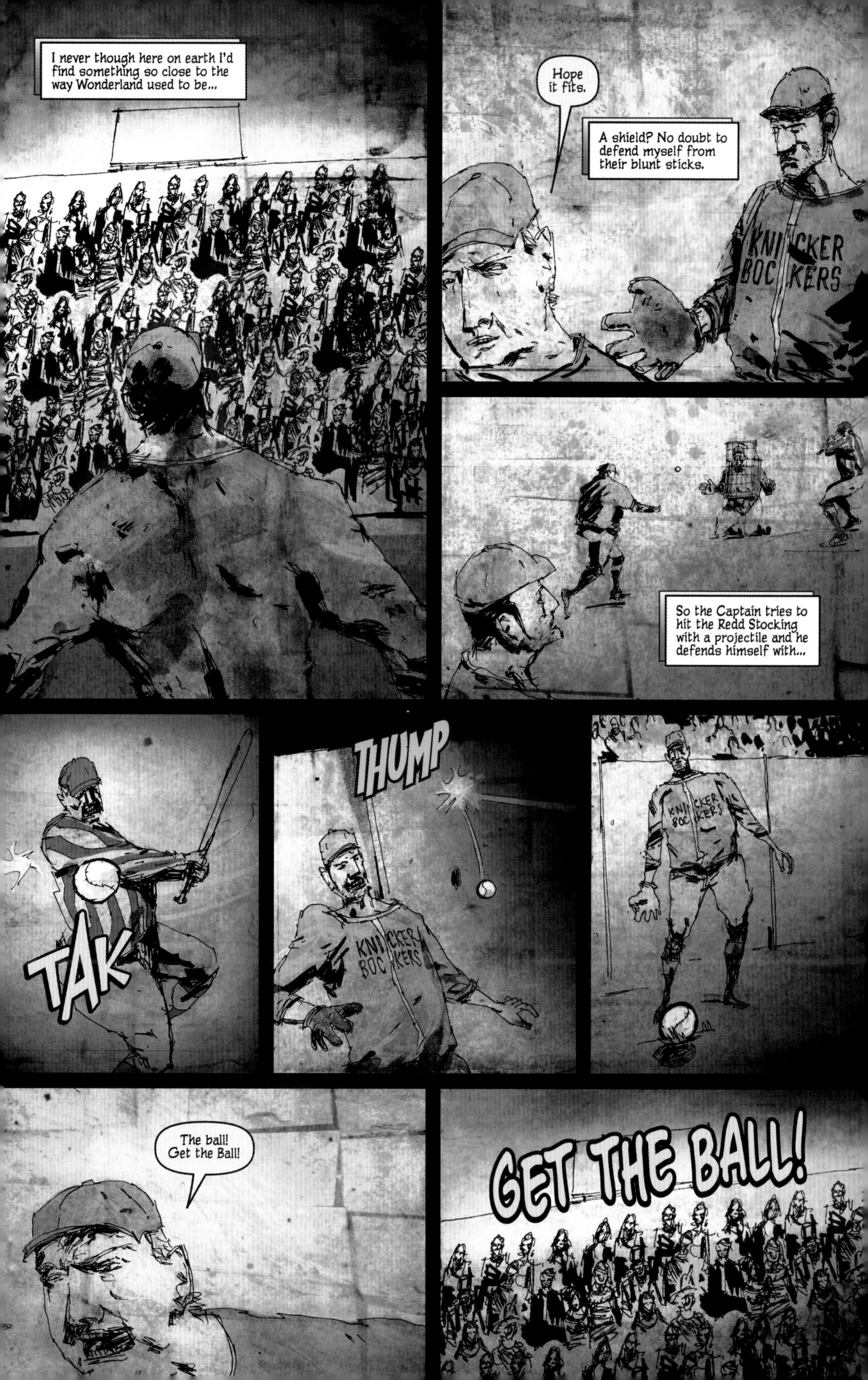
I never though here on earth I'd find something so close to the way Wonderland used to be...
Hope it fits.
A shield? No doubt to defend myself from their blunt sticks.
KNICKER BOCKERS
So the Captain tries to hit the Redd Stocking with a projectile and he defends himself with...
TAK
THUMP
The ball! Get the Ball!
GET THE BALL!

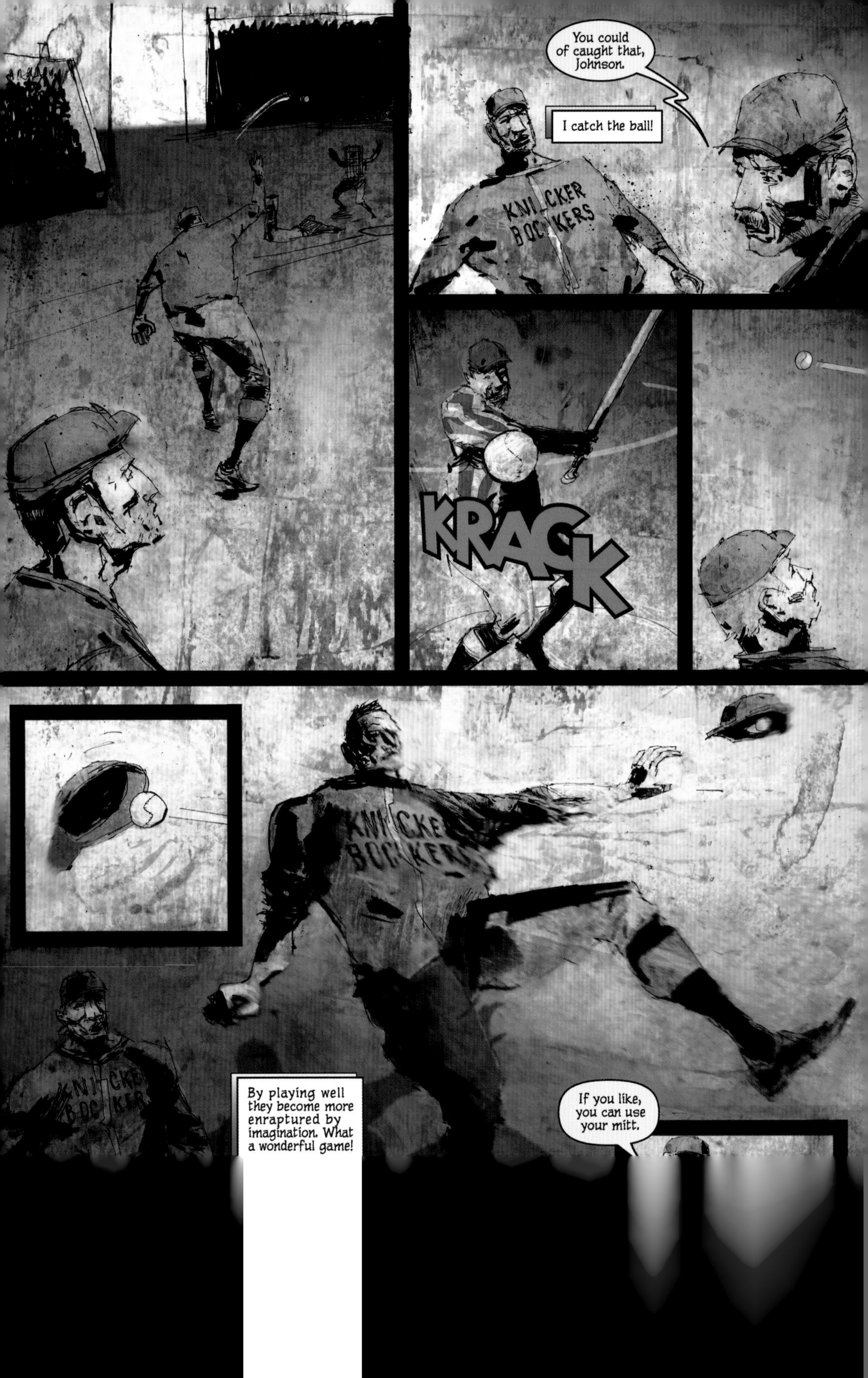
You could of caught that, Johnson.
I catch the ball!
KNICKER BOCKERS
KRACK
KNICKER BOCKERS
By playing well they become more enraptured by imagination. What a wonderful game!
If you like, you can use your mitt.

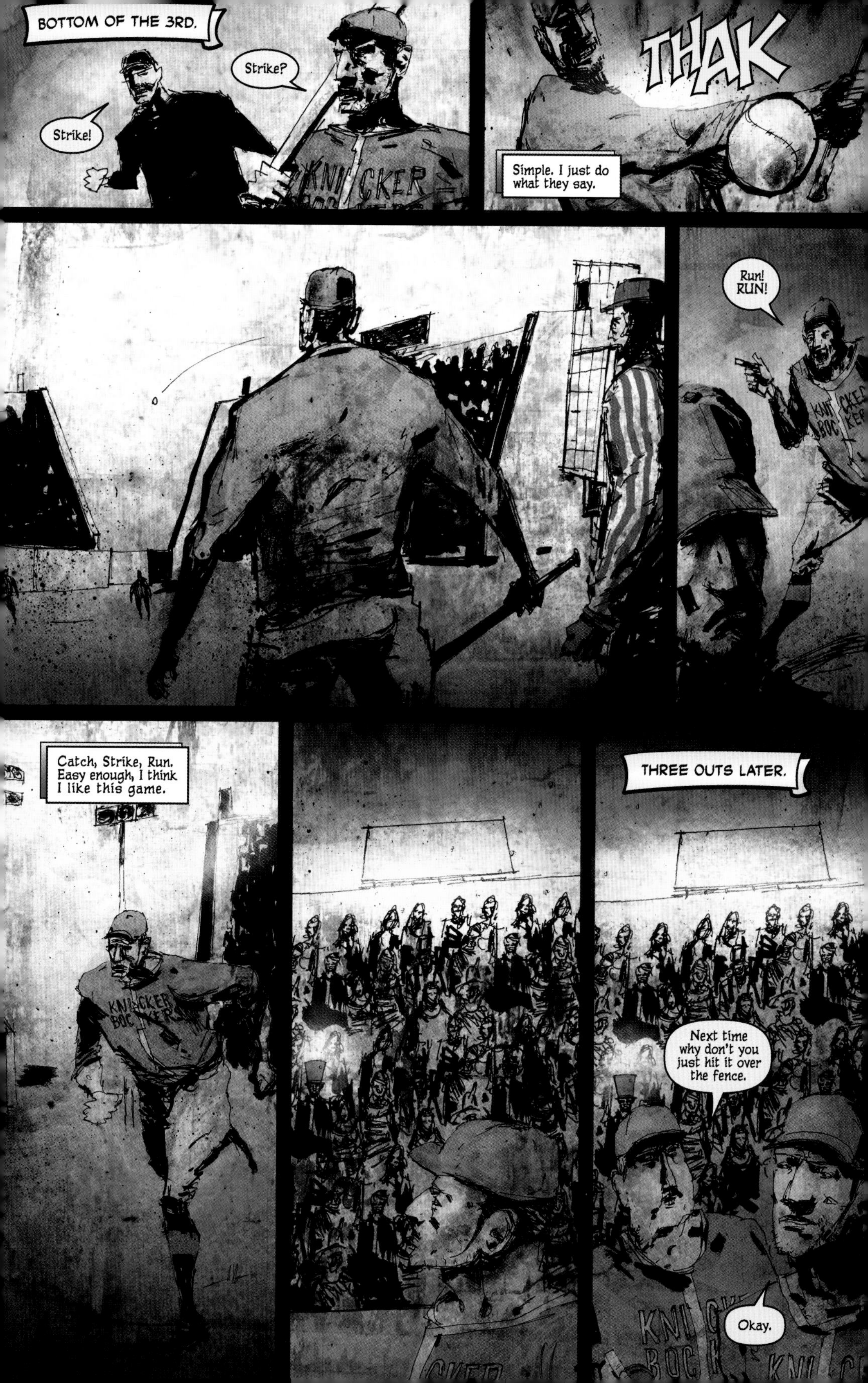
BOTTOM OF THE 3RD.
Strike!
Strike?
KNICKER
THAK
Simple. I just do what they say.
Run! RUN!
Catch, Strike, Run. Easy enough, I think I like this game.
THREE OUTS LATER.
Next time why don't you just hit it over the fence.
Okay.

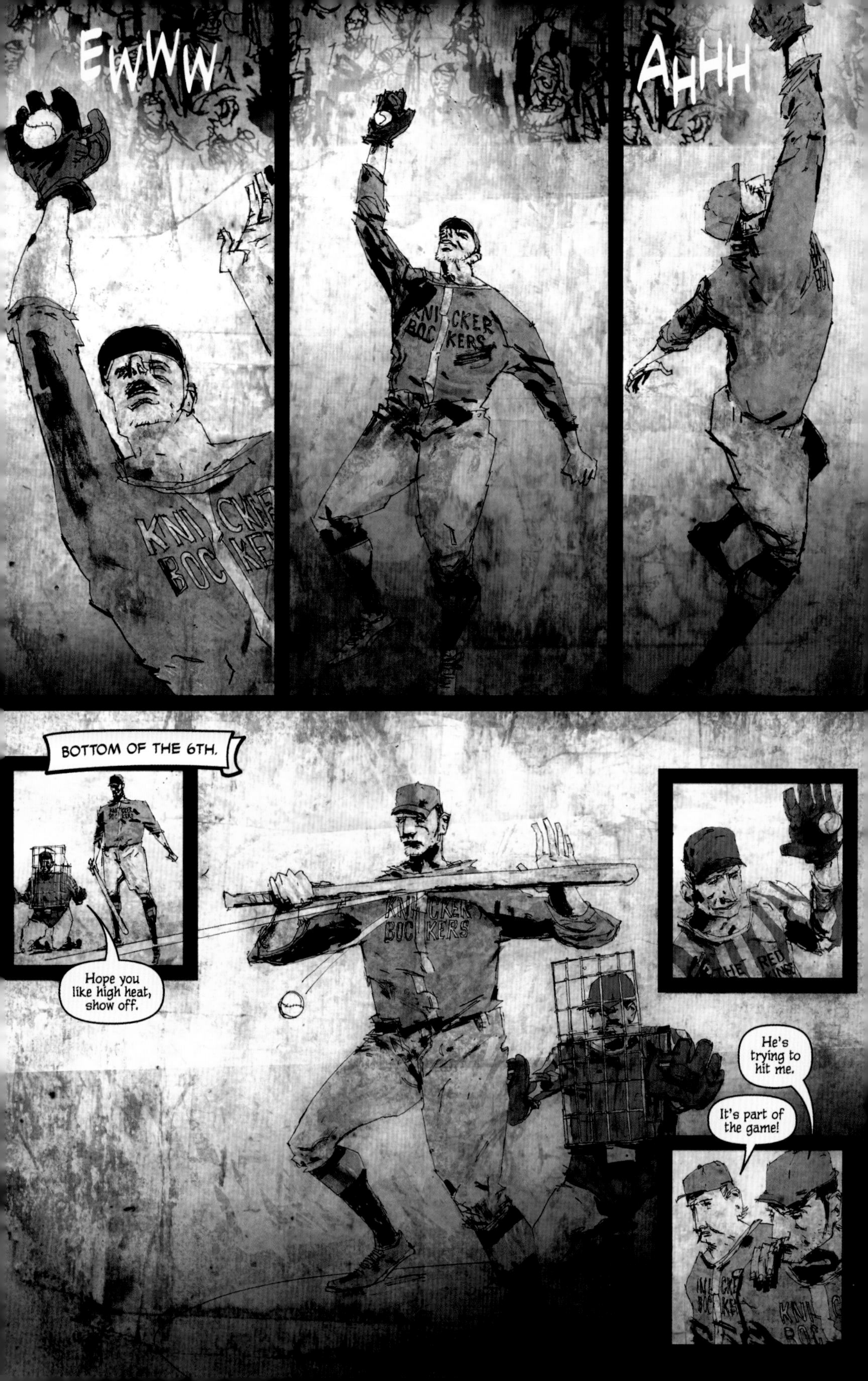
EwWw
AHHH
BOTTOM OF THE 6TH.
Hope you like high heat, show off.
He's trying to hit me.
It's part of the game!

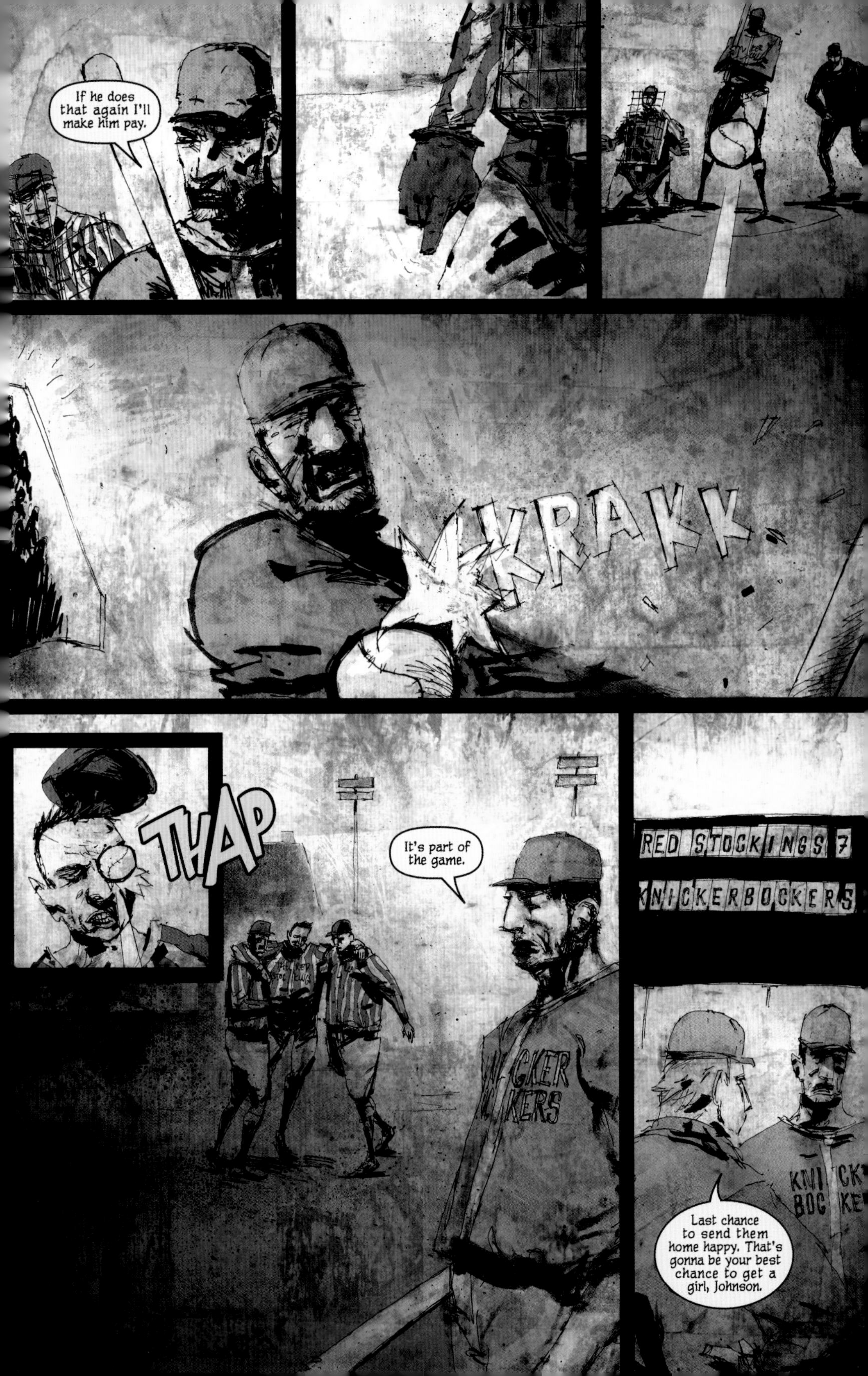
If he does that again I'll make him pay.
KRAKK
THAP
It's part of the game.
RED STOCKINGS 7
KNICKERBOCKERS
Last chance to send them home happy. That's gonna be your best chance to get a girl, Johnson.

BOTTOM ON THE 9TH.

KRACK

The winner is the team that sends the crowd home happy. If Princess Alyss made this game of course that would be the rule!

HORRRRAYYY

KNICKER BOCKERS

huh?

I overslept again... Captain's gonna kill me.

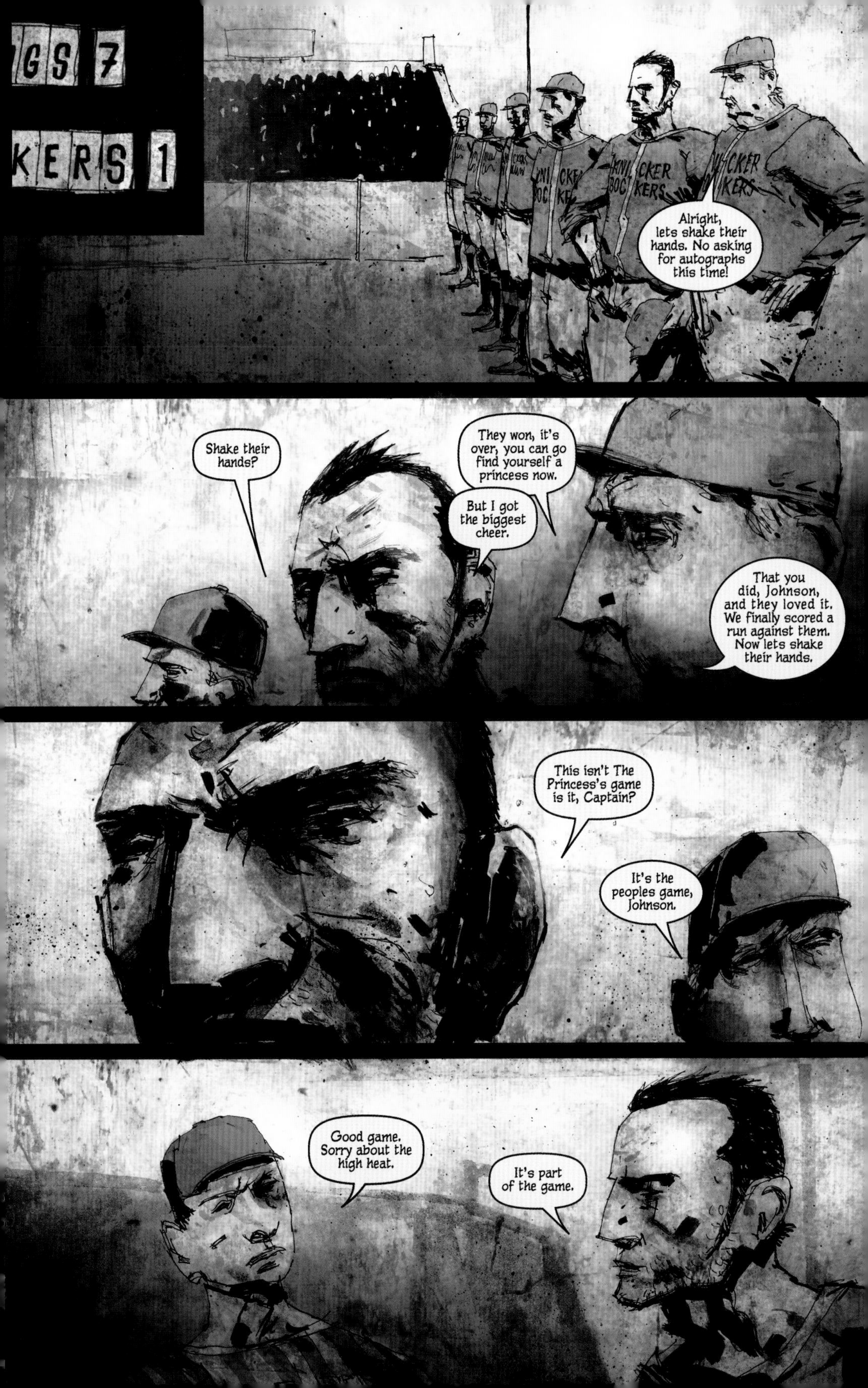
GS 7
KERS 1
Alright, lets shake their hands. No asking for autographs this time!
Shake their hands?
They won, it's over, you can go find yourself a princess now.
But I got the biggest cheer.
That you did, Johnson, and they loved it. We finally scored a run against them. Now lets shake their hands.
This isn't The Princess's game is it, Captain?
It's the peoples game, Johnson.
Good game. Sorry about the high heat.
It's part of the game.

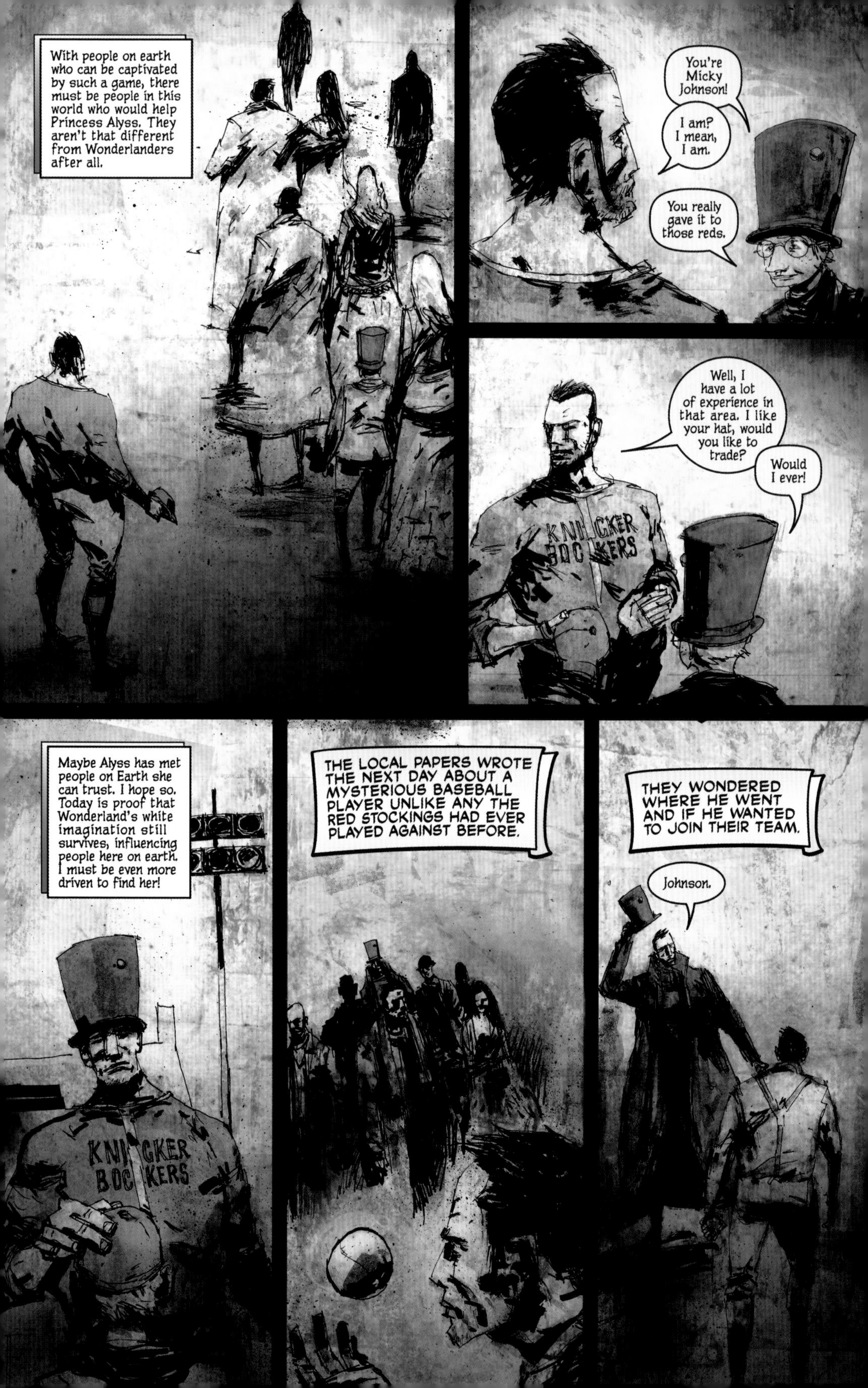
With people on earth who can be captivated by such a game, there must be people in this world who would help Princess Alyss. They aren't that different from Wonderlanders after all.
You're Micky Johnson!
I am? I mean, I am.
You really gave it to those reds.
Well, I have a lot of experience in that area. I like your hat, would you like to trade?
Would I ever!
KNICKER BOCKERS
Maybe Alyss has met people on Earth she can trust. I hope so. Today is proof that Wonderland's white imagination still survives, influencing people here on earth. I must be even more driven to find her!
KNICKER BOCKERS
THE LOCAL PAPERS WROTE THE NEXT DAY ABOUT A MYSTERIOUS BASEBALL PLAYER UNLIKE ANY THE RED STOCKINGS HAD EVER PLAYED AGAINST BEFORE.
THEY WONDERED WHERE HE WENT AND IF HE WANTED TO JOIN THEIR TEAM.
Johnson.

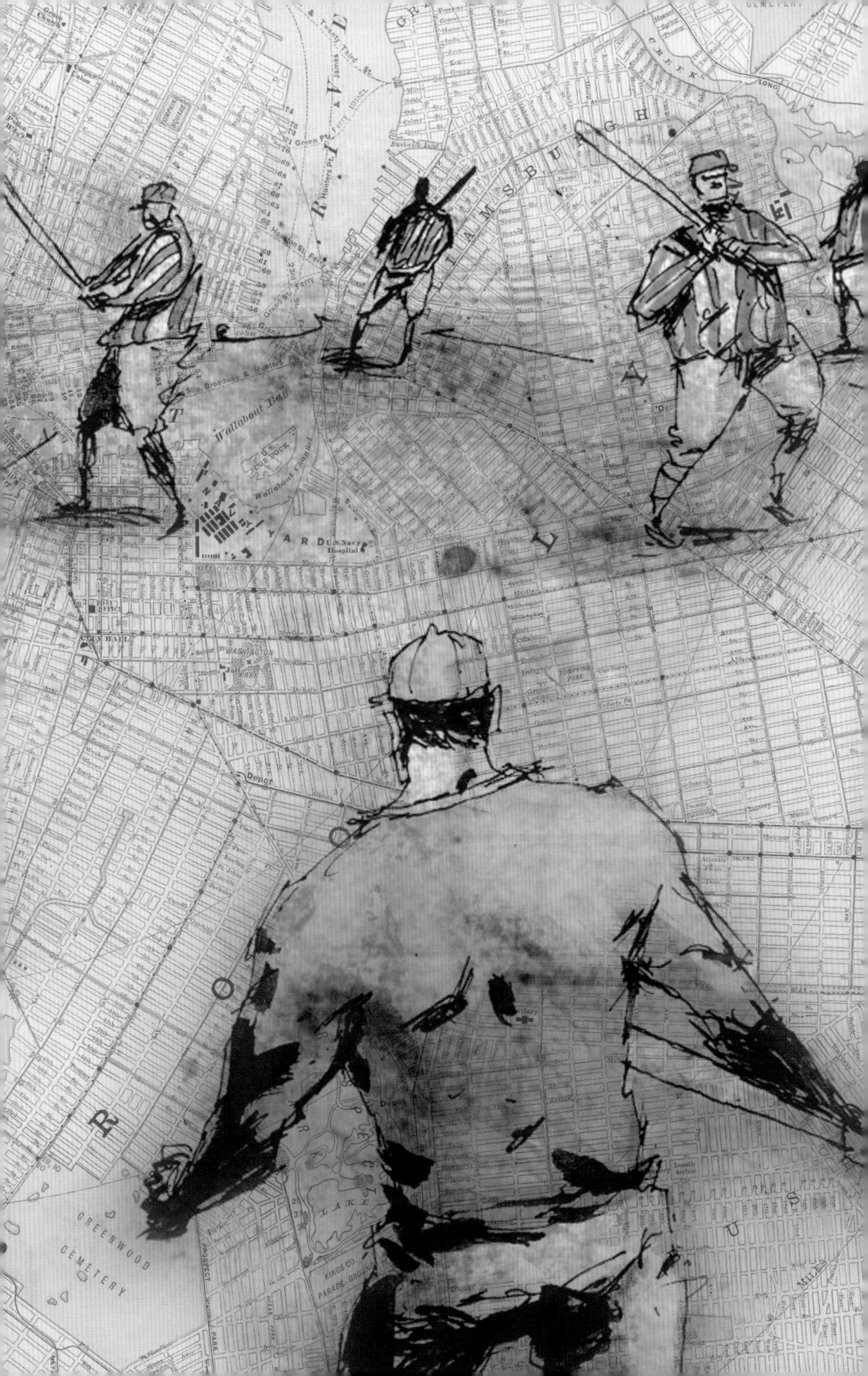

Wallabout Bay
Wallabout Channel
U.S. COB DOCK
U.S. Navy Hospital
WASHINGTON PARK
TOMPKINS PARK
GREENWOOD CEMETERY
KINGS CO. PARADE GROUND
LAKE

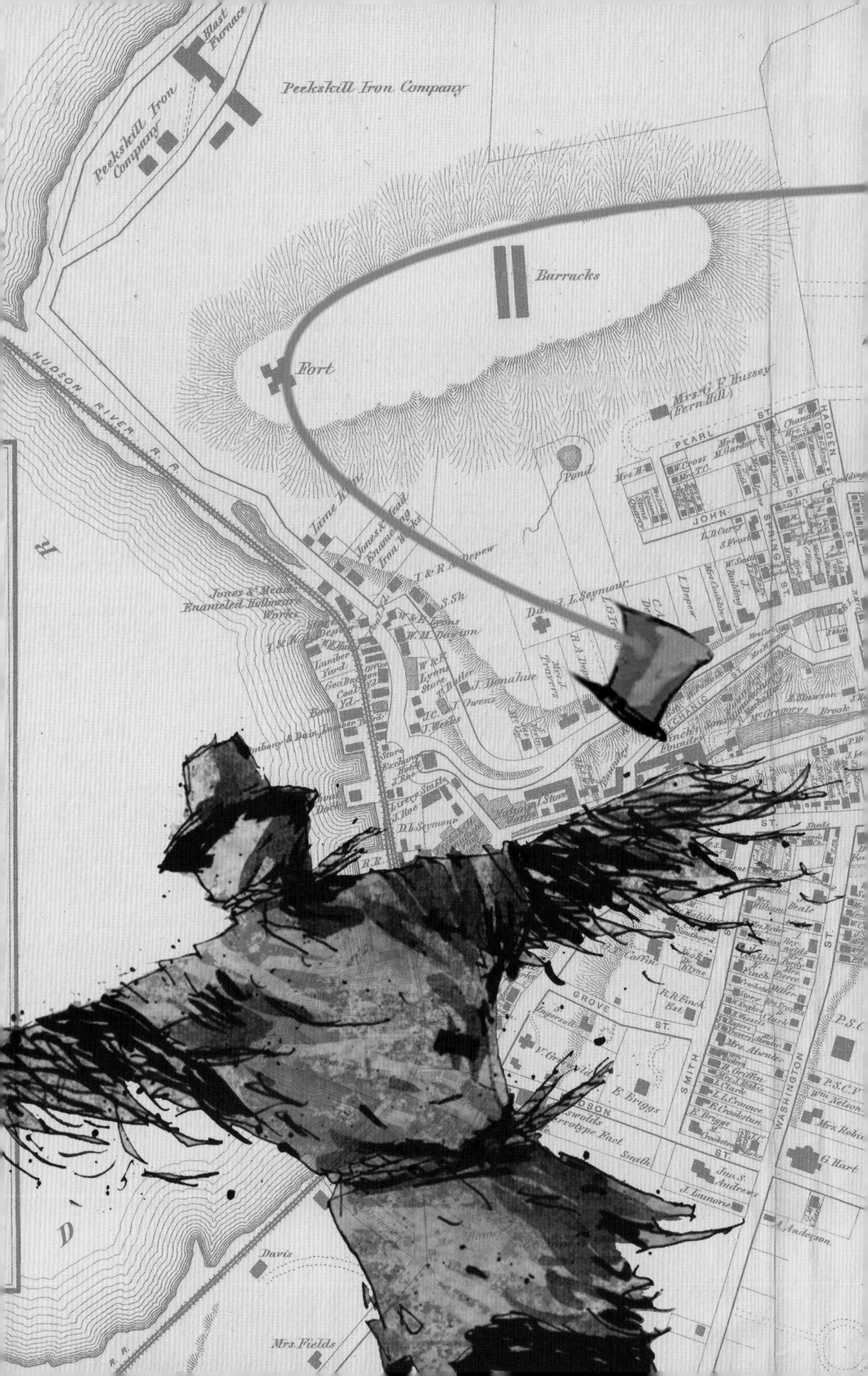
Peekskill Iron Company
Blast Furnace
Peekskill Iron Company
Barracks
Fort
HUDSON RIVER R.R.
Mrs. G. F. Hussey (Fern Hill)
Pond
Lime Kiln
Jones & Mead Enameling Iron Works
Jones & Mead Enameled Hollowware Works
PEARL
JOHN
SPRING ST.
GROVE
ST.
SMITH
WASHINGTON
HADDEN
E. Briggs
Davis
Mrs Fields

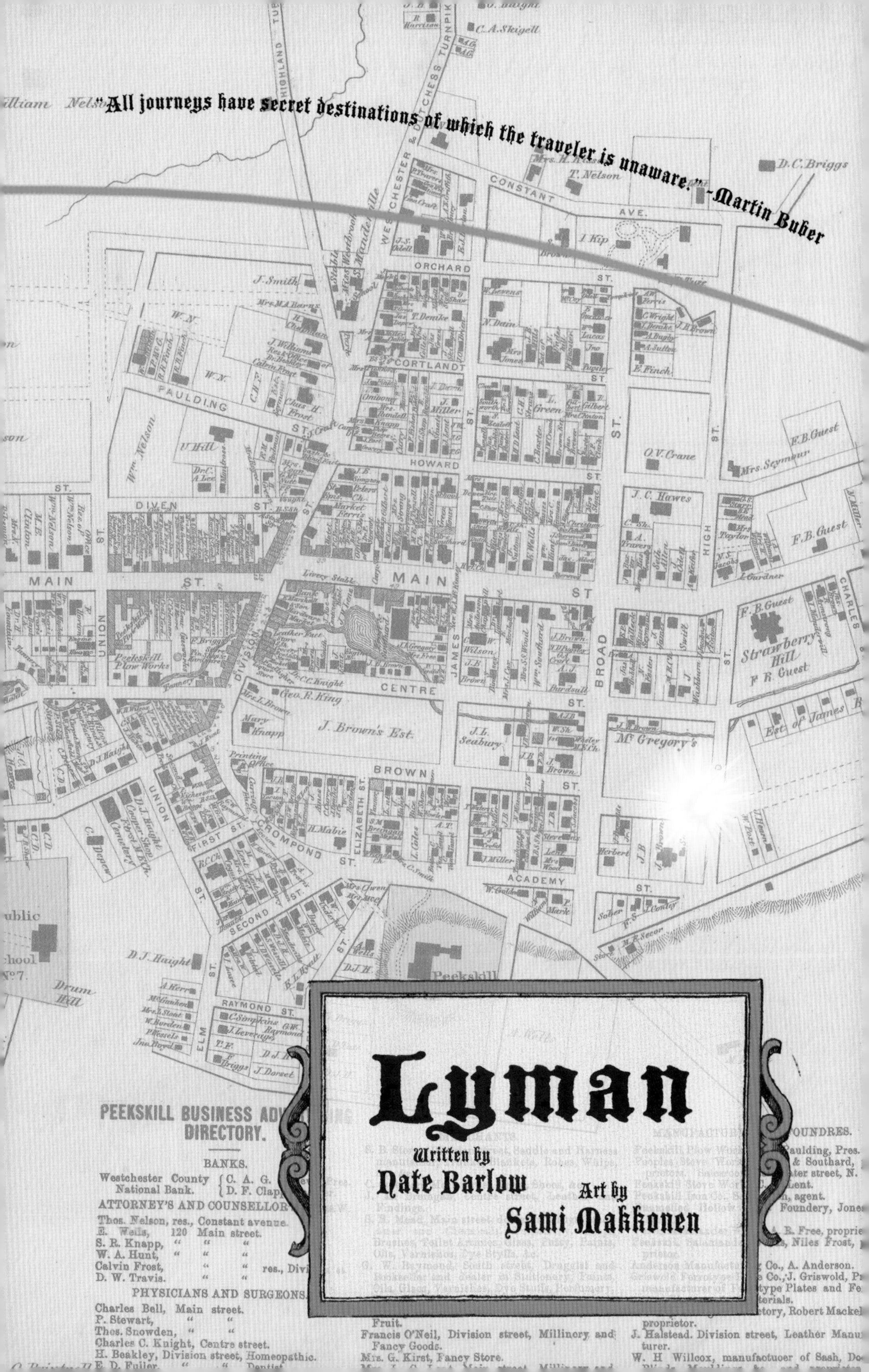
PEEKSKILL BUSINESS ADV
DIRECTORY.
BANKS.
MAIN ST.
BROAD ST.
HIGH ST.
UNION ST.
DIVISION ST.
CENTRE
BROWN ST.
HOWARD ST.
CORTLANDT ST.
ORCHARD ST.
PAULDING ST.
DIVEN ST.
CROMPOND ST.
ACADEMY ST.
RAYMOND ST.
CONSTANT AVE.
Strawberry Hill
J. Brown's Est.
Peekskill Plow Works

"All journeys have secret destinations of which the traveler is unaware." —Martin Buber

Lyman

Written by
Nate Barlow

Art by
Sami Makkonen

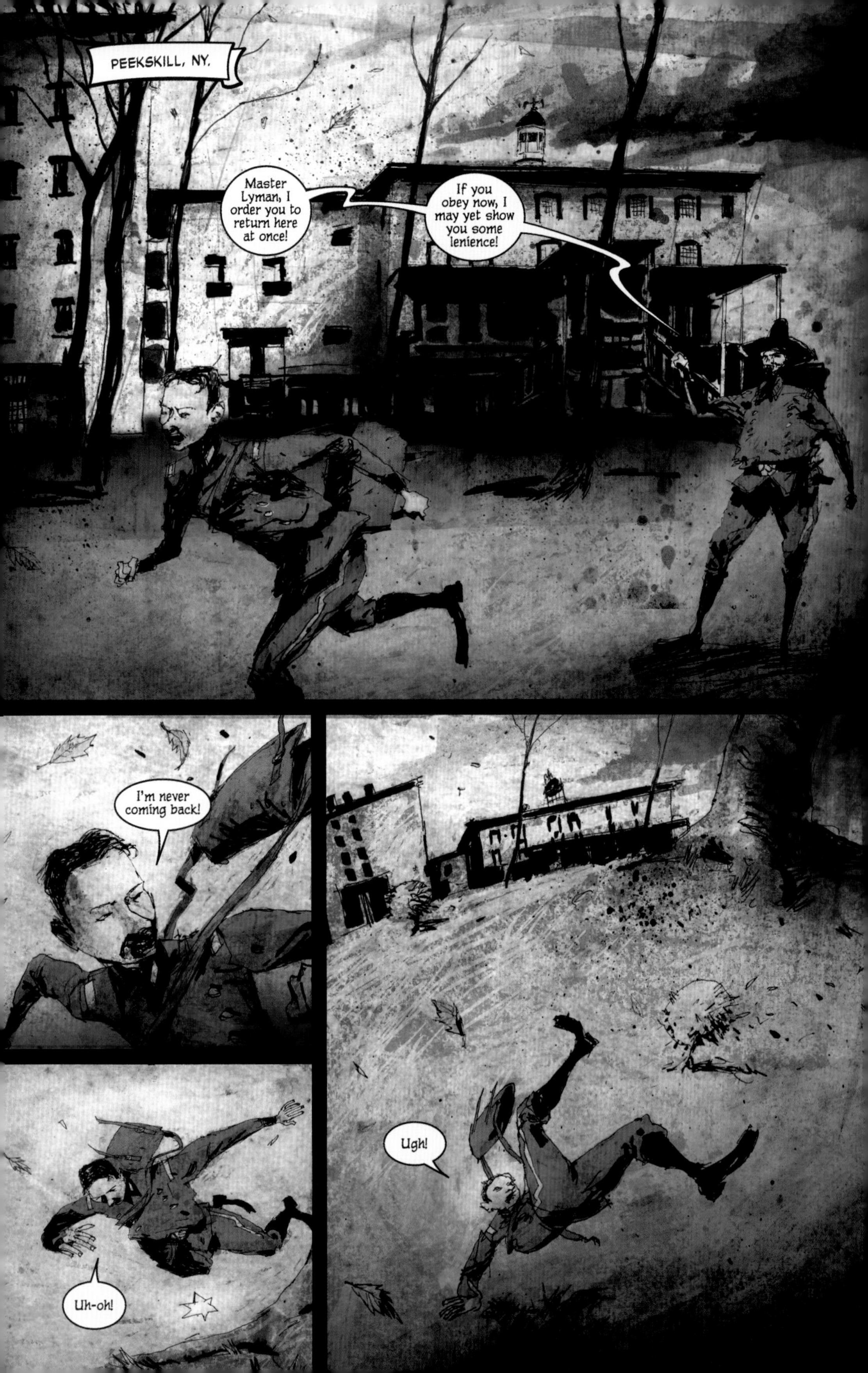
PEEKSKILL, NY.
Master Lyman, I order you to return here at once!
If you obey now, I may yet show you some lenience!
I'm never coming back!
Uh-oh!
Ugh!

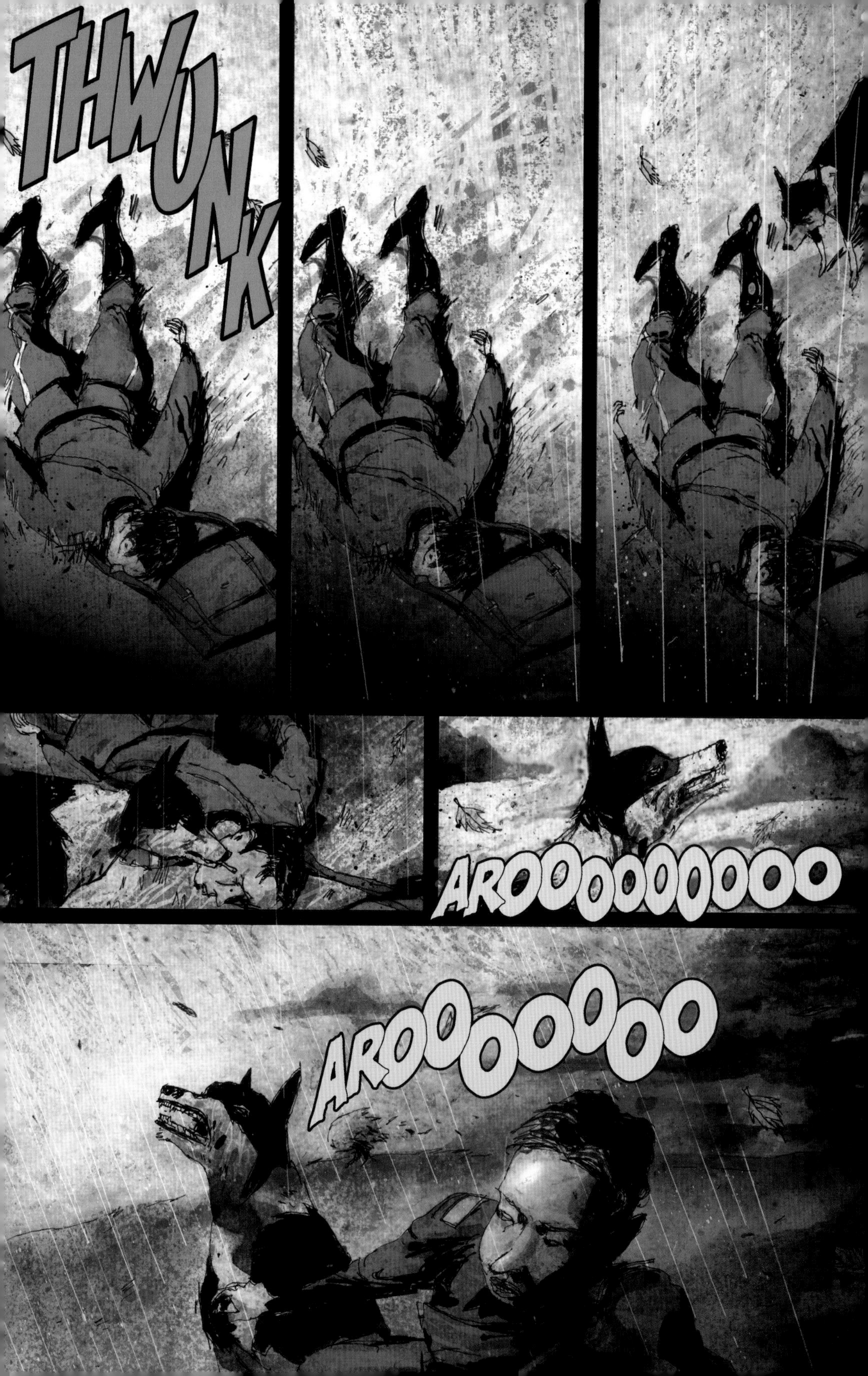
THWONK
AROOOOOOOOOO
AROOOOOOOO

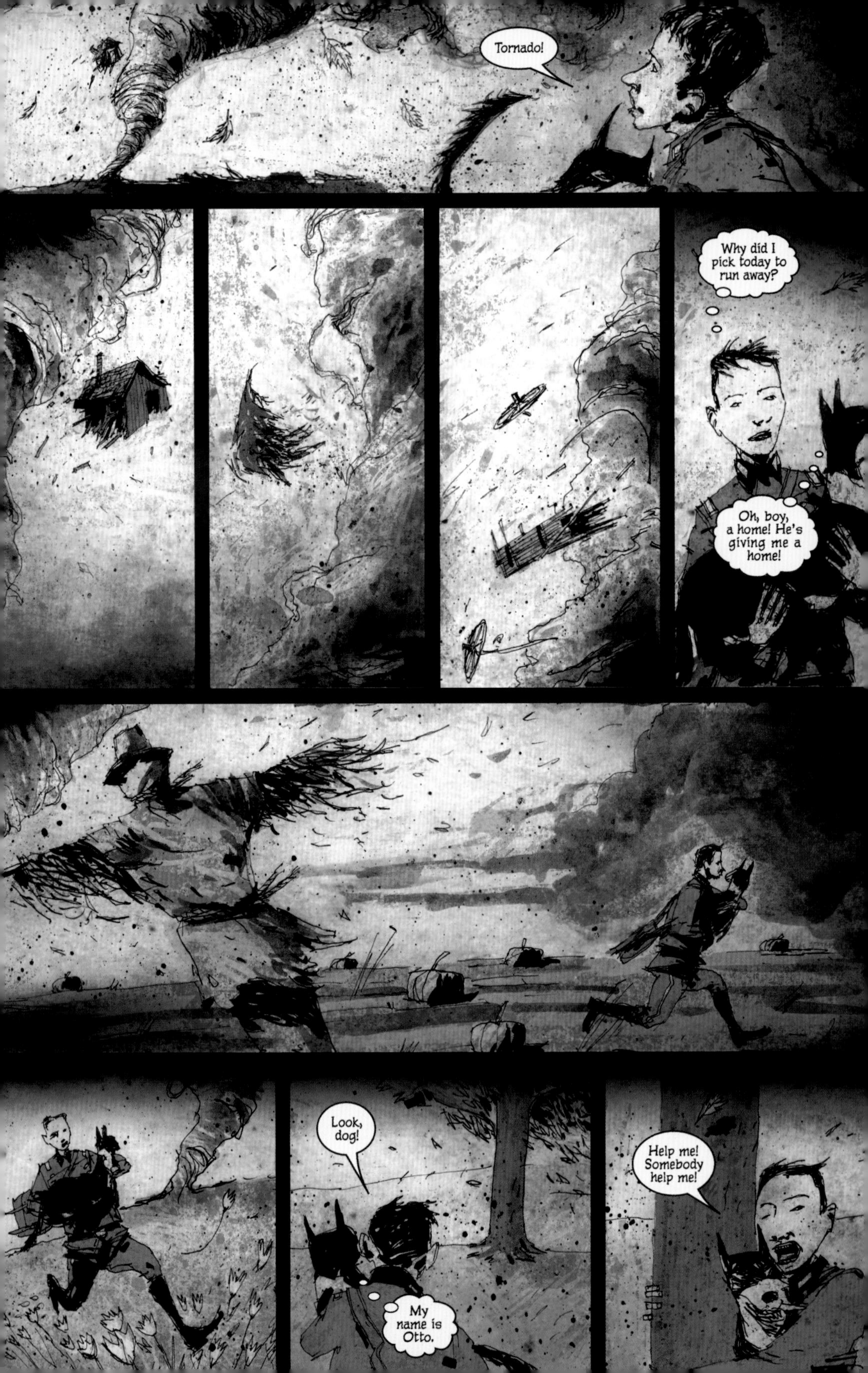
Tornado!
Why did I pick today to run away?
Oh, boy, a home! He's giving me a home!
Look, dog!
My name is Otto.
Help me! Somebody help me!

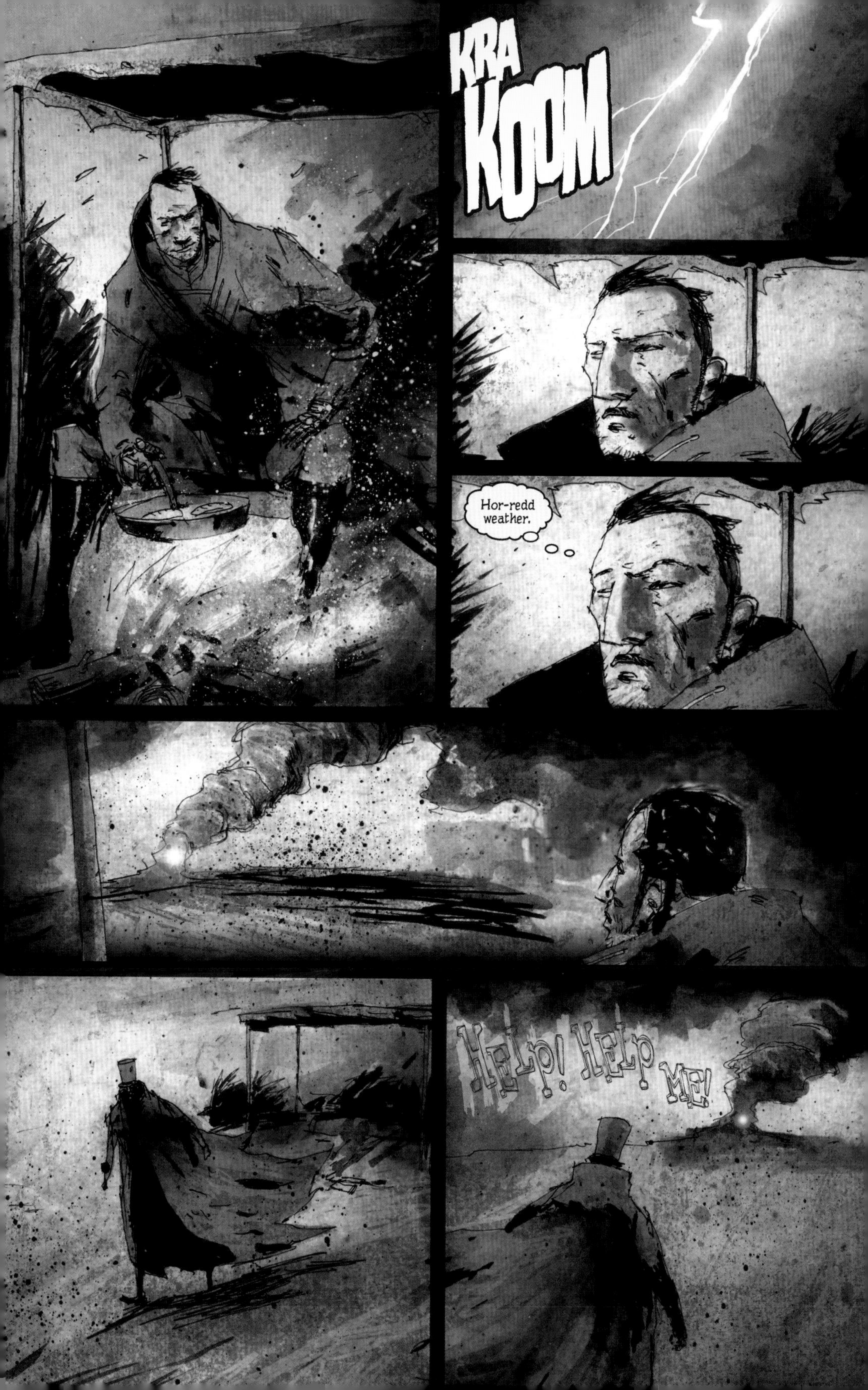
KRA KOOM
Hor-redd weather.
HELP! HELP ME!

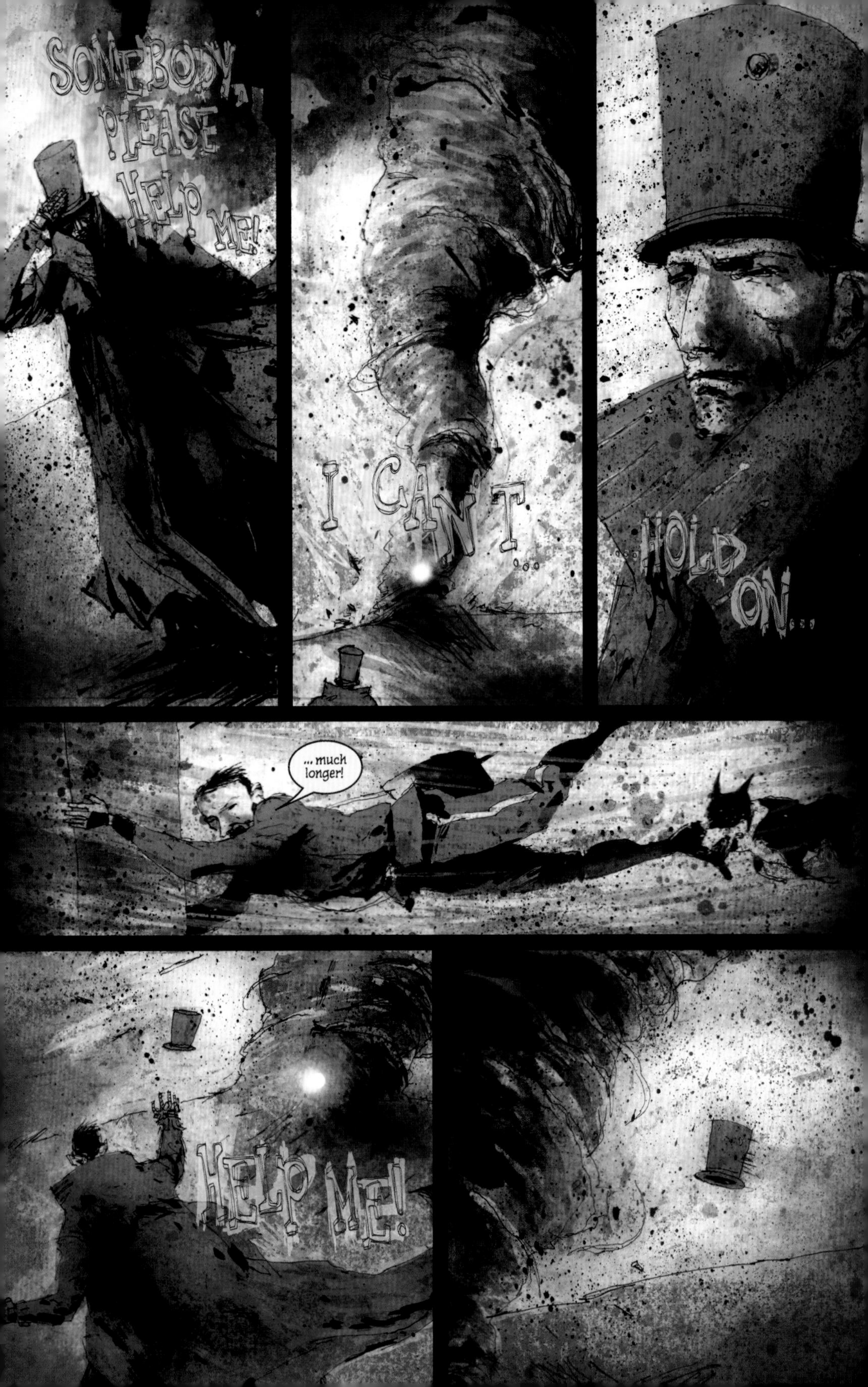
SOMEBODY, PLEASE HELP ME!
I CAN'T...
...HOLD ON...
...much longer!
HELP ME!

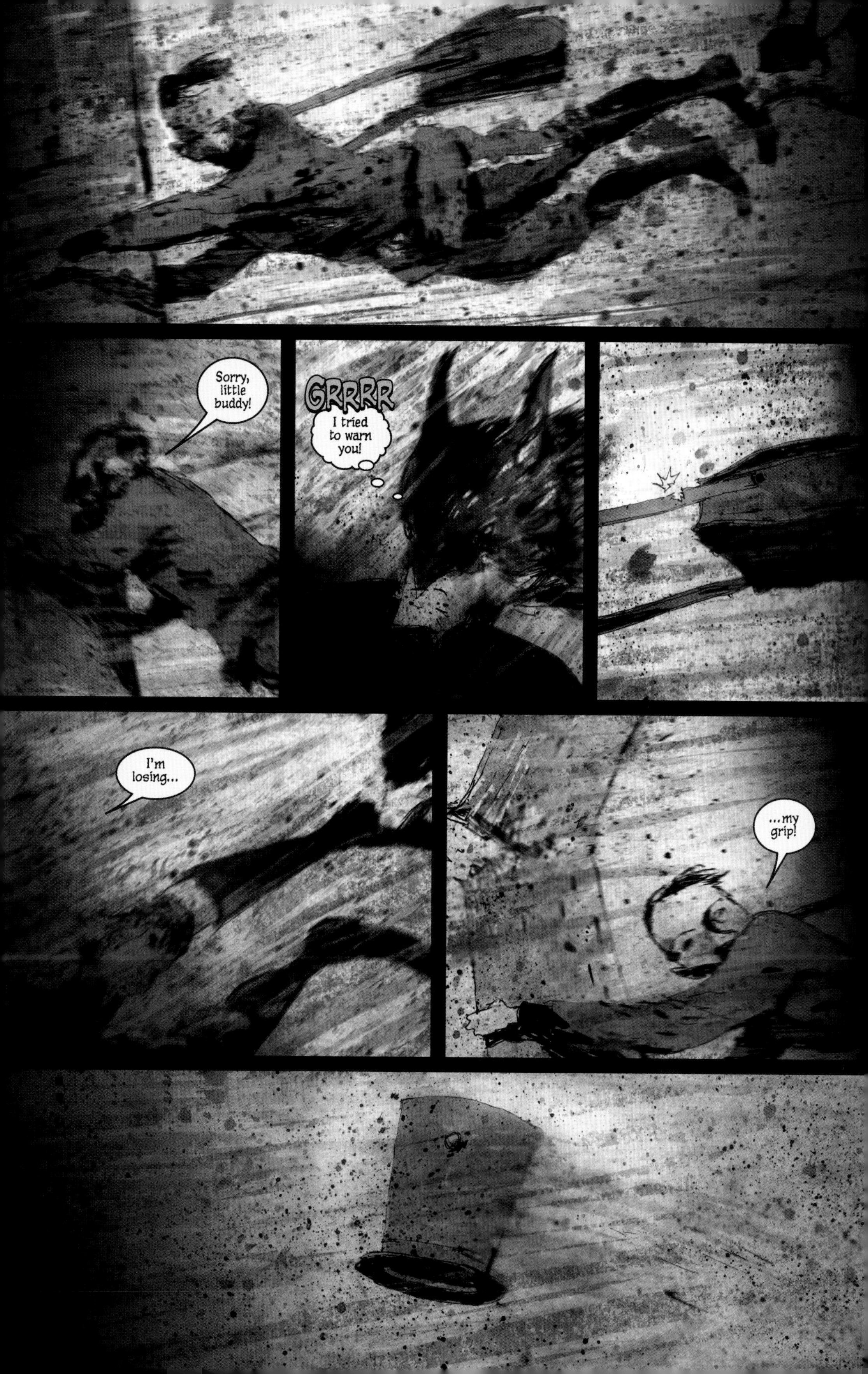
Sorry, little buddy!
GRRRR
I tried to warn you!
I'm losing...
...my grip!

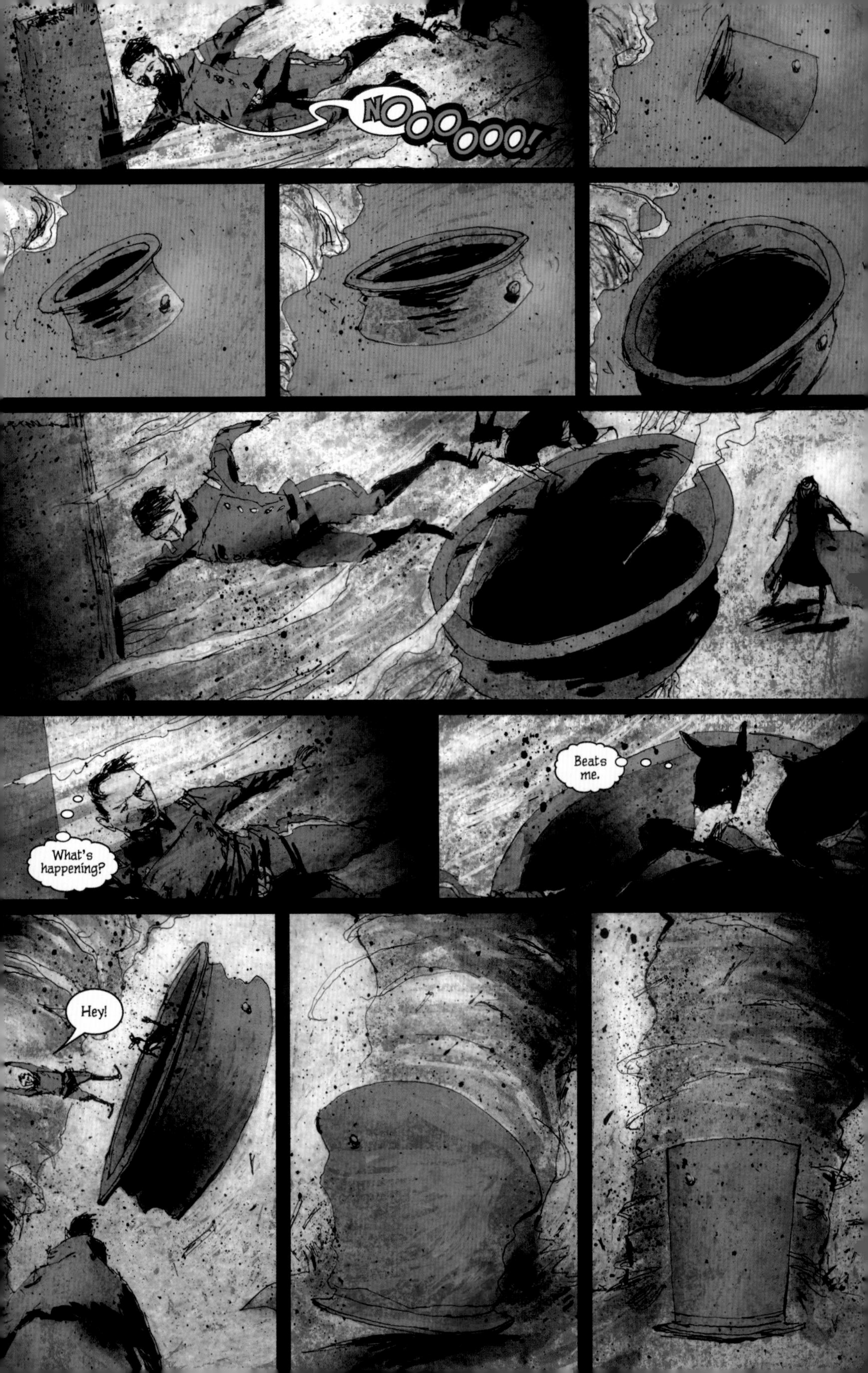
NOOOOOOO!
What's happening?
Beats me.
Hey!

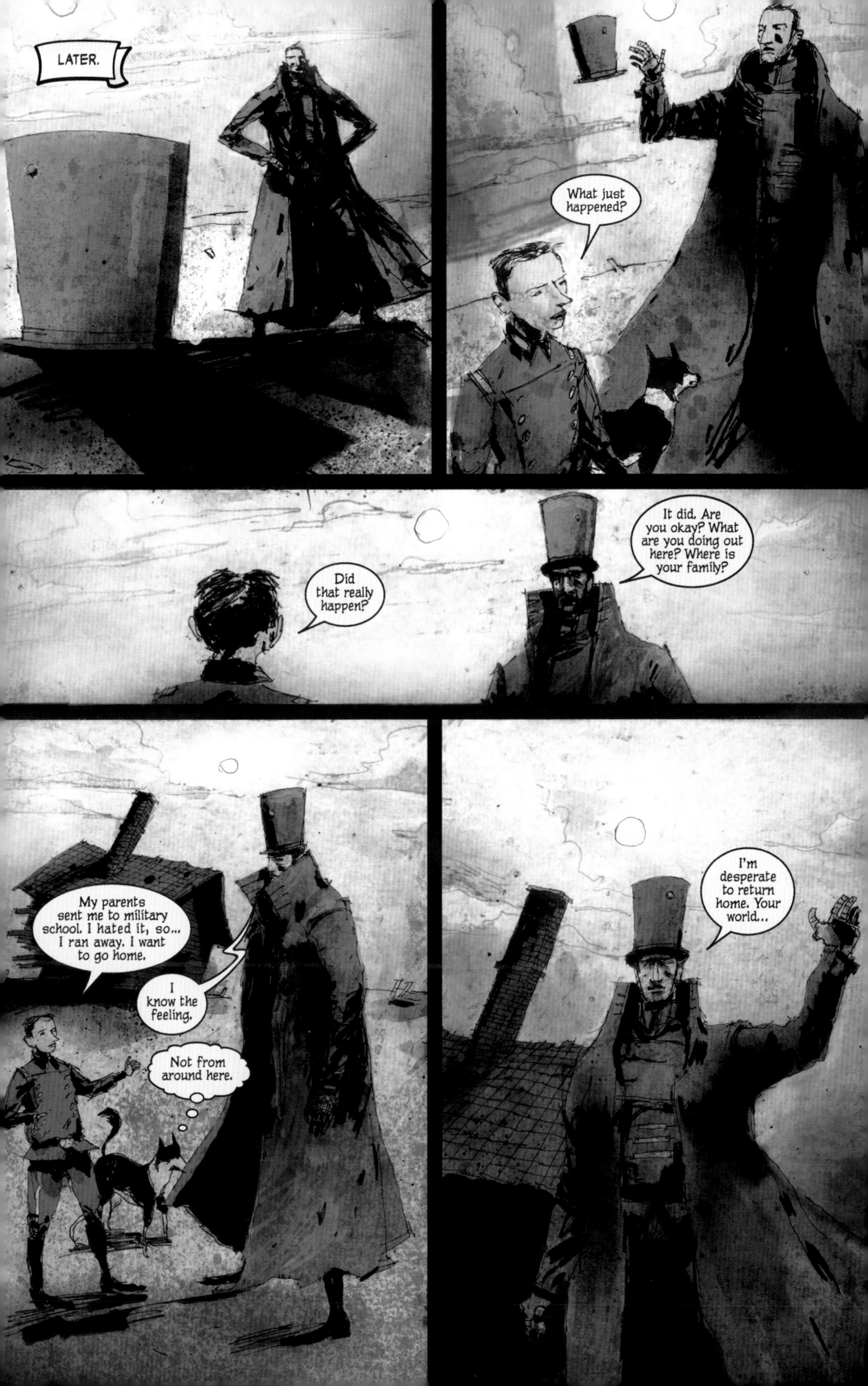
LATER.
What just happened?
Did that really happen?
It did. Are you okay? What are you doing out here? Where is your family?
My parents sent me to military school. I hated it, so... I ran away. I want to go home.
I know the feeling.
Not from around here.
I'm desperate to return home. Your world...

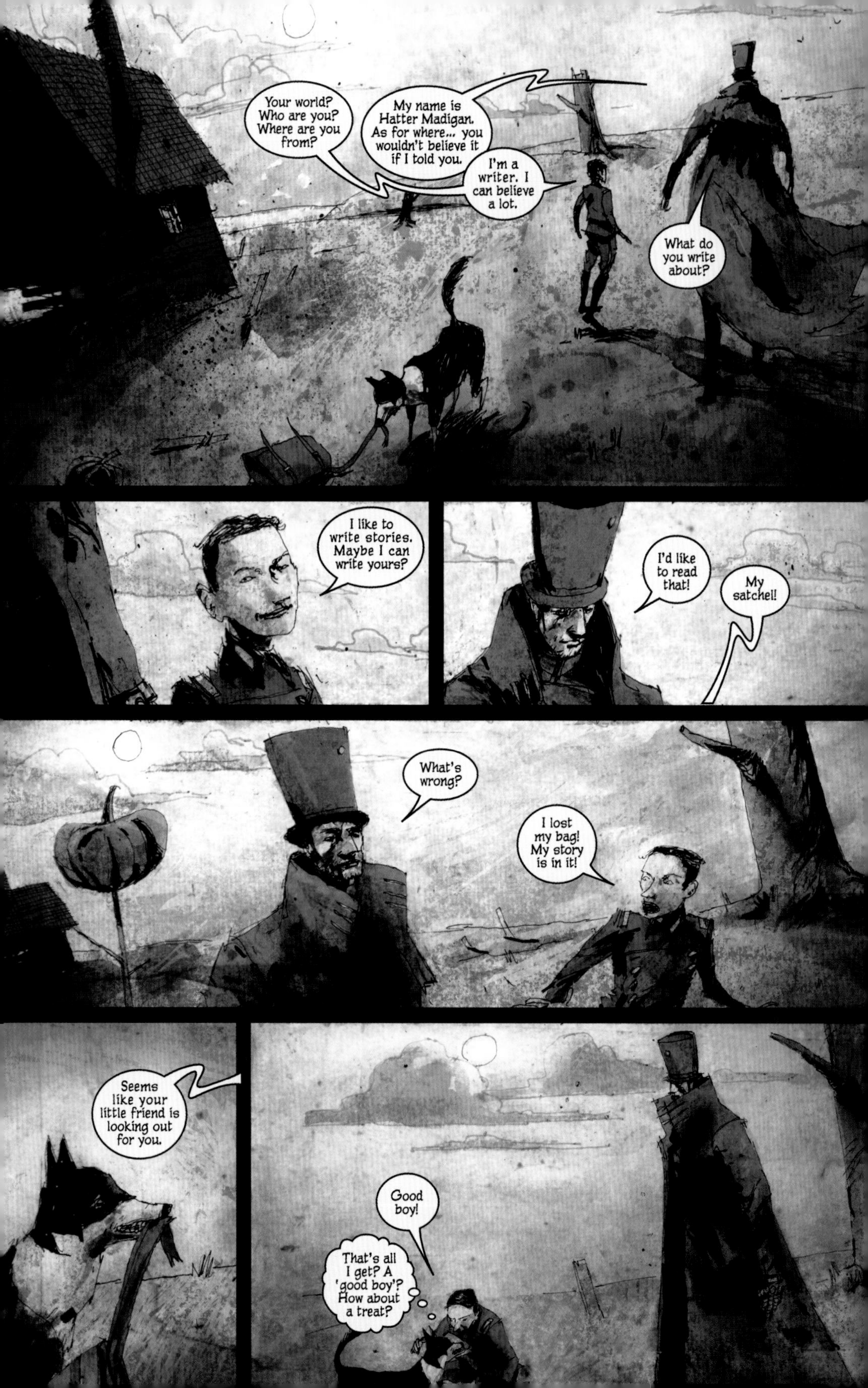
Your world? Who are you? Where are you from?
My name is Hatter Madigan. As for where... you wouldn't believe it if I told you.
I'm a writer. I can believe a lot.
What do you write about?
I like to write stories. Maybe I can write yours?
I'd like to read that!
My satchel!
What's wrong?
I lost my bag! My story is in it!
Seems like your little friend is looking out for you.
Good boy!
That's all I get? A 'good boy'? How about a treat?

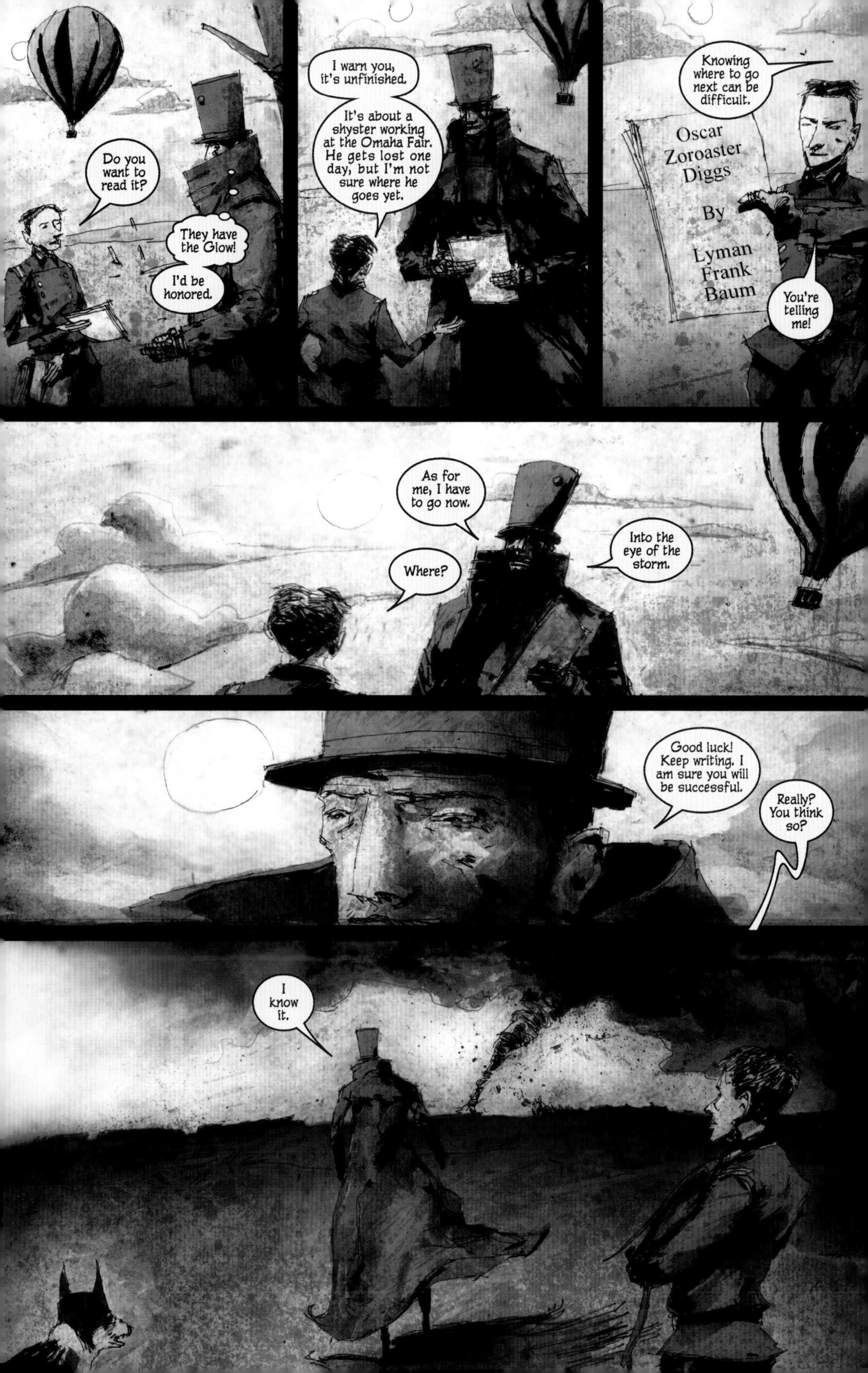
Do you want to read it?
They have the Glow!
I'd be honored.
I warn you, it's unfinished.
It's about a shyster working at the Omaha Fair. He gets lost one day, but I'm not sure where he goes yet.
Knowing where to go next can be difficult.
Oscar Zoroaster Diggs By Lyman Frank Baum
You're telling me!
As for me, I have to go now.
Where?
Into the eye of the storm.
Good luck! Keep writing. I am sure you will be successful.
Really? You think so?
I know it.

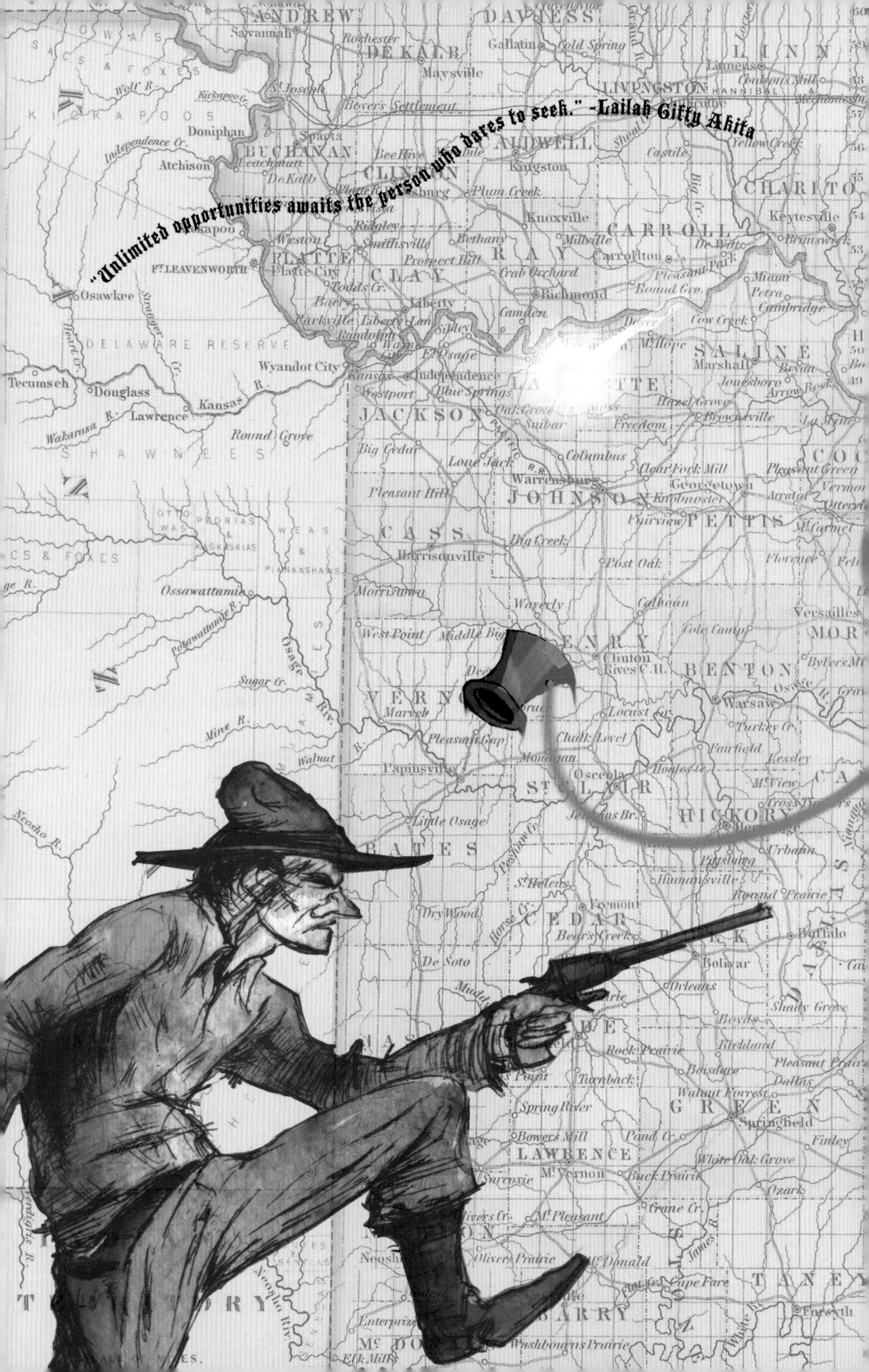
"Unlimited opportunities awaits the person who dares to seek." -Lailah Gifty Akita
ANDREW
DAVIESS
DEKALB
LINN
LIVINGSTON
CALDWELL
BUCHANAN
CLINTON
CHARITON
CARROLL
RAY
CLAY
PLATTE
SALINE
JACKSON
JOHNSON
PETTIS
CASS
BENTON
VERNON
BATES
HICKORY
CEDAR
LAWRENCE
GREEN
BARRY
TANEY
DELAWARE RESERVE
SHAWNEES

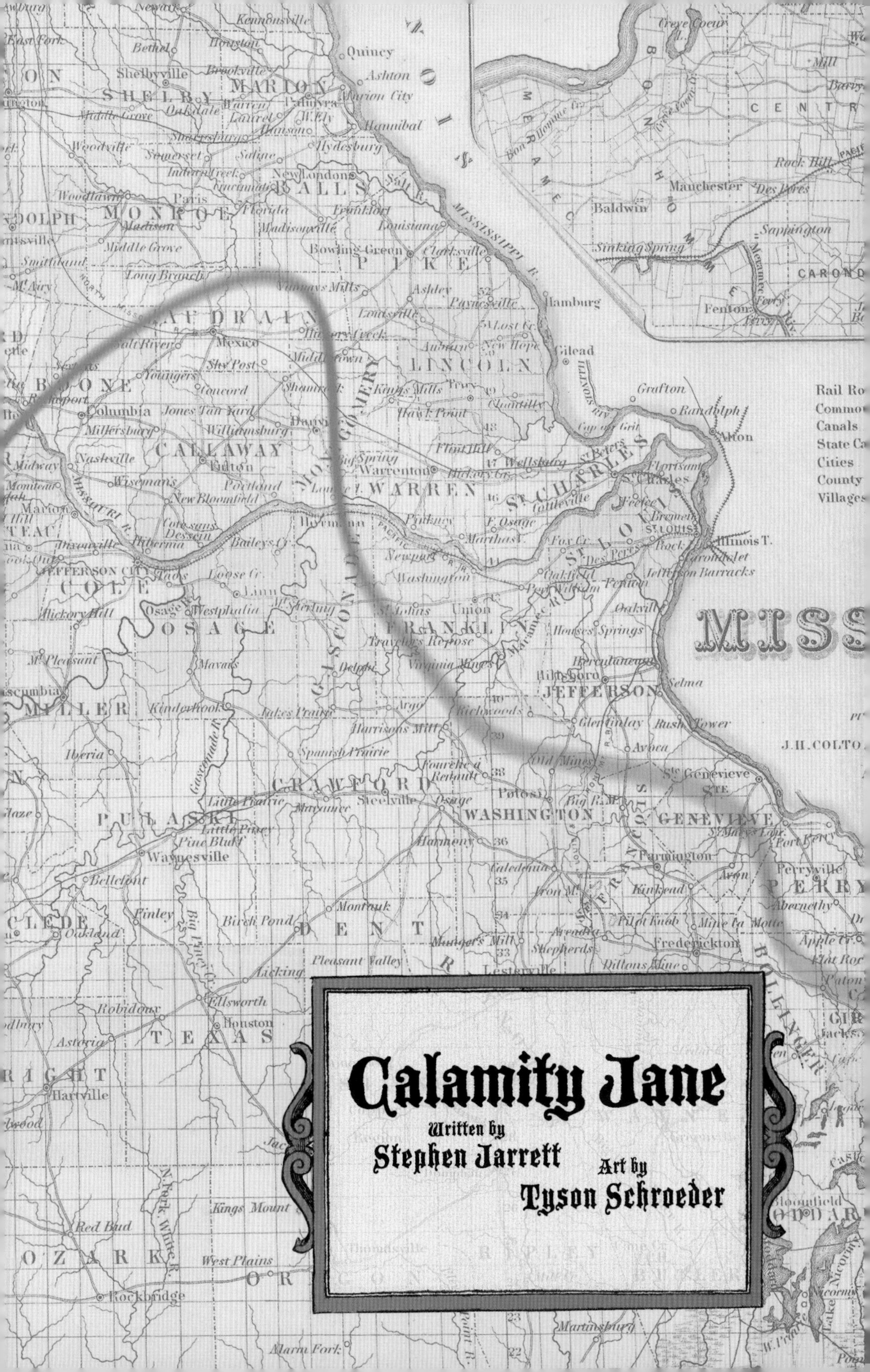

Quincy
Hannibal
MARION
SHELBY
MONROE
RALLS
PIKE
LINCOLN
AUDRAIN
BOONE
CALLAWAY
MONTGOMERY
WARREN
ST. CHARLES
ST. LOUIS
COLE
OSAGE
GASCONADE
FRANKLIN
JEFFERSON
MILLER
PULASKI
CRAWFORD
WASHINGTON
STE. GENEVIEVE
PERRY
DENT
TEXAS
OZARK
MISSISSIPPI R.
MISSOURI R.
Mexico
Columbia
Fulton
Jefferson City
Hermann
Washington
Union
Hillsboro
Potosi
Steelville
Waynesville
Houston
Hartville
Farmington
Fredericktown
Carondelet
Alton
St. Louis
Rail Ro
Commo
Canals
State Ca
Cities
County
Villages
MISS
J.H.COLTO

Calamity Jane

Written by
Stephen Jarrett

Art by
Tyson Schroeder

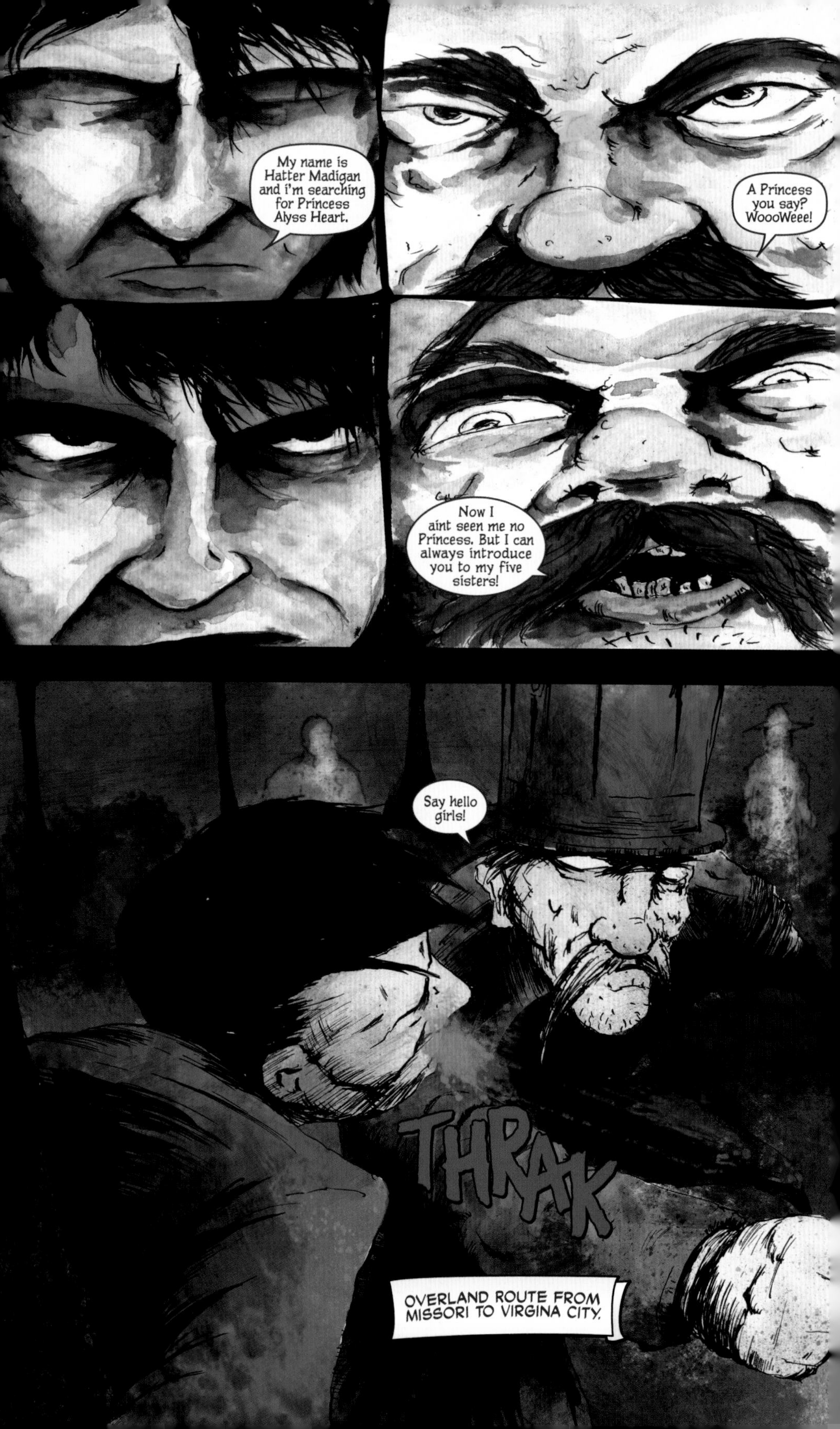
My name is Hatter Madigan and i'm searching for Princess Alyss Heart.
A Princess you say? WoooWeee!
Now I aint seen me no Princess. But I can always introduce you to my five sisters!
Say hello girls!
THRAK
OVERLAND ROUTE FROM MISSORI TO VIRGINA CITY.

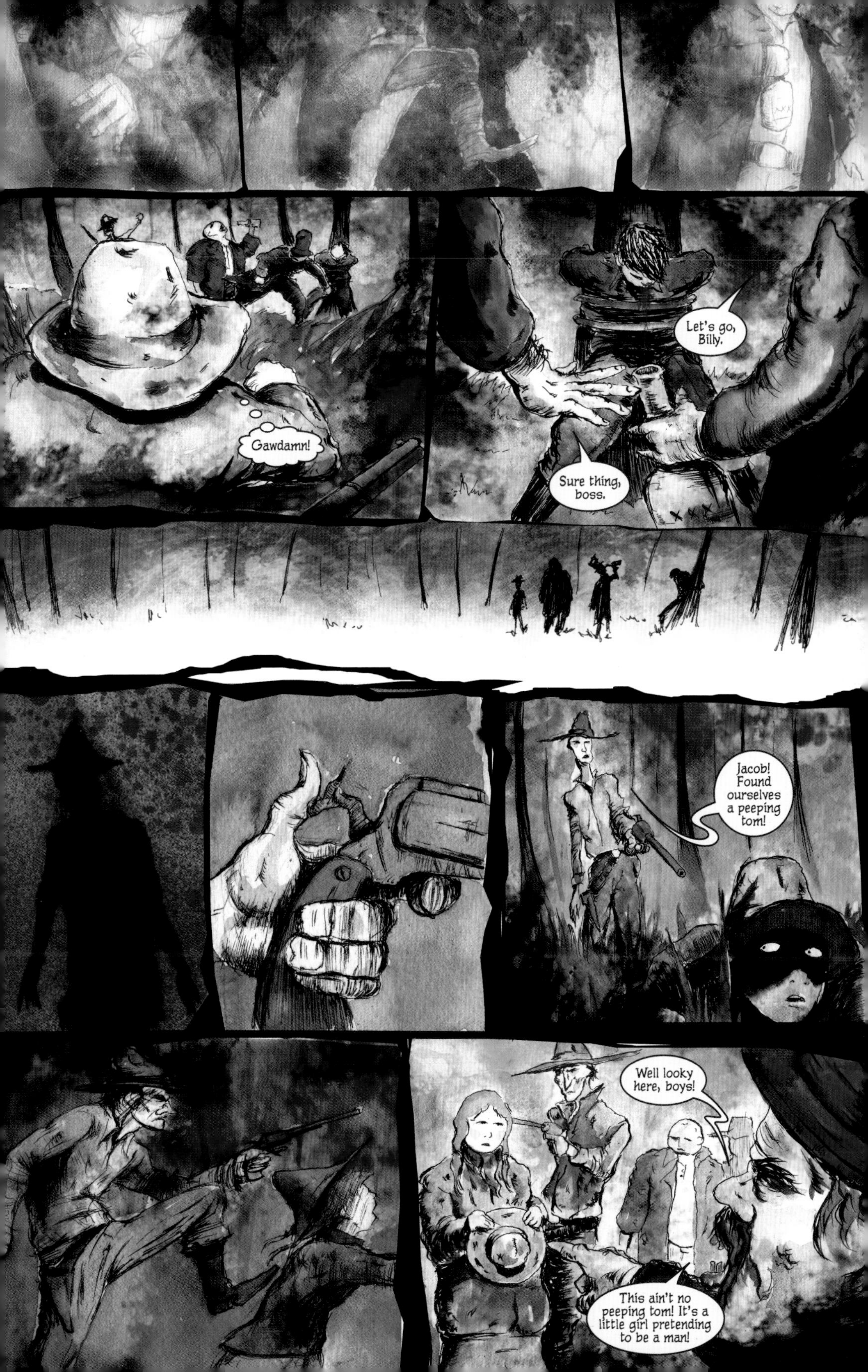

Gawdamn!
Let's go, Billy.
Sure thing, boss.
Jacob! Found ourselves a peeping tom!
Well looky here, boys!
This ain't no peeping tom! It's a little girl pretending to be a man!

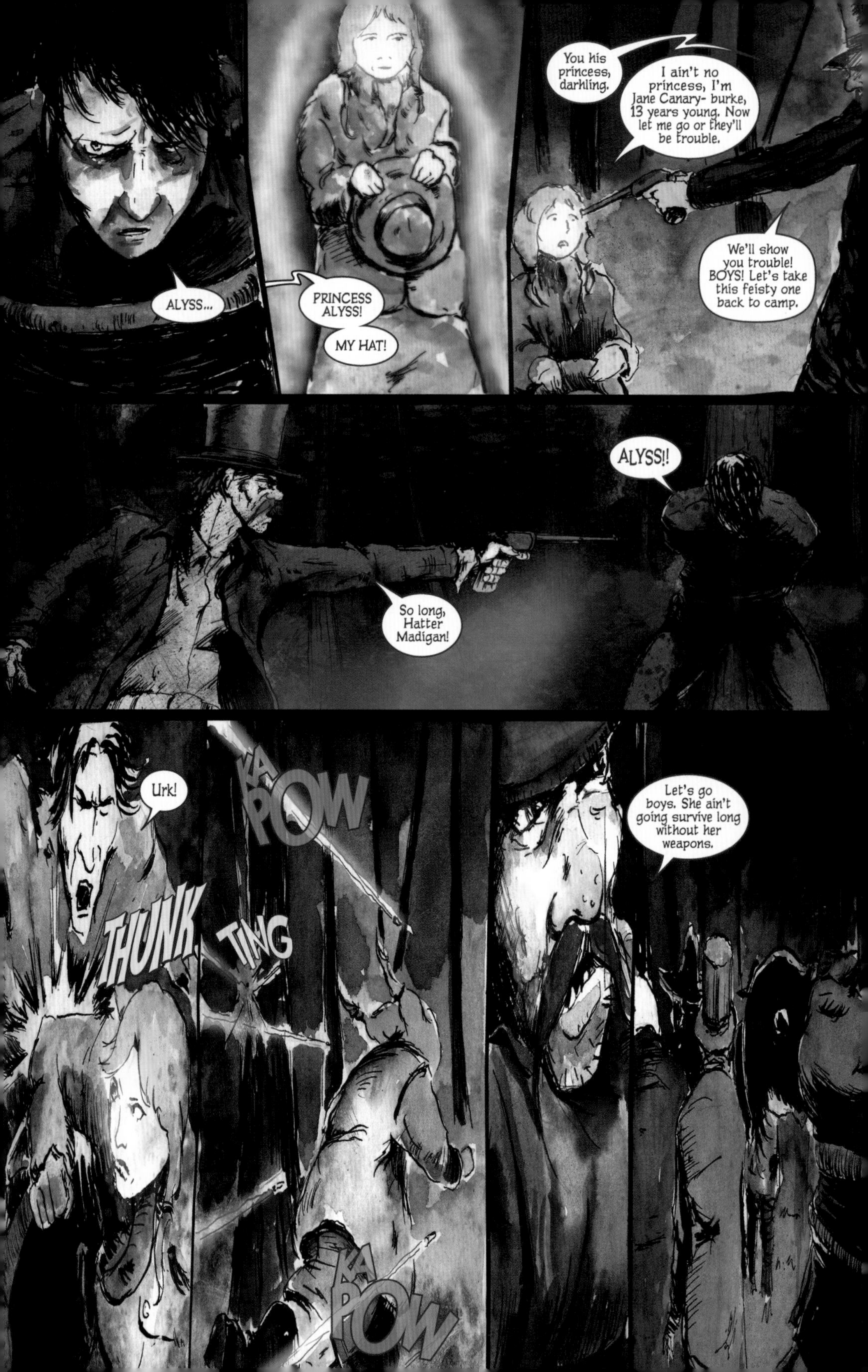
ALYSS...
PRINCESS ALYSS!
MY HAT!
You his princess, darhling.
I ain't no princess, I'm Jane Canary- burke, 13 years young. Now let me go or they'll be trouble.
We'll show you trouble! BOYS! Let's take this feisty one back to camp.
ALYSS!!
So long, Hatter Madigan!
Urk!
KA POW
THUNK
TING
KA POW
Let's go boys. She ain't going survive long without her weapons.

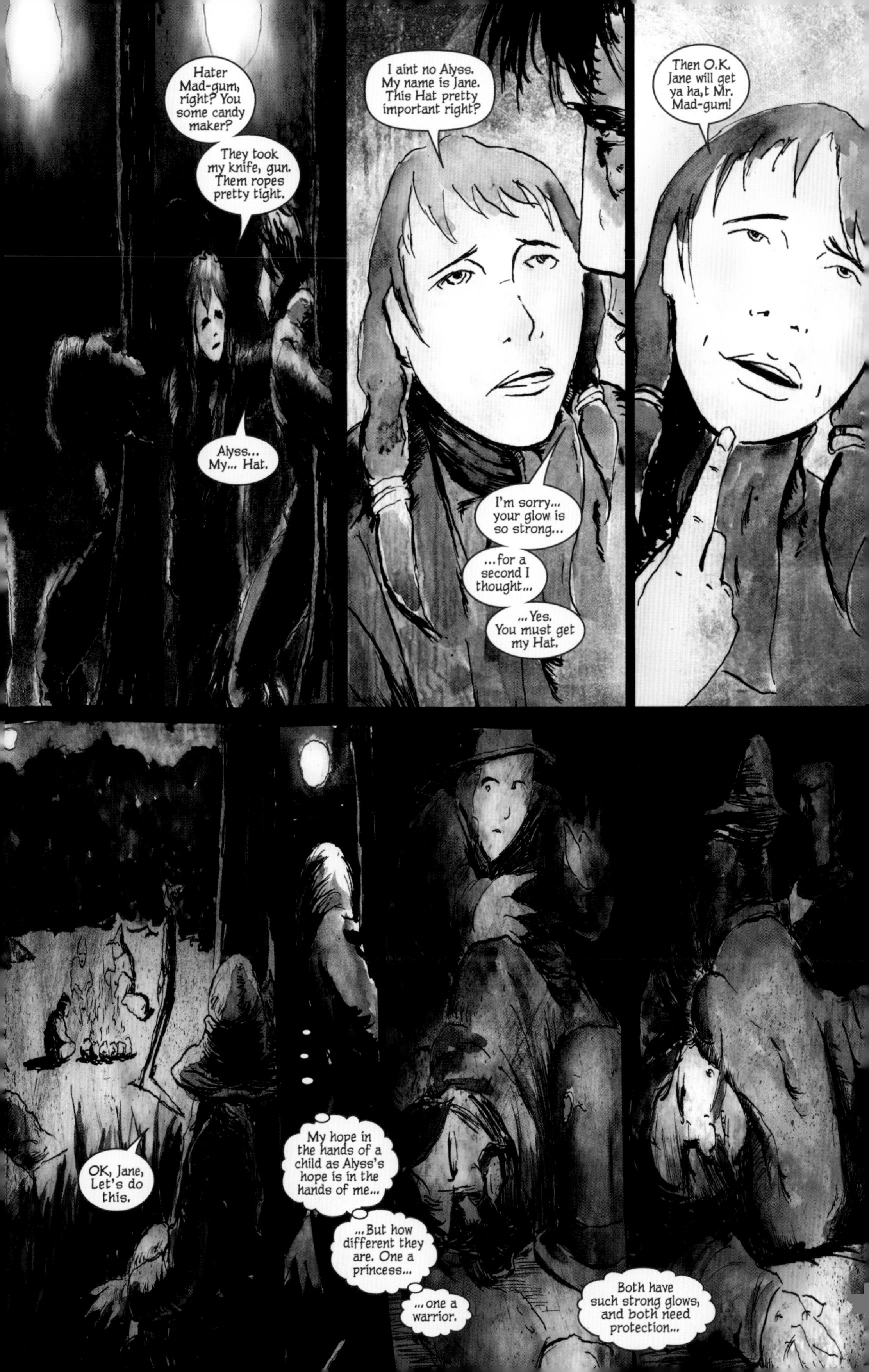
Hater Mad-gum, right? You some candy maker?
They took my knife, gun. Them ropes pretty tight.
Alyss... My... Hat.
I aint no Alyss. My name is Jane. This Hat pretty important right?
I'm sorry... your glow is so strong...
...for a second I thought...
...Yes. You must get my Hat.
Then O.K. Jane will get ya ha,t Mr. Mad-gum!
OK, Jane, Let's do this.
My hope in the hands of a child as Alyss's hope is in the hands of me...
...But how different they are. One a princess...
...one a warrior.
Both have such strong glows, and both need protection...

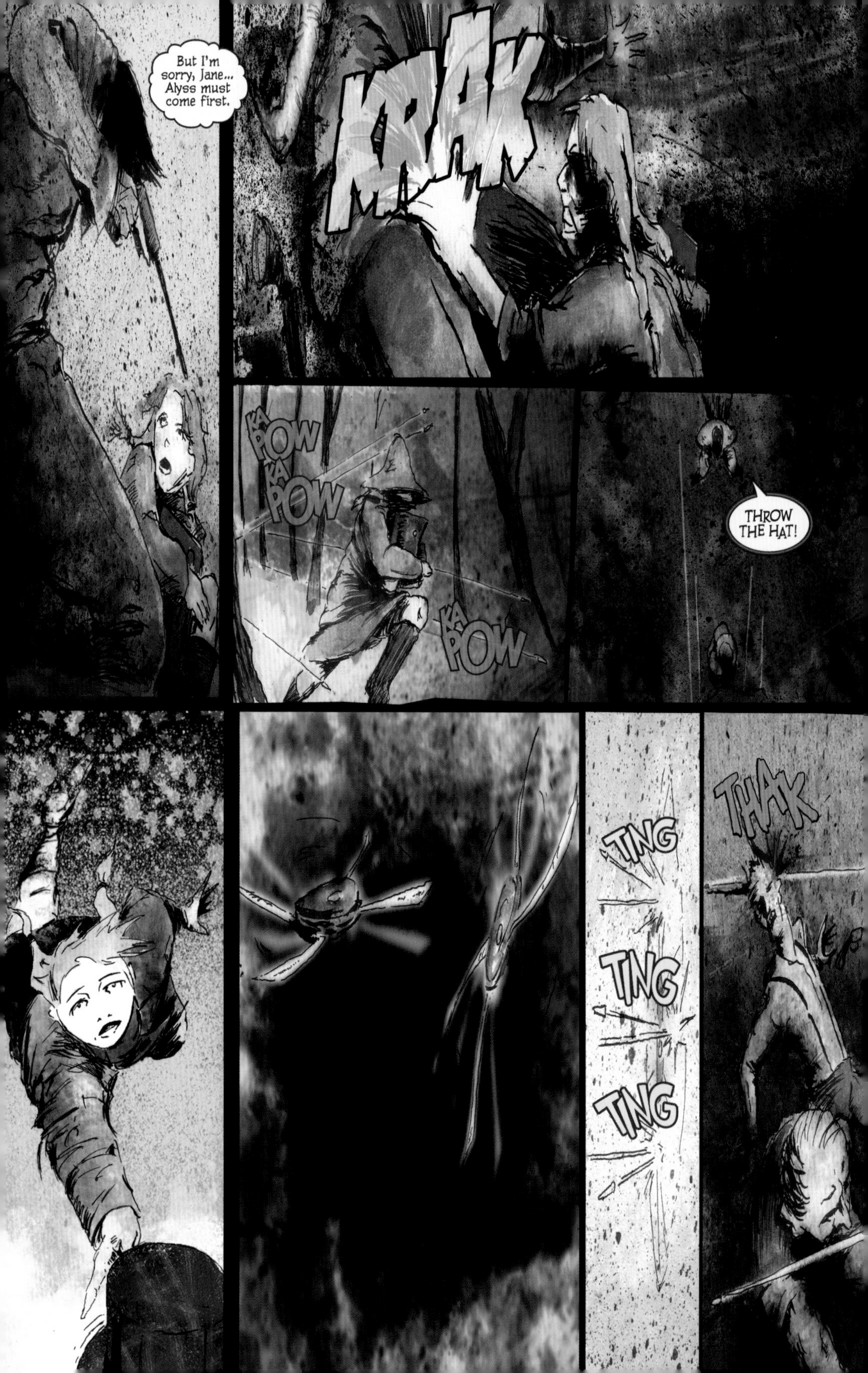
But I'm sorry, Jane... Alyss must come first.
KRAK
KA POW
KA POW
KA POW
THROW THE HAT!
TING
TING
TING
THAK

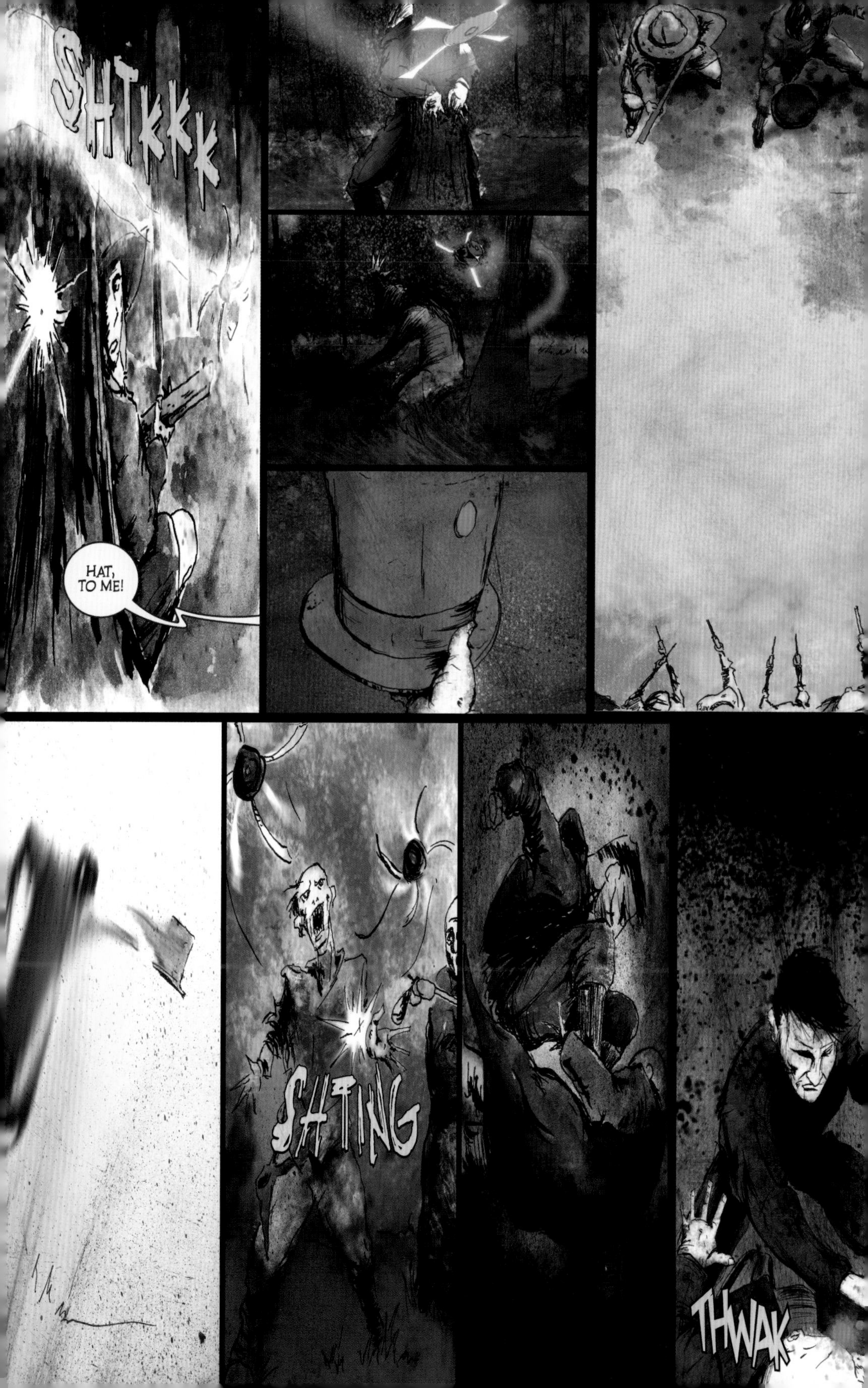
SHTKKK
HAT, TO ME!
SHTING
THWAK

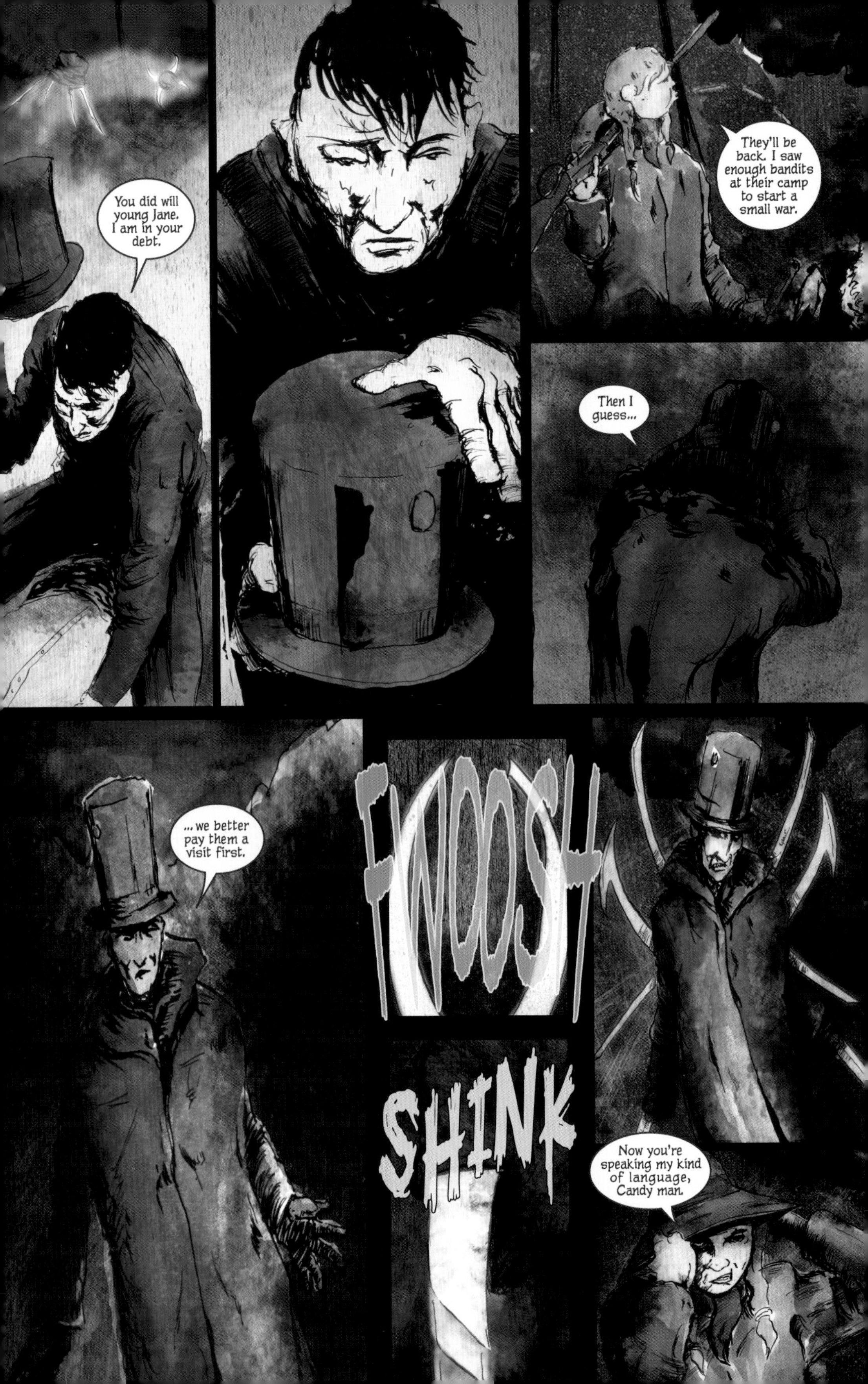
You did will young Jane. I am in your debt.
They'll be back. I saw enough bandits at their camp to start a small war.
Then I guess...
...we better pay them a visit first.
FWOOSH
SHINK
Now you're speaking my kind of language, Candy man.

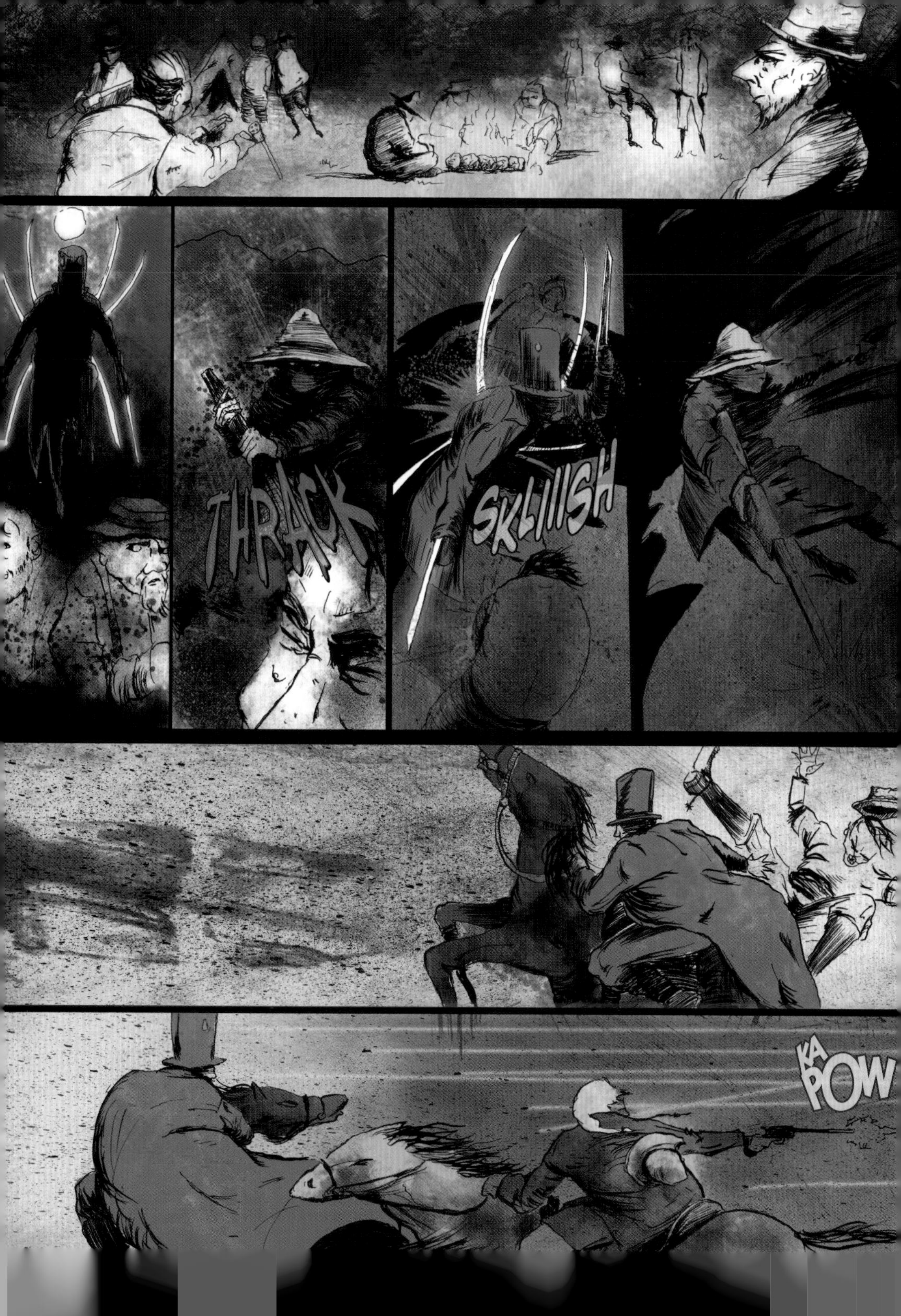
THRACK
SKLIIISH
KA POW

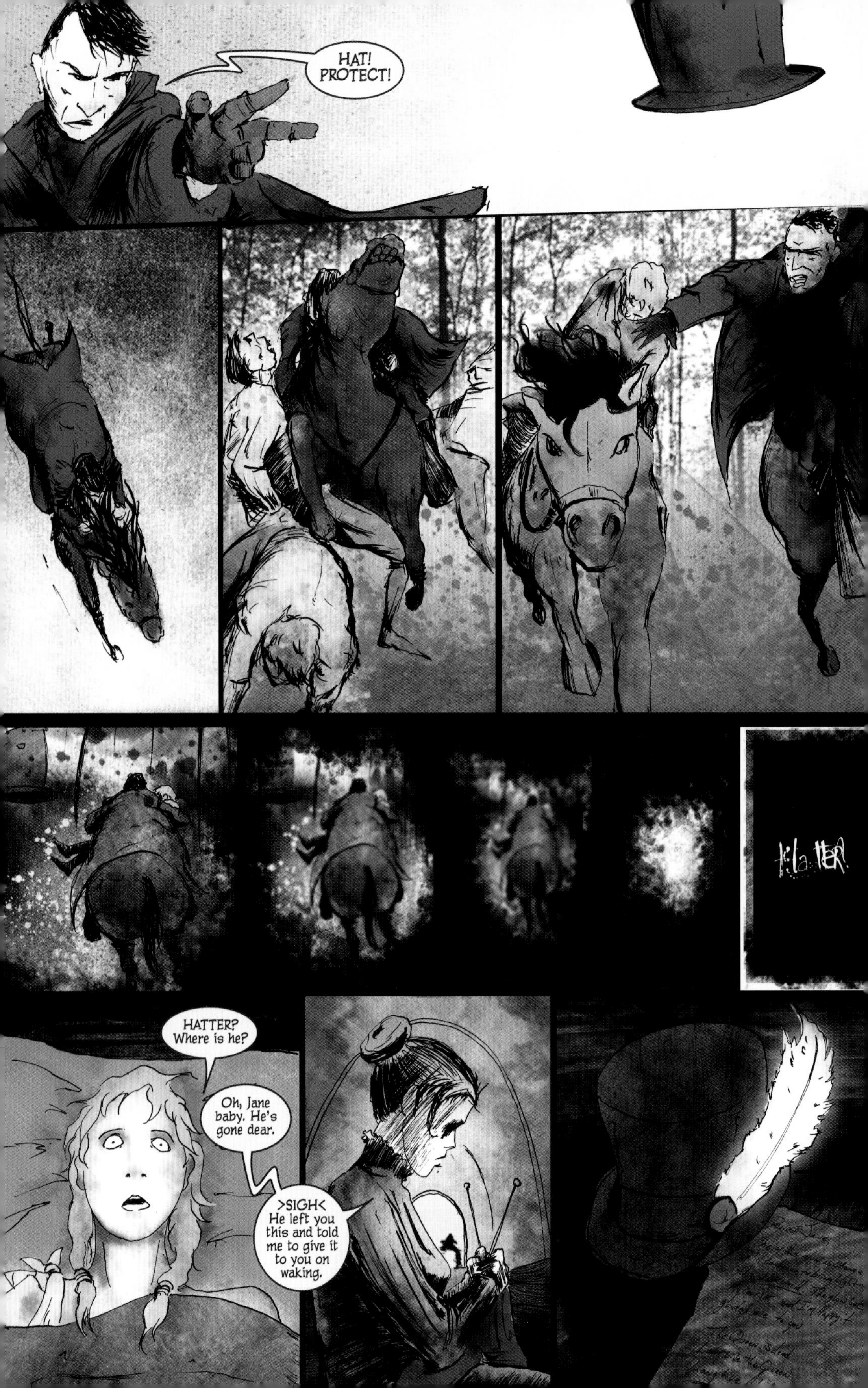
HAT! PROTECT!
HATTER? Where is he?
Oh, Jane baby. He's gone dear.
>SIGH< He left you this and told me to give it to you on waking.

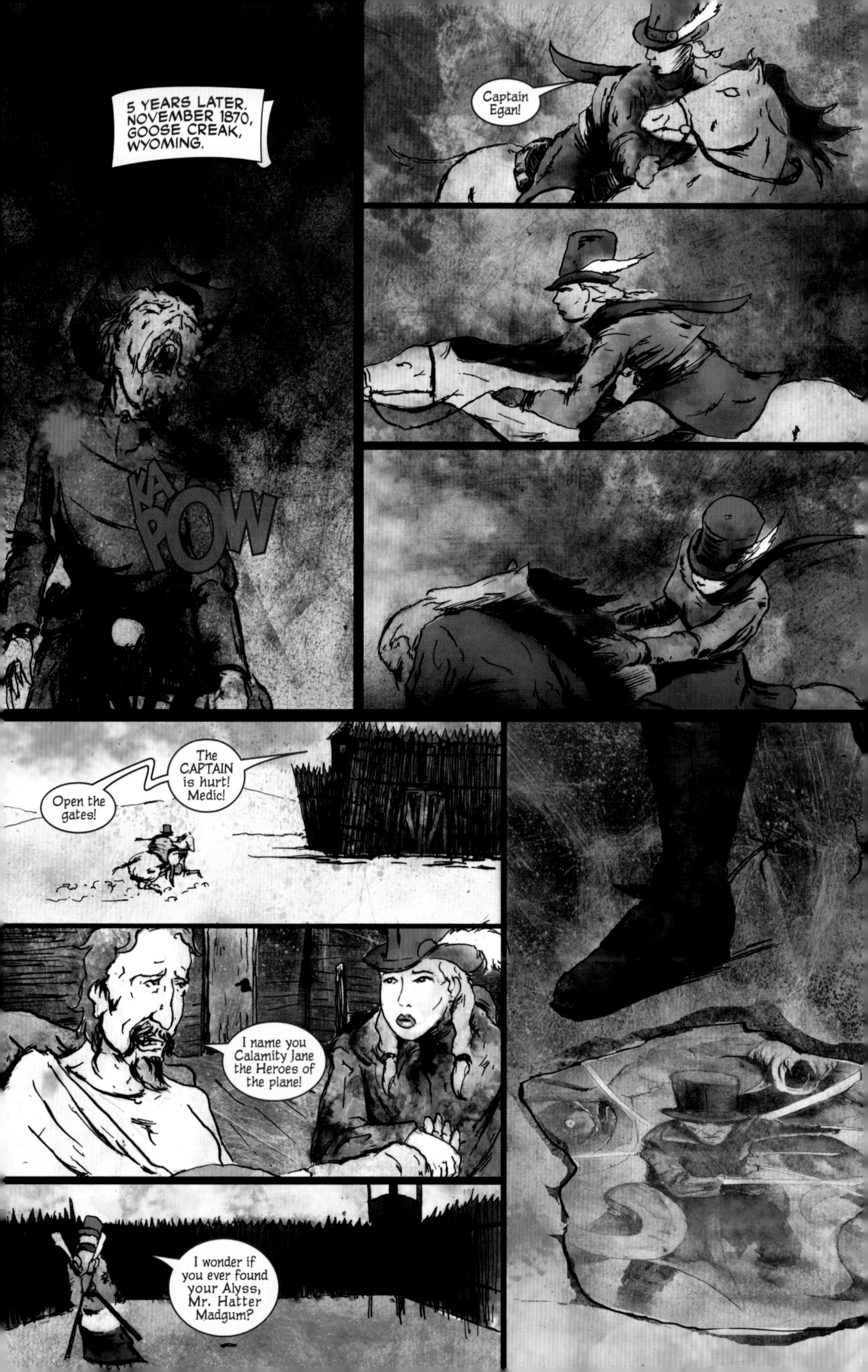
5 YEARS LATER, NOVEMBER 1870, GOOSE CREAK, WYOMING.
KA POW
Captain Egan!
Open the gates!
The CAPTAIN is hurt! Medic!
I name you Calamity Jane the Heroes of the plane!
I wonder if you ever found your Alyss, Mr. Hatter Madgum?

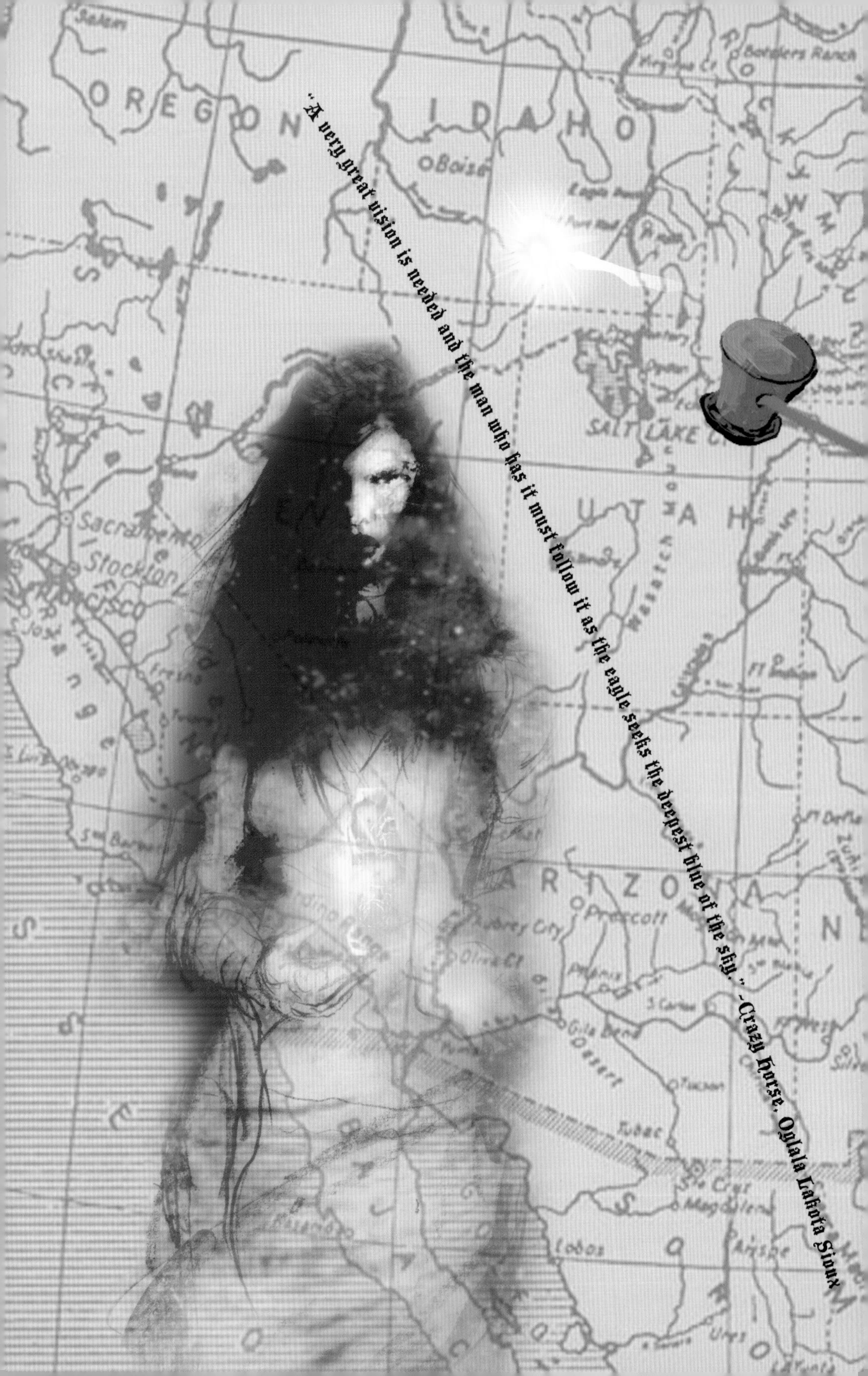
"A very great vision is needed and the man who has it must follow it as the eagle seeks the deepest blue of the sky." -Crazy Horse, Oglala Lakota Sioux
OREGON
IDAHO
Boise
SALT LAKE CI
UTAH
Sacramento
Stockton
ARIZONA
Prescott

Open Your Eyes

Written by
Sis Kipling

Art by
Tyson Schroeder

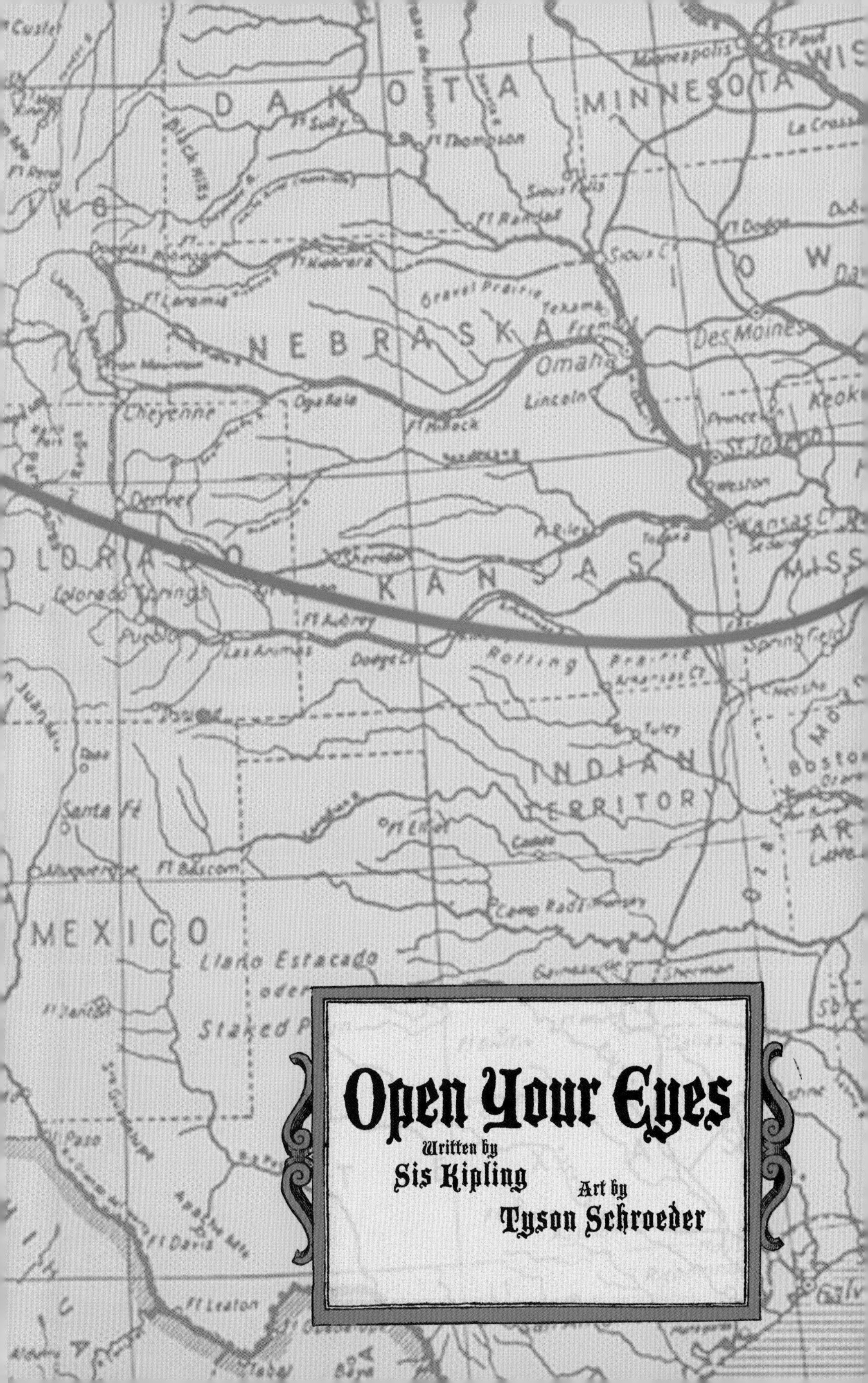

DAKOTA
MINNESOTA
Minneapolis
St Paul
Ft Sully
Ft Thompson
Sioux Falls
Ft Randall
Ft Dodge
Sioux C.
IOW
Gravel Prairie
NEBRASKA
Omaha
Des Moines
Lincoln
Cheyenne
Ogallala
Ft Laramie
Ft McPherson
Denver
COLORADO
KANSAS
Kansas C.
Topeka
Colorado Springs
Pueblo
Las Animas
Ft Aubrey
Dodge C.
Rolling Prairie
INDIAN TERRITORY
Santa Fe
Ft Bascom
Ft Elliot
Camp Radziminski
MEXICO
Llano Estacado oder Staked Plains
Ft Davis
Ft Leaton
Springfield
Boston

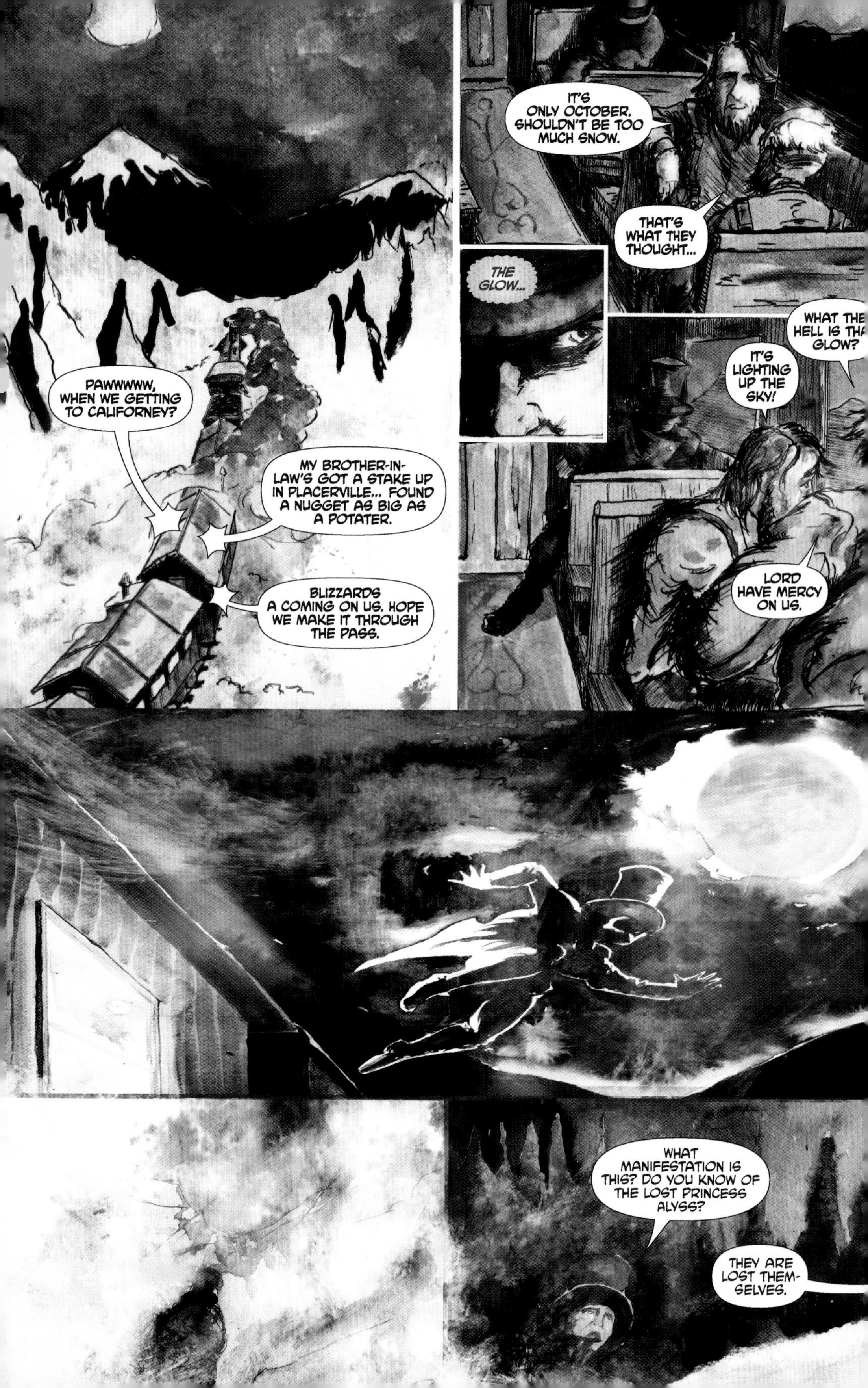
PAWWWWW, WHEN WE GETTING TO CALIFORNEY?
MY BROTHER-IN-LAW'S GOT A STAKE UP IN PLACERVILLE... FOUND A NUGGET AS BIG AS A POTATER.
BLIZZARDS A COMING ON US. HOPE WE MAKE IT THROUGH THE PASS.
IT'S ONLY OCTOBER. SHOULDN'T BE TOO MUCH SNOW.
THAT'S WHAT THEY THOUGHT...
THE GLOW...
WHAT THE HELL IS THA GLOW?
IT'S LIGHTING UP THE SKY!
LORD HAVE MERCY ON US.
WHAT MANIFESTATION IS THIS? DO YOU KNOW OF THE LOST PRINCESS ALYSS?
THEY ARE LOST THEM-SELVES.

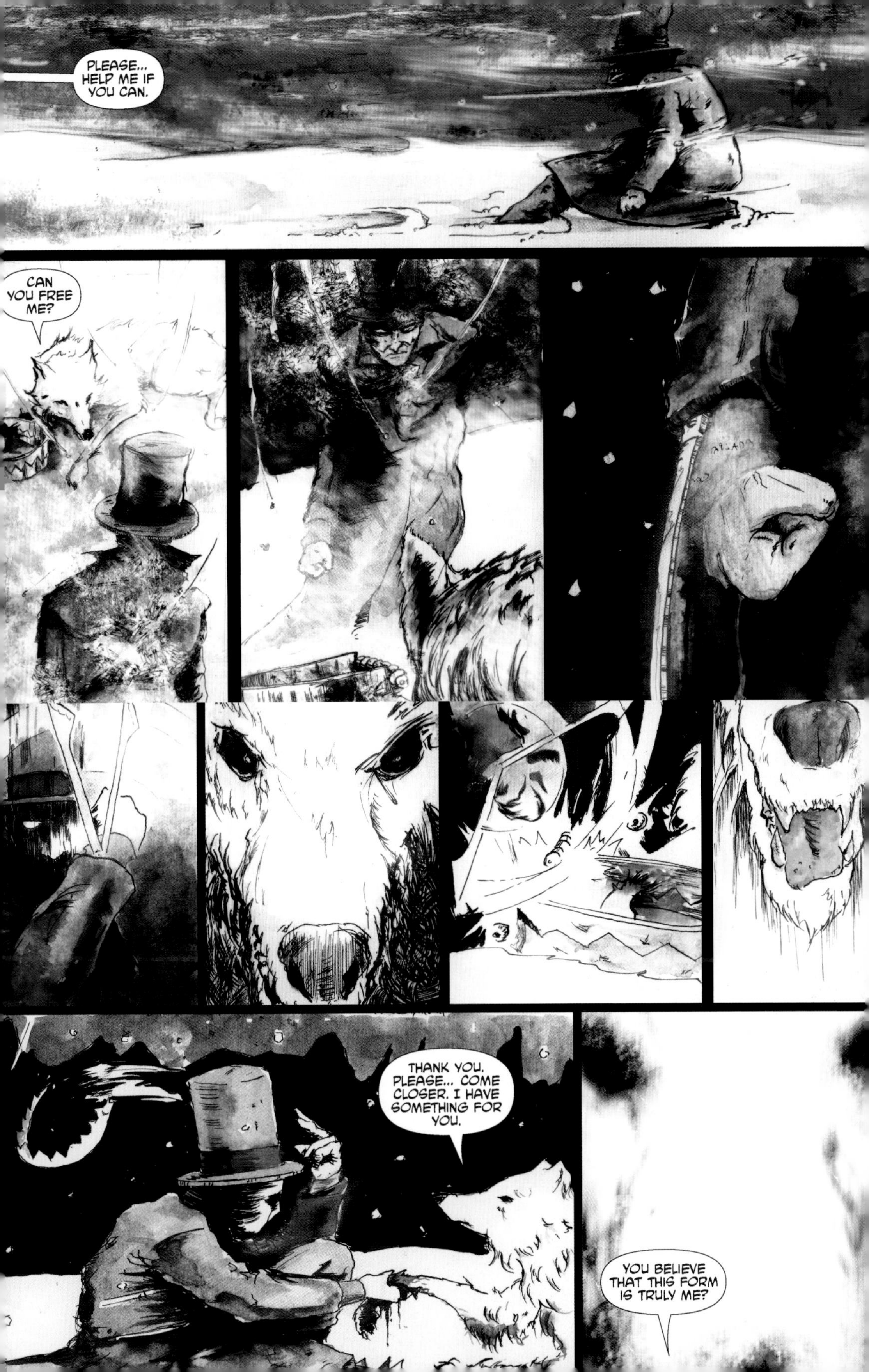
PLEASE... HELP ME IF YOU CAN.
CAN YOU FREE ME?
THANK YOU. PLEASE... COME CLOSER. I HAVE SOMETHING FOR YOU.
YOU BELIEVE THAT THIS FORM IS TRULY ME?

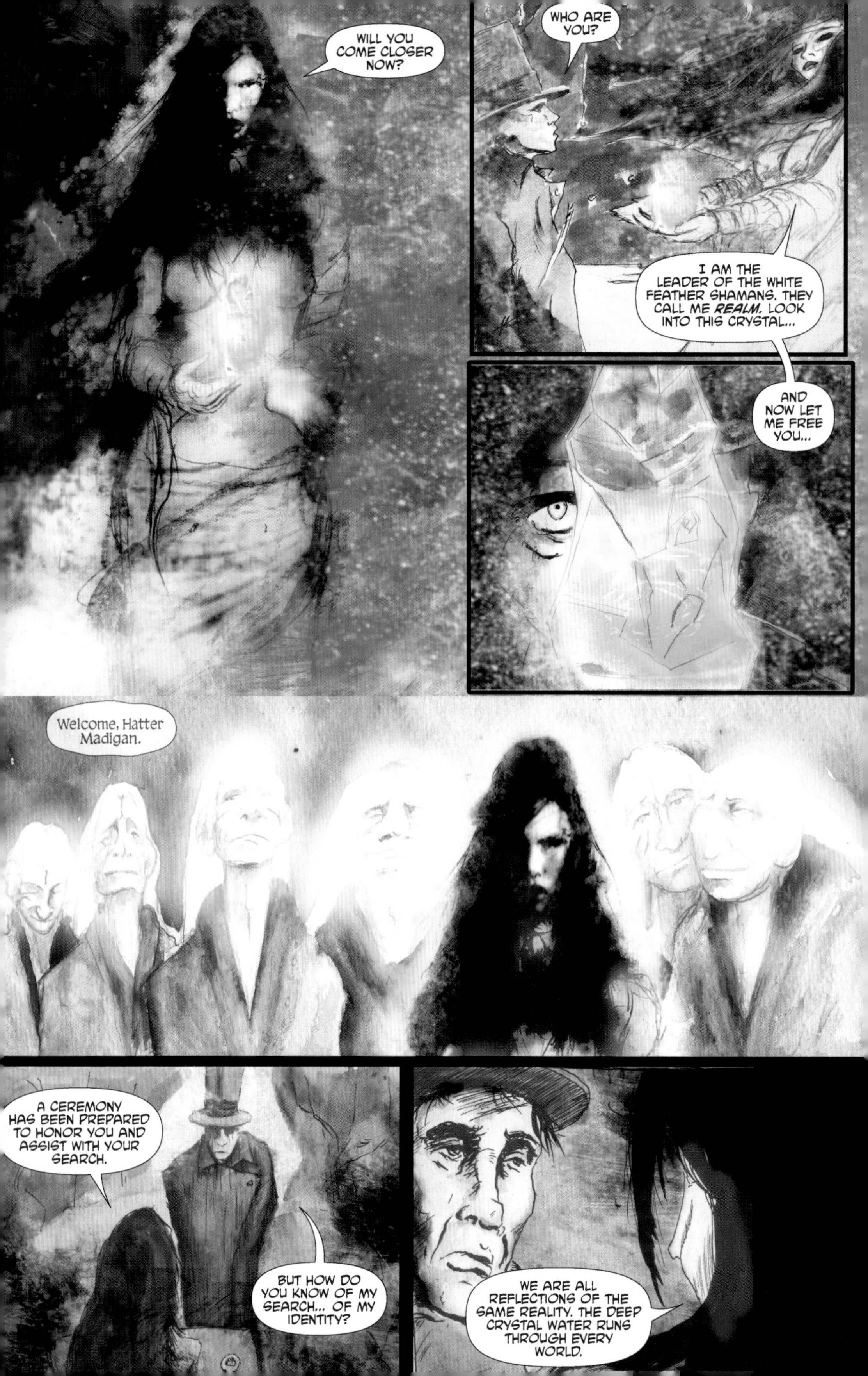
WILL YOU COME CLOSER NOW?
WHO ARE YOU?
I AM THE LEADER OF THE WHITE FEATHER SHAMANS. THEY CALL ME *REALM.* LOOK INTO THIS CRYSTAL...
AND NOW LET ME FREE YOU...
Welcome, Hatter Madigan.
A CEREMONY HAS BEEN PREPARED TO HONOR YOU AND ASSIST WITH YOUR SEARCH.
BUT HOW DO YOU KNOW OF MY SEARCH... OF MY IDENTITY?
WE ARE ALL REFLECTIONS OF THE SAME REALITY. THE DEEP CRYSTAL WATER RUNS THROUGH EVERY WORLD.

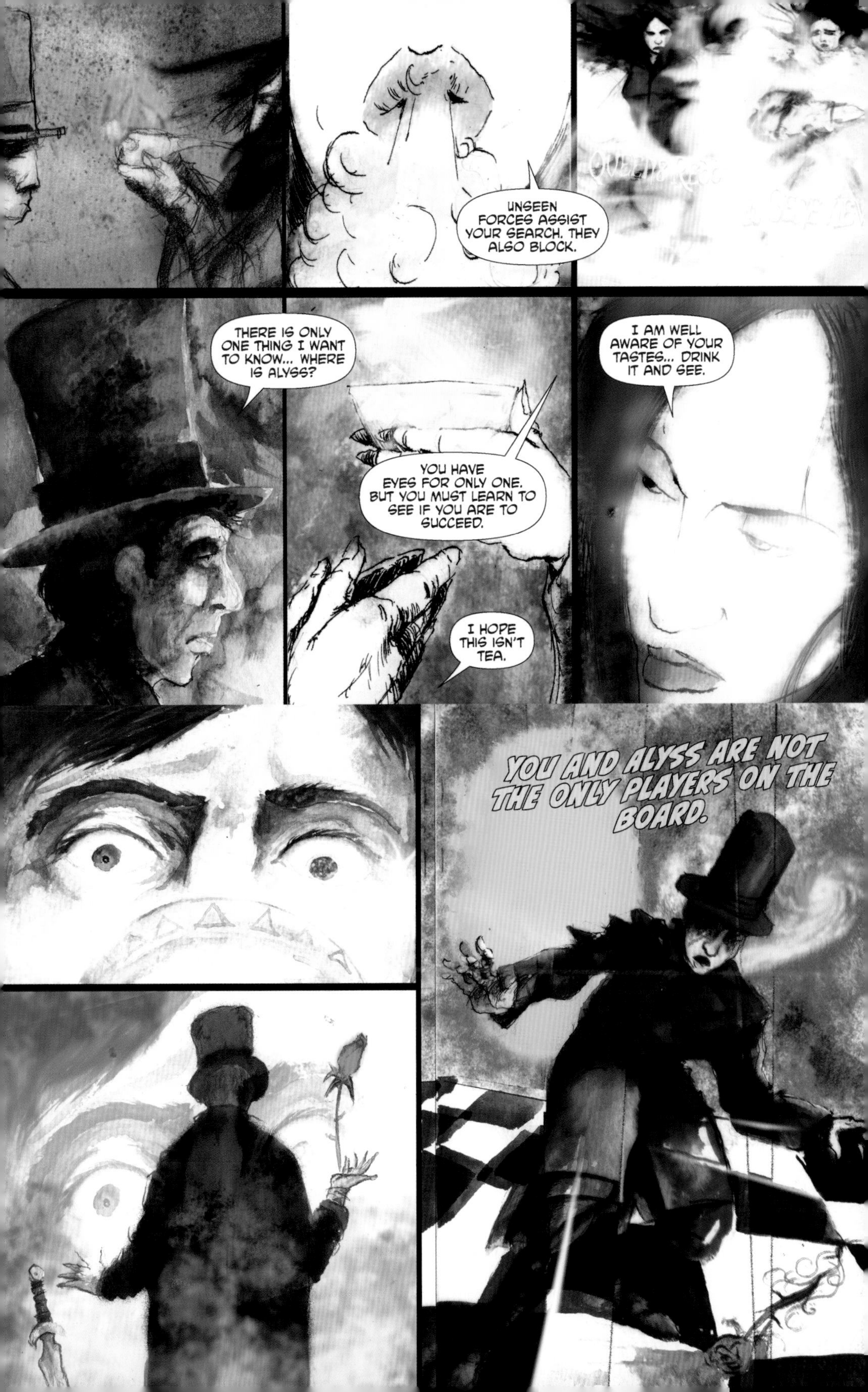

UNSEEN FORCES ASSIST YOUR SEARCH. THEY ALSO BLOCK.
THERE IS ONLY ONE THING I WANT TO KNOW... WHERE IS ALYSS?
YOU HAVE EYES FOR ONLY ONE. BUT YOU MUST LEARN TO SEE IF YOU ARE TO SUCCEED.
I HOPE THIS ISN'T TEA.
I AM WELL AWARE OF YOUR TASTES... DRINK IT AND SEE.
YOU AND ALYSS ARE NOT THE ONLY PLAYERS ON THE BOARD.

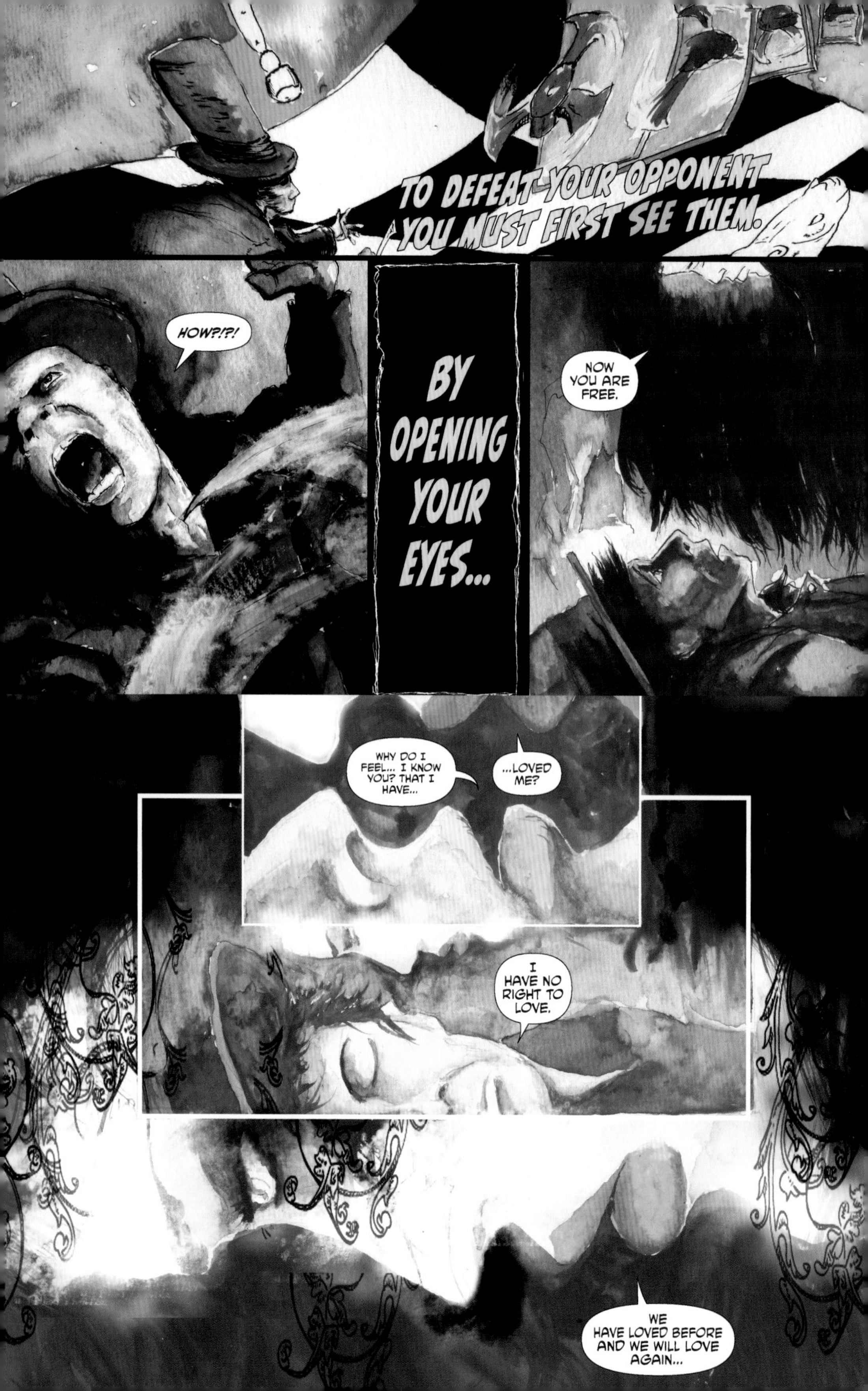
TO DEFEAT YOUR OPPONENT YOU MUST FIRST SEE THEM.
HOW?!?!
BY OPENING YOUR EYES...
NOW YOU ARE FREE.
WHY DO I FEEL... I KNOW YOU? THAT I HAVE...
...LOVED ME?
I HAVE NO RIGHT TO LOVE.
WE HAVE LOVED BEFORE AND WE WILL LOVE AGAIN...

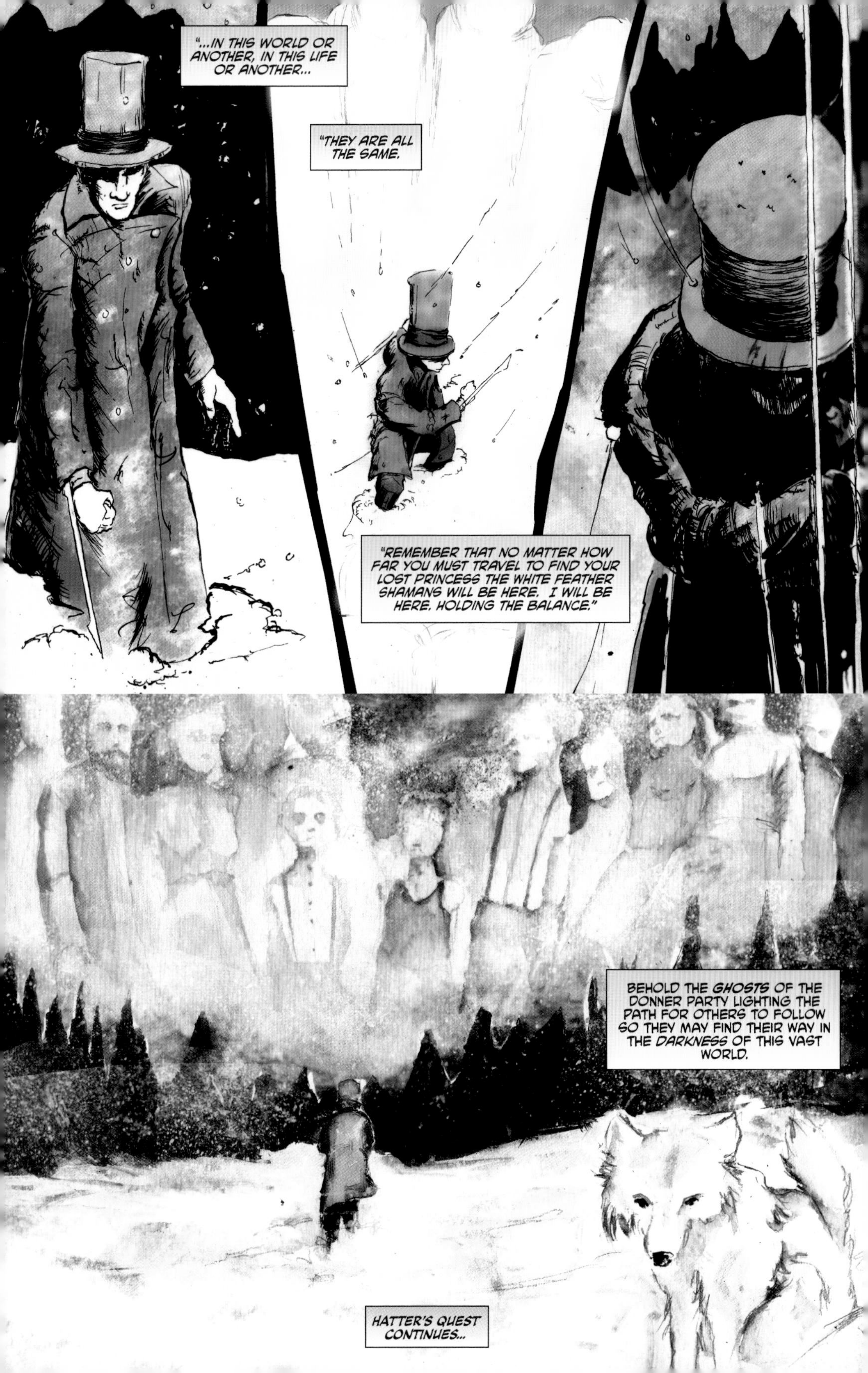
"...IN THIS WORLD OR ANOTHER, IN THIS LIFE OR ANOTHER...
"THEY ARE ALL THE SAME.
"REMEMBER THAT NO MATTER HOW FAR YOU MUST TRAVEL TO FIND YOUR LOST PRINCESS THE WHITE FEATHER SHAMANS WILL BE HERE. I WILL BE HERE. HOLDING THE BALANCE."
BEHOLD THE *GHOSTS* OF THE DONNER PARTY LIGHTING THE PATH FOR OTHERS TO FOLLOW SO THEY MAY FIND THEIR WAY IN THE *DARKNESS* OF THIS VAST WORLD.
HATTER'S QUEST CONTINUES...

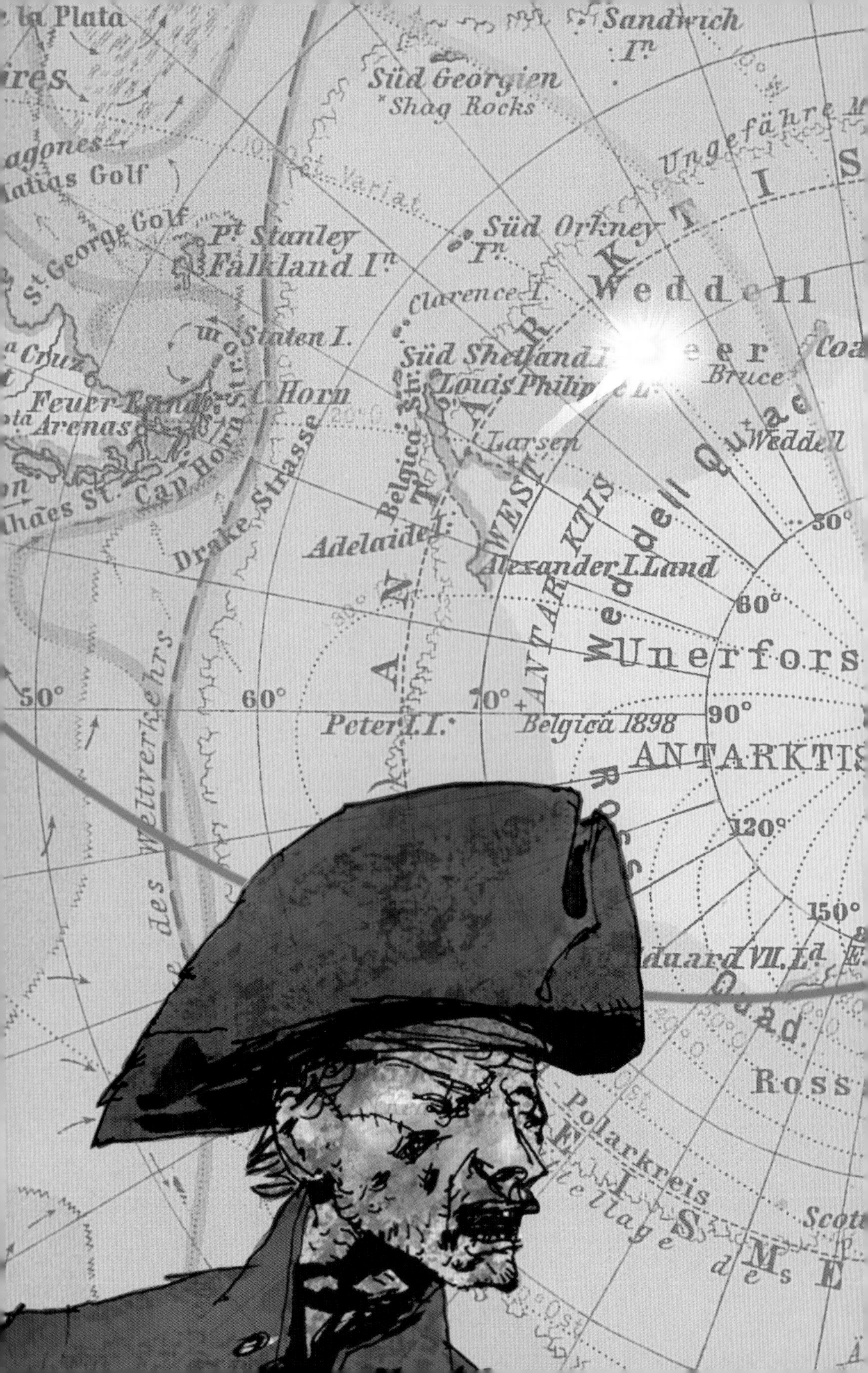

Sandwich I.n
Süd Georgien
Shag Rocks
Ungefähre
Patagones
Matias Golf
St. George Golf
P.t Stanley
Falkland I.n
Süd Orkney I.n
Weddell
Clarence I.
Staten I.
Süd Shetland I.
Louis Philippe L.
Bruce
Feuer-Land
Arenas
C. Horn
Cap Horn St.
Magalhães St.
Drake Strasse
Belgica St.
Larsen
Weddell Quad.
Weddell
Adelaide I.
West Antarktis
Alexander I. Land
Unerfors
50°
60°
70°
90°
Peter I. I.
Belgica 1898
ANTARKTIS
Ross
des Weltverkehrs
120°
150°
Eduard VII. L.d
Ross
Pollarkreis
Scott

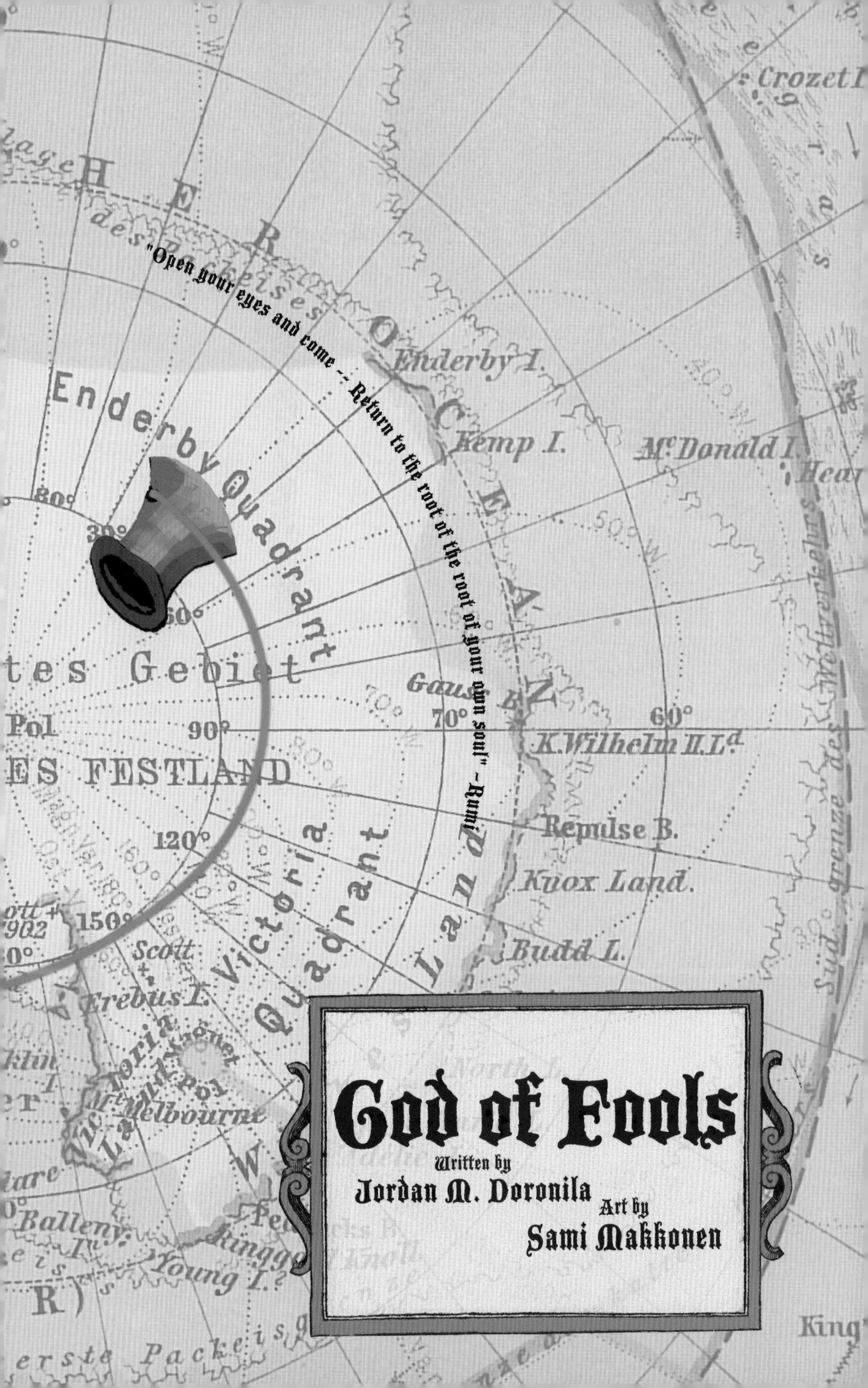
Crozet I
H E R
O C E A N
Enderby I.
Enderby Quadrant
Kemp I.
McDonald I.
tes Gebiet
Gauss B.
K. Wilhelm II. Ld.
Pol
ES FESTLAND
Repulse B.
Knox Land.
Budd L.
Victoria Quadrant
Scott
Erebus I.
Mt. Melbourne
Balleny Is.
Young I.
erste Packeis
80°
30°
60°
90°
70°
60°
120°
150°

"Open your eyes and come -- Return to the root of the root of your own soul" --Rumi

God of Fools

Written by
Jordan M. Doronila
Art by
Sami Makkonen

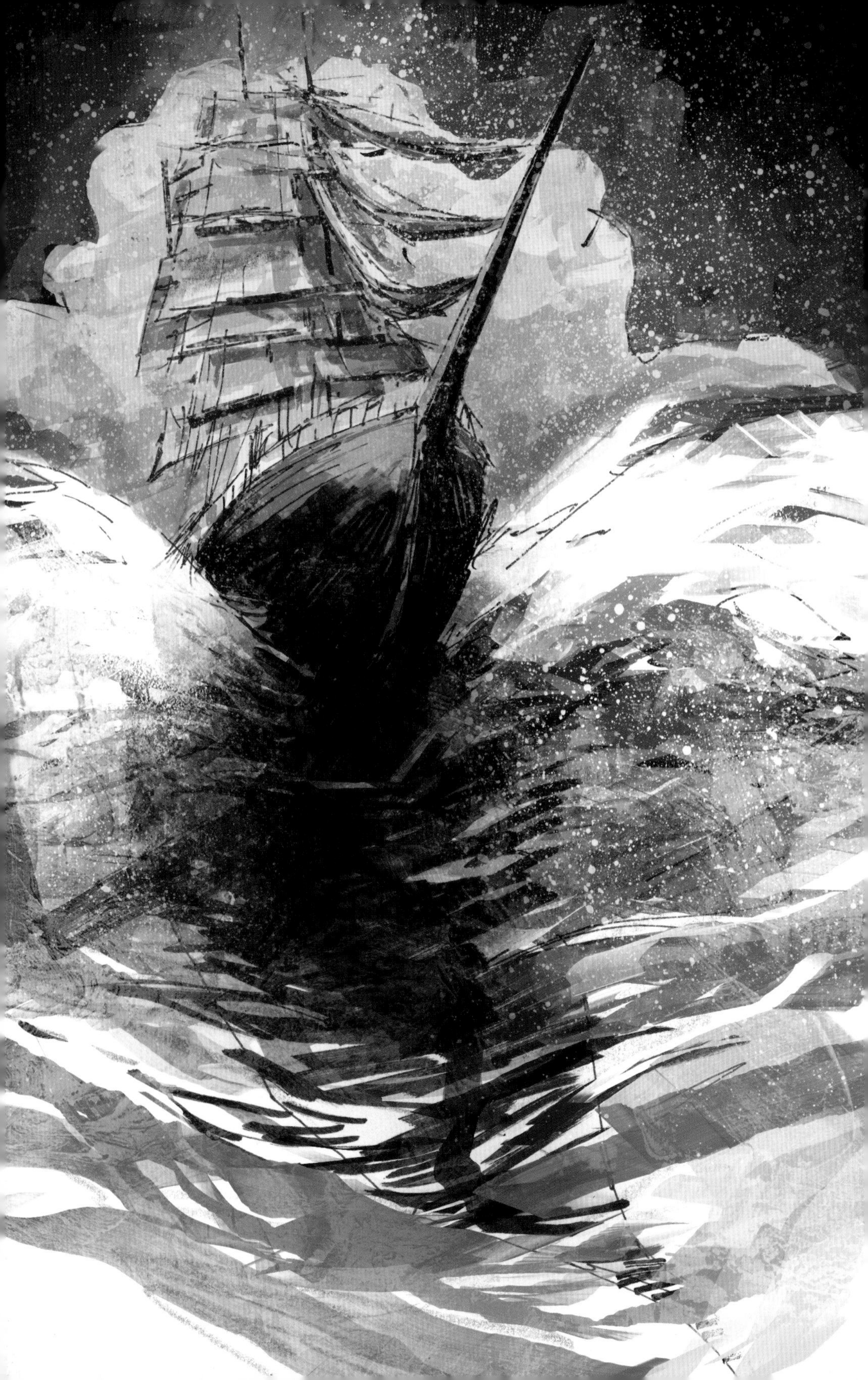

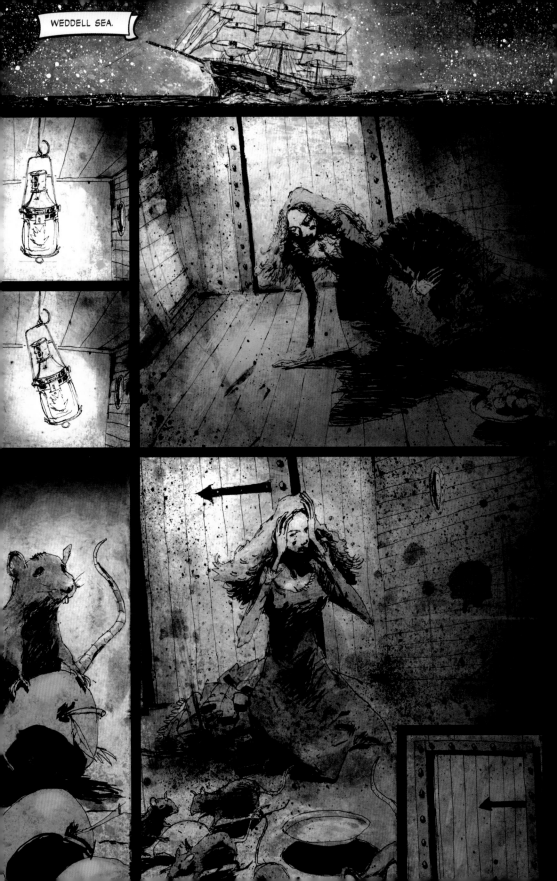

WEDDELL SEA.

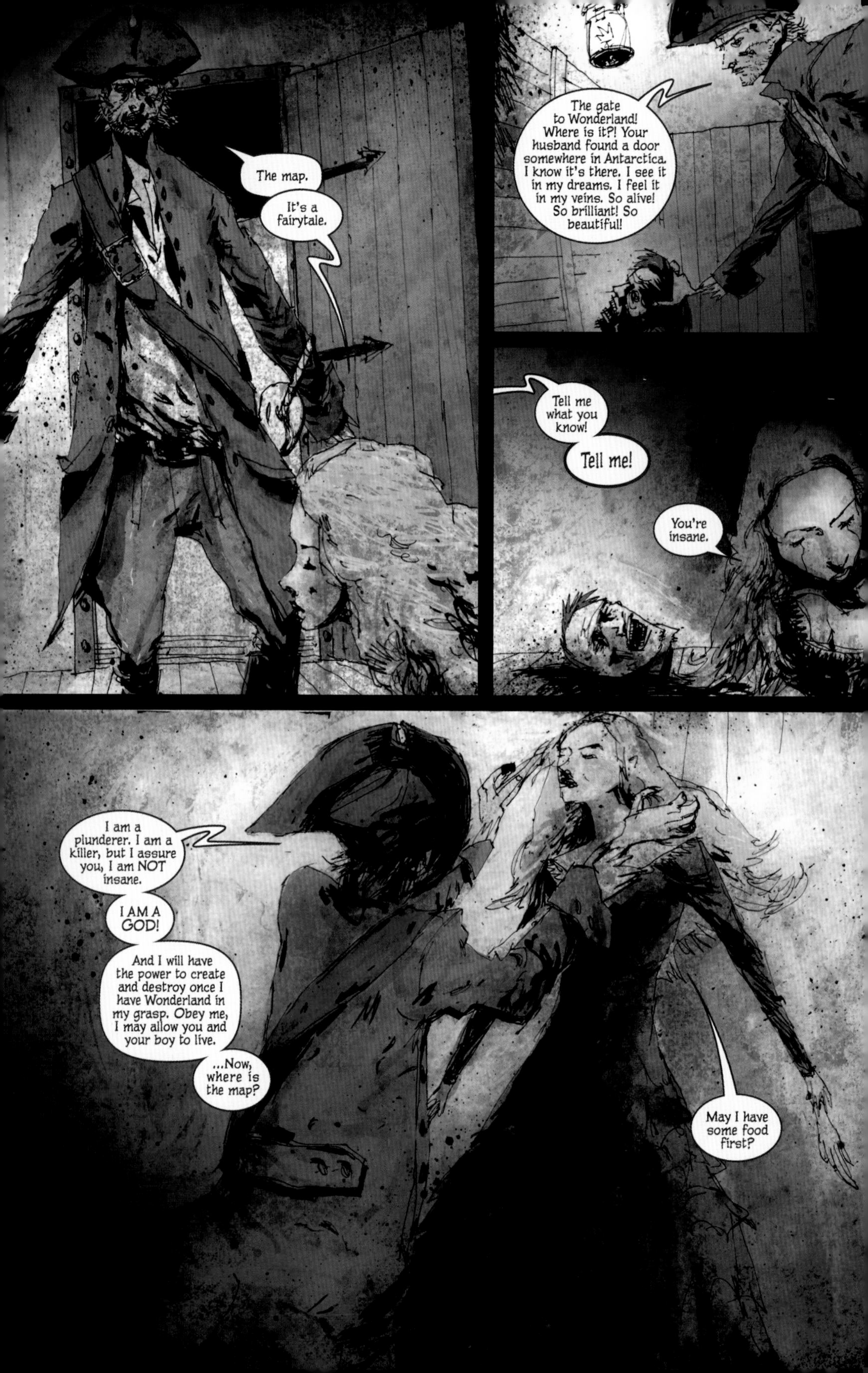
The map.
It's a fairytale.
The gate to Wonderland! Where is it?! Your husband found a door somewhere in Antarctica. I know it's there. I see it in my dreams. I feel it in my veins. So alive! So brilliant! So beautiful!
Tell me what you know!
Tell me!
You're insane.
I am a plunderer. I am a killer, but I assure you, I am NOT insane.
I AM A GOD!
And I will have the power to create and destroy once I have Wonderland in my grasp. Obey me, I may allow you and your boy to live.
...Now, where is the map?
May I have some food first?

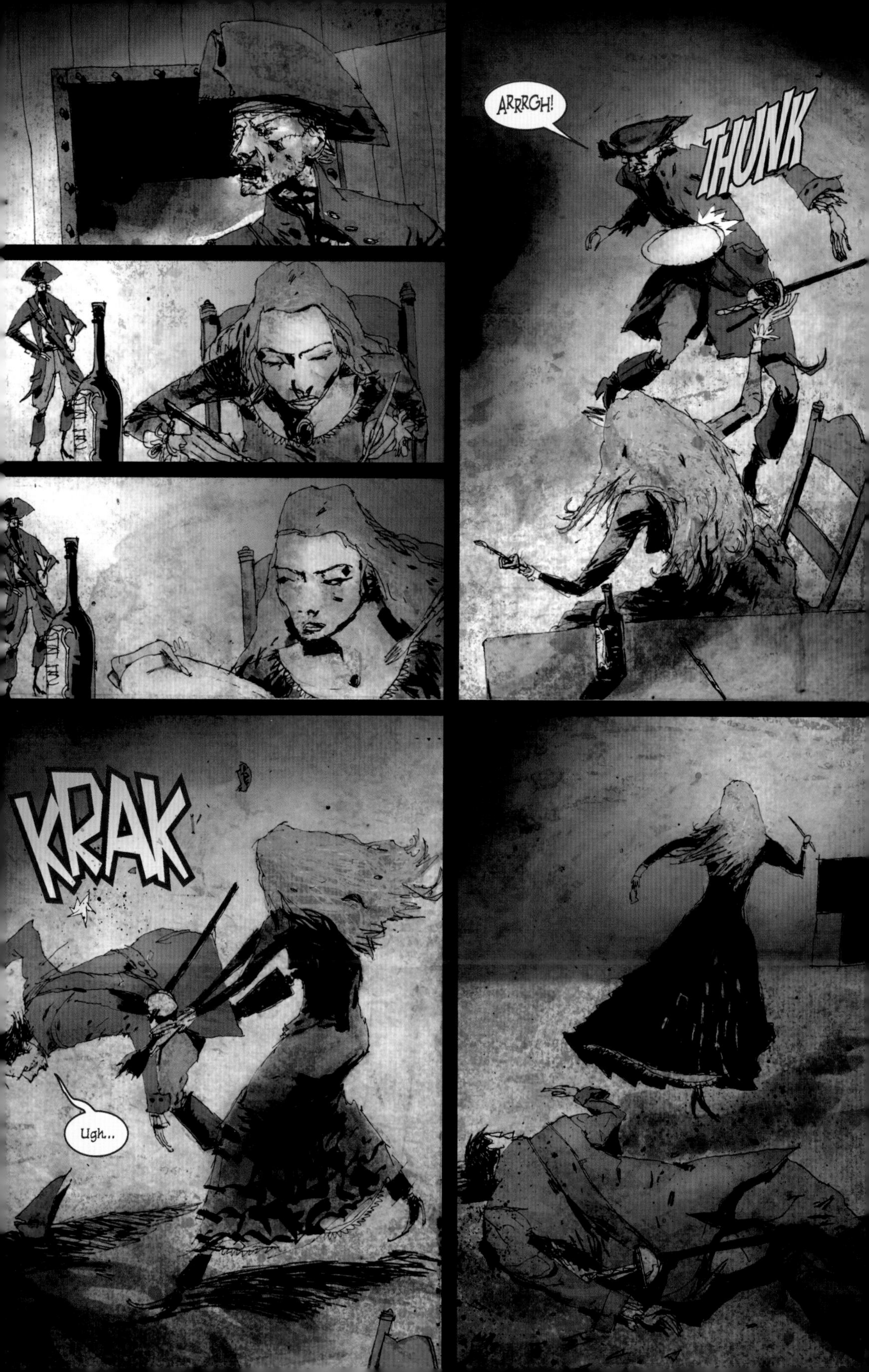
ARRRGH!
THUNK
KRAK
Ugh..

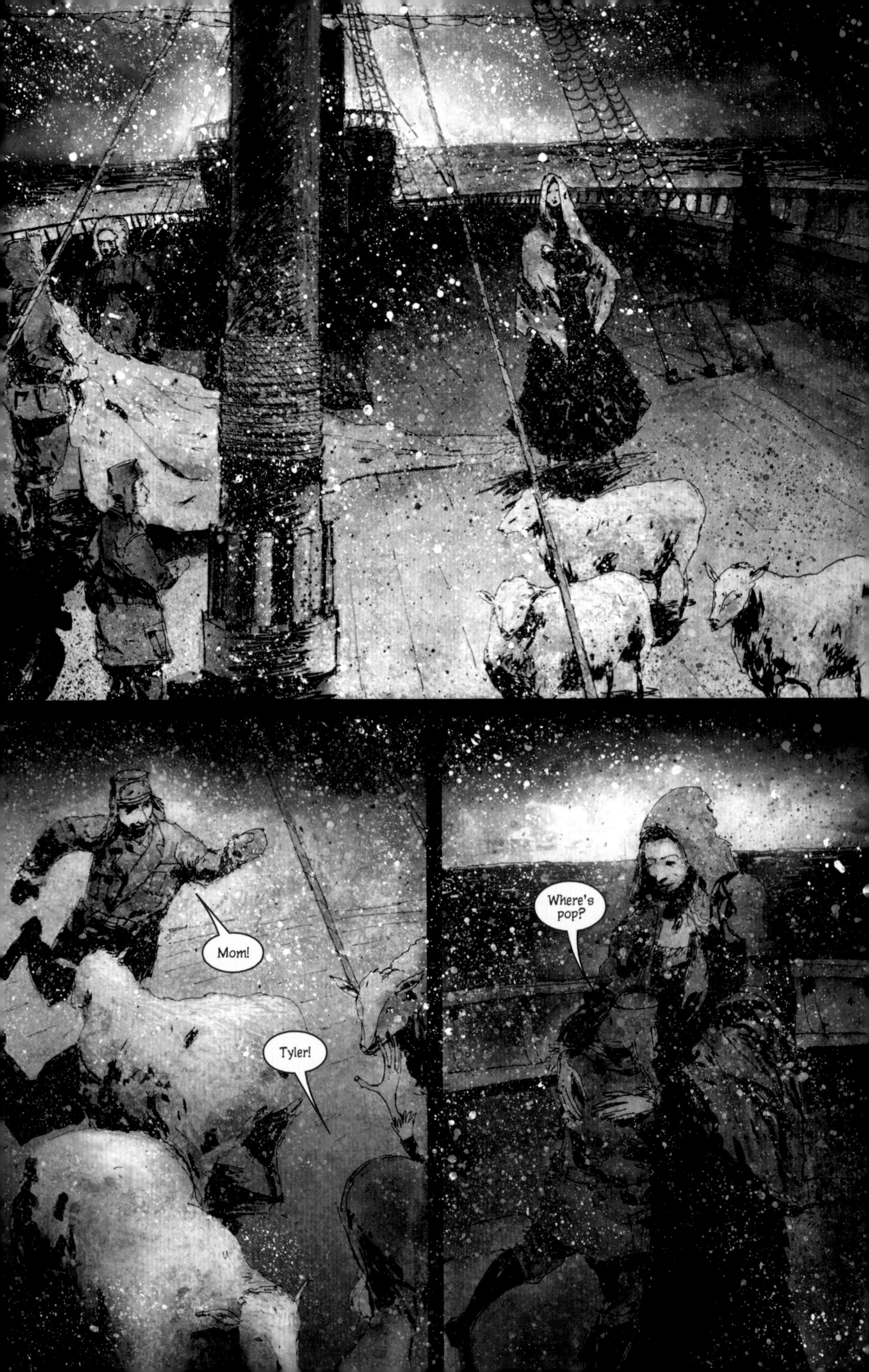
Mom!
Tyler!
Where's pop?

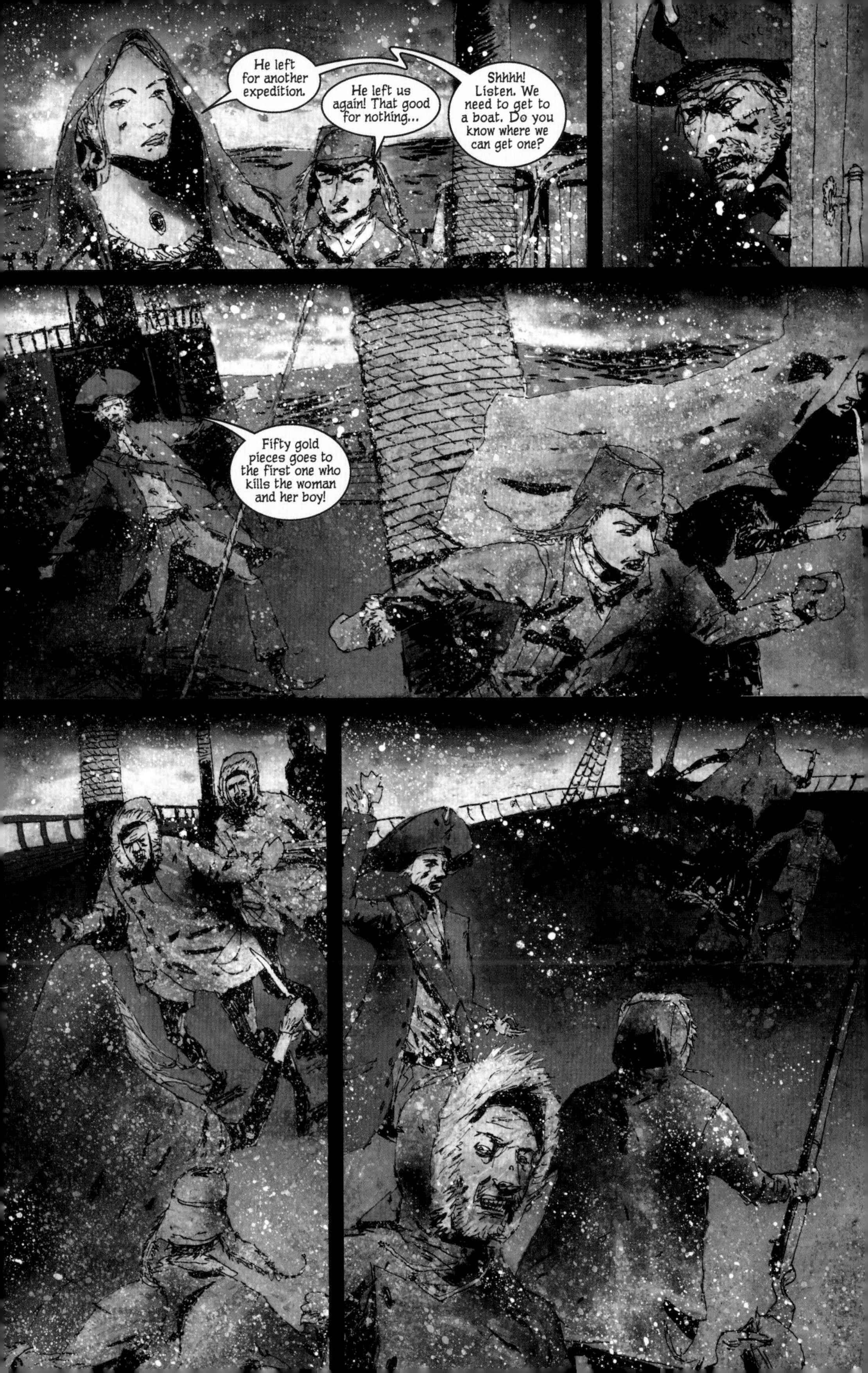
He left for another expedition.
He left us again! That good for nothing...
Shhhh! Listen. We need to get to a boat. Do you know where we can get one?
Fifty gold pieces goes to the first one who kills the woman and her boy!

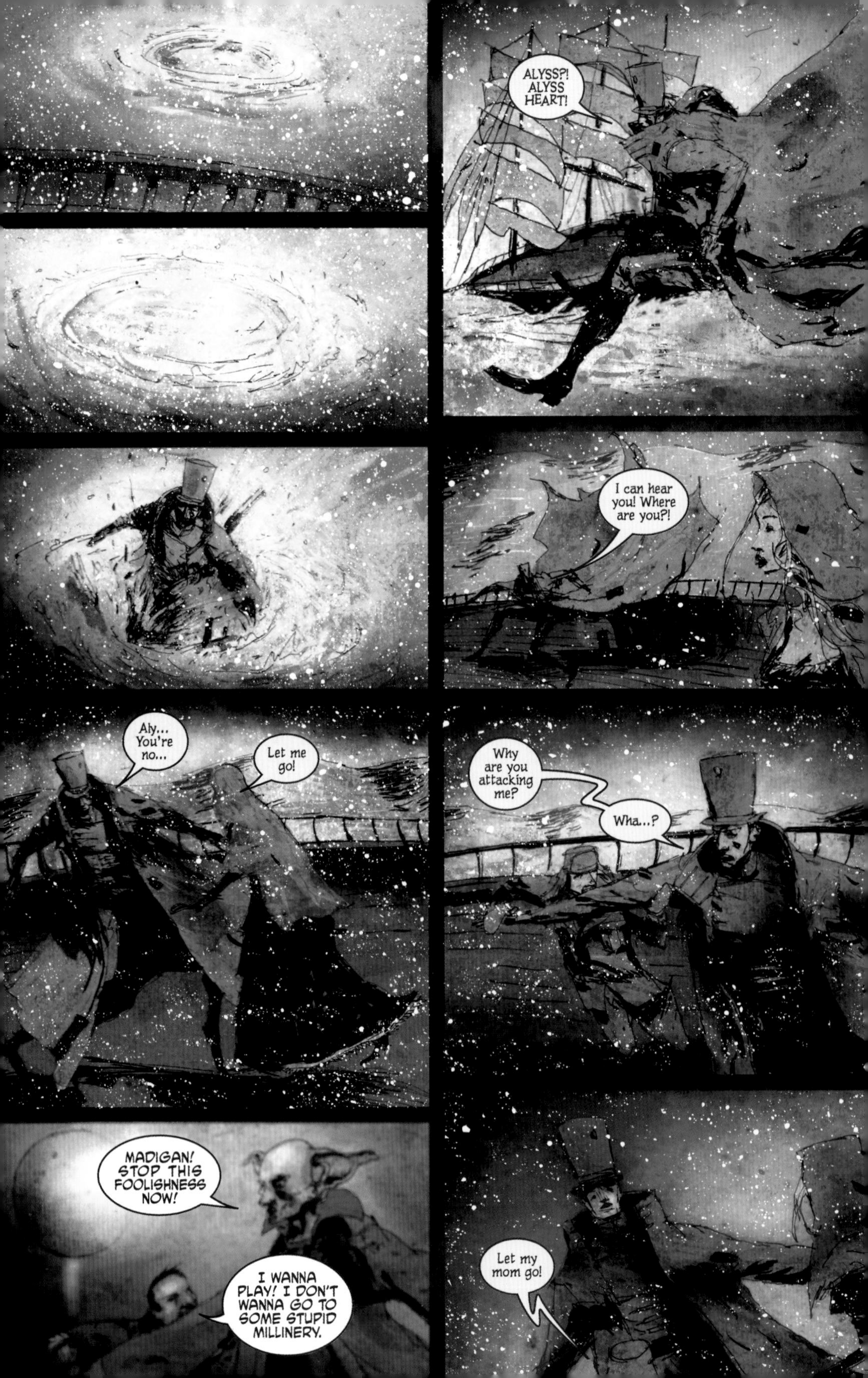
ALYSS?! ALYSS HEART!
I can hear you! Where are you?!
Aly... You're no...
Let me go!
Why are you attacking me?
Wha...?
MADIGAN! STOP THIS FOOLISHNESS NOW!
I WANNA PLAY! I DON'T WANNA GO TO SOME STUPID MILLINERY.
Let my mom go!

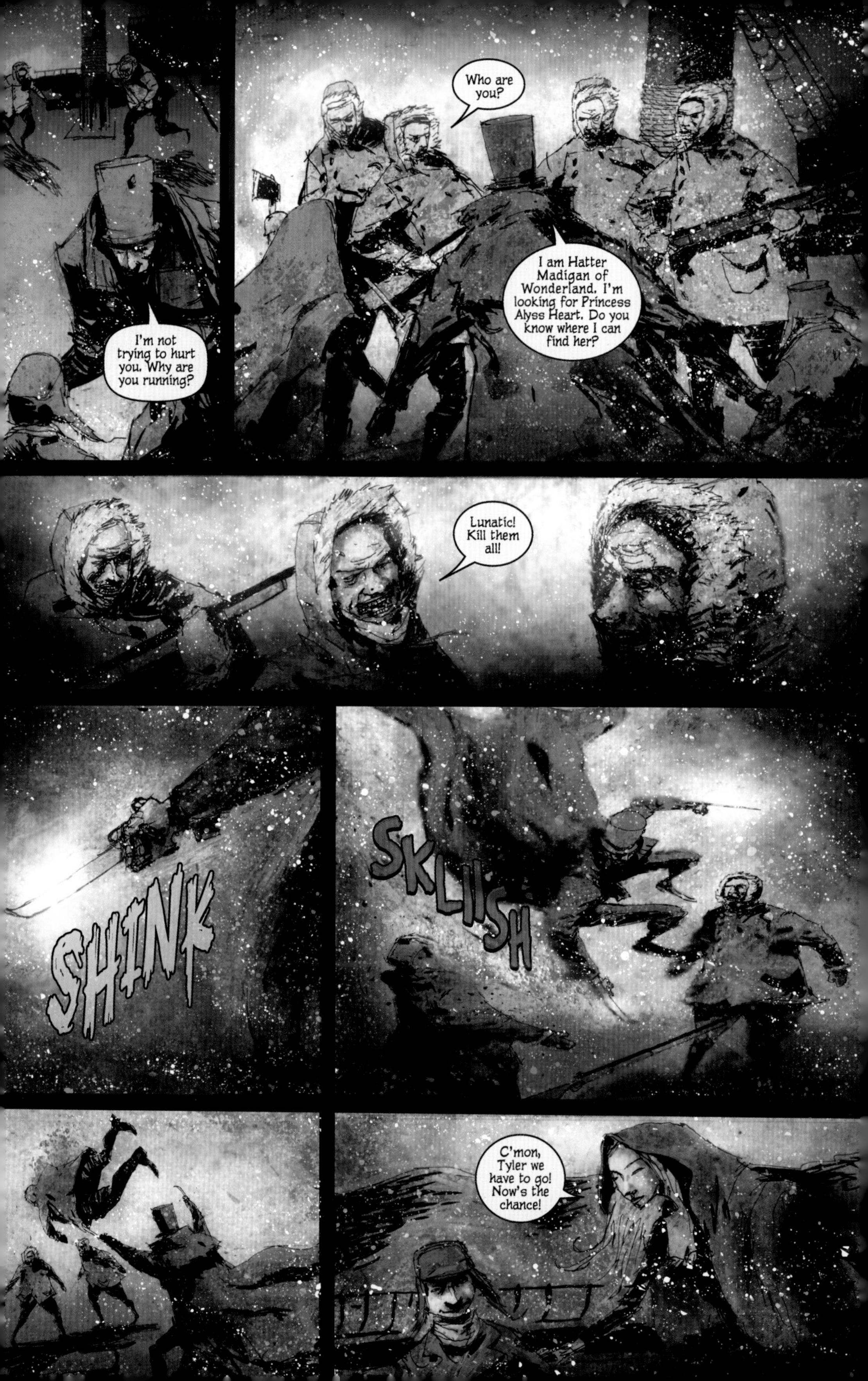
I'm not trying to hurt you. Why are you running?
Who are you?
I am Hatter Madigan of Wonderland. I'm looking for Princess Alyss Heart. Do you know where I can find her?
Lunatic! Kill them all!
SHINK
SKLIISH
C'mon, Tyler we have to go! Now's the chance!

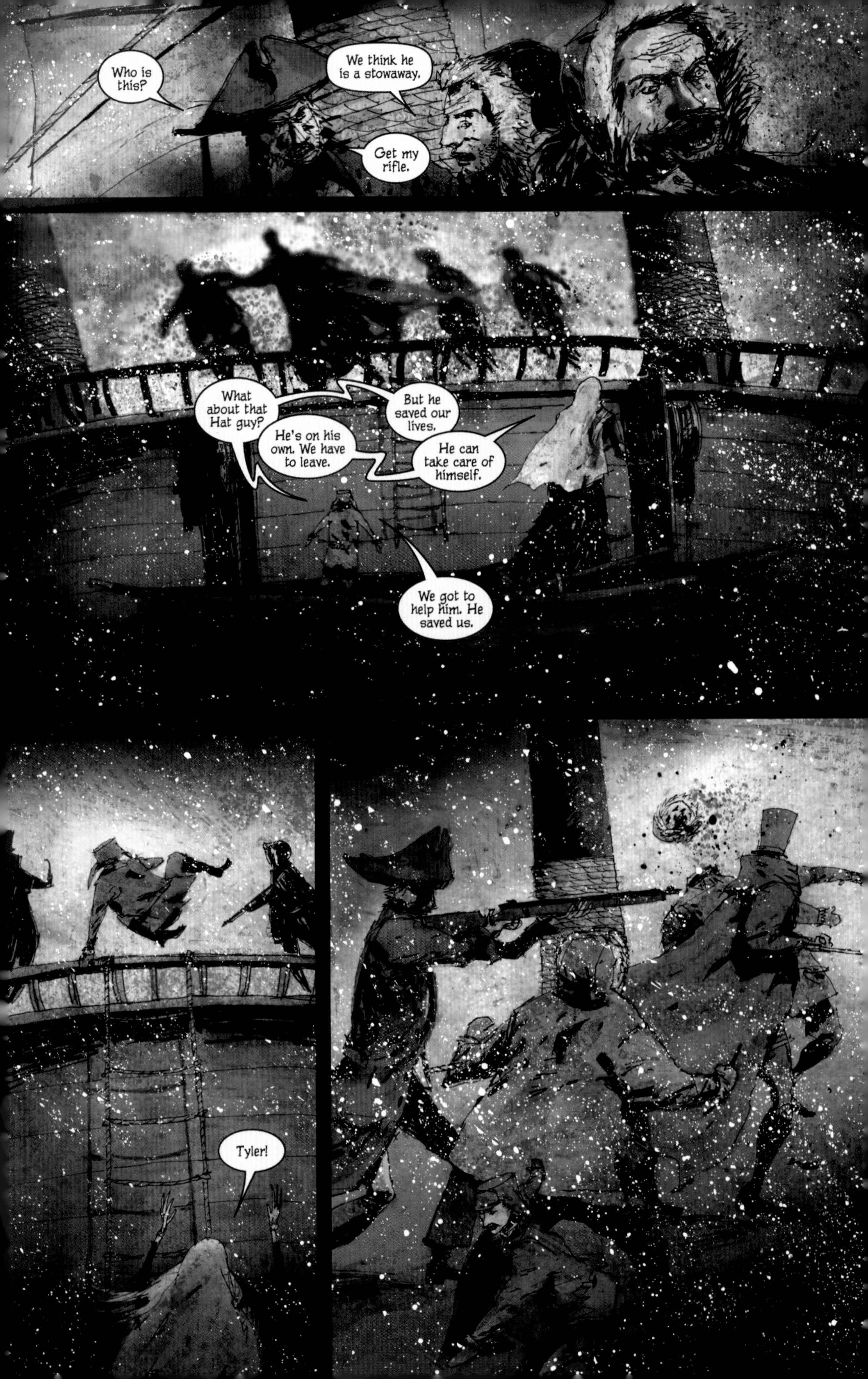
Who is this?
We think he is a stowaway.
Get my rifle.
What about that Hat guy?
But he saved our lives.
He's on his own. We have to leave.
He can take care of himself.
We got to help him. He saved us.
Tyler!

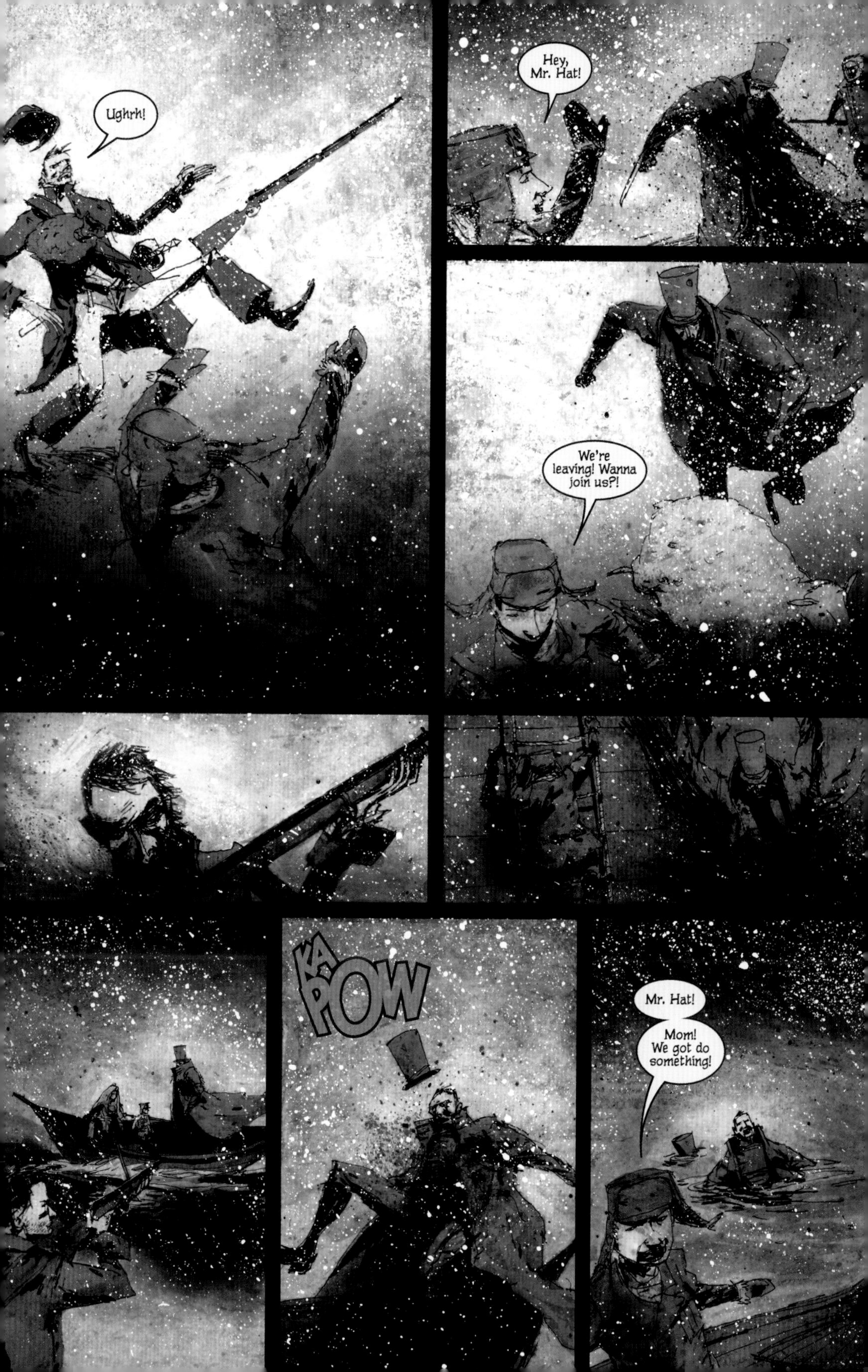

Ughrh!
Hey, Mr. Hat!
We're leaving! Wanna join us?!
KA POW
Mr. Hat!
Mom! We got do something!

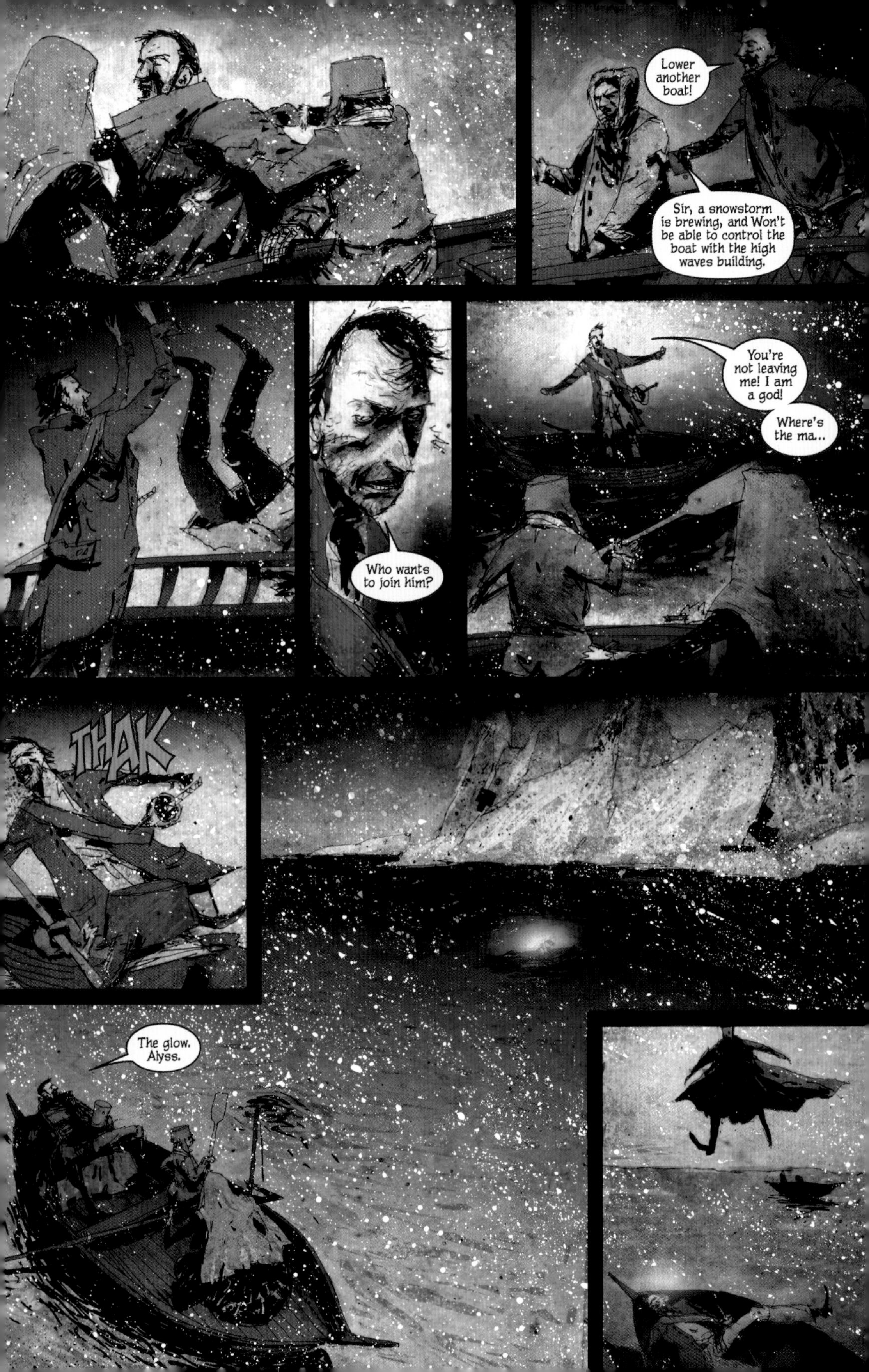
Lower another boat!
Sir, a snowstorm is brewing, and Won't be able to control the boat with the high waves building.
Who wants to join him?
You're not leaving me! I am a god!
Where's the ma...
THAK
The glow. Alyss.

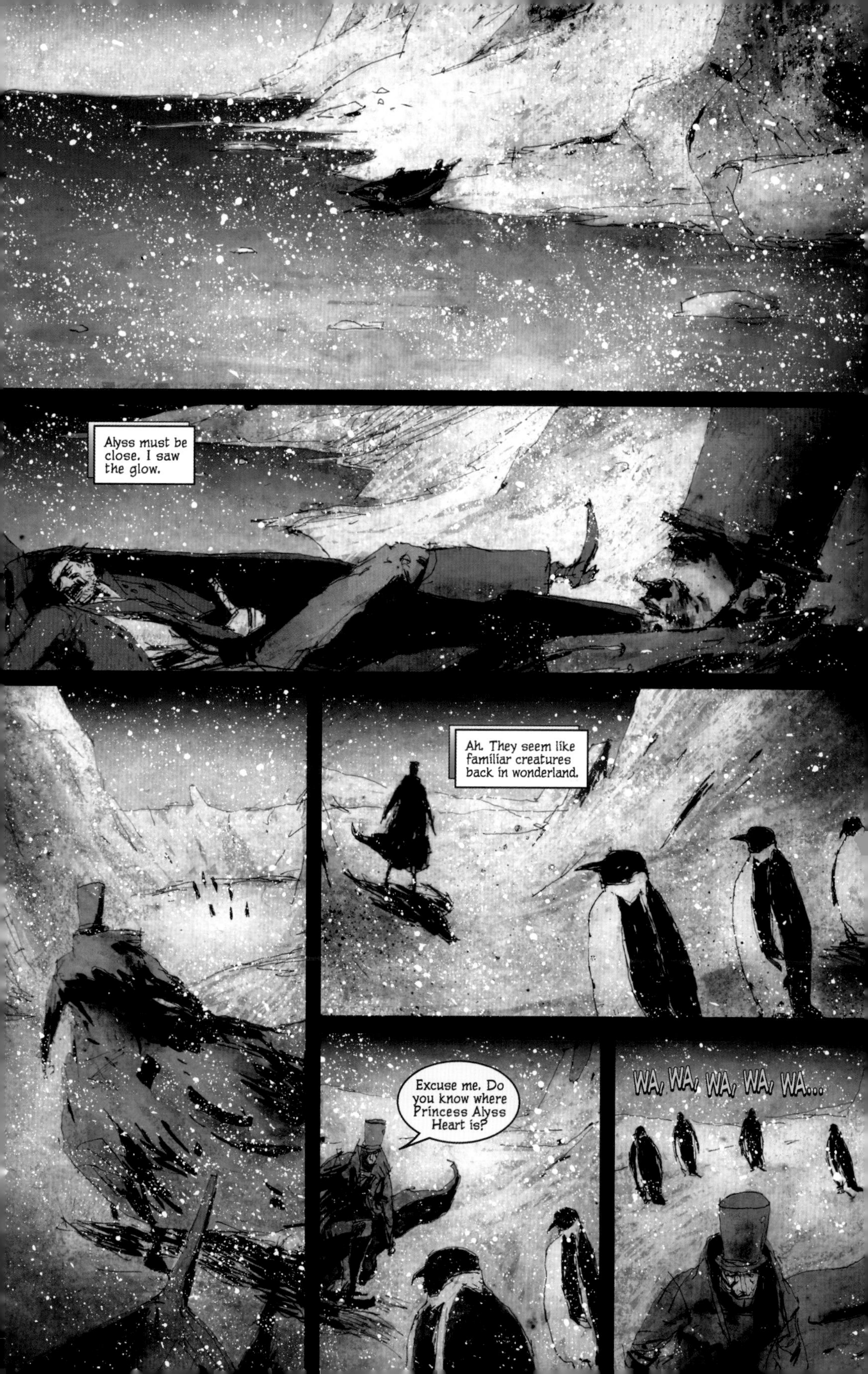
Alyss must be close. I saw the glow.
Ah. They seem like familiar creatures back in wonderland.
Excuse me. Do you know where Princess Alyss Heart is?
WA, WA, WA, WA, WA...

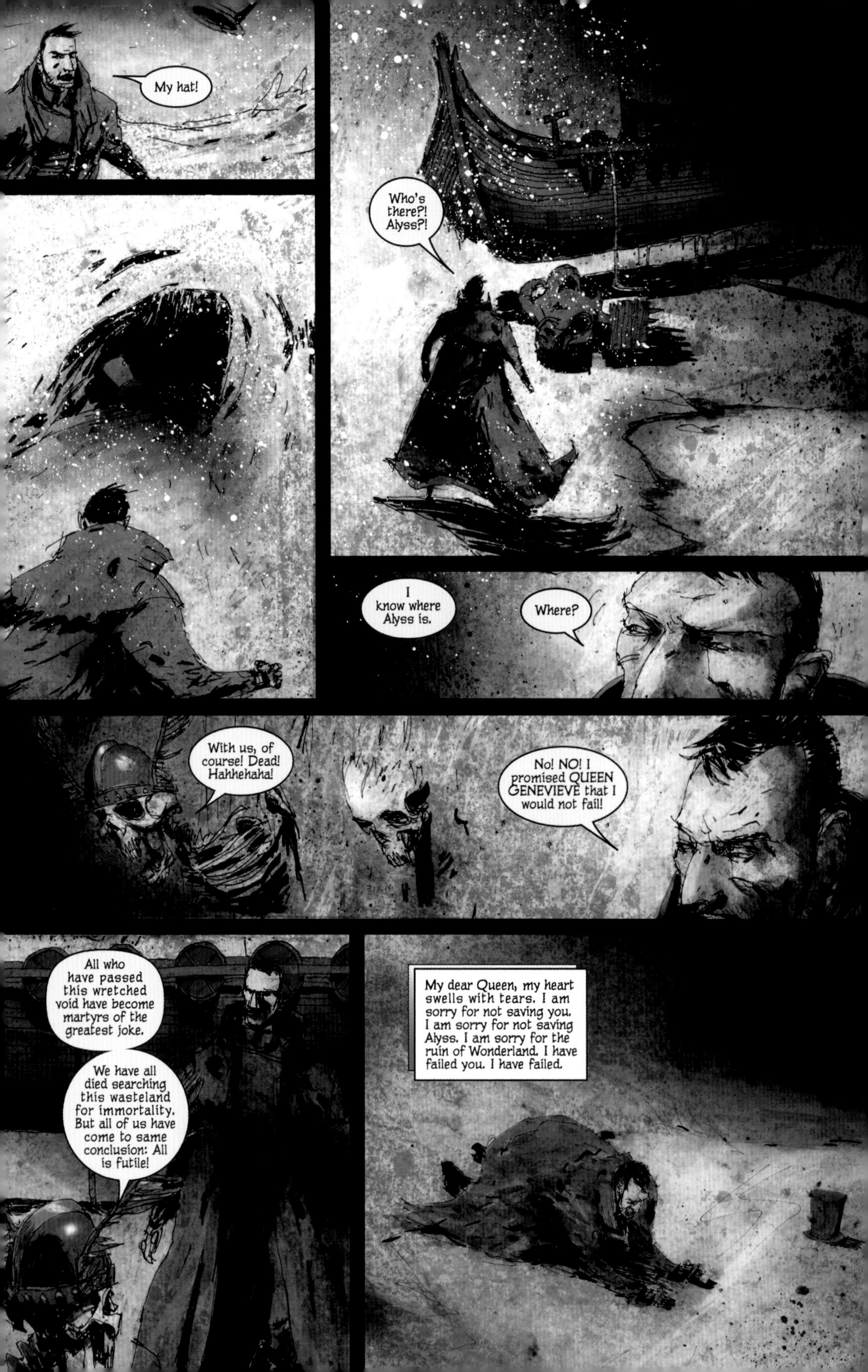
My hat!
Who's there?! Alyss?!
I know where Alyss is.
Where?
With us, of course! Dead! Hahhehaha!
No! NO! I promised QUEEN GENEVIEVE that I would not fail!
All who have passed this wretched void have become martyrs of the greatest joke.
We have all died searching this wasteland for immortality. But all of us have come to same conclusion: All is futile!
My dear Queen, my heart swells with tears. I am sorry for not saving you. I am sorry for not saving Alyss. I am sorry for the ruin of Wonderland. I have failed you. I have failed.

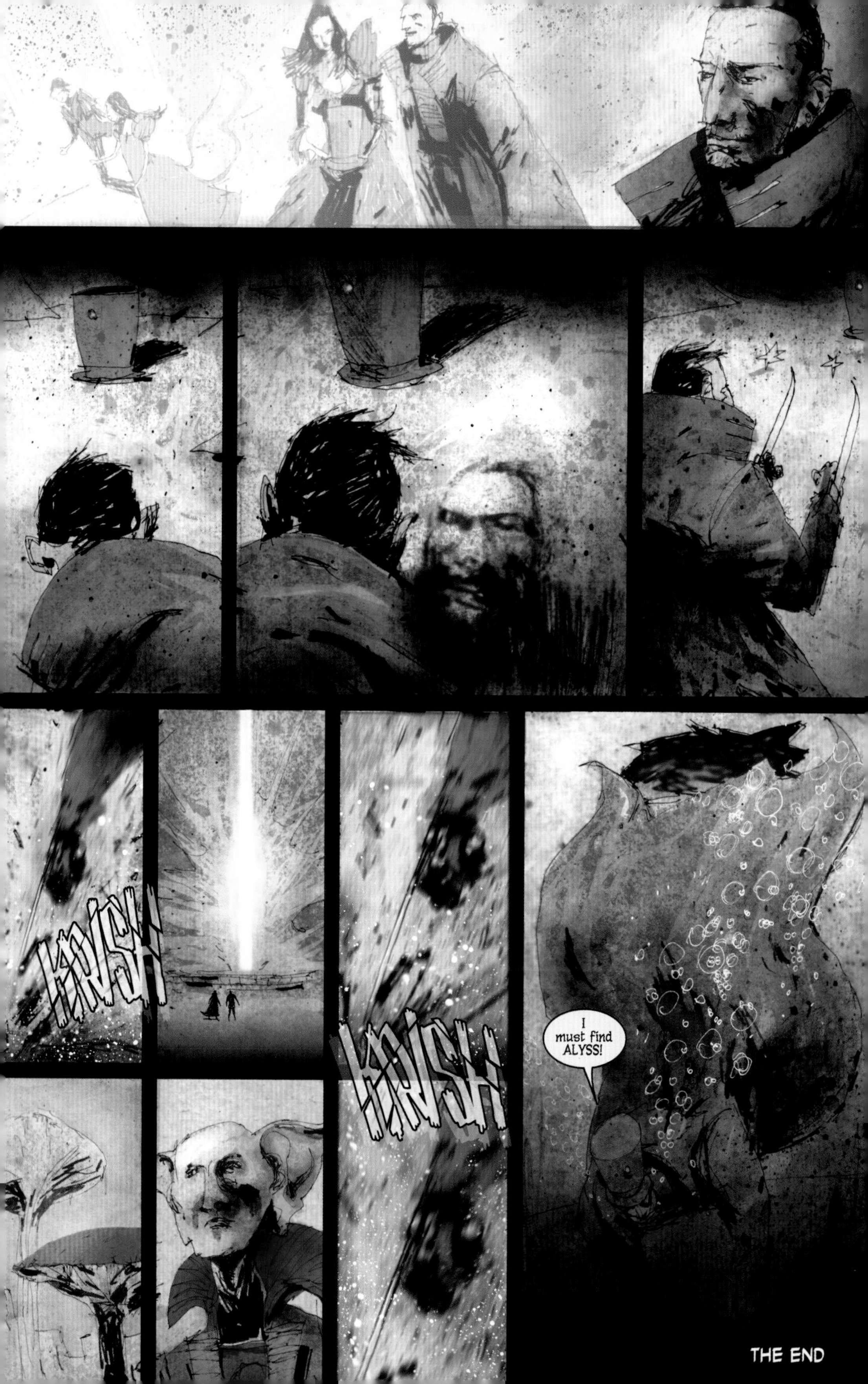
KRISH
KRISH
I must find ALYSS!

THE END

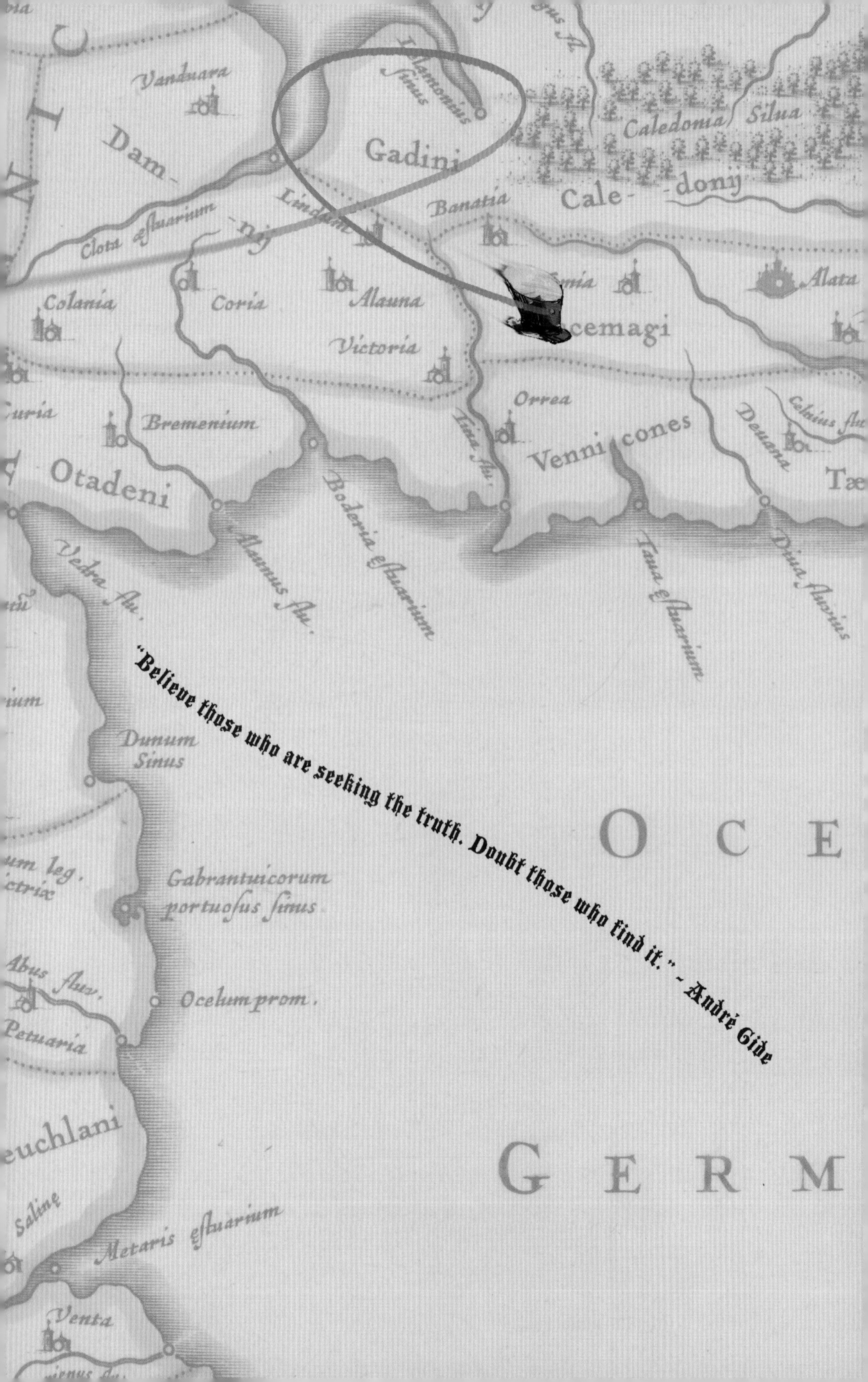
Vanduara
Dam-
Gadini
Caledonia Silua
Cale- donij
Banatia
Clota æstuarium
Colania
Coria
Alauna
Victoria
Alata
Orrea
Bremenium
Otadeni
Vennicones
Boderia æstuarium
Tava æstuarium
Diva fluvius
Vedra flu.
Alaunus flu.
Dunum Sinus
Gabrantuicorum portuosus sinus
Abus fluv.
Ocelum prom.
Petuaria
Saline
Metaris æstuarium
Venta
OCE
GERM

"Believe those who are seeking the truth. Doubt those who find it." - André Gide

Hatter M
Seeking Wonder

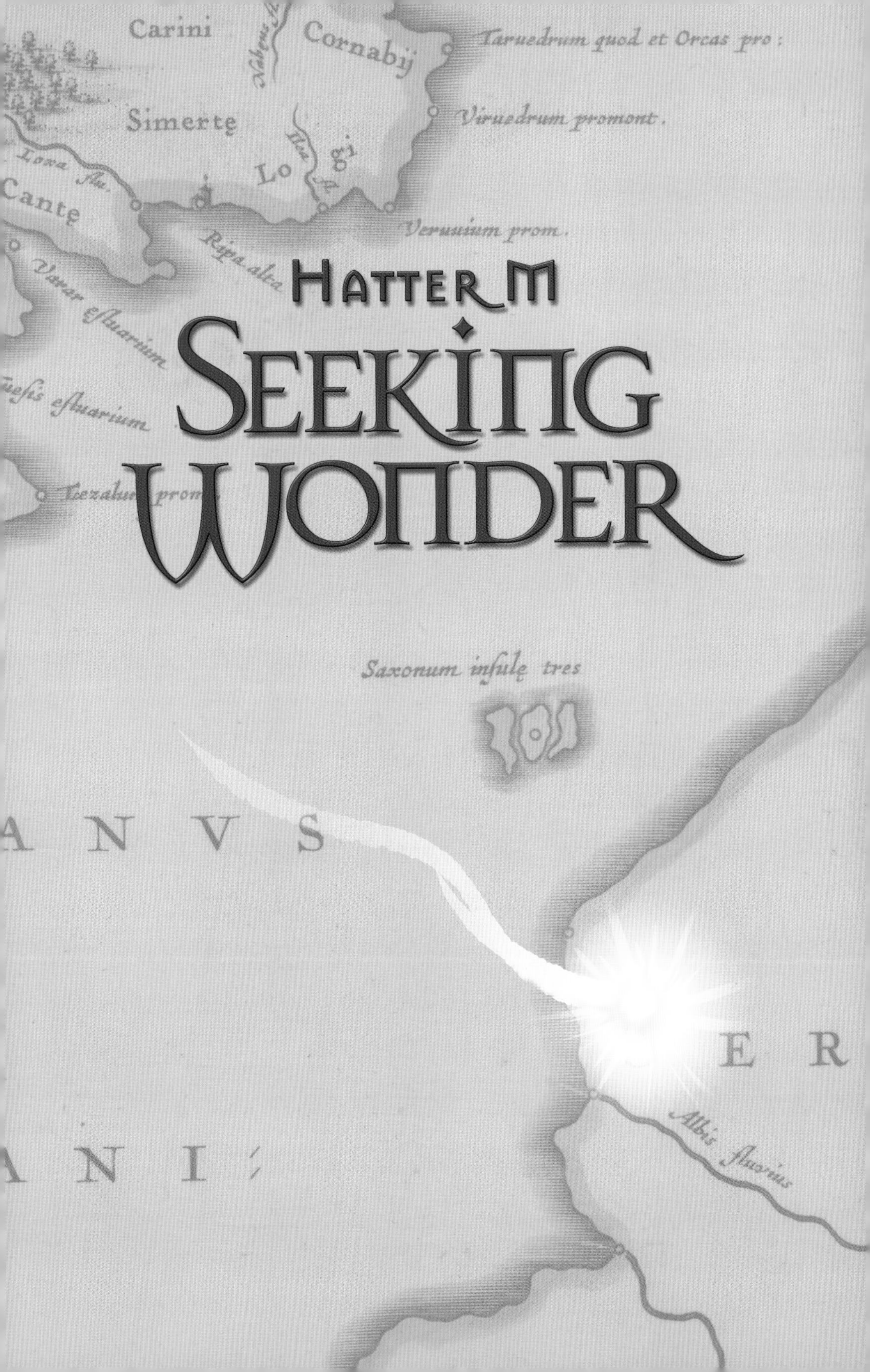
Carini
Cornabij
Taruedrum quod et Orcas pro :
Simertę
Viruedrum promont.
Lora flu.
Lo gi
Cantę
Veruuium prom.
Ripa alta
Varar æstuarium
æstuarium
Saxonum insulę tres
ANVS
ER
Albis fluvius
ANI

Hatter M
10TH
ANNIVERSARY
COLLECTORS
PLAYING
CARDS

HATTER M
TEMPLESMITH

In 2005, we launched the Hatter M series
with a single issue. 10 years and thousands of
pages of storytelling later, we invite you to
join our celebration with this anniversary
deck of playing cards featuring the art of
Ben Templesmith.

get in the game at
FRANKBEDDOR.COM/STORE!

AP
AUTOMATIC
PUBLISHING

FRANK BEDDOR

HATTER MADIGAN

Ghost in the Hatbox

A PREQUEL NOVEL TO
THE LOOKING GLASS WARS
COMING IN 2016

AUTOMATIC
PUBLISHING

Enemies unite in a WAR for WONDERLAND

IN THE THRILLING FINALE OF THE LOOKING GLASS WARS TRILOGY.

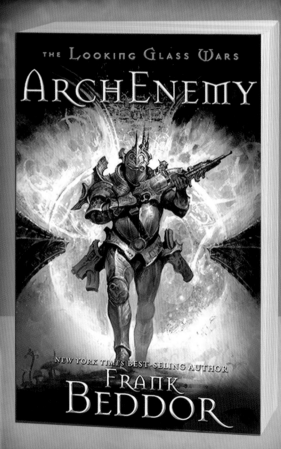

THE LOOKING GLASS WARS

ArchEnemy

NEW YORK TIMES BEST-SELING AUTHOR

FRANK BEDDOR

"Don't enter *The Looking Glass Wars* lightly. Once you're there, you can't turn back. Frank Beddor makes sure of that."

—Teenreads.com

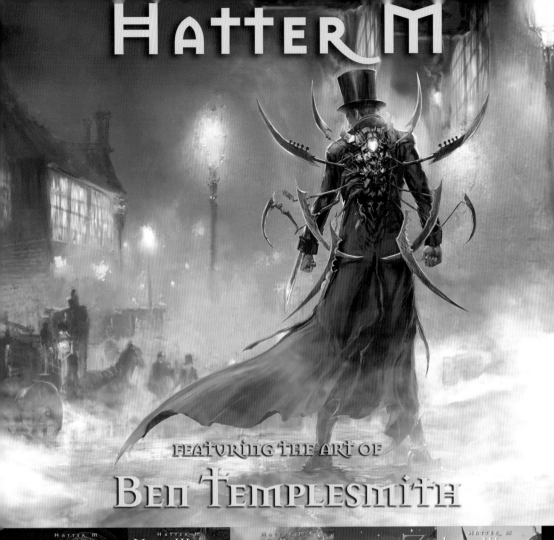

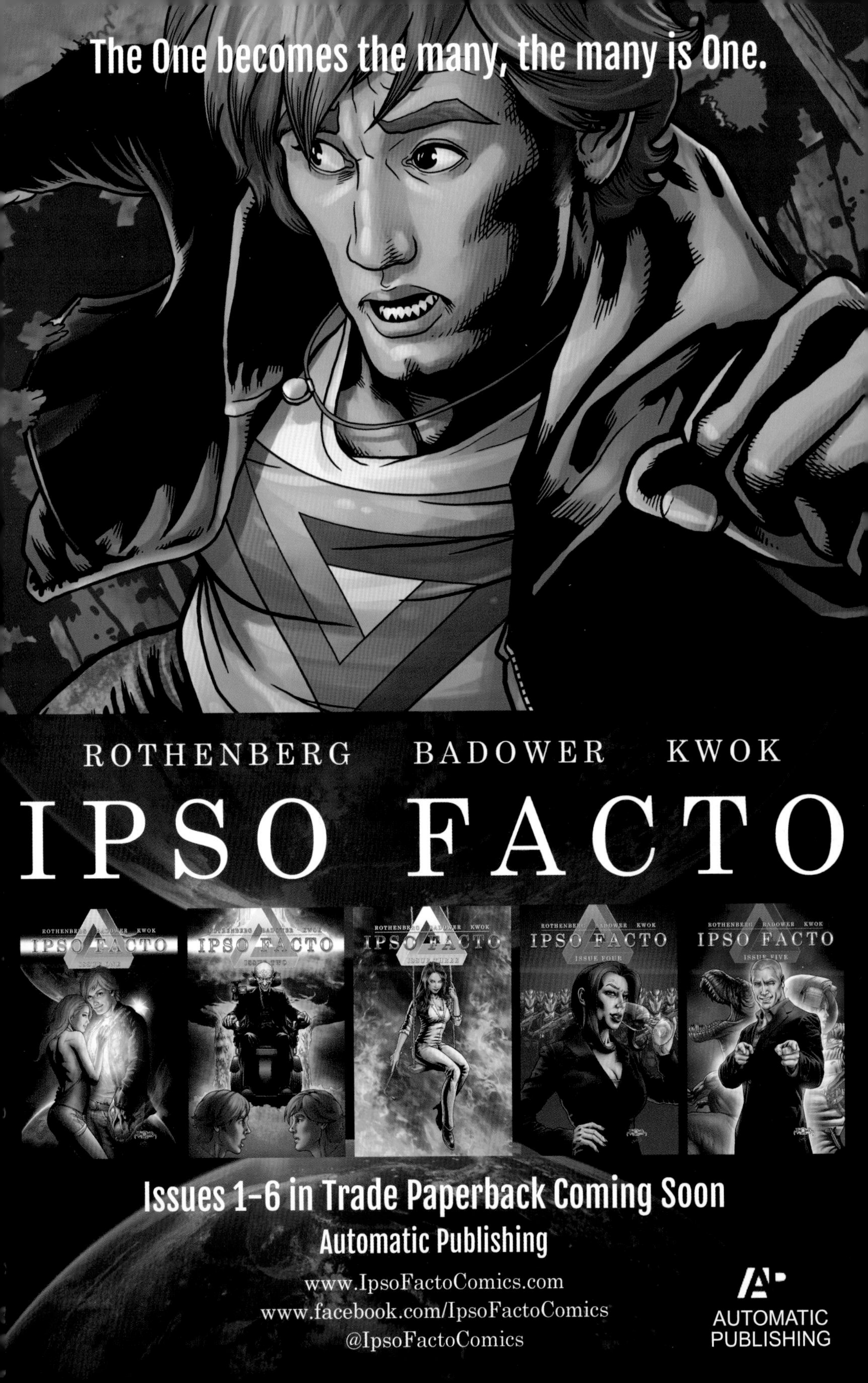

The One becomes the many, the many is One.
ROTHENBERG BADOWER KWOK
IPSO FACTO
Issues 1-6 in Trade Paperback Coming Soon
Automatic Publishing
www.IpsoFactoComics.com
www.facebook.com/IpsoFactoComics
@IpsoFactoComics
AUTOMATIC PUBLISHING

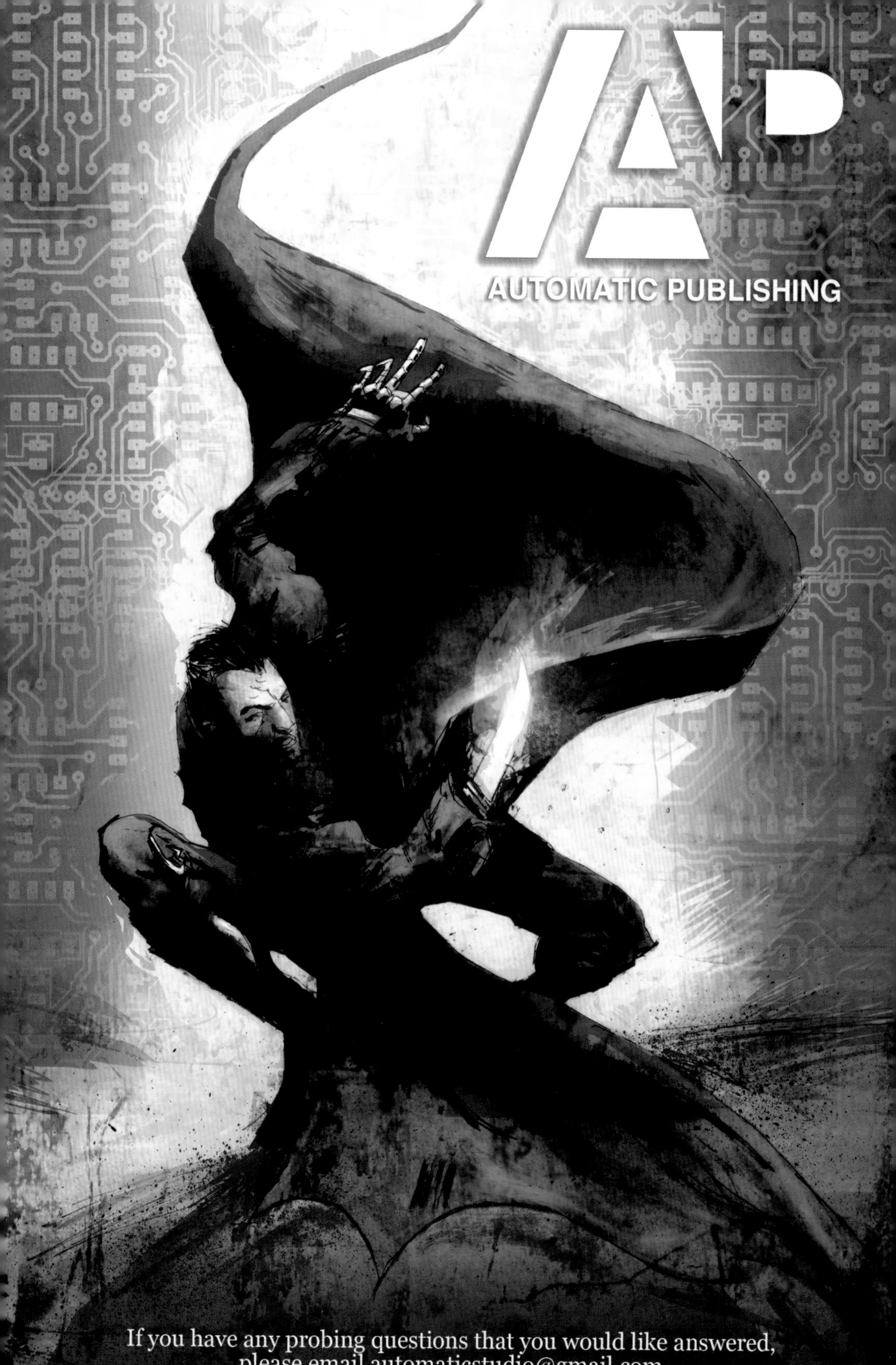
AUTOMATIC PUBLISHING